Longarm did as all hell busted loose, too close for comfort. He dove headfirst to the cobbles and horse apples, drawing his side arm as he landed on his left shoulder and rolled to land prone with his gun muzzle following every shift of his eyes as they took in a swirl of movement obscured by gunsmoke filling half the damned street.

A bearded raggedy cuss sporting a Texas hat, a Schofield .45, and red splashes on his dirty work shirt emerged from the gunsmoke like a shot-up battle cruiser from a fog bank, staring goggle-eyed at Longarm as he called him something in some outlandish lingo and swung his six-gun up to back his hostile words.

So Longarm shot him and he staggered back into the smoke—to whatever fate awaited him there.

TABOR EVANS

LONGARM

AND
THE DANISH DAMES

JOVE BOOKS, NEW YORK

LONGARM AND THE DANISH DAMES

A Jove Book / published by arrangement with
the author

PRINTING HISTORY
Jove edition / January 1999

The Penguin Putnam Inc. World Wide Web site address is
http://www.penguinputnam.com

ISBN: 0-515-12435-4

A JOVE BOOK®
Jove Books are published by The Berkley Publishing Group,
a member of Penguin Putnam Inc.,
375 Hudson Street, New York, New York 10014.
JOVE and the "J" design are trademarks belonging to
Jove Publications, Inc.

PRINTED IN THE UNITED STATES OF AMERICA

10 9 8 7 6 5 4 3 2 1

Chapter 1

It was raining fire and salt in Denver as the month of March went out like a lion. But U.S. Deputy Marshal Custis Long of the Denver District Court didn't care to eat and drink standing up in an oilcloth slicker. So he chanced a shop-front-hugging lope for the Parthenon Saloon, not so far from the Federal Building.

It seemed farther than usual by the time he ducked inside the steamy smoke-filled establishment in his dripping Stetson and a mighty soggy suit of tobacco-brown tweed. So he was standing by the free-lunch counter with his frock coat thrown open to let his wet vest have some air when an even wetter-looking individual in more rustic range-riding duds came in off the rain-lashed streets in an oddly ominous manner, his soggy boots planted wider and his knees bent more than any-body but a gunfighter on the prod would need.

He was packing a six-gun on either side, riding low in tied-down holsters. So Longarm, as he was better known to friend and enemy alike, had already thoughtfully shifted the ham and rye in his gun hand to the other hand as the stranger struck a stance and declared in a lofty tone, "I am the one and original Salt Lake Sam, a man to be reckoned with when he's out hunting skunks, and at the moment I have come all the way from Utah Territory in search of the skunk who gunned my cousin. They call him Longarm. Not my cousin.

He was called Bobby. Longarm is the cowardly skunk who backshot good old Bobby, and I've come all this way to clean his plow!''

Longarm had no recollection of backshooting any such cuss in Utah or anywhere else. But if there was one thing he'd learned in the six or seven years he'd been riding for the Justice Department, it had to be that it was better to have the drop on any armed and dangerous stranger before you told him he was full of shit.

So even as other noontime customers of the Parthenon were sort of edging clear of the line of fire along the bar from the front entrance, Longarm was casually reaching under the sandwich in his left hand for the Double Action Colt .44-40 riding cross-draw under his rain-soaked coattails.

The stranger with the mighty brag gasped, ''Hold on, there, pard!'' But after seeing that the two-gun man seemed to really know a thing or two about the opening moves of a showdown, Longarm showed him first, blowing the cuss off his boots and back out the front door with two hundred grains of hot lead in his right lung.

Nobody followed too closely as Longarm moved out into the rain as well, smoking six-gun in hand to cover the ferocious talker, who'd never made a serious try for either of his own guns on his way to the hospital or graveyard, depending.

As Longarm stood over the man he'd just shot, the sprawled but still-breathing loser stared thunderstruck up at him, spraying fine drops of blood as he gasped, ''Thunderation, Longarm! Didn't anybody tell you this was April Fool's Day?''

To which Longarm could only reply, ''I knew what day it was. What sort of a fool would come at a total stranger on any day of the year with two guns and the avowed intent of gunning him?''

The shabby stranger, oozing blood and rainwater on the sandstone walk he occupied at the moment, coughed and said, ''Aw, you know me from Dodge, Longarm. Don't you 'member that time I throwed that stink bomb under the crap table at Madam Moustache's house of ill repute? You laughed just as hard as anybody when all them soiled doves

2

run out of the cribs on the mezzanine in their shimmy shirts or less!''

''Practical Pete, you poor loco joker!'' said Longarm with a sigh as the not-too-distinguished features of a man he'd never met in Utah came back to him from other times and places.

Practical Pete, the joker of the western trail, coughed weakly, smiled sheepishly, and confessed, ''When they told me, over to the stockyards, you came here to this saloon for the needled beer and free lunch most every noon, I just couldn't resist reminding you it was April Fool's Day. Do you reckon you've killed me, pard?''

Longarm turned to tell a man he knew in the crowd to run up to Broadway and fetch a copper badge. Then he holstered his side arm and hunkered down to gingerly unbutton the front of Practical Pete's rain-and-blood-soaked denim shirt.

Once he had, he said, ''I was aiming to. But your threatening appearance inspired me to fire before I'd centered on your chest. From the way you're breathing at the moment, I suspect I hulled your lung. The fact that you're still breathing at all ought to signify I didn't hit nothing you can't get along without for a spell. Do you reckon we could roll you on your left side without it hurting all that much?''

Practical Pete sighed and said, ''I surely prefer rolling on my left side to rolling on my right, Longarm. But how come you want me rolling at all?''

As Longarm gently but firmly got the wounded man's right shoulder off the wet pavement, he explained, ''Want to see whether my round stayed in you or tore out your back. It's those exit wounds a man bleeds the most from, and it's hard to tell whether you've bled like a stuck pig, or more modest bleeding's been diluted and spread wider by all this rainwater.''

''That hurts,'' Practical Pete decided as Longarm got him curled up on his left side. A police whistle trilled in the near distance as Longarm said soothingly, ''The back of your shirt is still intact and only soaked with water. I'd say my round went through one lung and flattened against your right shoulder blade. That's likely what sent you flying out the door like so.''

Practical Pete replied through gritted teeth, "It felt like some big old mule kicked me full in the breast. How are we supposed to get that bullet out of me, pard?"

Longarm said, "We ain't. That's what they teach doctors in those fancy medical schools. You just stay put until the meat wagon can get here, and I'll be proud to bring you flowers, books, and candy at the hospital, you poor stupid cuss."

So that was about the way Longarm's superior, Marshal William Vail, found the two of them when he grumped over from the Federal Building on his way-shorter legs, under a big sensible umbrella, of course. For the somewhat older and much stubbier Billy Vail hadn't taken needless chances with his health since he'd survived earlier, more carefree days as a Texas Ranger in Comanche country.

Vail was smoking his usual stubby cigar under the drier brim of his own Stetson. So he was able to blow smoke out both nostrils like a bull about to charge before he declared, "We just heard at the office. What's that unfortunate at our feet charged with, if he lives?"

Longarm sighed and said, "Damn foolishness is the best I can come up with, Boss. I'd like you to meet the menace of the western trail, Practical Pete Clifton."

Billy Vail peered down at the shot-up practical joker while he decided, "I've heard tell of you, Mr. Practical. Is it true you once put a burr under the saddle blanket of Ben Thompson, and then somehow managed to stay alive?"

Practical Pete chuckled, choked, and managed, "I had a good old cayuse under me, and Ben's paint was wore down from bucking by the time he was able to chase me serious."

Glancing up at Longarm with an injured expression, the lung-shot joker added, "Some old boys have no sense of humor at all. Couldn't you tell I was just funning you with all that talk about a cousin from the Utah Territory? Great day in the morning, do I look like one of them Avenging Angels the Mormons send after anyone who guns a paid-up Mormon cousin?"

Longarm shrugged and said, "As a matter of fact, I have met up with some of those so-called Danites in my time. I lived long enough to shoot you today because I was told in

4

advance those boys dress and act like everyone else when they're hunting Gentiles. That's what they call anybody who ain't one of 'em, a Gentile. Mistaking a Danite on the prod for a saddle tramp or whiskey drummer has been known to take as much as fifty years off an average Gentile's life."

The copper badge tweeting the whistle sort of brainlessly was less than a block away in the rain now. So Billy Vail said, "You'd best take the rest of the day off, Deputy Long. I'll take charge here and explain as much as we want them to know to any local lawmen, the ambulance crew, the *Denver Post,* or the *Rocky Mountain News.*"

Longarm said, "I'd like to make certain my old Dodge City pal is fixing to live, Boss."

But Billy Vail snapped, "Nothing is certain in this vale of tears but death, taxes, and Reporter Crawford of the *Post* writing another one of those Wild West features he does on you every time he sees your big sombrero from across the street. I don't want you anywhere in sight as I pour us some oil on these troubled waters. So what are you waiting for, a kiss good-bye?"

Longarm shook his head and started to say where he'd be if they needed him. But Billy Vail cut in with: "Don't tell me if you mean to spend a rainy afternoon with a certain young widow woman over on Capitol Hill. I prefer to tell *my* own old woman I don't know whether you're still playing slap-and-tickle just down Sherman Street from us or not. Things seem slow right now with all the trails turned to axle-deep gumbo just outside of town. So take off until Monday morning, and we'll talk about this jasper some more then."

Longarm allowed that sounded fair, and ducked back inside to pay his bar tab and see if he could borrow a slicker or at least another fool umbrella.

As he left them, he heard Practical Pete asking the gruffer Billy Vail if he was likely to die.

To which Vail replied in a surprisingly jovial tone, "Sure you're going to die, sooner or later. Were you planning on immortality, you April Fool?"

Longarm had to laugh, and later, up at a brownstone mansion atop Capitol Hill, he was surprised a certain young widow woman with light brown hair and Junoesque curves didn't find old Billy's remark so amusing.

Those Junoesque curves were under a shantung kimono, along with the shirt-sleeved arms of her afternoon caller, as they hugged and swapped some spit in her entrance hall by the foot of the stairs. He could feel her soft flesh shuddering as she murmured, "I don't ever want to die, nor get old and ugly, Custis. It's not fair of Mother Nature to give us brains to think with if she means to let us wither and die as if we were just witless weeds or critters!"

Longarm kissed the part of her wavy hair, and ran one hand down to explore the crack between her soft buttocks as he said soothingly, "Don't blame poor old Billy Vail and me for the cruelties of Mother Nature, honey. You're way younger than Billy, and not as old as me, once you study on it. So you've got longer to enjoy life than the rest of us, and speaking of enjoyments, you say your household help has until Monday?"

"You said you didn't think you'd have to go out in the field until then," she demurely replied, adding, "What are you doing, you big oaf?" as Longarm swept her off her slippered feet and proceeded to carry her up the stairs to her bedroom suite.

He didn't answer on the stairs. It was a silly question, and if the truth were to be told, his old pal had put on a few pounds since first she'd become a rich widow with a warm nature it took a heap of manliness to satisfy.

But once he had her in her four-poster, and out of that raw silk kimono, Longarm found it easy as ever to rise to the occasion with a gal whose newfound padding overlay a mighty frisky body that spent a lot of time on horesback. Her late husband had left her a string of mining properties up in the Front Range that she liked to inspect in person. It kept her mining help honest, and didn't hurt her ample rump and slender waist worth mentioning. It was sort of nice to get aboard a pal who didn't need a pillow under her ass, once he had his own damp duds and six-gun, in need of its own reaming, out of their way.

She said his firmer flesh was cold as ice, and called him her poor baby as she hugged him tight with all four limbs

6

and did her best to warm him up. He warmed her some in turn, and a good time was had by all by the time he just had to stop for his second wind and a few drags on a three-for-a-nickel cheroot.

She didn't really mind. She shared most of his bad habits in bed. So as they cuddled under a sheet and cotton quilt to share a smoke without risking pneumonia in thin, damp air designed more for the active life than bare-ass repose, he elaborated some on Billy Vail's reasons for allowing them so much time together.

She allowed she was glad Reporter Crawford of the *Denver Post* was inclined to write blood-and-thunder whoppers about Denver's answer to the late Wild Bill. When Longarm protested that James Butler Hickok had never acted half that wild in front of *him* in Dodge, she snuggled closer and coyly reached down to fondle his virility as she purred, ''I only meant you were a wild thunder-whopper down here where it had best be our own little secret. Would you like to do me a real favor with this wicked thing, seeing you have until Monday at my disposal, you natural man?''

He held her closer and replied, ''I never came all this way in the rain to wave it out no window. But could I smoke this cheroot down first? You'll find I do bigger favors when I have my second wind.''

She laughed, tweaked him teasingly, and told him, ''I've noticed that, and I'll expect you to prove it as soon as you're done with that silly little cigar. But what I really meant was that I'd like to go up to Leadville this Sabbath, without advance warning to anybody. I hope it isn't true, but somebody wrote to warn me one of my shafts has been getting high-graded during church services, when nobody's supposed to be working the site.''

Longarm liked to think before he sounded off. So she took his few moments of silence harder than he'd meant them, and insisted, ''We'd be up there alone after dark, haunting our old hunting lodge like a pair of sex-crazed spooks, and there's something I've always wanted to try in one of those elk-antler rocking chairs in the living room, with a nice fire blazing on the hearth.''

He was inspired to snuff out his cheroot a tad early and

take her in both arms some more as he assured her, "I've always wanted to try it in an elk-antler rocking chair, and it ain't as if Billy Vail will have any other chores for me for a spell!"

Which only went to show, even as he was cocking a leg over to do her nice and dirty some more, that nobody riding for Justice really knew for certain what to expect in any given twenty-four hours.

Chapter 2

It was later in the day at the State Department in Washington. They were working overtime in Protocol as a severely pretty, and mighty confused, young stenographer entered the oak-paneled office of her superior, a lean and hungry-looking expert on international law, with the latest dispatches wired from Brownsville, Texas.

Her boss went on pacing the blue plush rug with a Havana claro puffing between his bared teeth like a Shay locomotive on a nine-percent grade as the girl who'd decoded the messages heaved a sigh and told him, "The Texas Rangers have refused our request as well, Mr. Chalmers. Something about them having no jurisdiction and not *wanting* jurisdiction on a *bet*. I fear I'm not too clear on the way cowboys seem to express themselves."

Hugo Chalmers Esquire exhaled an impressive billow of expensive smoke, removed the cigar from his mouth, and waved it like a huge smoldering match stem as he replied, "If only cowboys or even Indians had just murdered that Danish diplomat in Texas, we'd have no problem at all about jurisdiction. We could simply issue a federal homicide warrant, and a grand time could be had by all at the public hanging."

The stenographer, who'd never been to a public hanging, but had always wanted to attend at least one, sounded uncertain as she asked, "Do you think it was that Mexican grandee or that officer from the dead man's own Danish embassy who shot him in the driveway of that French embassy, sir?"

Her boss shook his head patiently and said, "Not an embassy, Miss Effie. Embassies are here in Washington. As a port of entry, Brownsville on the Rio Grande only rates *consulates* to help out travelers and businessmen from their own countries. So the killing took place in the driveway of the French consulate as their spring ball was just breaking up around midnight. I met the victim here in Washington one time. So his getting himself shot in the back comes as no great surprise."

The stenographer, who'd been decoding the heavy telegraph traffic to and from Texas over the past forty-eight hours, nodded and said, "He sounds as if he mustn't have been very popular, traveling with that royal carte blanche and a bodyguard of Danish marines after having to leave both London and Washington to avoid outraged husbands."

Chalmers sniffed and replied, "I just said I'd met him. The can of diplomatic worms they've handed us involves *who* shot him, rather than *why*. It boils down to most everyone still at the ball hearing a gunshot after the Greve or Count Svein Atterdag had just swaggered out. As those who can alibi one another rushed out on the veranda, they saw Atterdag down in the driveway as one of his marines struggled with his shied or wounded mount. There were two other men on the veranda, both standing there with drawn side arms. One was Don Hernan Obregon, a horse breeder and trader with stud farms on both sides of the Rio Grande and a grant of diplomatic immunity from Mexico City—lest the local border official try to shake him down, one imagines."

Chalmers expelled more smoke and continued. "The other man there with a gun in his hand was Captain Eric Steensen, a Danish cavalry officer attached to their trade commission in Texas. Something about trying to sell some of those famous Icelandic stock ponies to both American and Mexican ranchers. He not only had diplomatic immunity, but headed for the U.S. Customs House to demand political sanctuary instead of going home to his quarters at the Danish consulate.''

''Then he must have been the assassin,'' the stenographer decided, adding, ''Would you run and hide from your own government officials if you were innocent, sir?''

The more worldy protocol expert grimaced and replied, ''If they were Danish, and I stood accused of murdering a Danish nobleman? I think I would. Steensen is a long way from home, and the ocean in between is three or four miles deep in places. Others who were at the ball that night stand ready to afirm that Captain Steensen and the late Count Atterdag had a heated exchange by the punch bowl that evening. The Danish court may neither not know nor not care that Atterdag got into an argument with Don Hernan Obregon a few minutes later. Old Svein was like that when he'd been drinking.''

Miss Effie, who'd been reading the messages she'd been decoding, asked, ''What was that we asked the county coroner's office in Texas about bullets? I didn't understand those wires.''

Hugo Chalmers blew smoke out both nostrils and growled, ''Neither did anyone else we had on the scene! The Frenchmen with a dead Dane in their driveway didn't want him as a gift. So they called the local law. Once those outstanding peace officers heard the magic words 'diplomatic immunity,' they forgot about examining the weapons of the two prime suspects. But in its own good time Cameron County issued a death certificate so his nibs could be pickled and sent home in a lead-lined coffin. They had to go through the motions of a medical examination. So we know they found no bullets at all in the cadaver of the victim. One and only one round entered his back just under the ribs to sever his aorta on its way through him. But we know Obregon was carrying a Colt '74 of .45 caliber, while Steensen was holding a Belgian Nagant 7.62-millimeter pocket pistol. So we're talking about quite a difference. 7.62-millimeter would translate as roughly .30-caliber in our own terminology.''

She blinked behind her wire-rimed glasses and asked, ''But what difference could that make, since the fatal bullet went through the poor man and was never recovered?''

Chalmers explained, "There's a good chance the spent bullet wound up in the victim's mount, one of those tough Icelandic ponies he'd begged, borrowed, or stolen from Captain Steensen. Witnesses remember it bucking and fighting with the Royal Marine who'd been steadying it for the half-soused count to mount. But now the pony is missing, and so is that royal marine."

Chalmers blew a thoughtful smoke ring and decided, "His Majesty Christian IX seems to run his court with an iron hand. Nobody wants to wind up on the carpet there, it seems. Captain Steensen seeking political asylum is less hard to understand. The marine private, a Pall Njalsson, may have run off with that possibly wounded pony just because he seems to be an Icelander."

The stenographer looked totally confounded.

Her boss explained. "Iceland is ruled by Denmark, the way Ireland is ruled by England. Icelanders and Irishmen seem to feel much the same about that. The Icelanders staged an abortive revolt in 1808, and they've been sulking ever since. So this young royal marine may find himself in the same position an Irish guardsman might if he was helping an English earl mount up while somebody shot him."

"Then that young marine is a suspect as well?" she asked.

Chalmers shook his head and replied, "Not to anyone with any common sense. It's generally agreed Private Njalsson was standing in the drive, facing the veranda and Count Atterdag, with the reins of a pony, not a side arm, in his hands. You steady the mount with your left hand and hand the loose ends of the reins to the rider with your right hand. But anybody in Njalsson's position in the drive had a clear view of anybody standing anywhere on the veranda or front steps of the consulate as Count Atterdag was tottering towards his mount."

She gasped, "Good heavens! You mean Private Njalsson has run off with material evidence in the form of a horse after witnessing the crime?"

Chalmers shrugged and said, "He could be in on it, albeit I have it on good authority that an Icelandic marine private plotting murder with a Danish army officer would be stretching things. It's more likely Njalsson has his own ax to grind.

He knows who did it, but either doesn't want to be involved or doesn't think anyone will take his word if it doesn't fit either simple solution. So how do we go about recovering that material evidence and forcing a hostile witness to testify if we can't get anyone on the scene, federal, state, or local, to even try?''

Miss Effie frowned thoughtfully and asked, ''Why do *we* have to try, Mr. Chalmers? You just said the French consulate has washed its hands of the matter, and nobody else wants the bother of arresting a suspect with diplomatic immunity, only to see him swagger off with his lawyer and a writ.''

Chalmers sighed and said, ''We're the host country. Under the fuzzy logic of international law, we can't arrest either Obregon or Steensen for murder. But we can declare either *persona non grata,* with cause, and ask their own governments to take them off our hands.''

She asked what was wrong with just declaring *both* pests *persona non grata* and forgetting the whole thing.

To which he could only reply, ''Simple justice, with the case on the front pages of the infernal *London Times* and everybody waiting to see what we do next. We can't declare either suspect *non grata* without probably cause, or at least the suspicion they've committed a serious offense on American soil. If we send Don Hernan Obregon home, Mexico City will quite rightly demand that we put up or shut up. He's made public statements that he didn't do it. His story is that he heard a gunshot, drew his own gun, and ran outside to find Captain Steensen on the veranda, gun in hand, while Count Atterdag bled like a stuck pig as Private Njalsson struggled to control that small but mighty acrobatic pony.''

Chalmers took another drag on his claro and continued, ''On the other hand, should we accuse Captain Steensen without proof and deny him the political asylum he's entitled to under international law . . .''

''Why is he entitled to political asylum, sir?'' she asked.

Chalmers sighed and told her. ''I just said he'd be lucky if he ever made it home alive for as fair a trial as he'd be liable to get. I think they still chop your head off in Denmark. I know the royal governor of Iceland threatened to do that a lot back in 1808. We'd be sending a man to almost certain death after our own State Department had granted him diplomatic status, and how would *that* look in the *London Times* if it ever turned out he'd been innocent?''

She wrinkled her nose and replied, ''Oh, dear, we seem to have an impossible situation. Can't we just tell the Danes they can't have Captain Steensen and sort of call it a draw?''

Chalmers shook his bony head firmly and replied, ''Not unless we declared, and could *prove,* he was innocent. Since Customs officials in Brownsville have vouched for a diplomat they know and trust, the Treasury Department has granted him sanctuary *pro tem,* but they want State to back them, and I just told you why we can't permanently, unless we *can* prove him innocent.''

He waved his cigar expansively and added, ''Of course, if we had any proof he was innocent, nobody in Denmark would want to cut his head off and we wouldn't *need* to protect him.''

She nodded and decided, ''In sum, we're off the diplomatic hook as soon as we get somebody to prove that Mexican, that Dane, or somebody else entirely assasssinated that visiting nobleman!''

He smiled and said, ''I couldn't have put it better, and it would be a diplomatic blessing if we could blame the whole thing on Mister Lo, the Poor Indian. But with even the Texas Rangers refusing to help . . .''

She said, ''It seems to me the Justice Department ought to be more than willing to help us. I mean, they don't have to *charge* that missing marine with anything if they only bring him in as a material witness.''

Chalmers dryly asked her, ''Didn't you read any of those wires we got back from the Brownsville Federal District Court? Aside from not having jurisdiction, according to them, they claim their own deputy marshals are all busy running ragged in the hurricane season down yonder. So what are we going to tell Christian IX, or for that matter President Hayes, after they read the Monday morning papers and ask us what we intend to do about a hostile witness, with missing evidence on the hoof, somewhere north or south of the Rio

14

Grande, if we can't get anyone who knows that country to even *look* for them?"

She said primly, "We go over their stubborn heads and let me ask a stenographer I know here in the district who works for Justice."

"That just might work," Chalmers soberly replied. Then he shook his head and said, "On the other hand, it just might make a lot of people higher on the totem pole mad at us. Aside from intradepartmental rivalry, how could we be sure Justice would send a good man if they *agreed* to help us track that hostile witness down in mighty rough border country?"

She demurely suggested, "We could ask for a good man by name, Who was that diamond in the rough the Japanese Mikado wanted to pin a cherry blossom on after he'd helped *their* mission out that time?"

Chalmers gasped, "Bless you, my child! I'd forgotten that sticky situation with those renegade Japanese out on the West Coast! There was no way we could let them decorate that one-man wave of destruction with their Order of the Cherry Blossom, lest we admit right out that an agent of the U.S. government had made all that noise south of the border!"

He beamed down at her and added, "Now that you've reminded me, we *do* have something I can hang over Justice. That big deputy from their Denver District Court is more than noisy. He's *good.* So why don't we get out of this ridiculous vertical position while you take a wire, Miss Effie?"

"Mr. Chalmers! Whatever are you doing with that naughty hand on my derriere?" she protested, not too firmly, as he moved both of them over to his leather-covered chesterfield couch.

"I'm just overwhelmed by your bright suggestion, Miss Effie," he murmured. "Has anybody ever told you how beautiful you are without your glasses?"

Chapter 3

A cold gray dawn didn't have to feel so bad, going at it dog-style with a well-proportioned pal. But the sage who'd written the road to Hell was paved with good intentions had likely worked for Billy Vail one time.

For the breakfast she served him in bed restored the energy it might have taken to spend the day in bed with her if she hadn't kept at him about escorting her up to Leadville later in the day.

Billy Vail had given him the time off. But Longarm knew old Billy knew where he'd be if anything came up, regardless of what the sort of prim Mrs. Vail might have been told. So he told the younger gal who scandalized some of her older neighbors on occasion that he had to stop by the office before he really left town.

He told her this after she'd carried their trays to the dry sink and come back in the nude to rejoin him in her four-poster. So she forked a matronly thigh across his supine form and reached down between them as she coyly remarked, "I thought the Federal Building was only open half the day on Saturday, darling. What's the matter? Do you want me to kiss it and make it well?"

Longarm grinned up at her in the now-brighter morning light and reached for a bare tit as he replied, "That's exactly what I meant. If you want us to board the afternoon train to

Leadville, you'd better have mercy on me and let me tell my boss where I'll be before there's no *way* to tell him and *then* where will we be?''

"In Leadville, doing this in that old hunting lodge?" she suggested, as they went on playing with one another.

He pulled her closer and kissed her turgid nipple, which inspired her to stroke his old organ-grinder faster as he insisted, "There's no way I could excuse being out of town when they needed me, if ever they needed me and didn't know where in blue blazes I'd gone."

She sighed and said, "Oh, you're just getting bored with me, you brute. But make me come before you go and I'll forgive you."

So he rolled her over on her back and played with her other nipple, so it wouldn't feel jealous, as she guided his renewed erection into place between her welcoming thighs. His throbbing shaft had no trouble finding its way all the way home, once her wet, trembling love-lips parted barely wide enough to let him enter her.

But as lovely as she still looked and felt as she lay there with her hands locked behind her fine-boned head and careless light-brown curls, a man had to work at it a mite to come that many times in anybody, bless them all.

So it was just as well she took it as a compliment when Longarm locked his elbows to long-dong her with his own legs stiff while he silently counted under his breath, pounding his pelvis hard against hers for fifty thrusts without pause, then cheating just a tad with some moaning and grinding, as he rested his arms and let her take the load off them. He tried picturing that swell-looking actress, Miss Ellen Terry, laid out just as bare-ass and willing as he thrust. For a man who admired female anatomy could tell, just from pictures in the *Police Gazette,* what the tits of a famous actress in a low-cut bodice were likely to look like.

After he'd pounded Miss Ellen Terry fifty times, he closed his eyes and pictured other gals he knew better. For there was a lot to be said for variety, and the thing that kept a man curious was the simple fact that while doing it over and over with the same gal could begin to feel like a chore, those first few thrusts in any *other* gal you could get at were always a fresh thrill.

The familiar form he was fornicating with at the moment suddenly asked, ''Why are you smiling like that with your eyes shut, darling? Are you trying to imply I'm getting fat?''

He laughed sincerely, and assured her he liked her just as well no matter what she might weigh.

She looked away and almost sobbed as she murmured, ''Liar, liar, pants on fire, but don't stop, Custis. Don't *ever* stop, even though we both know I'm not getting any younger, and damn it, I *try* to watch my weight!''

He started to say he'd laid gals way fatter than her. But somehow he felt that might not cheer her all that much. So he pressed down against her to kiss her warmly and tell her, ''You're supposed to worry about such scary stuff as how high up might be, or how far out in the future forever might extend without you, when you're all alone, late at night, with nothing better to worry about. When you're in bed with a welcome guest, it's rude to remind him he ain't likely to live long enough to screw you as many times as he might want to. So would you like me to screw you, or fetch you a kerchief so you can weep and wail like an old maid bemoaning all her lost chances?''

She laughed despite herself and said, ''Pound me, you pragmatic brute!''

So he did, and by the time she'd come, ahead of him, she felt a lot better about the way her life was going at the moment, and agreed there was just no saying what tommorow might bring, so what the hell.

He'd have never caught up with her if her grim talk about old age creeping up on them hadn't inspired him to picture old Billy Vail and his gray and motherly old lady going at it just this way a few blocks down Sherman Street. It seemed likely they still did, since neither looked sick or insane, and Mrs. Vail had likely been a looker in her day. So what might old Billy think about to keep it up as he and his old gray mare went at it like this?

The picture of the rather prim and disapproving Mrs. Vail, posed the same way with her hands behind her tightly pinned-up hair, with her naked thighs flung wide and her elderly tits abounce the same way, struck Longarm so odd that he suddenly felt a thrill of forbidden longings and came all the way down to his toes as he committed wild imaginary adultery with his boss's wife.

So he was still feeling sort of guilty about that when he strode into the Federal Building less than a full hour later. The gilded lettering on the door of their second-story office, which read, "U.S. Marshal William Vail," seemed more stuffy, or accusing, than usual. As he entered, old Henry, the sallow youth who played the office typewriter out front, seemed to smirk up at Longarm as he told him, "I was just about to come looking for you. I was wondering whether I should pretend to be selling brooms or delivering a telegram. Marshal Vail is in the back and he wants a word with you right now!"

"How in thunder could he *know*?" Longarm muttered under his breath as he ambled on back to the private office of Billy Vail, paneled in that same dark-stained oak the federal government seemed to favor for supervising personnel.

The beetle-browed and bullet-headed Billy Vail was seated behind his own cluttered desk, puffing his own less-refined cigar, as Longarm seated himself uninvited in the one comfortable chair on *his* side of the desk and reached in self-defense for a smoke of his own.

Vail snapped, "Don't you dare light that pimp cheroot and scatter ash on my poor rug again! There ain't time. I have Henry typing up your travel orders, and you can still make the eastbound for Ellsworth if you get a move on!"

"Why do I want to go to Kansas, Boss?" asked Longarm as he lit a three-for-a-nickel cheroot just the same.

Vail said, "It wasn't my suggestion. It's your own fault you have to go to Texas because you were such a clever shit out California way that other time. The attorney general wired us a night letter, a long one, about lending you to the State Department for another one of your delicate diplomatic missions. State wouldn't have been able to twist the arm of Justice half as hard if you'd been more delicate about those rogue samurai you went after for that Japanese admiral at their West Coast consulate, you noisy rascal."

Longarm took a drag on his cheroot and asked, "Am I

19

supposed to arrest another Japanese outlaw in Kansas this time?"

Vail snapped, "We're borrowing a court recorder from my opposite number in Ellsworth. You'll find all the names, facts, and figures on the onionskins Henry is about to bestow on you. Then the two of you will head straight south to Brownsville on the Mexican border, where a Danish diplomat has just been murdered by either another Danish diplomat or an infernal Mexican granted diplomatic immunity."

"Does this court recorder from Ellsworth know any Danish?" Longarm asked.

To which Vail replied with a dirty look, "Why, no, we figured you could use a translator who spoke Greek. You're going to find it a can of worms whether you savvy a word of it or not. But ours is not to reason why, and they asked for you by name."

"Why can't we reason why?" asked Longarm, trying to remember one single thing about Danes or Denmark as he continued. "Why me? How come the Brownsville District Court, the Rangers, or the infernal old Danes themselves wouldn't do as good or better?"

Vail growled, "I just told you. It's a can of worms. Nobody else wants it for the same reasons I'd never send you if it was up to me. It's a fool's errand. There's no way any federal, state, or local lawman of these United States can arrest either of the two prime suspects and make it stick. A Mexican named Obregon might have shot the Danish diplomat with a Colt .45. He has diplomatic immunity whether he did or didn't. The other suspect is a Danish officer who may have shot the same cuss in the back with a 7-62-millimeter made in Liege, Belgium, by Nagant. He swears he never did, and he's demanded political asylum as an innocent man accused by political enemies. You'll get all that out of him once you get to Texas with your translator."

Longarm flicked ash on the rug, there being no ashtray on his side of the desk, and demanded, "How come? What am I supposed to do about anything I might see or hear down yonder if I'm not allowed to *act* on it?"

Vail said, "State doesn't want you to arrest either Obregon or the other suspect, a Captain Steensen. Everybody knows who they are. State wants you to track down and bring in a hostile witness, who has no diplomatic immunity and may be withholding material evidence. A Danish marine ran off or rode off with the murdered man's horse and possibly a bullet from the murder weapon, after possibly witnessing just who fired the shot from the veranda he'd have been facing at the time.''

Longarm whistled softly and said, ''That's who I'd want to talk to if I cared whether the killer was Mexican or Danish. But wouldn't you say a Danish marine would be more likely to be in with a Danish killer than a Mexican killer, Uncle Billy?''

Vail said, ''They never asked me for my opinion. They asked me for *you*. But I did wire State about that suspicion, and they just wired back it works either way. The abducted or hostile witness is not a Dane exactly. He's a Danish subject from Iceland named . . . let me see here . . . Pall Njalsson. State tells me Icelanders throw rocks a lot at the windows of Danish officials.''

Longarm took another drag on his cheroot, let fly a thoughtful smoke ring, and decided, ''When you're right you're right. I reckon I ought to hold that notion with slack reins until this Danish translator and me can have a word with our shy Icelander. You say he may be riding the dead man's horse?''

''Icelandic pony,'' Vail replied. ''Thirteen hands at the withers with distinctive coloration, like one of those Mexican palomino Arabs, only even blonder. We hope he's hung on to the dead man's mount, because it's not only distinctive enough for folks to notice and remember, but may be packing the same bullet that killed its original master. The U.S. State Department has sworn out the material witness warrant you'll need when you catch up with Private Njalsson, and the pony itself is naturally material evidence no matter who might be riding it right now.''

Longarm cautiously observed, ''Some old boys of red, white, or in-between persuasion may not cotton much to my demanding they give up a pony they may have paid for or caught wild, to their own way of thinking.''

Vail gruffly replied, ''I just said that. The pony, a mare

named Lille Thruma, is to be impounded as material evidence by the federal government, and we're counting on your powers of persuasion. Whether you track down the mare, the marine, or both, you're to bring them in and turn them over to State, not Justice, in Brownsville. I've just told you my opposite number down yonder passed the buck to me, and I am not about to let him share a fart's worth of credit.''

''What will State do with either the pony or the missing marine?'' Longarm asked.

Vail shrugged and said, ''Don't know. Don't care. It doesn't matter to us, or even to State, once they can tell Mexico and Denmark for certain and let *them* hash it out. As I recall my international law, the host country is off the hook as long as it can prove none of its own nationals did anything mean to a visiting diplomat.''

Henry came in with Longarm's travel orders. They shook on it, and Longarm lit out to make up a lot to a lady in the little time he'd have before that afternoon eastbound combination left town.

She wept and swore and told him she'd told him not to tell Billy Vail where he might be going. So he spread her out on her parlor rug to kiss away her tears, and after she'd come a couple of times, she calmed down enough for him to explain his unexpected field mission. Being smart as well as warm-natured, the young widow found the orders he'd read along the way in his hansom cab almost as interesting.

Sitting up to finish undressing on her sitting-room rug, she asked, ''Does this clerk from that Kansas court really know how to talk to your missing marine in his own country's dialect? I've heard some of those pheasants from outlandish parts can be hard to get through to.''

Longarm chuckled and replied, ''I suspect our hostile witness is a *peasant* instead of a game bird. But you heard right about old boys from the backwoods being tough to cope with. That's how come they want me to let this expert on Scandinavian notions tag along.''

She lay back down beside him and asked him to tell her more about the court recorder he was supposed to meet up with in Ellsworth.

Longarm allowed he'd yet to meet the fool pencil pusher, and that seemed to hold her. There was no saying *how* she'd have taken it if he'd told he was on his way to pick up Fru Sigridur Jonsdottir, a thirty-year-old lady from Iceland who'd somehow wound up in Kansas.

Chapter 4

Horses were not allowed to ride free or even half-fare aboard passenger trains. So Longarm almost always picked one up from a federal remount post or livery stable once he got to where Billy Vail wanted him to go. But he naturally preferred his own saddle, saddle gun, bedroll, and possibles as he rode new range or old. So he'd whipped home to his furnished digs on the unfashionable side of Cherry Creek to gather up his familiar McClellan army saddle, with his Winchester '73 and other things he might need along the trail lashed to the handy brass fittings that old George McClellan, a dreadful general but a swell quartermaster, had seen fit to stud his new saddle design with before they fucked up and put him in command of combat troops.

Longarm's boardinghouse was way closer to Union Station than the brownstone atop Capitol Hill. So Longarm made it easy afoot, with the awkward but not too heavy load braced on each hip in turn.

As he entered the cavernous gloom of the big brick-walled waiting room, the Regulator Brand clock on one far wall told him he had time to spare, and he was glad. For he'd noticed, packing his load those last few blocks, that he had to take a crap.

First things coming first, Longarm picked up his tickets and checked his saddle and possibles through to Ellsworth, hanging on to just the Winchester as he headed for the men's toilet through the crowd.

The former gold camp of Cherry Creek had gotten sort of fancy since they'd changed its name to Denver, made it the state capital, and paved most of its streets. So a tall, tanned figure with a pancaked Stetson and low-heeled cavalry boots at either end of a tobacco-tweed business suit tended to attract curious glances when it strode briskly with a rifle cradled over one arm and the grips of a cross-draw six-gun peeking coyly out from under a coattail.

Longarm wasn't out to shoot anybody as he headed for the men's toilet. He'd learned the hard way early on that a Winchester riding easy-draw in a saddle boot could present just too great a temptation to some railroad help as it rode all alone cross-country.

There was only one young cowhand pissing at the stand-up urinals as Longarm entered the fair-sized facility. The kid was leaving as Longarm let himself into one of the booths, bolted the door, and hung the Winchester on a hook by its trigger guard, along with his pistol belt and frock coat. There was no need to crap uncomfortably, as long as you got there soon enough.

So that was what Longarm was doing—it sure felt good—when he heard boot heels on the tiles outside, but he didn't think too much about them. You expected to hear boot heels in a men's toilet, and sure enough, there came the silken hiss of somebody pissing like he'd been holding it a spell.

Then somebody else came in to march over to the same bank of urinals as one or the other of them said, *"Hvenaer kemur lestin?"*

Somebody else replied, *"Klukkan halfur sex,"* and then they were headed back outside.

Longarm quickly rose, pants down around his boots, and peered through the slit above the door latch just as they were leaving. All he made out in the time they gave him was the impression of a heap of sheepskin jacket and a high-crowned gray Boss Model Stetson bringing up the rear. He hadn't seen the other cuss at all. He sat back down to study on their odd conversation as he wiped his ass.

They hadn't been talking Dutch, High or Low. But Longarm figured their lingo had to be related to Dutch, unless he was wrong about those last words sounding like the High Dutch *"Halb sechs."*

Longarm didn't know enough Dutch to get in trouble, but he had been snowed in for a mighty warm few days with a mighty friendly High Dutch homestead gal, and she'd naturally tried to teach him a few words of her native tongue, once they'd compared all the dirty words in Dutch and English.

It had stuck in his mind, being such an odd way to talk, that a body telling time in High Dutch didn't just use different words for the hours of the day, but *tallied* them differently as well. So instead of saying "five-thirty," you'd say "half six," and that was exactly the time his eastbound combination to Kansas was supposed to leave.

Longarm rose again to haul up his pants and button them as he muttered half aloud, "It's a free country. Where does it say in the Constitution that nobody else is allowed to catch that same fool train at five-thirty?"

As he strapped his gun rig on again, he frowned thoughtfully and thought back to the last time he'd been sent over to New Ulm, where all those Swedish homesteaders had settled.

"It wasn't Swedish exactly," he decided, even as he admitted to himself with a sheepish smile that he didn't know how to ask a gal for a dance in any of those outlandish tongues.

He put his coat back on and took the Winchester down from its hook as he severely warned it, "Let's not go getting our bowels in an uproar over a couple of funny-talking foreigners. Even if that *was* Danish, and even if they *are* about to board the same train in a few minutes, that doesn't mean you want to shoot them, or vice versa. We know at least one full-blooded Danish lawman, riding for old Judge Parker over in Fort Smith. His name's Madison, Madson, something like so, and he's never been accused of shooting anybody in the back."

He decided there was no law against other Danish riders pissing in the same public men's toilet, or even boarding the same train with a likely overly suspicious fool. But just the same, he kept an eye peeled for that Texas hat and sheepskin jacket as he climbed aboard that train a quarter hour later.

He didn't see either as he made his way to a coach seat that put his back to a bulkhead with the Winchester across his lap. He lit a cheroot before he spied the pretty little thing getting on alone with her carpetbag. But there were plenty of other seats, and she never looked his way as she primly sat herself alone with her back to him. So he just went on smoking until, sure enough, a hulking figure who had to stand seven feet tall when you included his gray Boss Stetson came Longarm's way wearing a sheepskin jacket big enough to fit two men of average build. The giant had flung the jacket open because of the balmy spring day they were enjoying, and this let Longarm read the narrow strap across his broad shirtfront. Shoulder holsters had been around a spell. But only serious shootists who didn't want to show the world what they were packing seemed to favor them.

The giant didn't glance Longarm's way in passing as he headed for the next car back. Longarm pretended not to notice *him*, or the much smaller cuss behind him with the same sort of jacket, a mustache the color of broom-straw, and eyes the color, and warmth, of raw oysters.

After they'd passed on to the car behind, Longarm reflected that neither total stranger had to have been pretending not to know him if they really didn't know him. They hadn't asked who might be taking a crap behind a closed door as they were pissing and comparing notes on railroad timetables.

He'd put the two American-looking foreigners on the back of his mental stove by the time the train started up with a jerk to clang out of the yards. The pretty gal had her cameo profile to him as she stared out her own window at the passing scenery. Longarm knew what the outskirts of Denver looked like as the shadows lengthened. So he was really starting to admire that profile as she commenced to smile out at the soft grassy folds of purple and gold that the High Plains turned into near sunset time.

Longarm could almost hear himself pontificating to her about the flora and fauna they were passing, mostly soapweed and cows, until he caught himself and sheepishly thought, "Do we really want to teach any more schoolgirls the lore of the West, old son? I know this is a night train, and I know you could likely hire a sleeping compartment before this night is over. But we'll be rolling into Ellsworth in the wee small hours, and that one's going to take a man a full six or eight hours to hold hands with, if she's willing to hold hands with anybody."

He made himself stare out at the scenery on his side of the car for a spell. Then the conductor read his travel voucher and stuck a paper stub in the holder behind his seat, and Longarm was free to roam the train. He got to his feet and headed back to the club car, where there would be less beauty to distract him and a man could order a pitcher of beer before they came to Kansas and its infernal dry laws.

Once he had his gallon of refreshment and a bowl of pretzels to keep him company, he went out on the rear observation platform, put them down on a bitty tin table, and took one of the two wicker seats provided for anyone who liked to count railroad cross ties as they receded to a point near where the sun was setting behind the Front Range west of the town they were leaving.

The mountains rose jagged-ass black against a sky that glowed as many shades of red and yellow as the coals in a locomotive's firebox while it held the first evening stars at bay. The range to either side of the speeding train smelled good enough for *folks* to graze as it sprouted fresh where the last snow patches of March had surrendered to the warm chinook winds of greenup. Longarm knew it would be even warmer by this time down Brownsville way. The Rio Grande emptied into the Gulf so far south that their winters were as warm as Colorado got by April. But at least he and that translating gal from Iceland by way of Ellsworth wouldn't have to cope with South Texas in high summer, when things could get from hot to hellish.

He was idly wondering how hot it got in Iceland in the summertime, and what that court recorder from there might look like, when the door behind him slid open and that other gal he'd admired up in their coach car came out on the platform alone, then gasped, "Oh, excuse me! I didn't think anyone else was out here, sir!"

He rose politely and removed his hat as he told her, "There's plenty of room and I ain't no sir, ma'am. I'd be Curtis Long. I ride for the Denver District Court as a deputy marshal, and I'm at your service, Miss . . . ?"

"Durler, Heidi Durler," she replied as he moved to swing the other seat around to sit in.

She hesitated. So he assured her, "You can leave just as sudden if you set a spell or not, Miss Heidi. In the meantime, I have beer and pretzels with an extra glass. I'd be proud to go inside and fetch you some soda pop instead, if you've taken the pledge or never started."

She laughed and sat down, saying, "Never ask a German-Swiss girl if she drinks beer, ah, Curtis. But they told me beer was not allowed aboard this train for some reason."

He poured her some suds in that extra glass he'd been smart enough to bring along, just in case, as he explained, "Kansas is the reason, Miss Heidi. They just voted their fool selves dry. That doesn't mean you can't belly up to the bar in most any Kansas cow town. It only means prissy hotels, railroad club cars passing through, and so on worry about such legislation."

As they clinked glasses, he added, "We're still in Colorado. I'll tell you when we cross the line, but I won't arrest you if you want to go on drinking. There's no *federal* laws against drinking, unless you happen to be an Indian, and you just told me you were . . . did you say Swiss or German?"

She took a sip of Colorado lager from up by Lookout Mountain and answered, "Both. I was born in San Francisco. But according to my elders our old country, small as it may be, began as a union of French, German, and Italian hill folk who got tired of paying taxes to a Holy Roman Emperor who was neither holy, Roman, or much of an emperor when we stood up to him. My elders came from the north of Switzerland, where everyone still speaks German, or High Dutch, as most English speakers put it."

He said, "Have some pretzels too. I met another Dutch-or-German-speaking gal one time who tried to teach me to tell time. Might you agree that *hover sex* means five-thirty?"

She laughed and sounded more foreign as she replied, "*Halb sechs* or half six would sound closer. But whom were you planning on asking for the time in German?''

He said, ''Nobody. Somebody already did, and I'm pretty sure they said something closer to *hover sex*. Might anyone you know of from the old country say it that way, ma'am?''

She shook her trim brunette head, then thought and decided, ''They might pronounce *halb* as *halbur* or even *halfur* in Low German or one of the Scandinavian languages.''

''You mean like Danish or Icelandic?'' he asked.

The girl who only knew some Swiss German shrugged and told him, ''I suppose so. I can't say for certain. Does it really matter?''

Longarm said, ''I hope not!'' as he rose to turn and peer into the club car through the grimy glass. It was dark enough by then so that he could see in better than anyone inside could see out.

Those two foreigners wearing shoulder holsters under sheepskin jackets were jawing with the colored barkeep at the far end. He was the only one of the three who glanced Longarm's way now and again. But that was enough for Longarm.

He told Heidi Durler to get out of her own high-backed wicker chair and move closer to him to one side of the sliding door. She did so without argument, but naturally wanted to know how come.

He said, ''It's safer than sending you inside in their direction. I hope I'm being an old maid and nobody is really fixing to roll out from under the bed. But tell me honest and tell me true, Miss Heidi. Didn't you ask inside if I was out here alone before you came out to join me?''

She didn't answer, but her flustered gasp inspired him to nod and say, ''Right. Make yourself flat as you know how against these few feet of shadowy bulkhead betwixt me and the side rail. Stay there until I tell you different, hear?''

She sobbed, ''What are you talking about? What in heaven's name is going on?''

To which he could only reply, ''Do as I say and let's hope I'm wrong. For heaven won't be the way to describe things if I turn out to be right!''

30

Chapter 5

It seemed to be taking forever to Longarm, but the bigger and blonder of the two inside wanted to wait longer as his short, dark sidekick murmured, "*Koma.* Let us get this over with."

The hulk with broomstraw-colored hair protested, "*Ekki dimmur nogu!*"

The dark one softly hissed, "How many times must I tell you to speak *Enskur,* softly? These people pay little heed to the murmurs of their own language at any distance. As for whether it is dark enough outside, the sun is down and the moon has yet to rise. We shall never get a better *hagnathur*— I mean advantage, damn it. You have *me* doing it and my orders are to stop that sly fox, not to give you language lessons!"

He put down his beer glass beside the generous tip he'd left on the club car bar, and started drifting back toward the sliding door to the observation platform. The car was crowded by this time, and nobody seemed interested. His hulking sidekick naturally followed, muttering, "What about that *stulka*? She knows nothing and presents no danger to us."

His darker and meaner-smiling leader muttered, "She is no *stulka*. She is a *vaendiskona* who travels this line in search of adventure. I naturally asked a porter when I noticed she was following him past us."

"She is *jung og laglegur* and I like this not!" The big one sighed as they made it to two empty seats near the sliding door and sat to let anyone who'd noticed them lose interest.

A million years later, the shorter one leaned forward to risk a quick glance through the grimy glass. As he sat back again, he told his sidekick, "Things could not be better. They told us he was a bit of a Don Juan, and she likes boys as well. They are seated close with their backs to the door. Get casually to your feet, and when I slide the door open, you shall aim low into the chair back to our left while I finish off the one to our right."

"I don't want to shoot the *stulka*! How can you be sure which one is seated right or left?"

"I can't, *thu bjani*! What does it matter? We can't leave her as a witness. Haven't you ever done this sort of thing before? Stay here and I'll take care of both of them if you are *hraeddur*!"

The big one gasped, "You call me a *ragur*? You dare? I'll show you who is afraid. But what about all these others? We can't kill every *Kanar* in this car, can we?"

His more experienced comrade in arms said, "Stop playing for time. You know that when he hears our shots, Snorri has orders to pull the brake cord and throw everything into confusion. You and me have only to leap off in the dark, get rid of these hats and jackets, and get back aboard, up forward, as the harmless immigrants we are!"

Longarm wasn't too worried about that barkeep, Snorri. He'd already taken care of him.

Not waiting for further argument from his cowardly partner, the dark professional got to his feet, took a deep breath, and slid the door open to step out on the platform as he drew his Starr .45-28 to blaze away at the wicker back of the barely visible chair to the right.

But there was just enough light from the ruby sky and lamplit interior for Longarm to slam the nape of his neck with the steel barrel of his own Winchester.

As he pitched forward through a blizzard of spinning stars, his bigger sidekick charged out with a confounded roar and fired wildly as Longarm used the Winchester on him more seriously.

The point-blank impact of two hundred grains of lead backed by forty grains of gunpowder staggered but failed to drop the giant, until he floundered into his dazed sidekick and grabbed for him as Longarm fired again to prove that a man out on his feet is not the most secure handhold. The two of them went over the rail as Heidi screamed like a banshee with her eyes shut and her hands over her ears.

Longarm turned and took hold of her as he lowered the smoking muzzle of his Winchester, saying, "Snap out of it and listen to me tight! I told you I was a U.S. deputy marshal, and I just found out the case I'm on has to be bigger than mere murder. I know you don't want to get mixed up in a game you never chose to play, and I mean to let you leave the table with all your chips as soon as I can. But I need your help right now. So do I have it?"

She weakly asked, "What do you want of me, Custis? Did your really kill those two men just now?"

He shifted the tin table with its refreshments back where it had been between the two wicker seats as he replied, "I couldn't have done either much good. We're going at least forty miles an hour on a level grade. Sit down here and let me do the talking, see?"

So there she sat, looking as if butter wouldn't melt in her mouth, when the conductor and a brakeman armed with a sawed-off ten-gauge came out to join them in the gathering starlight.

Bemused by the tranquil scene, Longarm having set his Winchester aside on the deck, the conductor stammered, "What's been going on out here? We just heard gunshots, a heap of gunshots, and the barkeep says two cowboys who talked funny were out here with you two."

Longarm turned with a smile, saying, "As a matter of fact, there *were* some old boys dressed cow out here a spell back. Don't see 'em now, though. Reckon they found this platform crowded and went somewhere else."

The conductor growled, "The hell you say. Sorry, ma'am. But nobody is ever going to sell this child such a fairy tale and . . . Say, aint you that lawman they call Longarm? The one who stopped them train robbers up in the south pass that time?''

To which Longarm was forced to reply with a modest nod that he was guilty as charged.

So the conductor winked and answered, ''Say no more. I'll tell the boys inside we just run over some track torpedos left by the repair crew to show they've finished with the next section. Let's go, Bull. Can't you see these passengers want to be alone out here?''

As soon as they were, Heidi asked, ''Repair crews? He meant those shabby men you see with tools along the track from time to time?''

Longarm said, ''Yep. They have to keep these rails we're rolling along neat and tidy, lest we all wind up upside down on the prairie. I hadn't considered rail torpedoes. That old bird must lie a heap. The track workers lay explosive caps on the track for their train crews to read like Morse code, with the space betwixt bangs filling in for the dots and dashes. The other passengers who don't really care will likely buy his big whopper. I don't know how long it will take any other gunslicks aboard this train to figure out who won back here.''

She gasped, ''Good Lord! You think there could be others after you up forward?''

Longarm shrugged and said, ''*I'd* sure send along some backing if I was planning to assassinate a federal agent aboard a train. Like I said, this game is turning out to be bigger, with more players in it, than anyone on our side figured.''

She shuddered and asked, ''What are we to do next? How are we to figure out who else might be after us aboard this train before they can try again?''

Longarm answered simply, ''We can't. I mean *I* can't, Miss Heidi. I told you I was fixing to deal you out as soon as I possibly could. They're out to stop *me*. They could hardly be after *you*. They'd have had no orders about anyone else on board but me. I'm still working on who could have told them *I* was headed for Ellsworth in any way, shape, or form. But you ought to be safe enough as soon as we part company at the next water stop.''

She gasped. "You're getting off?"

He said, "Have to. I don't know who or what I'm up against in the cars ahead or what's waiting for me on the Ellsworth platform with a big brass band. My baggage has been checked through. So it will be waiting for me in Ellsworth no matter when I turn up. I mean to turn up after I send me some wires at the next water stop and, whilst I'm at it, see if anybody else gets off to send any wires."

She said, "Most of my baggage has been checked through to Kansas City and, like yourself, I would feel much safer in some dear little prairie town than aboard this train with hired killers. But I have some personal things in the carpet-bag I placed in the rack above my seat up forward. Do I have time to fetch it?"

He said, "You'd doubtless be safer up forward than me right now. They'd never throw down on you with me and my badge unaccounted for. But weren't you listening just now when I said somebody else might try to send a wire from the next stop? You just now saw how noisy it can get when I meet up with such jaspers."

She said, "I certainly did. That's why I'd feel ever so safer with you, Custis. What's the matter? Don't you like me?"

He chuckled fondly and replied, "I've always admired brunettes and to tell you the truth, a strange gent walking into a small-town hotel with a lady after dark ain't as likely to excite the local vigilance committee. I ain't talking about getting separate rooms, no offense. I'm out to throw the other side off, not advertise my whereabouts."

She nodded soberly and replied, "They've been alerted to watch for a tall, dark lawman traveling alone, not a pair of tourists in no great hurry to get anywhere, right?"

He said, "I couldn't have put it better. But as grand as the notion strikes me, Miss Heidi, it wouldn't be fair to you. Aside from the danger, there's no future in it for a nice gal like yourself."

She demurely asked what made him think she was a nice girl.

He blinked and stammered, "We'd be parting company in Ellsworth no matter what kind of a gal you might be. What kind of a gal *might* you be, since you were the one to bring it up?''

She answered simply, ''I'm a whore. I used to call myself an adventuress. I often take a mark without even kissing him as I ride the cross-country trains to nowhere. But if a girl's going to take her chosen profession seriously, she has to call a spade a spade, and most men wind up calling me a whore whether they get any or not.''

He laughed uncertainly, and asked, ''How much were you fixing to ask me for the pleasure of your company, Miss Heidi?''

She smiled at him in the dim light and replied, ''Nothing. I knew who you were and I'd heard stories about your way with girls, good and bad. I'd be lying if I said I'd have passed up a likely mark to have a fling with you. But all the other well-dressed men on board seem to be traveling with other women this evening. So what was a girl with a restless nature and a long lonely ride ahead of her to do when there was a pair of shoulders like yours on board?''

He reached out to pat the hand she'd placed on the table by the beer pitcher as he said, ''You'll pay for that forward remark about my fair white body. I'll pay for the room. But it's understood this romance is betwixt two strangers under a full moon, costing nobody nothing serious and ending with no tears or recriminations as soon as it's safe for us both to tumbleweed on.''

She moved her hand from the table to his lap as she agreed she couldn't have put things more delicately.

He said, ''Let go of those buttons and just hold the thought, ma'am. Since that first water stop east of Denver was at Deer Trail, we'll be stopping next at Arikaree Wells within the hour. So why don't we talk about it some more after you fetch your bag from our coach car?''

She rose from her seat to bend and kiss him in a surprisingly sisterly fashion before she slid open the door and vanished—forever, if Longarm had anything to say about it.

For he'd lied about their time of arrival at the next water stop. He'd ridden this line often enough to know where he was once the moon was shining down this bright on familiar prairie. So he reached down for his Winchester and got up as, sure enough, the train began to slow down.

Longarm rolled over the rail before the locomotive up at the far end could hiss to a full stop at the water tower.

Getting his bearings from the glowing windows and dim street lamps of the dinky prairie settlement, Longarm legged it toward the Western Union office he recalled from an earlier visit.

He'd hit the ground running in hopes of heading off anybody else with a wire to get off. He hadn't deserted the adventurous Heidi Durler because he was shocked by her forward way of putting things. He'd meant what he'd said about wanting to deal her out of a mighty dangerous game. For whores had as much right as anyone to go on living, and things were getting downright spooky.

He made it to a storefront catty-corner from the dimly lit doorway of the small Western Union office near the freight office. Like the shop behind him, the railroad facility had already closed for the night. They tended to close everything early in Arikaree Wells.

Nobody came anywhere near the Western Union there during the short time it took the night train to refill its tender tank and roll on, with a long lonesome wail of its steam whistle.

Longarm had never decided whether locomotive whistles sounded so wistful on purpose, or whether his own mind made an otherwise natural sound that haunting because it dredged up memories of small boys in bed, listening to a distant railroad whistle as they wished like hell they could follow it through the night to parts more interesting than a tiny West-by-God-Virginia hollow with its chores, church, schoolhouse, and such.

He shifted his Winchester to a less-threatening position as he gave up on the Western Union and stepped out from the storefront to head for the one hotel in town.

As he did so he heard a familiar voice call out, "Custis Long! Where are you? I thought we had an agreement and . . . you haven't stranded me in this one-horse town, have you?"

Longarm stepped into the circle of light cast by a street

lamp and waved at the smaller figure toting her carpetbag up the far side of the one serious street.

As she almost ran across to him, he soberly assured her, "It was your continued safety and comfort I had in mind, ma'am. But seeing you wouldn't stay safe and comfortable aboard that train, let's see if we can find some safe and comfortable place to spend the rest of the night here in the middle of nowhere."

Chapter 6

Along the way to the Majestic Hotel, she coyly confided there'd been no other baggage checked for any particular destination. She said she traveled light, and bought what she needed to replace the soiled traveling duds she discarded along the way.

When she confided the carpetbag he was toting for her held what amounted to a chemistry set, he soberly replied, "I wasn't trying to leave you aboard that train because I thought you were a *dirty* whore, Miss Heidi. I told you there were others after me that I'm still confounded about. I'd never forgive myself if I got an innocent party killed by a person or persons unknown!"

She said she'd be the judge of how innocent she might be, and told him she hosed herself out every day, whether she'd been with anybody else down yonder or not.

He sighed and said, "If you're trying to make me feel romantic, you're going about it all wrong, no offense. Some of my best friends lay other gents about as often as I lay other women. But we don't go bragging on it, and it's understood that any fun-loving child with a lick of sense keeps his or her horny privates in good working order."

She laughed softly and purred, "I'm glad you'll have something clean as a whistle for me to play a love song with.

How far is this hotel you promised me back there? These heels were never made for this dusty street.''

He waved ahead at the unlit sign of the Majestic Hotel, which could have passed for a shut-down warehouse if there hadn't been a few lamps dimly gleaming out from scattered windows upstairs and down. He surmised she'd stayed in hotels as often as he had, from the way she moved off to casually examine the Boston fern in one alcove while he signed the register and hired them the only room with a bath.

The old gray clerk never let on he found two total strangers in a remote prairie town at all unusual, but apologized for not having a bellboy to see them up the stairs. He said they just didn't get enough quality folks at the Majestic to justify keeping a bellboy.

Longarm allowed he could pack their baggage upstairs, seeing he'd packed it all the way from the train stop. So Heidi drifted over to join him as he headed for the stairwell, and the next thing he knew they were alone up yonder and she was trying to unbutton his fly in the moonlight coming through the open window as she knelt before him on the threadbare carpet.

He said, "Hold on. It's early and I'm holding a loaded Winchester at port arms, for Pete's sake!''

She giggled and said, "I know. I think it was all those big guns of yours that first piqued my interest. I read somewhere that both men and women tend to confuse gun barrels with potent peckers.''

He laughed and said, "My real pecker's feeling potent enough at the moment, honey. But I want to wait and see if we have visitors coming before I take my pants down, see?''

She rose back to her feet, moving over to make certain the door was bolted on the inside as she protested, "You told me we got off here to throw those killers off our trail, Custis!''

He said, "We did. It should have worked. No matter what they wire ahead down the line, neither they nor the master-mind they're riding for ought to know just where we got off, and where we headed after that.''

"Then who . . . ?" she asked.

He said, "Town law. It depends on how tame this town

40

might be and what time he turns in for the night."

He placed the Winchester across the foot of the bed and hung up his hat and coat as he explained. "You heard the night clerk say how seldom anyone fancy enough to need a bellboy stays here. They'd mostly hire rooms to stock and produce folk off the surrounding range, just in town for business or pleasure. So we might strike Arikaree Wells as exotic in our store-bought duds, bay rum, and that French perfume you're wearing."

He hung his gun rig over a bedpost, took a small square linen pouch from the frock coat hanging nearby, and sat down on the bed to pick up his Winchester and cradle it across his knees as he told her, "I ain't trying to act shy, honey. If nobody comes before I clean and reload this saddle gun, I'll figure it's safe for us to act a mite more neighborly."

She sat down beside him with a laugh, saying, "Well, I suppose I could go into the bath and clean my *own* weapon, but to tell the truth, it's not healthy to douche more than you really have to."

He said other pals had told him that. He began to empty the Winchester as she muttered remarks about nervous lawmen.

Longarm shrugged and levered the action all the way open as he confided, "I ain't nervous about having somebody pounding on yonder door to ask what we're doing in here. I just prefer to devote all my powers to one pleasant chore at a time, and this infernal gun needs a good cleaning anyway."

He opened the gun-cleaning kit and tied a fresh patch of cloth to one end of some fishing line as he continued. "I want to get that over and done with early. So I'll know, should anyone rattle our door latch later on, whether I want to open up with my .44-40 in hand or not."

She started to ask a dumb question. Then she nodded and said, "Once you've clarified whether it would be the local law or another tourist after dark, can I count on you to treat me rough? Honest to God, I'm really gushing for you, Custis! Don't ask me why. I've never been able to understand these sudden changes of mood either. I mean, it seems I no sooner make up my mind that all men are frogs before I suddenly meet a prince again!"

He set the Winchester on its butt plate between his boots on the carpet, and dropped the fishing weight tied to the other end of his line down the barrel, as he dryly asked what happened when a pretty little brunette kissed a prince instead of a frog.

She sighed and said, "A lot of the time, he turns into a frog. Why were those men aboard the train trying to kill you, Custis?"

He stood the Winchester on its muzzle to pull the cleaning patch up through the barrel as he told her, "I wish I knew. When I got on that train, I thought I was on my way to Texas to see if I could shed some light on a fairly cut-and-dried backshooting. The case is only supposed to be complicated by the two main suspects playing games with international law. I thought all I had to do was round up a third party who could implicate either a Mexican stockman or a Danish officer. I thought, like everyone else, I'd been sent to track down a scared young Danish marine private who'd run off on his own. But how often might a marine private on the dodge have the wherewithal, or the know-how, to hire his own assassination team?"

She suggested the private might have sent home for money.

Longarm laughed and said, "I mean to have my own pals check the cable offices for massive money orders. The international cable can be a fuss about giving away private messages. But they have to tell U.S. Customs about serious transfers of wealth from . . . Hold on, the Mexican government won't let you wire money across the border in secret either. They have a twenty-percent export tax on silver, gold, or paper that can be converted to either!"

He ran another patch through, the other way, as he told her he was glad he'd let her tag along after all. He said, "I find I talk smarter to others than I talk to myself."

He swiftly reloaded the Winchester's magazine, replacing the few rounds he'd fired with fresh brass from his well-stocked frock coat as he explained, "When you tell yourself a story or a joke, it ain't the same. Your mind runs along the tracks it followed the first time. It's the little surprises of another body's words that jar your brain into thinking afresh.''

She leaned back across the bed in her dark but summer-weight dress to dreamily reply, ''I see what you mean. It must be a lot like the difference between masturbation and fornication with some sweetly surprising stranger. No matter how well you know how to tickle your own fancy, it's nothing really *new* to come that way!''

He set the saddle gun aside as he smiled down at her and asked, ''Do you really wind up playing with yourself that way, seeing the line of work you're in, no offense?''

She raised her high-button shoes to brace her heels wide on the edge of the mattress as she spread her upraised knees and hoisted the hem of her skirt, moaning, ''More often than you can imagine! I told you I try not to bed my marks unless I like them, and most men I meet on trains are such clumsy clods!''

He decided, ''Well, if that town law meant to come and question us, you'd think he'd have come by now,'' as he began to unbutton his own duds.

Most men would have, faced with a hairless little ring-dang-doo smiling up at them from between such shapely little thighs.

As she followed his drift, she shucked her summer dress off over her head without rising from the bed. Neither one of them made any dumb suggestions about trimming the bed lamp, and the rest of her was trim and petite for a full-grown woman. He knew she was a full-grown woman when he lay down beside her to take her in his naked arms and suddenly found himself being raped, with her on top and whimpering like a bitch wolf in heat as she literally milked his raging erection with her astoundingly muscular innards.

It felt swell, and it didn't occur to him before he'd rolled on top to finish right with her high-buttons crossed over the nape of his neck, that no gal had ever learned to screw that fine without a lot of practice.

That was the trouble with having a lusty organ-grinder and a romantic nature, Longarm knew, resisting the impulse to ask her who on God's Green Earth had taught her that sort of deep-throated growl with her vagina as they paused a moment to share a smoke and catch some cool evening breeze.

She told him he had as nice a cock as she'd ever vibrated around, and he allowed she was pretty too. Gals always thought it was better to be considered pretty than a good lay. It was a wonder the two sexes agreed on anything. He didn't want her telling him lies about his old organ-grinder. He'd gone swimming naked with enough other growing boys to know about where he stood in the scheme of things. Knowing he had enough was enough. He never accused women of being downright freaky-twatted. He gently but firmly asked if they couldn't just up and *do* it, without trying to convince one another they'd never done it with anybody else they hadn't just hated.

She laughed, and got on top again before he'd finished the smoke. He reached out to snuff it out as he admired the way her small but perfectly fashioned breasts bounced by lamplight. Little Heidi was built as different from that widow woman back in Denver as two women could get without one of them being ugly. As he thought about that, he felt better about this one being such a sass. Because that made for yet another contrast as he shut his eyes and pictured a bigger, softer brown-haired gal who'd gone to her marriage bed as a virgin.

When he suddenly laughed, Heidi stopped bouncing to ask him why. He said, "I was just now considering that whether a gal learns to pleasure a man from one or two husbands or a whole army of different men, she still winds up bouncing with about the same enthusiasm."

"Were you thinking about another woman just now?" she demanded.

He said, "Everybody does, now and again. I was comparing you in a favorable way to a fine lady who's been putting on a little weight of late. You can compare me with anyone you fancy, as long as you keep moving like so!"

She laughed, low and dirty, and declared she'd show him something he'd never had from any other damned woman.

So he never told her he'd been sucked off before he was old enough to shave regular. Gals who gave French lessons seemed to want to feel they were pioneers, and it sure felt grand her way.

So a swell time was had by all, and when Longarm suddenly woke up, surprised as hell when he saw he'd been asleep, he couldn't have gotten it up again with a block and tackle.

That wasn't what worried him. He saw at a glance she'd trimmed the bed lamp. He had to prop himself up on one elbow in the moonlight to make sure he was really alone in there. The door to their adjoining bath was open. Unless she liked to crap in the dark with the door open, she'd lit out on him!

He swung his bare feet to the carpet and reached for the end table to strike a match and relight the lamp. He saw her carpetbag was where she'd left it by the dresser. But there was no sign of her summer dress or the organdy rose she'd been wearing in her black hair in place of a proper hat. So she'd gone out. It was pushing three o'clock in the morning when he consulted his pocket watch.

"Asshole!" Longarm grumbled as he rolled to his feet and, first things coming first, checked to see whether she'd taken his wallet.

She hadn't. He still had his money, his badge, his guns, and even the onionskins Henry had typed up for him back in Denver.

"That doesn't excuse letting yourself fall asleep in bed with any self-confessed railroad whore and con woman!" he declared aloud as he rapidly got dressed, strapped on his .44-40, cocked his Stetson cavalry-style, and trimmed the lamp again before he let himself out into the dark hallway.

"I'm missing something here," he told himself as he eased down the stairs and strode past the dozing night clerk to find it was downright cold outside this late in the day in the month of April on the High Plains.

He knew she'd be even more goosefleshed as he hugged the shadowy storefronts in the moonlight. All the street lamps had gone out by that hour, bless them. So the only lamplight in sight ahead came from that Western Union office closer to the tracks.

He saw her first, coming home from that direction at a rapid pace, as if in a hurry to get back in bed with a man she'd screwed to sleep before he could wake up.

45

He froze in a doorway and let her get close before he stepped out to say, "Howdy. I hope you were smart enough to send your message by night-letter rates. Or was it too urgent?"

She gasped, "Oh, it's you, darling! You startled me!"

To which Longarm sadly replied, "You startled me too. So now you are under arrest, and if you think you can wiggle off the hook back in Denver by compromising the arresting officer, you just don't know Judge Dickerson of the Denver District Court."

Chapter 7

The adventuress stared down aghast at the handcuffs Longarm had whipped off the back of his gun rig to snap around
her wrists.

She pleaded, "Surely you jest! What are you trying to
accuse me of, darling? I only went out for a breath of fresh
air. I needed to sort my own thoughts after some of the things
that have happened in such a jumble since first we met."

Longarm said, "Sure. First we'll take you back to the
telegraph office and see what their night clerk has to say
about fresh air. Whether the message you sent makes any
sense or not, the town law ought to be willing to hang on to
you for me until I can get someone from the Denver District
Court to pick you up and store you away for me in the Federal House of Detention. Lord only knows when I'll be back.
But at least I ought to get there alive, without you keeping
tabs on me for the other side."

She protested, "How could I have been in with those killers on that train? Have you forgotten they tried to kill me
too?"

To which he could only reply, "Not hardly. I studied on
that as I was leaving our hotel. You don't seem dumb enough
to remain loyal to anyone who set you up for a killing,
whether they had a reason or just didn't care what happened
to anyone in my company."

"I swear I have no idea who those men were. You have to believe me, darling! You have to believe I'm not in league with any enemy of you or your government!"

"Who *were* you working for?" asked Longarm, herding her toward the telegraph office she'd just left as he added, "I use the past tense because there's just no saying when you'll be free to work for anybody again. I know the smart boys told you arresting officers ain't supposed to bring in suspects they've known in the biblical sense. But I'm sure Judge Dickerson will work something out after he chews me up, down, and sideways."

She protested, "I haven't done anything else you can arrest me for! All right, I fucked you and I sucked you and maybe I sent a wire bragging about it to a friend. Show me where I violated any federal law!"

He moved her along as he said, "I'll know better after Western Union hands me a transcription of that sneaky wire you just sent at this outlandish hour. I know the same smart boys likely told you Western Union operators get fired if they disclose any paying customer's message. But they forgot to tell you any clerk who causes the company to be served with a federal writ can be in even *more* trouble! So we'll just see what you wrote about fucking me, and who you addressed it to. Then I'll have them picked up, and we'll give what we have to Reporter Crawford of the *Denver Post*."

She pleaded, "Please! You don't know the sort of people you are dealing with!"

Longarm chuckled dryly and told her, "That's all I'm trying to find out. I'll be mighty surprised if your message to them ain't in code. But we can still arrest anybody we find at the address you sent your message to."

He paused between street lamps to swing her around so she stared up at him with frightened eyes as he tried, "I'd be lying if I said I wanted to alert both Western Union and the town law here as to where I headed after I evaded their trap. So tell me honest and tell me true, and we'll just go back to our hotel and say no more about it."

She sobbed, "You have no idea of the trouble I'd be in if they found out I'd told you!"

He said, "You must have no idea of conditions in our few

federal prisons for womankind. Dealing my cards faceup, Miss Heidi, I don't want to produce a federal witness who's sucked me off to old Judge Dickerson, and their lawyers would make you look bad in court as a known whore. So I give you my word I'll let you off and never put your name in any report if you'd like to tell me what in the blue blazes this is all about!''

She licked her lips, took a deep breath, and licked them some more before she said, ''Most of what I've already told you was true. I may have changed my name to protect my elders, but I am an American of Swiss-German descent and I do work the trains for fun and profit.''

He said, ''It's been lots of fun. Get to the point.''

She sighed and said, ''Sometime ago I met a man, a handsome man who, like yourself, neither paid for pussy nor got into card games with friendly strangers aboard trains. After we'd gotten to know one another better, in the biblical sense, he told me how much he admired my German. You see, we, ah, had a little fun speaking German, once I detected his accent. As a matter of fact, that's how I managed to . . . break the ice with him in the dining car.''

Longarm grimaced and said, ''I noticed how innocently you can pick a gent up. Which one of the High-Dutch-speaking countries did this sporting blood hail from?''

She hesitated again, heaved a defeated sigh, and said, ''Prussia. I've been passing on conversations I might hear in my travels to the Prussian General Staff, by way of their military attaché in Washington.''

''Jesus H. Christ! I took you for an innocent whore, and all this time you've been a Prussian spy?''

She answered simply, ''You have no idea what a girl who understands German may hear on cross-country trains. As you say, Prussia is not the only German-speaking power, and even some of Der Kaiser's own subjects plot against him when they don't think any of his agents can overhear them. But naturally, I often ride the trains for days without even getting the chance to eavesdrop on a farmer interested in our American Homestead Act.''

He said, ''I get the picture. Get to your orders about *me*.''

She smiled timidly and confessed, ''Teaching you French

was my own idea. They wanted me to find out just how much you knew about that assassination down in Texas. I just wired them you didn't know very much and that you and your office were treating it as a simple case of murder, complicated by diplomacy.''

He smiled thinly and told her, ''I'm glad to see you tell the truth on occasion. Now tell me what we've been missing. What might the backshooting of a Danish diplomat by either a Mexican or another Dane have to do with the Prussian General Staff?''

She took a deep breath, shuddered, and said, ''Missing guns. Nobody who will admit it seems to know how many, or who diverted them from Oberndorf to Brownsville, Texas. But somebody must have if a Danish count they'd asked about it was murdered in the very seaport the ship they suspected of running guns ran into!''

Longarm shopped for guns more often than he could afford to buy any. So he nodded soberly and said, ''Oberndorf, Prussia, is where that Royal Wurttenberg outfit makes those single-shot Mauser breechloaders the Prussian Army has used on the Austrians and French—so far. It's a good gun. Its bolt action allows a trooper to reload six rounds a minute flat on his gut. But you can do that with the trapdoor Springfield, the Remington rolling block, and heaps of other current breechloaders. So what's so special about a shipment of Mauser bolt-actions headed for the border country, where such guns command way higher prices?''

She said, ''I don't know much about guns. But I understand these brand-new Mauser rifles somebody begged, borrowed, or stole are not single-shooters. I'm supposed to listen for anyone in any language mentioning a rifle that combines the rugged design of a bolt-action with the tube magazine of a Henry or Winchester.''

Longarm whistled softly and said, ''Somebody already did, a year or so ago. I remember reading about it in *Scientific American*.''

He thought, then recalled, ''It wasn't the Mauser brothers. Fruwirth, in Austria, and our own Hotchkiss and Chaffe-Reese have experimented with combinations of the Mauser, the Spencer, or Winchester patents.''

He tried to decide which way they were heading as he went on to say, "That bolt-action allows for a man-sized cartridge like our army .45-70 the Winchester patent just can't stand up to. But up to now, no army ordnance department seems to be in the market for a serious repeating rifle. They ain't just acting crusty. Lead and brass are both heavy metals, and even at a firing rate of six rounds a minute, a trooper in the field uses up ammo faster than ordnance can get it up to him. So they're still arguing about the merits of rapid fire at short range versus slow but serious fire out past four hundred yards."

He caught himself and asked, "Never mind all that. Are you trying to say the Prussian General Staff has come down on the side of rapid fire in heavy caliber and somebody else has been helping themselves to the rifles?"

She shook her head and replied, "As a matter of fact, the General Staff considered Mauser's new design, ordered some experimental models, then shelved the idea until such time as they can figure out that ammunition problem you just mentioned. The Mauser brothers *say* they delivered the few dozen repeating rifles they made up to the Prussian Army. Maybe they think they did. But thanks to the rather fussy record keeping of the Prussian authorities, it's been discovered that at least a boxcar load of the same-model Mausers was shunted into a train of farm produce bound for the seaport of Hamburg. The cases seemed to have turned into windmill parts and irrigation pipes by the time they were loaded aboard an American flag freighter bound for Brownsville. Naturally no Prussian customs agents would have inspected Prussian exports unladen from an American vessel in an American port."

Longarm let go of her wrists, and got out his notebook to scribble a few lines in the dark as he muttered, "That Danish officer asked for political asylum at U.S. Customs down in Brownsville. This sure gets curiouser and curiouser."

She looked up hopefully and asked, "Do you think your own government could have wanted a carload of those new repeating rifles for its own reasons?"

He put the notebook away, muttering, "Not hardly. The trouble with such notions about government conspiracies is that governments don't have to behave so silly. If President Hayes or even General Sherman wanted to order ordnance experiments with a new military rifle and some Danish diplomat was in the way, they'd hardly need to have him murdered. They'd just have a dozen witnesses declare him a crazy-mean drunk and ask Denmark to recall him as *non grata*."

"Unless he knew too much," she pointed out.

He snorted in dismissal and said, "*Bueno*. Let's say the country is being run by murderous crooks in high places who don't worry about the next elected administration uncovering any dirty little secrets in the files, or anybody involved in the plot coming forward for fun or profit once they're out of office. Let's say they had Greve Svein Atterdag murdered in public when they had all the federal facilities in and about Brownsville at their command, if they just wanted him to die naturally or disappear into thin air. Let's say they killed him sloppy and gave sanctuary at the U.S. Customs House to one of his killers. What in tarnation would *I* be doing here tonight?"

She tried, "Wouldn't they have to at least go through the motions of a full investigation, darling?"

He said, "Call me Deputy Long. I'm still studying on that as well. The State Department is run by a cabinet member who could send in as many or as few investigators as he liked. State asked for me by name. Why would they have done such a thing if they didn't want me looking into the killing? Neither me nor my boss, Marshal Vail, ever up and *volunteered* my services. Whether anyone in our government high enough to matter has any notion of what's going on, they'd have no need to put this child in his grave. Me and Billy never heard of any Danish bigwig getting killed before Washington told us. They never had to tell us, and they could *still* stop me, easy, just by ordering my boss to order me back to Denver, see?"

She did. She said, "Those two on the train couldn't have been on Der Kaiser's payroll. I just wired *that* side you didn't know half as much as they do, and *they* don't know what's going on! They'd never send anyone to *stop* you. They'd *want* you to get safely through to the scene of that assassination and turn over all the wet rocks you could manage! Count Atterdag was working with Prussia on the mystery of those missing Mausers. Prussia is anxious as Uncle Sam to know what's been going on down in Texas. It's not nice to murder members of the diplomatic corps. It's even worse to divert shipments of still-secret weapons to another country. But you're right about gunsmiths in America, Austria, and even Switzerland already knowing how to combine the strong Mauser action with the ammunition tube of a lever-action repeater. So the Prussian General Staff is really more worried about the audacity of some person or persons unknown running off a private issue of such weapons and sneaking them out of the country with forged export papers, see?''

He said, "I'm commencing to. Let's head back to our hotel."

She beamed up at him and exclaimed, "Goody! How about taking these handcuffs off me now?"

He said, "I'm still studying on that. We'll talk some more as we await the morning eastbound. I ain't about to let you put me to sleep again."

As they started back to the Majestic Hotel, she groused, "Don't be mean, honey. You know how much fun it can be for a man and a woman to kiss and make up after a little misunderstanding."

He laughed despite himself and said, "I understand you way better now, no offense. We'll go over your story some more as we wait up for that train. If I buy half of it, we'll ride on to Ellsworth and you can stay aboard as I get off. I reckon playing the cards you've just dealt me close to my vest has arresting you on cloudy evidence beat. So just behave yourself for a change, if you still know how."

But she didn't, and since that train wasn't due in before seven in the morning and they'd commenced to talk in tedious circles about the little either knew, Longarm naturally decided he might as well make up with the pretty little thing. So he did, but this time he left his socks on as he threw it to her dog-style, keeping an eye on his saddle gun and .44-40 as he admired the trim little rump he was having so much fun with.

53

Chapter 8

They were much more friendly when they parted as their second train paused at Ellsworth the next afternoon. As he had at Arikaree Wells, Longarm dropped off running, with his rifle, well short of the passenger stop, and circled wide to see who might be waiting for him there.

Nobody was. When he reported in to the Ellsworth District Court, Billy Vail's opposite number there told him they'd been so worried when he hadn't shown up at the crack of dawn that they'd wired all along the right-of-way to send local lawmen out to look for him.

It answered some other questions on Longarm's mind when he found out nobody had found the mortal remains of anybody anywhere along the tracks. Whether those two who'd come after him aboard that earlier train had lived through the results or not, it was a safe bet the other side had its own riders out to make sure nobody brought them in dead or alive.

Longarm told the Ellsworth marshal most of what had happened since he'd left Billy Vail's jurisdiction. He left out some of the personal habits of Miss Heidi Durler, but told the older lawman all she'd told him about gunrunning. He added, "There's little call to keep such secrets for Der Kaiser. I've found the more cards you lay out faceup, the less call anyone else has for shooting you before you deal 'em."

54

The somewhat leaner and hungrier-looking but just as crusty cuss in Kansas—the Justice Department seemed to get them out of the same barrel—asked, "Ain't them square-heads likely to take it out on the Swiss miss who told you about them newfangled Mauser rifles?"

Longarm nodded, but said, "We had us a long talk about that as we were, ah, making up after I'd caught her spying on me. They're just as likely to suspect she blabbed no matter what the rest of us say, once we start our own investigation of import duties, bills of lading, and so on. That missing hostile witness may or may not be able to tell us who shot Count Atterdag. Finding out how much the dead man might have known, about who and what, might give us a motive whether that marine can point out the killer or not."

The Ellsworth marshal nodded thoughtfully and said, "The mouth of the Rio Grande would be where *I* might run some fancy guns, if I was in the gunrunning trade. Am I correct in assuming a heavy repeating rifle you can handle easy from a prone position—say, behind some mesquite—would be an ideal weapon for a rebel guerrilla?"

Longarm had already thought of that. He nodded. "Such a rifle would make an ideal defensive weapon. Those old boys at the Alamo would still be holding it against all comers if they'd started out with repeating long-range rifles and all the ammunition they could store up ahead of time. I suspect the Prussian General Staff has been hesitating because they are downright *offensive* rascals who can't affort to issue more than eight or ten pounds of bullets to an advancing conscript in Prussian blue."

The older lawman shoved a cigar box across his desk to his younger visitor and stated flatly, "The Mex *federales* are armed with those old single-shot trapdoor Springfield .45-70's, or the British Martini-Henry chambered for the same rounds. I understand some Turks recently made hash of the Russian Army with underpowered but rapid-fire Winchesters, though. I'd sure hate to be trudging across the Chihuahua desert with my thrifty single-shot toward a bunch of them *Mejico Libre* boys armed with repeaters that could nail my ass at six hundred yards!"

Longarm helped himself to a nickel cigar as he replied,

"That would likely smart, and I know for a fact there's a heap of pissed-off Mexicans who never voted for El Presidente Diaz, because I've had supper with some of 'em."

He left out his relationships with some of their rebel sisters or daughters, and pointed out, "I know one of our prime suspects is a big-ass Mexican who'd hate to see such rebels win. But that takes us to how come a member of the ruling junta would gun any Danish officer who was trying to *stop* the suspected flow of arms to the riders for *La Revolución*. That leaves us with the other prime suspect, and I'm having trouble making *him* fit either."

They both lit up. The marshal shook out his match as he asked Longarm, "Didn't Billy Vail wire us that Captain Steensen, working for that Danish trade monopoly, had argued with Count Atterdag just before the count wound up dead and *he* wound up demanding political sanctuary from us?"

Longarm took a drag on the cheap cigar, wishing it was one of his even cheaper cheroots, and said, "He seemed to think his own government might hang him first and ask questions later. Whether an officer and a gentleman or not, Captain Steensen ain't no highborn Danish greve. That's what they call a count, a greve, and by any name his shit don't stink and you ain't even allowed to insult him. So Steensen could be as pure as the driven snow, and still have good cause to hole up with American pals at the Customs House. I mean to question him a heap once I get there."

The marshal let fly with an expanse of cheap blue smoke and asked, "You say there's already something about this trading officer that sticks in your craw, old son?"

Longarm nodded. "His possible motives. Unless Steensen is one of those thin-skinned assholes who'd gun a man over words at a ball where the punch has been laced enough to matter, Steensen is a Dane. And he rides for Kongelig Handel Afhaenge, which I looked up back in Denver, and which means Royal Trade Department. When they call the KHA a monopoly, they ain't whistling Dixie. They didn't allow anyone but KHA members to import or export a spool of thread to Iceland until recently. You still ain't allowed to even *visit* Greenland, their Faroes, or the Danish Virgin Islands without their permission. So a loyal agent of the Danish government makes a lot more sense trying to *control* the sales of rifle guns than selling them in secret to rebels, Mexican or Icelandic."

The older American lawman blinked and asked, "They got rebels in *Iceland,* for Gawd's sake?"

Longarm confessed, "I'm still working on how many and just how serious. Those missing Prussian rifles slipped out of any Prussian control once they were laden aboard an American flag vessel. Said vessel put in at a river port where *Danish* flag vessels may put in to load most anything, with U.S. Customs only asking you to declare what you're bringing *into* the country. Mexico levies export duties. We don't, so far."

The Ellsworth lawman nodded soberly and said, "I'm commencing to follow your drift, old son. But wouldn't a loyal member of this here Danish trade monopoly be as anxious to keep guns out of the hands of Icelandic rebels as a Mex in cahoots with Diaz would want to bar the same from *La Causa Mejico Libre?*"

Longarm said, "That's about the size of it. Neither prime suspect had any call to block Greve Atterdag's investigation there in Texas. But I'm hoping, like the old song goes, that farther along we'll know more about it. When do I get to meet that court recorder who speaks Danish, Marshal?"

The older lawman rose from his desk, saying there was no better time than the present, lest old Sigridur quit early that afternoon.

Longarm followed him out, and down a courthouse corridor, his Winchester pointed politely at the floorboards, until they got to a smaller office with one dinky window.

A severely pretty blond gal was playing a typewriter at a flat-top desk near the window. Her wheat-stem hair was straight as an Indian's, and braided over the top of her head like a straw tiara. She had on a white blouse she filled out considerably, and as her boss introduced Longarm to her she got up from her desk, then up some more.

Longarm hadn't been introduced to all that many ladies taller than himself by a good two inches. But he managed not to laugh or ask how the weather might be up there as she held out her hand as if she expected him to shake it instead of kiss it. Her towering figure was saved from being bearish by a surprisingly trim waist. Otherwise, it seemed ample enough. The voluminous buckskin-colored whipcord skirt extending down from her cinched midriff might have made a swell play tipi for a bunch of Cheyenne kids, once you propped it empty over a circle of broom handles.

Sigridur Jonsdottir said she'd been expecting to meet up with him, savvied their mission, and had her own possibles packed to go over at her nearby cottage.

Longarm said, "*Bueno.* I was hoping we might just make the supper-time train coming through here in a spell. My own baggage is over to the railroad stop. If you're ready to move out, we'd better see about getting your own stuff over by the tracks."

He turned to her boss to politely add, "That's with your permission, of course, Marshal."

The older lawman beamed and replied, "I told Billy Vail the two of you could borrow Miss Jonsdottir with our blessings. But are you certain you'll make connections with that southbound express you want at Junction City if you get in after dark?"

Longarm said, "I've studied the timetables, and we'll make the connections we need to, changing more than once along the way."

He turned back to the big blonde to add, "It's going to take us better than forty-eight hours if we start right now, ma'am."

So she swung around the desk and led the way out the door as she asked what was holding him up.

Outside, she led the way as quickly, swinging along on her long legs on high-button shoes most men could have worn. Longarm was able to keep up without panting, but he wasn't used to walking so fast down a street with a woman. From some of the looks they got along the way, it was safe to assume not many folks in Kansas were used to such a sight.

Her hired cottage was up a side street behind a picket fence and a neat but not too fancy front garden. As he followed her in, Longarm complimented her on her English,

58

and allowed that she spoke it with hardly any accent.

She waved him to a seat in her small front parlor and went to fetch her own things as she raised her voice to call back, "Thank you. I am an American citizen now, and of course I have to pay attention to English spelling and grammar if I am to keep the transcripts at the federal courthouse. I have a Harrington Richardson .24 packed with my riding habit. Do you think it would be better if I carried it in my handbag aboard the train to Texas, considering the trouble you had getting here?"

He called back, "We'd best pick you up at least a .36 along the way, ma'am. You look strong-wristed enough to fire a .45, no offense, and while I'm hoping you won't need a gun at all, it can be a mortal insult to fire a bitty .24 at a grown man. Mortal for all concerned."

As she came back out with a soft leather traveling grip in either hand, Longarm rose and said, "Hold the thought a moment before we head over to the railroad, Miss Sigridur. We've got a few minutes to talk and some serious matters to sort out if you're to go along with me at all."

She put down her bags, but demanded, "What are you talking about? They told me about the mission and asked if I wished to volunteer. You want me to go to Texas with you and question suspects in Danish, Icelandic, or Norse. They are all closely related, and I can assume the right accent if you want to trick anybody. I am, as we say in Iceland, a well-sailed traveler."

He said, "That was the original notion. None of us expected one missing witness to have a whole gang spread out betwixt us and him. I'm still working on whether they're trying to help him stay missing or trying to get to him first and shut him up. Either way, it's a safe bet he's still out there somewhere."

She nodded soberly and said, "Dead men tell no tales, *ja*?"

He said, "My sentiments exactly. If you're willing to come along anyway now that the party's gotten rougher, I'm going to have to ask you to stick tight as a tick and do just as I say, no matter how odd or improper it might sound to you. Agreed?"

She raised a thoughtful brow, but nodded.

He said, "*Bueno*. To begin with, I want to try something with you that not even your boss at the courthouse is to know about."

She hesitated, shrugged, and began to unbutton her blouse as she calmly told him, "We had better make it a quick one then, if you really expect us to catch that next train out."

Chapter 9

It would have been neither polite nor truthful to tell a no-longer-young and never petite blonde that you didn't find her misunderstanding mighty tempting. But she'd been right about the time they had to work with. So he tried to sound just as worldly when he told her, "I'm glad we're going to be such friendly traveling companions, Miss Sigridur, but we'd best keep our duds on till we change trains up the line at Junction City."

"This is a secret we must keep from everbody else?" she demanded with a puzzled smile, although without a trace of embarrassment in her well-sailed eyes of cornflower blue.

He explained, "We will be catching a southbound Pullman train, and the nights get chilly on the prairie at this time of the year. But the really sneaky part is our exact route to Brownsville."

He handed her his Winchester and picked up her two heavier bags as he continued. "I can tell you along the way to the railroad stop, seeing you seem so willing to go along with my suggestions."

She pinned on a straw boater and gathered up a knit wool shoulder wrap to guard against the evening ahead of them. Then she locked up and said, "I'm still listening. But you sure do beat about the bush for a man of your reputation, Custis Long."

He grinned sheepishly and said, "I never kiss and tell, but I see someone else must have. What I had in mind, for right now, was a move to shake off anybody laying for us along our sensible route to that border town almost due south of here. By this time any mastermind who sent a team after me at the Denver Union Station has to know I got past them. But he, she, or it can't know exactly when I planned to get here, pick you up, and move on."

She said, "The marshal and some of us were talking about that before you got here. The marshal told his deputies to keep their eyes peeled for any strangers getting on or off the trains passing through."

Longarm nodded and said, "The other side would expect that, if they're another side worth worrying about. They're more likely to have somebody staked out at Junction City, ready to board any train bound for Brownsville right behind us."

She asked, "Would that be wise on their part? It didn't work the first time, and this time they should expect you to be more alert!"

He shrugged and explained, "It's tough to be alert when you don't know who to watch out for. They know what I look like. Since they knew I was making this detour to Kansas, they likely know what *you* look like, no offense. So there we'd be, two targets, as any other passenger of any description waited for the chance to try and deal us out of a game we didn't even know the name of."

She shuddered and asked, "Are you sure you really want us to catch that night train to Brownsville?"

He shook his head and cheerfully said, "We ain't about to. We're fixing to ride on *through* Junction City and catch another southbound later further east, out of Manhattan, Kansas."

She protested, "Listen, I am a court recorder, and people rob our Kansas trains a lot. So I have a grasp on the way the tracks run east of here, and that line out of Manhattan won't take us to Brownsville."

He said, "If you know that, our secret enemies ought to be able to figure it out as well. We ain't boarding any Brownsville-bound train because they might be watching it.

We're headed south to Galveston. They'll never expect us to head *there*."

She laughed incredulously and replied, "You're right. The State Department wants us to investigate an assassination that took place in Brownsville!"

He nodded. "On the same Gulf of Mexico, with coastal steamers following the Inland Waterway all the way from east of the Mississippi to Matamoros, Mexico. I wasn't planning on such a romantical sea voyage when first I thought that alternate route up. But either way, we ought to get much closer than they expected us to before we pop back into sight and commence to question everybody we can get at about that killing and the missing marine who witnessed the killing!"

She agreed that his sneaky plan sounded safer and might not delay them by more than an extra day. So they enjoyed a snack and some soda pop at a trackside stand before Longarm reclaimed his loaded-down army saddle from the nearby railroad shed. Sigridur didn't have to have him explain why he didn't want to check their baggage through this time. Well-sailed gals knew how little time a traveler might have to manage unusual travel connections.

They boarded the eastbound passing through just after six P.M. without incident, and found facing seats where they could pile all their possibles across from their knees. The sun wasn't anywhere near setting that late in the spring, and it would have been dumb to start anything they couldn't finish right before they had that Pullman car after dark to work things out like grown-ups. So along the way to Manhattan, Longarm questioned her about the Icelandic dialect that hostile witness might be more willing to talk to them in.

Sigridur said the good news about her native tongue was that it was related to English. So while the spelling was wilder, it wasn't tough to grasp that *Hin mothir og fathir* lived in a *hus* with their *sonur og dottir*.

The bad news was that Icelandic was only *related* to English, so that many a word was entirely different, and worse yet, lots of words that meant one thing in English meant something contrary in Icelandic.

Sigridur said a *barn* was a child, you climbed up a *fell*, and if you stepped on a *trapp* you were heading upstairs.

He asked how she could manage Danish as well as Icelandic and English.

She confided, "Everybody can, whether they want to admit it or not. Danish, Icelandic, and Norwegian are just dialects of Old Norse, as English has divided into, let us say, Broad Scots, Texas Twang, or high-toned Oxford English. An Icelandic fisherman may feel the same way about the Danish trader in town as an Irishman feels about his English landlord. But they can speak to them, or even speak *like* them if they have to. Why do you ask?"

He said, "I speak fair Border Mexican. I don't know how well Captain Steensen and his Danish pals speak English. It's good to know that betwixt us we ought to be able to question anyone we can manage to catch up with."

She said all bets were off if any suspects turned out to be High Dutch, and she had trouble getting through to Swedes.

He said he doubted there were any Swedish suspects waiting for them in Texas, although that angle about Prussian repeating rifles might turn out to be a linguistic bother.

Sigridur hadn't been in that other office while he'd filled her boss in on those Prussian repeating rifles. He decided it had been just as well when he saw how little she knew, or cared, about that subject.

She told him none of her kith and kin had been allowed to own anything but Danish muzzle-loaders made for Eskimo fur hunters and other such backward subjects of Denmark before she'd been old enough to worry more about boys.

He asked her to stick to firearms, and she told him the monopoly imposed on Iceland by that Danish KHA had been eased a bit a few years back after considerable hellfire and brimstone from the late Jon Sigurdsson, who'd roused his fellow Icelanders to demand free trade and at least some home rule or else.

Longarm asked how come this Icelander who sounded like Thomas Jefferson was *late*.

She allowed he'd died of natural causes a year or so back, long after she'd left home.

He said he'd heard Icelanders felt about their Danish king about the same way Irishmen felt about Queen Victoria, and seeing they had nothing better to jaw about as the sun went down outside, he asked her for a thumbnail sketch of the current situation in her old country.

He wound up with a history lesson instead. Sigridur said she had to start at the beginning if he was to make any sense out of her sagas of gloom and doom beneath the midnight sun.

Somebody had sure done something gloomy to that Danish count. So he told her to just spoon the medicine out to him, and she did.

She said Vikings had discovered Iceland and then Greenland back in the Dark Ages, and had gotten their names backwards, likely from it being so dark on the North Atlantic when a sea rover was liquored up on honey wine. She said Greenland was just about covered with ice, while Iceland was almost as green and a tad larger than Ireland.

Then she started to talk about ocean currents and prevailing winds, and he said he only wanted to know what made Icelandic rebels so rebellious.

She said the Vikings hadn't found anybody worth robbing on either big island. Then farming and fishing folk had settled mostly in Iceland to get away from the kings of Norway, who'd gotten too big for their britches and commenced to tax folks instead of just robbing them the old-fashioned way.

Moving out to the middle of the main ocean with nobody telling them what to do, the early Icelanders had taken to feuding and fussing as bad as gold-rushers without a vigilance committee. So the survivors of what they called sagas had gotten together every June in this big canyon to hold an open-air congress they called the Althing to settle feuds, make up laws they called *logs,* and drink lots of the honey wine.

She bragged on the Althing being older than the British Parliament and far more democratic. But she allowed that without a written constitution, some sessions of all those honey-wine drinkers could turn to shouting matches and end in sword fights. So after a web of feuding and manslaughter led to an Althing recalled as the ''Stone Throwing Summer,'' the king of Norway stepped in with the blessings of the Pope and many a bruised Icelander to restore some law and order, inspired by the way the king of England had done as much for Ireland a hundred years earlier. Norway, the same as England, just took over and put its own royal governors in place after they'd restored more order than the local folks had ever asked for.

Sigridur sounded as if she was still bitter about something recent as she groused that the Icelanders had sold their birthrights for a mess of pottage and never gotten the pottage.

She said the Norwegian strangers had lorded it over them bad enough. But then Norway and Sweden had both come under Danish rule and the Danes, who'd never done anything to deserve it, took Iceland over to oppress the natives considerably. She said that Icelandic seamen had been world traders in the Middle Ages, with many an English, Dutch, or Hanse vessel putting into Icelandic waters to swap all sorts of the good things in life for Icelandic wool and stockfish.

Longarm wasn't surprised to hear that the Royal Danish trade monopoly, the KHA, had barred Icelandic ports to everybody else and forced the Icelanders to trade with them and nobody else. But he thought the other aspects of Danish rule sounded mighty piggy.

Sigridur told him that whenever a Danish official or KHA trader wanted to go anywhere, he was allowed to commandeer the pony of the first peasant he asked. If he wanted to cross a river, those folks living near it had to drop whatever they were doing and ferry him across. Free. It went without saying the Danes never paid for the favors of any Icelandic gal they fancied, or took no for an answer. Longarm wondered if that might account for the way a country gal from Iceland had commenced unbuttoning her blouse when a rider for the U.S. government suggested he might want a sneaky favor.

She said that the one-sided trade restrictions imposed by the KHA had been even rougher on a folk who were having enough trouble getting by on marginal range with volcanoes out back. She said the trading posts set up by the KHA set the prices on trade goods and anything the local Icelanders might have to swap. She said the Danes tended to hold Danish hardware, notions, and tobacco dear, while dismissing Icelandic wool and smoked fish and mutton as inferior. And they made sure Icelanders couldn't shop for fairer prices anywhere else, including in Iceland. A certain Pall Torfasson had had the entire contents of his house confiscated after he'd swapped some wool socks his wife had knitted for some fishing lines an English trawler had had to spare.

Another Icelander called Holmfast Gudmundsson had been flogged in public for selling fish to *another Icelander* who lived outside the bounds of his own KHA trading post.

Longarm stopped her and said, "I follow your drift. If *you* remember those names and the tales of injustice that go with 'em, I can well imagine how Icelanders who never applied for American citizenship must feel. So now this Icelandic leader who'd been standing up for their rights has up and died on them, meaning many a disgruntled or just ornery cuss could be plotting something more direct, and a man hunkered down behind some volcanic rocks with a repeating Mauser would be able to deliver death directly at six hundred yards for certain, and further with a little luck!"

She asked, "Then you think it is possible those missing Mauser repeaters were meant for Icelandic rebels, based in *Texas* of all places?"

He shrugged and said, "Mexico has more rebels than you can shake a stick at and they're way closer. But in the meantime, there ain't anything unusual about rebels from all sorts of climes holing up in this land of the free to plot and solicit funds at leisure. So it works either way, and like the old song goes, farther along we'll know more about it. Farther along, we'll understand why. I like that old song, I've run across the oddest things farther along just by following its advice to be patient and keep plodding farther along."

Chapter 10

April nights were cold in Kansas. So even though they had
a stove lit down the aisle a piece, and the oil lamps all along
the car gave off some heat as well, Sigridur got out her wool
spring coat, and still bitched about American weather next
to the warm clammy sea breezes of her old country.

She wound up colder by the time they rolled into Junction
City. For it was commencing to snow outside. Longarm
knew they'd never be able to make anybody out on the platform while they paused there. He knew anyone peering into
the lamplit car could see they were aboard and not getting
off. So he moved them and their baggage out on the forward
platform of their coach car, just behind the dining car the
line had shut down for the night.

As they stood there in the dark, wisps of snow drifting in
to swirl around their ventilated forms, the big blonde protested that he was out to freeze her to death.

He took her in his arms to see if he might warm her some
as he told her they only had to stay out there while the train
pulled on in, stood in the station just a spell, and moved on
out.

Sigridur unbuttoned the front of her coat and partly
wrapped the two of them closer, shuddering as she pleaded,
"Hold me *closer* then. I'm not wearing any undergarments,

and these bitter drafts are blowing up under my skirt beyond endurance!''

He ran a tweed-clad thigh between her long legs to pin her loose whipcord skirting to the bulkhead she was braced against. She thrust her big pelvis forward, and there was no mistaking what she was groping for with her sort of amazing crotch. As he found himself rising to the occasion, the big blonde actually grabbed hold of his bulge with what felt like skillfully forked fingers down yonder. So it seemed only natural to kiss such a friendly gal, up above where she was smiling at him so innocently.

Sigridur kissed like she was out to swallow him alive at *that* end too. She stuck her tongue halfway to his tonsils, and rolled it all around his teeth and gums, while she reached down between them to go for the fly of his pants.

He pulled his head free to warn her, ''We're coming to a town, and this is likely to get us stared at if any new passengers get on at this end!''

She moaned, ''They can't see anything if I hold my coat-tails all the way around you. Please don't tease me like this, Custis. We've both known what we wanted since the first time our eyes met back in Ellsworth!''

As she unbuttoned his pants with what had to be practiced skill, Longarm protested, ''It's early, and I told you we'd be aboard a real Pullman train up the line at Manhattan, honey!''

She purred, ''I'm looking forward to that. But we won't get to Manhattan for *hours,* and would you have me waste this much passion on my own hand? There is simply no way I could ride as far as that transfer point without climaxing one way or another, now that you have gotten me started!''

He was too polite to say he thought it was she who'd gotten *him* started. She had a point about how hard it was to stop once a big old gal was hauling your cock and balls clean out of your pants.

He returned the favor by hoisting her skirt for her, under the screeen of her darker coat. He could see why those upward drafts had been pestering her, once his questing hand found nothing at all but a whole lot of naked flesh above her mid-thigh garters.

Their train rolled into Junction City just as he thrust into her, deep as hell for a wall job, thanks to her out-thrust pubic bone and her legs actually being longer than his own.

Like most men tall enough to matter, Longarm usually found that position a tad awkward, calling for him to spread his own feet wide as the gal stood tippy-toe and seldom managed to take it all. But it was much different with such a long-limbed and ingeniously built gal.

Sigridur Jonsdottir didn't come with a bitty little twat despite her other proportions. She was a big old gal with a big old twat, and she could have likely taken his fist past the wrist, had either one of them wanted to try that. But she was muscular as well as gigantic. So she was able to sort of suck him up inside her and bite down hard to offer them both considerable friction as they both thrust their hips like hoochy-coochy dancers and got back to kissing like long-lost lovers. They were going at it hot and heavy when the train hissed to a stop at Junction City.

She pleaded, "Don't stop! I'm almost there!"

He said, "We got to. We ain't almost there. We're standing in the station!"

She pleaded, "Keep going! I don't care if anyone suspects anything! What can they really see of what we're doing under this coat?"

He pressed her hard against the bulkhead, his shaft in her deep but not moving, as he insisted, "The ones I'm worried about ain't out to *embarrass* us. They're out to *shoot* us."

So he got his gun out as he left his organ-grinder in, and after at least a million years had passed while they stood there throbbing on the platform, the train moved on some more, and nobody seemed to have noticed them out there in the dark.

So Longarm made it up to old Sigridur by pounding her hard until she bit down and climaxed, with him spurting in time to her inner pulsations.

As the trail rolled on through the snowstorm and they began to notice that again, Longarm kissed her sincerely, and told her he had never had a better quick one standing up with all his duds on.

She clung to his semi-erection with her moist inner lips as she shyly confided, "I have always liked it standing up.

70

Back home a bad boy used to tease me, as I passed him and his friends, by calling me a Hallgerdur Langurfotleggur!''

She suddenly laughed and said, ''That is funny. They call you Langurhandleggur! What a saga the skalds could have made up about the two of us if we had met in the days of Njall's Saga!''

He truthfully told her he had not the least notion what she was talking about. So they somehow wound up screwing some more while she explained that any limb sticking out of a body was a *leggur* in Icelandic. So what he called a leg was a *fotleggur* or foot leg, while an arm was a *handleggur* or hand leg.

He shoved it to her as he mused aloud, ''Let me guess what *lang* likely means. You're saying they called you Longlegs back in your old country?''

She coyly confessed there were times long legs came in handy for a warm-natured gal, but explained that the more famous Miss Hallgerdur Longlegs had been the cause of the considerable blood and slaughter they told about in Njall's Saga, a tale of blood and slaughter Icelanders told their children on long winters' nights.

It being nighttime, and snowing like hell as they tore through the night on an open railroad platform, Sigridur insisted on telling it to Longarm as she helped him move in and out of her with a firm hand on either of his tweed-covered buttocks.

She kept her version terse, but included all the dirty parts, so Longarm could see what a Jezebel that Hallgerdur Longlegs must have been in olden times. She'd had two husbands murdered by her kinsmen by the time she'd married up with a retired Viking called Gunnar. An easygoing gent as long as you didn't cross him, but inclined to come at you waving a sword in one hand and a big battle-ax in the other if you did.

Gunnar's beautiful bride, who likely did it swell standing up, lying down, or hell, flying, got into a neighborhood feud with the wife of Njall Thorgeirsson, another respected chief who never liked to draw his sword in anger, but who'd only take so much shit off anybody.

Sigridur told him that for quite a spell that was hell on all the *others* in those parts, neither Gunnar nor Njall took sides in the fight between their wives. But being the wives of Jarls, or big high-and-mighty landlords, the gals acted high-and-mighty with each other's *thralls,* or servants. Killing the servant of somebody you didn't like was not only fun but insulting, to their way of thinking. So with all the folks getting murdered having kith and kin who'd as soon eat shit as let the spilled blood of a kinsman go unpunished, old Gunnar was called before the Althing to explain how come he just couldn't control his beautiful but bitchy wife.

Gunnar told them all to go fuck themselves, and the next thing he knew he was holed up in his farmstead with enemies all around and yelling for his blood.

Holding Longarm deep inside her, Sigridur said, "Gunnar held them at bay with his bow and arrows until his bowstring of human hair broke. He asked his Hallgerdur Longlegs for a hunk of her own hair to fashion a new bowstring. That was when she suddenly remembered she was vexed with him about a quarrel of their own sometime earlier. So she refused, and reminded him she'd warned him she would get back at him some day. So he cursed her and drew his sword to just go down fighting as a proud Viking was supposed to."

Longarm said, "He should have just snatched her bald-headed and fixed his busted bow. How come they call it Njall's Saga if it's all about Gunnar and his sassy wife?"

She said, "It wasn't half over with the death of Gunnar. The sons of Njall Thorgeirsson set out to avenge the killing of Gunnar."

Longarm blinked and said, "Hold on. I thought you just said the two families were at feud!"

She said, "Move a little faster, please. You'd have to be born an Icelander to understand how complicated our affairs of honor can get. Njall's three sons and their followers ran down and killed the ones who'd slain their father's honorable enemy. Then they ambushed one of Gunnar's relatives because they considered him boastful. Then they were talked into another absurd act of murder by another one of Gunnar's kinsmen, a two-faced troll who makes Shakespeare's Iago seem a true friend."

Longarm said, "You're right. You'd have to be born Icelandic to make any sense of *that*. Could we go inside again?''

She purred, ''You *are* inside, and I love it. Njall's three sons caught the orphaned son of the chief they'd ambushed in a corn or wheat field near Ossbaer. The boy's name was Hoskulder, and he had no reason to be on guard against any attack because he was harmless, popular, and Njall himself had taken him under his personal protection.''

Longarm said, ''Old Njall sounds like a nice gent. Don't you want to save some of this for that nice Pullman compartment later on?''

She said, ''Just do it this way one more time. Njall's murderous sons surrounded Hoskulder in the open field and cut him down. They were denounced at the Althing, and everyone was against them now. A posse of a hundred men descended on Njall's farmstead, calling for their blood. Njall knew his sons were in the wrong. But they were still his *sons*! The avengers set the houses on fire, but offered to let Njall come out and leave alive. Oh, that feels good. Njall chose to stand by his horrid sons. They all died together in the flames. The good and the bad together and I'm comingggg—*minn stor karmannsk hrutur!*''

That made the two of them, and once they were back inside, both sets of long legs a-wobble and glad to get in from the cold, Longarm was pretty sure they were through for the night.

But it took a good while before they'd changed trains at Manhattan and found themselves headed south after midnight in that cozy private compartment she allowed she'd been looking forward to.

He figured she meant it when she proceeded to undress with the wall fixture burning bright, as if this had been their third or fourth night getting ready for bed together.

Longarm still felt a mite shy, despite all that huffing and puffing on that dark platform, because they'd been dressed as well as in the dark and . . . Lord have mercy, there surely was a lot of Sigridur to see stark naked as she stood there, hands on hips, with her blond head nearly brushing the ceiling, and asked him, ''Do you still think you can't get it up for us again tonight?''

He not only could but did, unconcerned by the less-earthy

notions of his own politer society now. For he could see, as the big blond farm girl hopped naked on the bunk bed to spread her big country thighs and flaunt her blond cunt hair, that Sigridur wasn't all that impressed by the Danish princess who'd married up with the Prince of Wales, or the manners of the Danish redhead's mother-in-law, Queen Victoria. Those sagas Sigridur had been raised on hadn't had prissy morals about the lusty men and women who'd come west-over-seas, as they put it, to live as free and natural as they could manage on their mid-Atlantic island.

She welcomed him aboard with a natural moan of animal pleasure, and it was something like easygoing slap-and-tickle with a friendly old Lakota gal, save for the fact that Sigridur was a blue-eyed blonde with high-toned Nordic features. He could see how that other long-legged gal in that saga about poor old Njall might have driven many a man wild out yonder under the northern lights and . . . "Thunderation!" he exclaimed.

Sigridur kept bumping and grinding under him as she asked what was distracting him *now*.

He went on humping her, as most men would have, as he explained, "I've been trying in vain to come up with a motive for men without a sensible connection to any rebel movement having it in for a man out to stop a shipment of lost, strayed, or stolen rifles. I completely forgot what the French lawmen advise when you can't come up with any other motive. They say *cherchez la femme*. See if there could be a woman mixed up in it."

He kissed her some more before he explained. "I know Mexicans can get excited over a woman at a dance, and you've convinced me Scandinavians have been known to brawl over them at least as much. Wouldn't it be a bitch if all this mystery was inspired by nothing more than one drunk cutting in on another at a fancy ball?"

Chapter 11

They finally got some sleep, which he needed more than she did, and spent most of the next day lounging bare-ass in their private compartment, admiring the passing scenery outside and pulling down the shades when the train was standing in a station, for the views inside would have struck a lot of folks as far more interesting.

When they weren't viewing one another in interesting ways, Sigridur liked to tell him stories. He found her old-time sagas more to his taste than her confessions. That was what a well-sailed farm gal who'd started young liked to call her bragging. Confessions. Women were inclined to call it confessing when they just couldn't keep their mouths shut about the wild things other men had done to them, or vice versa.

Longarm had noticed most men either came right out and said they'd had a swell time with some old gal, or said no more about it. You hardly ever heard men admitting they'd been at their kid sister or even their kissing cousins, while many a gal seemed sure that if her daddy or big brother hadn't really molested her, he'd sure as hell been thinking about doing it. Gals told the damnedest tales about older women who'd tickled their fancy while combing their hair, and seemed to feel it made any man in bed with them feel good to hear about those other brutes who'd beat them up

75

and made them commit crimes against nature until now they might enjoy them, although only with such a sensitive and understanding simp.

Longarm hadn't figured Sigridur had taught herself to take it so many ways so often. So he kept changing the subject back to Iceland and the folks who hailed from there, whether she was a hostile witness or not. Next to knowing a lot of positions and the rustic attitude that went with them, Sigridur knew all those old Icelandic sagas and *eddas* by heart.

She said plain stories were called sagas, while the *eddas* were supposed to rhyme. They didn't rhyme when you repeated them in English. So she mostly stuck to the sagas, explaining they were older than most folktales in the younger English language.

That likely accounted for so many of them sounding like earlier versions of familiar legends about noble but doomed outlaws, monsters who'd had to be tracked down and hacked apart, or mysterious elfen maidens who lured men out into the heather and ferns to Lord only knows where, since they'd never been seen again.

Even though they were just folktales, Longarm encouraged her to go on as he tried to get a better handle on her almost unknown kith and kin. For as she talked about them, Longarm commenced to see they were a tough dry-humored breed that reminded him of the more written-about Scotch Highlanders.

They'd dressed even odder in those saga times, although Sigridur said they hadn't indulged in sword fights at the supper table back in Viking days. For they'd have never built all those seaworthy dragon ships, or fashioned long swords with names like *Baralogi* or Waveflame, if they'd fought one another all the time. She said the Vikings who'd gone off to raid all the way to Russia had never been a majority of a mostly hardworking bunch of farmers, fishermen, and craftsmen, and that Mr. Wagner and other modern romantics made the wild bunch look wilder than they'd really been.

She said none of them had worn horns or wings on their helmets, and allowed that much of the blood and slaughter in the sagas had been added later, seeing how seldom real folks in the middle of a sword fight were likely to make dry comments about their mortal wounds.

Longarm said he'd noticed Ned Buntline tended to put words in the mouths of dying cowboys and Indians, come to study on it. So he wound up with a mental picture of a rugged breed of hard workers and stubborn fighters who were good at holding grudges.

The fact that they *thought* real men were supposed to comment that they could see why broad spear heads were back in fashion, just as they'd been speared, told more about Icelanders' notions on fighting than about any real fights in the old days.

Like most self-educated men, Longarm read more than he let on at the office. So he knew ''laconic'' meant the way the ancient Spartans of Laconia had talked when things got sort of tough. He told Sigridur about the Spartan king Leonidas, who'd shrugged when they'd told him the oncoming Persian hordes shot so many arrows they blotted out the sun, and just said, ''Then we'll get to fight in the shade.'' She said he sounded like an old-time Icelander.

Whether any of those three hundred Spartans who'd fought to the last against impossible odds had ever said such a fool thing or not, it showed what Spartans *expected* of a man. So men brought up under such manly codes could be expected to neither ask nor give quarter.

Longarm hoped for the sake of the current king of Denmark that old Svein Atterdag had been killed over a woman at that fancy ball down Texas way.

It took Longarm and Sigridur another enjoyable night aboard their Pullman car to wind up in Galveston, Texas.

Once they had, they found the April breezes off the Gulf of Mexico far warmer. So after he'd bought the big blonde a Colt Detective .38 and spring holster, he suggested she wear a loose-tail middy blouse over the more serious six gun tucked in her waist cinch.

They didn't tarry long enough to take in all the sights of Galvestown. They boarded a side-paddle coastal steamer, and booked a seaward-facing stateroom ahead of the portside paddle box. Longarm had been aboard a sister ship following the same course one time, and so he knew all about the mistake you could make when you first got aboard in Galveston. Sigridur wanted him to *make* it, until he explained that their jalousied window would only be aimed into the sunny south as they started west along the inland passage. After that, he explained, they'd be catching sunlight and sea breezes from the east as the vessel steamed more and more to the south into more and more torrid latitudes. So heading south, you didn't really want to turn in aft the paddle box on the starboard side, with the afternoon sun and paddlewheel mist turning your stateroom into a sort of clambake.

She said she was glad *he* was so well-sailed, and proved it to him with a French lesson after an early supper in the aft salon. Had he been traveling alone, he might have spent more time on deck or in the forward salon, where there were always a few card games going. But the whole point of approaching the scene of the assassination the long way around was approaching it discreetly, and it was tough enough to sneak up on folks in the company of a six-foot-six blonde, never mind getting into a public poker game.

The next morning dawned sunny enough for Sigridur to cuss him. But the sun came through the jalousies with a brisk sea breeze, and only lasted until noon. So they opened the shutters wide to admire the view to the southeast as they lounged in the nude and sipped mint juleps.

Sigridur had never had one before. She said hers was mighty nice, and that she saw why folks in a climate such as this one had invented mint juleps.

He told her nobody in Texas had done any such thing. "Julep is a word twisted out of the Arab for rose water," he said, "which I for one wouldn't want to drink on a hot day or a cool one. Mint juleps are made out of mint sprigs instead of rose petals, with the mint water mixed with sugar, bourbon, and shaved ice so the planters of the Old South could survive the heat as they admired their happy darkies laughing and shouting out in the cotton fields."

He sipped his own experimentally, and allowed, "You have to admit sucking mint-sweetened whiskey through shaved ice has hot toddies beat on a day like this."

She said she did, rubbing ice on her bare tits as she blessed

78

the pioneers who'd brought the mint julep west from Dixie with them.

He said, "They had to. It could get even hotter out in the West than back in the older South. So they kept on drinking mint juleps as they slowly turned in to Texicans."

He chuckled and added, "They hadn't known they were fixing to wind up Texicans when they applied for Spanish land grants west of the Sabine. Neither did the Spaniards, or they'd have never granted a fool thing. But Spain was run at the time by some mighty odd elder statesmen who were worried about the way the former British colonies kept crowding ever westwards. So some of 'em who likely didn't speak English came up with this grand notion that Spain might be better off with a whole lot of tough Anglo-Saxon-hating Irish Catholics settled betwixt their more solidly held Mexican colony and the expanding U.S. of A."

She said, "I didn't know most Texans are Irish Catholics."

Longarm smiled thinly and replied, "Neither do they. A heap of the early Texican settlers may have been. But others might have been as willing to say a Hail Mary for a section of Texas range, and His Most Catholic Majesty seems to have mixed up the Catholic Irish with the Scotch Irish. Both kinds of settlers thought of themselves as more American than *any* sort of Irish, and Comanche, Kiowa, Kiowa-Apache, and such kept them from arguing religion with their less truculent neighbors. So by the time Old Mexico busted off from Spain in '21 and cast a more jaundiced eye on the Texas gringo, it was a mite late to stem the flow, and when they tried, Mexico lost New Mexico, the Arizona Territory, California, and the great Utah-Nevada basin as well."

Aiming his cheroot at some passing barrier-island dunes, Longarm continued. "History took the bit in its teeth on those early Anglo-Texicans too. They'd planned on being Southern planters west of the Brazos. But they found the climate too dry for cotton, indigo, taters, or tobacco. You could likely grow *some* cotton in *Iceland* if you really set your mind to it. But to show a profit you have to grow what grows easy where you are and those would-be Southern planters soon discovered their new Mexican neighbors were right about most of Texas being cattle country."

He waved his smoke at the barrier island off to the southeast and told her, "They started modest, grazing Afro-Iberian longhorns they bought off the Mexicans out on those islands, where they couldn't stray or get run off by Indians. They didn't bother to brand them at all until a part-time cattleman called Doc Maverick learned the error of his ways. Other Texicans learned other tricks of the trade off the Mexican *vaqueros,* until they got good enough at it to call their fool selves *vaqueros*, which they pronounced buckaroo. But to hear them tell it these days, Sam Houston, Jim Bowie, and even old Davy Crockett headed west because they meant to be cowboys when they grew up. Like I said, history has a way of surprising us all."

He didn't know how right that observation could be before they disembarked at Port Isabel, after a pleasantly sensual voyage down the inland passage, and he hired two ponies and an extra saddle so they could catty-corner across Cameron County and ride into Brownsville from the landward side.

As they lit out for the hard day's ride, he explained to Sigridur, leaving out the dirty parts, that by this time those Prussian spies who'd been keeping tabs on him had likely figured out why they'd missed that direct rail connection from Junction City. Sigridur asked about those other sneaks, the ones who'd been out to kill him.

Longarm said, "Them too. I don't want anybody meeting us on the dock at Brownsville when our steamer swings up the Rio Grande. This dustier approach ought to get us there just after dark. We'll go to a *posada* I know. That's sort of a Mexican inn. Sort of quaint, but clean enough, and safer than some of the waterfront hotels in town. After we set up a safe base of operations, I'll make the few courtesy calls I can't get out of, and then start asking sensible questions about that missing or hostile witness, Pall Njalsson. Do you reckon he could be descended from that Njall in the saga?"

She laughed and explained as she bounced along beside him that few Icelanders had regular family names. She was called Sigridur Jonsdottir because her father's name was Jon and she was his daughter. She said it was obvious to any

Icelander that Pall Njalsson was the son of some cuss named Njall. Njall was a popular first name back home.

When he asked about Captain Steensen, she said that wasn't the same thing. Steensen was a Dane and Danes had settled on some early ancestor and kept his name, trade, estate, or whatever as a regular family name, like most Christians did these days.

She said her own folks got along just fine *their* way, and asked him why her pony trotted so uncomfortably.

He said that was the way most ponies trotted. She said she liked the ponies back home better, and so it went most of the day, save for a mighty friendly noon break in a shady palmetto grove as their unsaddled mounts cooled and grazed a spell.

They saw stock and riders in the distance as they rode on, but the country was wide open and empty for the most part, with most of Cameron County claimed by one big cattle outfit. Nobody cared where you rode on such range, as long as you behaved yourself.

They got to Brownsville after sundown. Longarm deposited Sigridur and all his other precious possibles at the *posada* he'd told her about, and legged it over to the federal district courthouse to call on Billy Vail's opposite number in Brownsville.

The marshal who hadn't seemed interested in the killing of Count Atterdag had gone home to supper. Longarm didn't care. He was just going through the motions as he pulled night duty because of all the longer-than-usual telegraph messages. He just glanced at Longarm's warrant and snorted, "You could have saved yourself the trip. It was the greaser as shot that Scandahoovian in the back and the case is closed. You've come all this way for nothing."

81

Chapter 12

Longarm took a deep breath, and silently counted to ten as he let it out slow. Then he quietly asked, "Who solved the murder if none of you gents were interested, no offense?"

The paper pusher lounging behind the night desk off the courtroom answered easily, "That witness everybody was asking about, Private Njalsson. He sent his own consulate a letter, postmarked Laredo, and they sent a transcript to us, translated so's we could read it. You want a copy? They sent us a whole mess of carbon-copied onionskins."

Longarm said his boss back in Denver would doubtless want one. So the gruff but neighborly cuss slid open a desk drawer and got it out, allowing they'd expected Longarm to ask for it once he got there.

As he handed it over, the Brownsville man asked where Longarm had been all this time. Longarm said, "Ducking Dutch spies and some other gents who didn't seem to want me to get here."

He scanned the transcribed letter he held in one hand as he fished out two cheroots with the other. In the message, Private Njalsson said he was sorry he'd run off, but what was done was done, and he meant to try his hand as a Texas cowboy lest they put him to work making little rocks out of big ones back in Iceland.

Longarm handed the night man a smoke, and thumbnailed

a match head alight for his own as he read on.

The nonchalant deserter said it had come to him, as he'd finally steadied that pony way down the road, that they were likely to think he'd had something to do with the assassination, the late Greve Atterdag being so unpopular in Iceland and he, Njalsson, being the son of a man who'd risen against the Danes back in '08. So he said that was why he'd just forked himself aboard the calmed-down pony and kept going up the moonlit road after midnight. He added that there was no sense looking for him because he'd sold that fancy uniform, along, with the pony and its bridle and saddle, for enough to dress more Texican and ride on up to Laredo.

Longarm took a thoughful drag as he mentally pictured a greenhorn trying to deal in horseflesh somewhere along the border between Brownsville and Laredo, a good two hundred miles upstream.

He exhaled and observed, "That's a whole lot of Texas and a whole lot of Mexico to canvass, and he never mentions that pony having any bullets in it."

The court clerk suggested, "Mayhaps it was never hit after all. The county coroner says the fatal round went through that human victim. He never said for certain it wound up anywheres else in particular."

Longarm raised the transcript more to the light and muttered. "I noticed. That helpful sawbones didn't seem to notice the diameter of the entry wound either. So we're talking about a heavy .45 slug that might slow a pony some, or a bitty .30 that might not. So Njalsson says he witnessed that Mexican throw down and fire with his .45, and then never bother to aim at either an eyewitness or that Danish officer dashing out to nearly catch him in the act. Atterdag was only hulled by one bullet, and nobody else heard any other shots. So Obregon should have had at least four more rounds in his wheel, and yet he just stood there like a big-ass bird in front of the two of them?"

The court clerk shrugged and suggested, "Try her this way. The scamp we already had down as a hostile witness lied. It was that other cuss with the whore pistol that shot the Danish count, and what difference does it make? There's not a damned thing we can *do* about it either way. The Mex has run down to his spread in Matamoros and the Dane's holed up in the Customs House. If we could arrest either one, this court don't have jurisdiction.''

Longarm pointed out, "You just said the case was closed.''

The older federal employee nodded easily and replied, ''It is, as far as we're concerned. Be it recorded a dead diplomat got shot out of our jurisdiction and he's on his way home with everyone but you satisfied he was gunned by that Mex. Others at the fancy French ball have come forward to say that that pissed-off count and Don Hernan exchanged some heated words over who got to dance with a sassy French lady that night. A kid holding the count's pony out front couldn't have known that. So his story that he just saw the Mex throw down on the count has a ring of truth to it.''

Before Longarm could say anything, he quickly added, ''Have it your way and say he's covering for a killer from his own outfit. Nobody *cares*, old son!''

Longarm said, ''*I* care. Njalsson and Steensen ain't from the same outfit. Njalsson is a Royal Marine assigned to the dead diplomat's personal guard. Steensen is a glorified horse trader assigned to a Danish trade mission. Likely that KHA monopoly your average Icelander hates like fire.''

He snorted some smoke and added, ''Even if nothing I just said was true, Billy Vail sent me to round up that hostile witness and, if possible, that missing pony.''

The court clerk puffed some more for enjoyment, then replied, ''Suit yourself. There's more than one shallow-draft paddle wheeler that can take you upstream to Laredo, Lord willing and the river don't fall too far.''

Longarm said, ''I like to eat an apple a bite at a time. Before I head for Laredo, I'd like to know I have good cause to head that far up the river. Anybody could hop a steamboat up to Laredo and drop a letter in the post office slot. I want a more expert opinion on that sudden revelation before I go tear-assing far and wide on what could well be an invite to a wild-goose chase.''

The older man asked, ''Why would anybody want *us* to think Njalsson mailed a letter to his own pals from Laredo?''

Longarm growled, ''I just told you. You don't send a

sucker after a real goose when you only aim to green him. So I reckon I'd best get over to that Danish consulate before they close for the night, if they haven't closed already.''

They shook on it, and the local man offered directions, despite Longarm allowing he had the address in his notebook. Brownsville was about twenty miles up the estuary from the Gulf of Mexico, but like Matamoros, a ferry-boat ride to the south, it was a deep-water seaport. So its waterfront ran east and west along the salty estuary, and was built up to handle anything from a tugboat to a warship that had any call to dock there. The port was named for a Major Jacob Brown, who'd taken the De La Graze land grant from Mexico and held on to it against all comers back in '46.

The Danish consulate, like most of the others, was near the waterfront, but up a more refined side street. Longarm knew he'd come to the right place when he saw the big white cross on a drooping red flag. But he had to bang on the big front door awhile before somebody opened it a crack and told him they were closed.

Longarm flashed his federal badge and insisted, ''Anyone can see you folks are quartered upstairs in this same modest building, no offense. I am U.S. Deputy Marshal Custis Long, and I've come all the way from the Denver District Court to talk to somebody about that dead count of your own.''

The door slammed shut and stayed that way a spell. Then, just as Longarm was set to pound some more, it opened again and a handsome gal in a black silk dress, with hair to match, ushered him in and led the way to a book-lined study where a white-haired man in a smoking jacket sat smoking a big meerschaum pipe in a big morocco leather chair. The secretary, play-pretty, of whatever introduced him to the Baron Senderborg, and the old gent rose to shake hands and offer Longarm another morocco leather chair facing his own across a knee-high birchwood table by the unlit fireplace.

The petite brunette scampered off for the moment as the baron and his guest sat down. Senderborg said they'd been expecting him for days. Longarm dryly remarked he'd been delayed by problems with his cross-country connections, and repeated his conversation across town at the federal courthouse.

The baron sighed and said, "I don't know why Captain Steensen is still barricaded in the U.S. Customs House, now that young Njalsson has cleared him of all suspicion."

Longarm said, "Maybe he ain't certain nobody suspects him. I was hoping you could let me have a copy of that letter from Laredo as it was written in Danish, or was it Icelandic?"

The older man smiled easily. "He naturally wrote to his Danish sergeant of the guard in Danish, albeit with a few grammatical errors. I just sent my secratery for a file copy, along with a few refreshments, of course."

Longarm relaxed a tad more in his own chair as he said, "The, ah, grammatical expert I'd like to show his message to wouldn't know the kid's handwriting from my own. But whilst we're on the subject, might you still have the original on hand?"

The diplomat shook his distinguished-looking head and said that the letter and everything else Private Njalsson had ever brought across the main ocean with him was headed back to Copenhagen, along with his unit and the body of the count they'd been detailed to guard.

The gal came back in with an envelope, some glasses, and a bottle of *akvavit* on a silver salver. You had to watch Scandinavians and that white lightning they liked to hit you with. It tended to make Holland gin or tequila seem smooth. Will Shakespeare had noted in one play how serious Danes could get about their drinking habits.

Longarm tried not to show his alarm as the baron poured him one hell of a jolt of medical-proof alcohol. He put the Danish transcript of that letter from Laredo away while he still had feeling in all ten fingers. As they clinked glasses and the baron made a remark about their skull, Longarm casually asked who was in charge of their safety if those Royal Danish Marines had carried their dead boss home.

As he tasted his drink and tried not to cry, the baron told him in that same easygoing way, "Captain Steensen was in command of our few guards, before he ran off to his friends at the Customs House and refused to even talk to us. This is only a consulate, and we only need a handful of guards to guard the actual property and, of course, those horses KHA

86

has been trying to sell to your American cowboys.''

He drained his glass and leaned back with no visible distress, to puff on his pipe some more and dryly add, ''Without much success, I fear. Icelandic ponies are not very large, and some of you Americans have wicked senses of humor.''

Longarm tried not to grin as he replied, ''I just had an Icelander tell me the cow ponies we rode in on were fair-sized, and neither was more than fifteen hands at the withers. Somebody told me the captain was a trader with your KHA. You say he's running a military unit for your government as well?''

The baron leaned forward to pour more *akvavit* as he explained how Denmark was sort of a family-owned business corporation with its army, navy, trade monopoly, and public utilities all on the same books and run more for *profit* than *form*.

As Longarm pretended to be putting away that second drink, the older man, who seemed to have a hollow leg, made no bones about the methods, of his neither unkind nor overly democratic King Christian IX. The king was inclined to send his army or navy to collect bills, and saw nothing at all wrong with having a naval vessel deliver trade goods to Eskimos or asking a cavalry captain to peddle horseflesh. For, as the baron felt Longarm ought to see, an officer who trained cavalry troopers and their mounts surely knew as much about horses as any fool civilian horse trader.

Longarm put most of his second drink on the table. *Akvavit* was as clear as a glass of water. So with any luck, an older gent who'd just put away two glasses of it might not notice.

Getting back to his feet, Longarm allowed he had to get back to his other chores. The baron didn't try to stop him or ask just what they might be. So they shook again, and that nice-looking gal took Longarm back to the big front door and showed him out. If the gal had noticed he was walking funny, she was too polite to say so.

Longarm wasn't staggering as he headed back to his *posada* along the riverside waterfront. If anything, he was walking straighter, with more dignity, than usual. A shot and a half of *akvavit* could make you feel dignified as all get-out when you first stood up.

But Longarm was a big man who'd made it home in his time with a skinful of down-home-aged-in-the-jar. So the effects were wearing off as he passed an open cantina and a lady holding up one corner of it called out, "*A 'onde va,* sailor?"

He resisted the impulse to tell her she'd had too much to drink if he looked like a sailor to her. Gals who rode the ferry across the estuary to peddle their pussies at higher prices likely had no clear notion what half the English words they yelled really meant.

That was only fair. Mexican shoeshine boys were always suggesting a visiting gringo could get a good haircut by saying *"Chinge tu madre,"* or "Fuck your mother," to the barber.

He found the corner he was looking for, and turned up it towards that *posada* where good old Sigridur waited to read Danish and teach him some French, as she put it. The moon was up, but low to the east. So if anything, the narrow street seemed darker, with inky shadows spread from one pitch-black row of walls to halfway up the moonlit stucco on the far side. Most of the houses in the older parts of Brownsville were laid out in Spanish Colonial style, with blank walls facing the streets and most of the windows opening on inner patios. It made for lonesome night strolling, as well as privacy on all sides.

But Longarm suddenly became aware he was not alone on that dark and seemingly deserted side street. He heard the scuffle of leather on brick pavement and the loud clank of a metal object bouncing off the pavement. He crabbed sideways into the angle formed by two walls a tad out of plumb as he turned, got the .44-40 out, and softly called, *"Quien es?"*

Nobody answered, and a million years went by as Longarm waited, then waited some more, and finally began to inch forward on the balls of his feet, figuring they couldn't see him any better.

It only took him another million years to make out a darker patch of blackness sprawled like a bear rug on the pavement. Longarm kicked the six-gun on the ground between them before he got to the body.

Hunkering down over the very still form, Longarm softly told it, "I don't see how robbery could have been the motive. How bad are you hurt, pard?"

There came no answer. Longarm felt for a pulse. Whoever this might be, he, she, or it lay as dead as a turd in a milk bucket.

Chapter 13

The siege of Petersburg had taught a younger Custis Long
there were times and places you just didn't strike a light after
dark. So he studied the dead man by Braille as he tried to
decide what the poor cuss had run into, or vice versa.

The body was dressed about right for Texas riding, and
whoever the stabber had been, the single wound was tidy
and small, in the back just over the kidney. So to lie so dead,
the good-sized cuss must have bled inside considerably, and
that accounted for all the thrashing as the killer had held on
to the victim from behind, no doubt with one hand clapped
over his mouth.

Longarm muttered, "*Strong* son of a bitch, whoever he
was."

The dead man had been packing a knife of his own, an
eight-inch bowie, along with that six-gun he'd dropped and
a billfold in his hip pocket.

Longarm opened the leather and ran a thumb over the bills
the dead man had been packing. He put the billfold in one
of his own coat pockets, murmuring, "Robbery couldn't
have been the motive if those turn out to be singles and
Mexican. The strongman or strongmen who jumped you tonight were after you personally. They dropped you and faded
away in the dark before or just after they could have known
I'd be interested."

He got back to his feet and felt his way along the pavement to that gun he'd kicked before. He picked it up, and it felt like a Colt '74, loaded with five in the wheel. Army .45-28 rounds if he was any judge by feel alone. He put that away as well before he moved on, trying to decide whether he ought to report the killing himself or let the neighborhood folks call the law. He sighed, turned around, and headed back for the brighter lights along the waterfront. It was none of his business as a federal deputy, as far as he could tell. But he was still a paid-up peace officer and somebody local, state, or federal had just committed murder. So the sooner the town law or Texas Rangers started looking for the rascal, the better the chance they'd have of catching him.

But as he approached the first lamplit corner closer to the Rio Grande, another lady holding up a wall with her back called quietly out to him, "*Pero no, Brazo Largo.* You are going the wrong way. Your big *gringa rubia* must be worried about you by this time, no?"

Now, since Brazo Largo translated as Longarm and *rubia* meant blond, it was safe to assume the shadowy female of Mexican persuasion had to know who he was and who he was staying with at that *posada*. Nobody would tell a man he was headed the wrong way if they didn't know where he was staying for the night.

As he moved toward her, Longarm asked how long she and her friends had been following him.

She hissed, "*Auséntese!* If I wished for you to see me better I would light a candle. For why are you so *testarudo*? I just gave you good advice. Be good enough to *take* it, *por favor.*"

He stayed where he was and asked, "If I don't pester you about which *cuadrilla* you belong to, might you tell me why I just tripped over another Anglo, spread out on the pavement betwixt here and that blond friend of mine you mentioned?"

She said, "The *pendejo* was no friend of yours, Brazo Largo. He was moving up behind you with a gun in his hand when someone who likes you better thought it was time for to stop him."

"*Muchas gracias,*" said Longarm dryly, adding, "Now

91

tell me who in blue blazes he was and we'll say no more about it to the town law."

She sounded sincere as she told him, "We don't know who he was or for why he was about to shoot you in the back. When it was first reported El Brazo Largo was in town this afternoon, a certain friend of yours you may not know ordered that you be protected, but allowed for to go about your business until we could find out what it *was.*"

Longarm smiled thinly and replied, "That sounds fair. Tell El Gato, La Mariposa, or whoever I seem to owe my life to that I'm not here in connection with *La Causa Mejico Libre,* or even looking for one of those straw *vaqueros* to take home as a souvenir. I'm here looking into the murder of a Danish diplomat over by the French consulate. If you've had somebody tailing me, you know I just paid a visit on the Danish consulate. When did that other jasper commence tailing me? Before or after I dropped by the Danish consulate?"

She hesitated, shrugged, and said, "If he was following you for more than a few minutes, none of us saw this. As I said, he followed you along the waterfront to that darker *calle,* and when we moved in on him he already had his gun out. It appeared as if he was waiting for to shoot as soon as you stepped out into some light while he could remain in the dark. He could not have been a brave *hombre.* I think our world is well rid of him."

Longarm said, "You could have a point, *señorita.* But no offense, it's my duty to report dead bodies on the street to the powers that be."

She shrugged and said, "Go ahead. Nobody will be able for to find any dead bodies now. I only wished for to save you the extra steps out of your way, *comprende*?"

Longarm laughed in spite of himself and said, "I do now. You only wanted to stall for time here whilst others tidied up, right?"

She coyly replied, "*Quien sabe?* You do as you wish. I understand you most often do. I have to go home and wash my hair now. So I shall say *buenoches* and ask you for to pay my respects to that big *yegua rubia* you have been riding."

Longarm grimaced after her as she flounced off, wonder-

92

ing why the sass had made that rude remark about poor old Sigridur. Then Longarm shrugged and headed the other way toward their *posada*, reflecting that the Mexican gal had at least called Sigridur a big blond mare, instead of a cow or worse.

It came as no great surprise when he came upon the death scene to step in a great big puddle of water. It hadn't been raining, but a couple of buckets of well water could sure wash away a little blood.

When he got to the *posada*, things were quiet downstairs in the taproom, which meant they knew. He'd told Sigridur when they arrived that he'd stayed there before and knew the Mexican folks who ran it could be trusted. He'd never tell a federal court recorder about a few favors he might have done in the past for *La Revolución*.

By lamplight he saw he'd guessed right about the dead man's Colt. The billfold contained twenty-three dollars and a library card made out to a Mr. John Brown of Kansas. That made two John Browns of Kansas who would never bother anybody again.

He looked in on their two hired mounts in the manger out back, and saw they were just fine. So he went up the back stairs, knocked the way he'd told Sigridur he would, and the big blonde was all over him, blubbering, as he kicked the door shut behind him, made sure the oak latch-beam was back in place, and moved them both over by the one bed lamp as he told her, "Let go of my damned dong and let me show you something first."

She pulled him down on the bed beside her, pissing and moaning about the singing and guitar music he'd just missed down below.

He said, "You ain't heard nothing until you've been down this way in really hot weather. Mexicans ain't crazy. They just sleep all day when it's too hot to go out, and stay up all night after things cool off. I suspect the party's over downstairs for now. I'll tell you why after you read this transcript of a letter Private Njalsson is supposed to have sent from way up the river."

He got out the envelope that much smaller gal had given

him, and handed it to Sigridur. She read the first few lines and told him, "This is in Danish."

He said, "Well, it was addressed to the Danish Royal Marines, and can't you Icelanders talk Danish if you have to? I mean, when you'd want to enlist in the Danish Royal Marines, for instance."

She read it all the way through, and began to translate it before Longarm said, "I have me a copy in English. I'll give it to you so you can compare them in a minute. Let's worry more about how correctly an Icelandic marine of humble stock might write in Danish, clearing a Danish officer by blaming a killing on a Mexican."

Sigridur nodded soberly and said, "That is about what this letter says. I can tell nothing about the handwriting from this typewritten transcript. I have never met this Pall Njalsson. So I know nothing of his education. But I can say he expresses himself in Danish as well as if he grew up in Copenhagen."

Longarm got out a smoke, that *akvavit* having just about worn off by now, as he pointed out, "You told me before that Danish, Icelandic, and Norse are fairly close."

She nodded and said, "Perhaps as close as American English and a Scotch brogue, if both parties tried to spell words as they pronounced them."

Longarm grimaced and decided, "Mr. Robert Burns did, and his Broad Scots poetry can make for rough going if you ain't used to observing it's a *braugh bricht nicht, tonicht.*"

She smiled and explained, "You have hit the nail on the head, I think. If a Scot was writing a letter to an American, most of it would agree about spelling and grammar, but since they speak such different versions of English, there might be some confusion as to whether wall or *dike*, man or *mon,* hill or *brae*, and so forth were the proper usage."

As he lit his cheroot, she added, "I keep learning new things about English grammar working as a court recorder in Kansas. Icelandic and Danish grammar are not quite the same. But whoever wrote this note from Laredo uses Danish grammar not only correctly, but as a native working-class Dane might speak."

Longarm nodded soberly and said, "Njalsson might not

94

have sent it from Laredo. I reckon I follow your drift about the grammar of regular folks. When you look it up in a textbook, the way you say good night in Spanish would be *buenas noches*. Mayhaps they say it that way in Spain. I've never been there. But border Mexicans say *buenoches* as often, and *'onde va* as often as *a donde va* for where are you going. Wouldn't a farm boy from Iceland be more likely to look things up and write correct textbook Danish than Copenhagen slang?"

She said that had been her exact point. Then she spoiled it all by adding, "We can't be certain Pall Njalsson is an ignorant peasant. We do send some of our brighter Icelandic youth to college, and that calls for at least four years in Denmark. Even if he has no higher education, Private Njalsson has been serving with Danish marines, who would naturally speak their own Copenhagen slang."

Longarm sighed and said, "I wish you hadn't said that. It takes us clear around the damned barn. A Texas cowboy serving in that Black Watch in Scotland would be likely to say *hoot mon* now and again. So I have to allow it's possible Pall Njalsson really wrote that fool letter. But I ain't about to hop a paddle wheeler upstream to Laredo before I snoop closer to the scene of the crime."

"Do you mean you suspect someone has been trying to drag a red stockfish across his trail with a forgery?" she asked, reaching for his old organ-grinder again.

This time he let her—it felt good—as he replied, "I suspect red *herring* was the word you were groping for."

Then she was groping him clean out into the lamplight. It was half hard, and she was calling it a poor thing as she swung off the bed to kneel between his boots and bend lower to see if she could kiss it and make it swell.

She could. Longarm hissed, "Oh, Lord, I'd forgotten how nice you do that. Just go ahead and pay me no mind as I undress us both, you friendly little thing!"

So she did, and he did, and there sure seemed to be a lot of her spread out in the lamplight by the time he was back in the saddle, admiring the considerable view as he thought about that joke where the midget winds up crowing, "Acres and acres of it, and it's mine, all mine!"

She looked up at him adoringly and asked why he was grinning so. He told her he hardly ever felt like crying while he was having so much fun. So that inspired her to move her big hips even more, and a good time was had by all, with that *akvavit* he'd had across town slowing him just enough for her to take it as a compliment. Most gals thought a man was trying to be considerate when he seemed to be waiting for them to catch up. So when you studied on it, a man getting some on the side could be said to be pampering his wife as well.

He pleasured her good, and relit the cheroot he'd had to set aside to do so before he brought her up to date on that other mystery on a dark street somewhat closer than Laredo.

She took it mighty seriously, and couldn't understand why any Border Mexican bandit, as she called whoever the order had come from, would have risked his own neck to save an American lawman.

Longarm patted her big bare shoulder and snuggled her close on the fortunately big bed as he replied, "*Bandit* may be putting it too harsh, honey. As to sticking his neck out, his poor momma stuck his neck out when she gave birth to him in Mexico. The late Benito Juarez had it right for a few short years. But he'd no sooner saved Mexico from that loco Austrian grand duke and the French Foreign Legion, when he up and died so one of his generals, Porfirio Diaz, could take over as a dictator."

She snuggled her blond head on his shoulder and murmured, "If you say so, *unnusti*. All I know about Mexico is what I read in your own papers, and they seem to feel President Diaz is an improvement over some of the earlier Mexican governments."

He repressed a yawn, snubbed out the cheroot some more, and told her, "Mayhaps he is. Some of them have been real bastards, whilst some others didn't know what they were doing. Suffice it to say, they never sent us down this way to mix up in Mexico's political mess. Whether Don Hernan Obregon was the killer or not, he has diplomatic immunity because he's in so tight with the powers that be. So about the only thing I'm certain of is that the late Count Atterdag couldn't have been assassinated by Mexican rebels!"

But as he reached out to trim the lamp in hopes of getting some sleep at last, he suddenly blurted out, "Not as far as I can see so far, I mean!"

After that, he got to lie there quite a spell in the dark, listening to Sigridur's breathing as she fell asleep without a lick of care.

He hadn't told her half of what he knew about Mexican rebels, or even those repeating rifles the Prussians seemed to be missing.

He couldn't see how either fit in with the murder of a Danish diplomat. But what the hell, he had all night to worry about that.

Chapter 14

U.S. Customs in Brownsville was much closer than any stud spread in Mexico. So Longarm headed there the next morning. Sigridur Jonsdottir wanted to tag along. But he convinced her she ought to shop for a summerweight riding habit, a more practical sombrero, and a spell in a beauty parlor.

Her spring outfit wasn't all that bad, and she was one of those natural beauties who could get by on soap and water. But he wanted to keep her and her arcane knowledge of Scandinavian matters secret for a spell. So he said they'd get back together around noon.

When he got to the Customs House near the dry docks, a distinguished gent who could have been a prim Don Juan if he put his mind to it took Longarm aside in a cubbyhole and sat him down with a Havana perfecto and a tumbler of bourbon and branch water. They seemed to teach such manners in government official's school. Longarm said he still wanted to see Captain Steensen.

The man, who worked for the Treasury Department, said, "We've given him political asylum *pro tem*. Nobody can see him before we get a ruling on his status from Washington, Deputy Long."

Longarm asked to whom he had the honor of speaking,

and the sort of stuck-up cuss repeated he was their Harold Andersen in charge of Protocol.

Longarm nodded pleasantly and said, "Well, to begin with, you are full of shit, Mr. Andersen. Political amnesty does not protect any refugee from a foreign power from officials of your own government. And I'm not only working for it, I was sent here specifically to look into this mess. So do you aim to trot the captain out, or do I have to come back with a search warrant and a real hard-on?"

Andersen sniffed and demanded, "A warrant sworn out against who by whom? As I understand your government rank, you work for Justice, not Treasury, and I outrank you."

Longarm was sorry he'd lit the prick's cigar as he smiled across the desk at him incredulously and marveled, "I swear, I'm getting a hard-on for you already! Have you ever taken it into your head to make money?"

Andersen blanched and sputtered, "See here, you can't talk to me that way, you glorified court bailiff!"

To which Longarm replied, snuffing out the fancy smoke in a copper tray on the desk, "I ain't even wound up yet. The Secretary of State outranks the Secretary of the Treasury, the Attorney General, and everybody else below the Vice President. So rank me no ranks because that's who I'm riding for on a special assignment. By the way, might Andersen be a Danish name?"

Andersen looked away and murmured, "It might have been, way back when. Why do you ask?"

Longarm snorted, "I figured it might be, and a rose by any other name would sound as thickheaded. Can't you see it's up to the State Department and nobody else whether your asshole buddy from your old country gets to stay in this country or not?"

"They'll kill him if we let them have poor Eric!" Andersen almost sobbed, adding, "You don't know that Baron Senderborg. He's charming as a friendly housecat and deadly as a cobra!"

Longarm smiled thinly and replied, "I suspected as much. But fair is fair, and as the host country, we have to produce the real killer of that Danish nobleman, murdered whilst un-

99

der the protection of the red, white, and blue, or let Denmark settle the score as best they see fit.''

Andersen tried, ''The French flag is red, white, and blue too.''

Longarm shook his head and insisted, ''I looked that up as I was riding a steamboat with time on my hands. Under international law the French could deal themselves in if they *wanted* to. But they don't want to, and who can blame them? Nobody connected with the French government is on anyone's list of suspects or eyewitnesses to anything worth a summons to court, whether here or in Copenhagen. Captain Steensen has diplomatic immunity from us, even if we could prove him guilty. If we can prove him innocent, this asylum you've extended on your own may stand up despite Danish requests for his extradition. If he's guilty, it won't. Your own boss will defer to the State Department; State will deport him, and whether they hang him or cut his head off won't matter that much to anyone on this side of the pond.''

''It will matter to me!'' Andersen rasped, adding, ''It's a frame-up! Baron Senderborg was behind all the trouble poor Eric has been having since he first arrived here! The baron seems to have taken an instant dislike to him. It was his idea to have that arrogant Count Atterdag come here in all his pomp and glory to investigate the captain's trade mission.''

Longarm shrugged and said, ''Those are serious charges. You'd best let me talk to your sweetheart and thrash out just what that late Count Atterdag was looking for, and whether he found it.''

Andersen's face got red, as if he'd been caught jerking off in the outhouse, and he rose from his seat and thundered, ''Are you insinuating I'm a fairy, you son of a bitch?''

Longarm's voice stayed calm as he smiled up at the angry Andersen. ''Don't get your bowels in an uproar whether you are or you ain't. Nobody sent me all this way to determine which side either of you boys part your hair on. If you ain't in love with Captain Steensen, you're sure acting silly as hell about him, and by the way, don't ever call me a son of a bitch again. I mean that.''

Andersen said, ''We're just old friends, and all right, business partners. We met at school in England. Cambridge, class of 1863."

Longarm remarked, not unkindly, "It was us ignorant farm boys in the field that long hot summer. You say you went into business after the war whilst you were taking courses over yonder?"

Andersen shook his head and said, "More recently, when Eric and I met here in Texas. You see, he and his trading company have been working on this breeding project and . . . You're right. I'd better let you talk to him. But I have your word you won't try to arrest him, no matter what he says?"

As Longarm rose, his drink barely tasted, he stated soberly that he hardly ever arrested anybody who seemed innocent. But that that worked much the same the other way.

When Andersen hesitated, Longarm said, "Aw, for Pete's sake. If you insist on me serving you with a telegram for your own superiors, I'll go wire for one! I just said I was on his side if he looked at all innocent, and so far, that dreadful Baron Senderborg just told me *he's* convinced the killer was that Mexican."

Captain Eric Steensen didn't seem to buy that notion either as Andersen introduced Longarm to him, up under the mansard roof in a newly well-furnished storage loft.

Captain Steensen was naturally about the same age as the draft-dodging Andersen. But the Danish cavalry officer was more wiry and much tanner than the dapper customs man. Like that Danish gal at his consulate, Steensen was as dark as many an Italian, proving not all Scandinavians had to be blue-eyed blondes.

Steensen had a firm handshake and a way of looking you in the eye as he talked. As the three of them sat down around a small garden table with some more tumblers and a pitcher of iced sangria, a sweet red Mexican punch that could sneak up on you, Steensen dismissed the letter postmarked in Laredo as a crude forgery. He hadn't seen it, but Baron Senderborg had sent that secretary over to tell him all was forgiven and tell him why.

Steensen, whose English was as good as you'd expect from anyone who'd graduated from a fancy English university, asked many of the same questions Longarm had about a farm boy from Iceland writing in educated but casual Danish. Steensen had the advantage of having known the missing marine to talk to. He backed what Sigridur had said about tricky grammar, and made it clearer by explaining, "Like English in all its dialects, the western Scandinavian descendants of Old Norse have evolved in different directions. Icelandic has stayed closer to the original language of the sagas, and don't think they are not proud and touchy about *that*! Njalsson is from a fishing village, a small one, on the Vestmannaeyjar or Irish Islands off the south coast of Iceland. We shared a common interest in the *Islenzkur Smahestur* or Icelandic pony. He was a shy but friendly *fiskimathur*, but he could barely make himself understood in modern Danish, and I simply can't picture him sitting down to write a *letter* in *any* dialect!"

"Why might anybody else have done so for him?" Longarm asked with no beating about the bush.

Steensen was just as direct. "It's a trap, of course. To get me to leave this sanctuary. Once Baron Senderborg has me in his power, he can cheerfully admit that he or that slut of a secretary wrote it and thus repudiate all it says in my favor. You have to understand that our own constitution is closer to the Napoleonic Code and the burden of proof is on the accused!"

Longarm sipped some sangria and asked, "What was that count that *somebody* surely murdered accusing you of, Captain?"

Steensen answered just as directly, "Gunrunning. He was out of his mind, or somebody put him up to it for some insane reason of their own. As Harold here can verify, I've been trying to establish a market here in Texas for the Iceland pony we have in greater supply than Iceland, Norway, or Denmark could ever need. The breed is tough, yet intelligent, and easier to train than your Western cow pony."

"It gives a better ride too," Andersen chimed in with enthusiasm.

Longarm said, "Let's just say the ponies are swell and stick to what Count Atterdag said about gunrunning."

It was Andersen who said, "The man was an arrogant ass. We here at U.S. Customs would know if anyone tried to land contraband in any quantity for a goddamned screw clipper tied up at any goddamned dock in Brownsville!''

Longarm said, ''I heard tell about some new Mauser rifles, last seen going aboard an American flag vessel.''

Andersen nodded and said, ''The *Trinity* out of New York. I just told you we kept tabs. Any and all oceangoing vessels are boarded and inspected as they put in here. What did you think they built this Customs House for, a gambling casino? Count Atterdag complained to me personally that Eric here had imported close to a thousand repeating bolt-action Mausers from Hamburg aboard the *Trinity*. I naturally had to tell him he was wrong.''

''Did he know what old school chums the two of you were?'' asked Longarm.

Andersen shrugged and said, ''I suppose he could have found out easily enough. As I said, I've been introducing Eric and his KHA team around Cameron County. But that gives nobody the right to say U.S. Customs or any part of it has been party to any gunrunning!''

Longarm said, ''What the count suspected and what he found out for certain don't have to jibe. I'm more interested in how come he wound up so dead.''

Facing Steensen, Longarm flatly stated, ''I've been told that you KHA trade monopolists play rough. Something about cutting off the heads of customers who trade at another store?''

Captain Steensen grimaced and suggested, ''Why don't we talk about the Salem witch trials, the Yankee slave trade, and the only good Indian being a dead Indian? KHA was established in the *sixteen hundreds,* and to date it's never sold opium to the Chinese at gunpoint or asked an Eskimo to pay for a rifle by piling furs flat from the floor of the trading post to the tip of the muzzle.''

Longarm smiled sheepishly and said, ''I've never done business with your outfit. An Icelander I've been talking to . . .''

''I'd rather you asked an Eskimo or a cane cutter on our Virgin Islands!'' the apparently loyal KHA man shouted.

When he saw he had the floor, Steensen continued. ''Icelanders have neither forgotten nor forgiven their Wagnerian grudge fights. They were killing one another with glee; and picking lice out of their beards, when we took over. Of course we established a trade monopoly. Of course some Danish merchants took advantage of this. Danes are human beings, not creatures of light and mercy. Meanwhile, the so-called free traders of the times were exploiting everyone they could, and if you think we overcharged Icelanders in the sixteen hundreds, you don't know much about the triangular trade. We traded them tobacco and pink ribbons for their wool and stockfish. We never sold anyone to your gracious Virginia planters at a time the English were selling Irish wenches to them cheap."

Longarm said, "Touché. But could we get it up to more modern times and the way Icelanders feel about you Danes today?"

Steensen shrugged and said, "I told you, they like to complain. A royal governor, Count Trampe, did abuse his authority during the Napoleonic Wars, when Denmark had more important worries than a few thousand fishermen and sheepherders in the middle of the ocean. The idiot tried to raise a private army to disband their Althing. But it was the Danish government, not the Icelanders, who put a stop to his abuses. We gave them representation in the Danish Rigsdag. Then, when that wouldn't shut them up, we let their native Althing legislate local matters. They demanded and got free trade just before your Civil War. KHA still has trading posts in Iceland and Icelanders still trade with us. Does that sound as if we're cheating them blind?"

Longarm shrugged and said, "You remind me of some English gents who've explained their Irish problem to me. What's your view on the recent death of that Icelandic rebel leader, Sigurdsson?"

Steensen answered simply, "He died. Everybody dies, sooner or later. Jon Sigurdsson presided over the Icelandic. Althing and openly advocated an independent republic. But it wouldn't be fair to call him a rebel. Neither he nor any members of his nationalist party are known to have broken any laws."

Longarm was sorry he'd asked. He smiled sheepishly and confessed, "Asking about politics in any country is like asking what time it is and getting a lecture on watchmaking, no offense. The government I ride for only wants to know who killed Count Atterdag. Since neither of you gents want to tell me who did it, I'd better get on down the road.''

As he rose, Andersen demanded, ''Just what might you mean by that veiled remark, Deputy Long?''

To which Longarm replied, ''It wasn't a veiled anything. It was a simple statement of fact. I wasn't expecting anybody to own up to a killing whether they were innocent or guilty.''

Chapter 15

As they were eating their noon dinner of tortillas and chili con carne at the *posada*, Sigridur was careful not to spill any on her new outfit of hemp sailcloth the color of her hair. She said it felt much cooler for April on the Gulf of Mexico.

As they ate and sipped *cerveza*, Longarm brought the big blonde up to date on his own morning, adding, "I know I'm running around like a kid's top on a bumpy walk. But I don't see how we'll bring in that hostile witness unless I can make an educated guess as to what in the blue blazes he could be out to hide."

She said, "I like this Mexican beer. Private Njalsson wrote us he saw that Mexican shoot the count in the back, right?"

Longarm said, "Wrong. The letter was addressed to the sergeant of that marine guard, whether Njalsson wrote it or not. I ain't the only one who's considered that notion. I'm still working on whether the letter was designed to get Captain Steensen off the hook or bring him in to be double-crossed and court-martialed. Steensen thinks it's all a plot on the part of that Baron Senderborg. Some of those sagas you told me about coming down from Kansas are starting to make more sense. You Scandinavian folks sure enjoy feuding with one another! I wish I knew whether the captain or the baron decided they should have a feud."

He washed down some chili, made just right by a Mexican

cook who seldom served Anglos and thus had nothing to prove about red pepper. Then he told Sigridur, "I ain't ready to traipse all the way to Laredo before I have more evidence Njalsson headed that way. That pony he may or may not have sold by now looks more distinctive to local eyes. So we might do better asking around about a small blond pony than a tall blond deserter from the Royal Marines. My papers on Pall Njalsson only describe him as standing a tad over six feet, with a long, lean build, gray eyes, and blond hair. None of which are all that rare in any Texas cow camp."

He swallowed some more grub as he tried to picture such a bland-sounding suspect, then asked, "How come they just told me those wester-whatever islands are *Irish* islands? Might Njalsson be more Irish-looking than most of your folks?"

The gal shook her blond head and explained. "To the Old Norse the Scots were the South Men and the Irish were the West Men. So *Vestmannaeyjar* means West Man Islands literally, or Irish Islands in the sagas, because some Irish war prisoners escaped to those volcanic crags off our south coast and managed to hold out a while."

She sipped more *cerveza* and went on. "Iceland was settled mostly by fugitives from Norway. They found a few settlements of celibate Irish monks who must have really wanted to be alone. The sagas say my pagan ancestors allowed them to leave in peace, whether or not they might have *wanted* to. Over the years a Celtic minority from Ireland and the Scottish Highlands and offshore islands joined the Norse in Iceland, as captives or volunteers. We have a whole village of Scottish Jacobites who took refuge up a fjord after Bonnie Prince Charlie lost, just before your own American Revolution. But I doubt Pall Njalsson would strike anyone as an Irish immigrant. The fishing folk of the Vestmann-aeyjar are just plain Icelanders, and as you say, tall slender cowboys with blond hair are not looked upon as freaks in Texas."

He agreed it was safer to keep an open mind about the appearance of that hostile witness. He almost let it pass him when she mentioned that she'd almost taken a Danish gal at the beauty parlor for Creole, or even a lighter Mexican.

But he backed her up and made her go over it again, even though she said she hadn't caught anybody acting or talking sinister.

She said she'd been lying back under a hot towel when the gal in the next chair over commenced to chat in *Danish,* of all tongues, with another customer.

Sigridur explained, "I naturally said nothing to her as I waited beside her. The last thing I would have taken her for would have been a *Danskona*! She was small and dark, and as I said, I took her for some Latin breed."

Longarm asked, "Was she somewhere betwixt twenty-five and thirty, with delicate features and a taste for black silk?"

Sigruder said that sounded exactly right, and asked if he'd been peeping through the beauty parlor windows.

He explained about the baron's secretary at the Danish consulate, and asked Sigridur to keep going about the pretty little thing.

The big pretty blonde said some other gal she couldn't see from under her hot towel came in and commenced jawing with the brunette in Danish. But then it got less interesting. Sigridur said they'd mostly jawed about how hot it was getting so early in the year, and how much it cost to eat unless you were willing to settle for local groceries.

Longarm decided, "I doubt anyone would dictate a murder confession to a secretary in any lingo. But I'm glad they didn't spot you as a former subject of their king. Have you had enough, or would you like me to order you some tuna pie and coffee for dessert?"

She said the mere thought of a fish pie on such a warm afternoon made her ill. He was in a hurry, so he never told her a tuna pie made Texas-style tasted more like baked cherries mixed with figs, *tuna* being the crimson red and juicy fruit of a local version of prickly-pear cactus.

As hot as it was for April anywhere else, it was a cool day for Cameron County. So even though La Siesta had officially commenced, they got their ponies saddled out back, mounted up, and rode them at a walk through the sunny deserted streets of Brownsville.

As they did so, Longarm told her how he'd used La Siesta in the past to move about sneakily. He said, "With most everybody, Anglo or Mexican, holed up in the shade with or without the bed partner of their choice, you can sneak around town like a burglar up north at four in the morning, with the added advantage of broad daylight to keep you out of bear traps.''

She said she'd heard most Mexicans were lazy, but asked why other locals indulged in the time-wasting Mexican siesta.

He said, "It's hot this early in the year, and it aims to get way hotter quickly. It ain't no waste of time to catch up on your sleep betwixt noon and late afternoon, when you'd be a total fool to try any hard work in any case. Some Mexicans are as lazy as some of our own, I reckon. Others can get a whole lot done by working twelve or more hours, spread out and broken up into four-to-six-hour shifts. A heap of Anglo Texicans have learned the hard way to keep the same odd hours. For the same practical reasons. So on a more reasonable day like this one, we ought not to meet many nosy pests. While at the same time, anyone trying to follow us very far in broad daylight is going to face a real chore!''

She followed his drift, as he'd taught her to say, and so just a few minutes later, they'd circled around to the back of that Danish consulate and reined in.

As Longarm had expected, since they had to have them somewhere, the consulate's carriage house and stable faced the alleyway running along behind it. Longarm was hoping Baron Senderborg and that pretty brunette would be enjoying their own siesta, along with all the other bigwigs posted there.

But as always, some poor soul was always stuck with watching the store. So when they dismounted and led their ponies under the shady overhang of the stable, an older man sporting a gray beard and a manure fork came to meet them, fussing in uncertain English.

He calmed down considerably, and even smiled, after Sigridur got to talking to him in Danish. Longarm had told her what to say, but he was only able to follow a word or so here and there as she lied for him. Longarm wasn't sure, but it seemed to him that Danish was a tad less singsong than Icelandic, although you had to almost sing a lot of words in both to pronounce them. So he was in the position of, say, a Greek listening to a couple of English speakers who might or might not talk with Irish brogues or Texas drawls.

It only took Sigridur a few such outlandish words and phrases to find out what they really wanted to know. By introducing Longarm as a horse trader interested in Icelandic ponies, Sigridur got directions to the farmhouse, barn, and paddock on the outskirts of town where the captain she'd asked for had his remuda of *Islenzkur Smahestur* stock on tap.

They rode out that way, with Longarm keeping a casual eye on their backtrail, until sure enough, they spied a white-washed pole fence wrapped around what looked to Longarm like a whole bunch of kid's toys come to life.

As they rode closer on regular cow ponies, some of the fuzzy little Iceland ponies came over to the rails to nicker and peer over the barrier, friendly as pups in a pet shop window.

Longarm had seen Shetland ponies galore, of course. So when he'd been told the related Icelandic stock was closer in size to a serious mount, he'd pictured a runty Indian pony proportioned like a "Shelty." But the real thing didn't look like a cow pony or any other sort of pony. It looked just plain . . . unusual.

As they rode along the fence toward the buildings, with some of the ponies on the far side tagging along as if they expected to be given at least some apples, Sigridur told him that the funny way some of them were either walking fast or trotting slow was called the *tolt* gait in Iceland. She said they could keep that up for hours, and it was easy on both themselves and their riders. Longarm said a grown man would look silly riding such a runty mount at any gait. Icelandic ponies might be bigger than Shelties, once you measured them, but they didn't *look* any bigger at any distance, and Shelties, bless their little hearts, were meant for little kids.

Sigridur told him he was wrong as they reined in by the farmhouse. She was explaining how grown folks in the Shet-lands, Faroes, or Iceland had brought strong, shaggy, runty Nordic horseflesh with them from the mainland with the avowed intent of riding or working them the same as any other brutes. She said she didn't know why the ponies on those Shetland Islands had evolved to become sort of dwarf-ish. She wasn't certain she bought all that talk by Professor Darwin. But it made some sense to Longarm when she explained how all the North Atlantic island folk had bred their riding stock for ease of handling and thrifty foddering on rough pasture that spent a lot of time under snow.

He'd noticed all of them looked furry enough to play in snow, and how their coloration ranged from chocolate and white paints to near creamy white, with most the sort of autumn shades the original wild horse had likely been.

As a gent in a snuff-colored business suit and planter's hat came out on the porch of the house to look them over, Longarm told Sigridur, "See if we can get photographs of any cream or palomino stock. It doesn't have to be that mare called Lille Thruma. No Mexican or Texican would be able to see much difference in detail, once he or she was shown a picture of such an outlandish critter!"

Sigridur hailed the KHA dealer in Danish, and like the older hostler back in town, he seemed pleased as punch to jabber in his own lingo with a pretty lady.

If he detected any Icelandic accent in her speech, it didn't seem to bother him. Longarm wondered if, like the Irish, some Icelanders tended to feel that strangers lording it over them were more snooty than your average Englishman or Dane might feel. For when you'd been raised to feel superior to folks, you didn't feel much need to grind them under. American Northerners and Southerners tended to compare apples with oranges when they argued about the way white folks were supposed to talk to colored folks. When a well-meaning Yankee chided a Southerner for being mean to his contented darkies, the Southerner was likely to reply in honest indignation that he'd never been mean to any coon who knew his place.

However the Danish KHA man felt about Icelandic peasant folk, he waxed enthusiastic about their ponies, and wanted to sell Longarm some fine breeding stock right then and there.

With Sigridur translating, once the KHA man had decided

her Danish was way better than his English, Longarm said he had to study some before he tried crossing the colder-blooded Nordic stock with his own warm blooded Arab barbs up the river a piece.

The horse trader allowed the Arab barb was bright as a button and quick-turning as spit on a hot stove. But after that, he said, a man needed a seven-pony string to work cows with such high-strung and easily tired riding stock.

He said Captain Steensen, who wasn't available at the moment, had already crossed an Arab mare with an Icelandic stud, back in their old country, to produce a filly of astonishing speed and endurance. Sigridur never blinked, Lord love her, when Longarm asked her to ask more about that and the KHA man told them they'd named the critter Lille Thruma!

Sigridur kept the ball rolling with desperately casual questions about such a grand mount. The Dane explained that the captain's prize mount had been borrowed by a visiting dignitary, and wound up strayed or stolen after that shooting incident they'd likely heard about.

Longarm was sure glad he'd brought Sigridur along when, before he could even ask, she'd wrangled a photograph of the famous Lille Thruma out of the horse trader!

He seemed happy to oblige, even before she'd told him a picture of such a crossbreed might help some Texas stockmen make up their minds.

He'd been teased some by the few Texicans who'd seemed at all interested in the runty stock out back.

So in no time at all they were back in their saddles, riding off with a much better idea and a literal picture of that pony the missing Private Njalsson had lit out with.

Lille Thruma, as described on paper earlier, was a sort of pale palomino with honey-blond hide and almost snow-white mane and tail. All in all, she looked like the sort of pony every kid wanted for a Christmas present, although she was fourteen hands at the withers and less freaky than most Icelandic mounts.

But there'd be no confusing it with any Texican cow pony, and most anyone who'd seen Lille Thruma in passing would be sure to say so—unless they aimed to lie, of course.

Chapter 16

"You said it would get cooler after three or four o'clock!" said Sigridur in a pouty tone as she lay stark and sweaty on the wilted bedding in their shuttered but sweltering room at the *posada*.

Longarm was just as stark, but seated at a corner table, going over the papers he'd spread out beside the sepia-tone print of the prized as well as missing Lille Thruma. For as voluptuous as Sigridur was built, she'd have likely killed him had he tried to mount her in such sticky heat, and he'd have deserved it as a suicidal maniac.

He said soothingly, "It happens like so down here along the Gulf at most any time of the year, honey. With any luck we're fixing to have us a hurricane. That'll cool things off considerably, and if it's any consolation, it never stays the same more than three days in a row. Don't you get heat waves in Kansas anymore?"

She sat up to wave a magazine like a fan in hopes of cooling her big sweaty nipples as she sighed, "*Guth a him-inn,* not *this* hot! How do the people who have to stay here stand it?"

He said, "They don't. They take all their duds off and lie down. I wonder if that other Icelander, Pall Njalsson, has been having as much trouble adjusting to this climate that's warmer than he's used to. The little I have on him says he just got over this way with that dead count in March. So this would be the first Texas heat wave he's been through. I hope it hits him as hard and he doesn't have any pals smart as me to teach him La Siesta. With any luck he'll have a heat stroke and wind up under a doctor's care. It's tough to cut the trail of a want when you start so cold. I have a better mental picture of the *pony* he may or not be riding, thanks to this photograph of Captain Steensen's pet mare.''

He sipped some of the sangria he'd had delivered from downstairs, and mused, ''You reckon that could have inspired some of the malice the captain feels for Baron Senderborg? He'd have never offered his own favorite mount for the late Count Atterdag to ride. He was more than likely ordered to do it.''

He leaned back in his chair and lit a fresh cheroot as he recited, half to himself:

I had a little pony,
His name was Dapple Gray,
I loaned him to a lady,
To ride upon, one day.

Sigridur moaned, ''Must you, in this heat? What is your point?''

Longarm continued:

She whipped him!
She lashed him!
She rode him through the mire!
I wouldn't lend my pony now
For anybody's hire!

Sigridur sighed and said, ''Neither would I. Are you suggesting Captain Steensen assassinated Count Atterdag for abusing his private mount?''

Longarm shrugged and told her, ''I recall a sad love triangle up in Denver a spell back. The Denver police took the call, Lord love 'em. I only tagged along for the excitement.''

She asked how many horses were involved.

He said, ''None. It was a bitch sheepdog. Her owner came

114

home early to catch her *en flagrante* with a neighbor who'd been peeping in his window and knew she put out. Her owner and outraged lover shot the both of them, and would have shot himself if he hadn't used up all the rounds in his double derringer. Some of the copper badges were laughing as they led the poor old coot away. But I couldn't help feeling sort of sorry for the weeping and wailing degenerate. His story is sort of tragic as well as disgustingly comical."

Sigridur laughed weakly and said, "Have it your way. The whole thing was an affair of honor over the favors of a beautiful mare, and the best man eloped with the bride! Don't you think that is really outlandish Custis?"

He shrugged his bare shoulders and replied, "It's as sensible as any other motives I can come up with. Look how *loco en la cabeza* the whole bunch have been talking and carrying on! Count Atterdag accusing the younger officer of being in cahoots with U.S. Customs to smuggle guns into Texas for Icelandic rebels!"

She pointed out, "We don't know Count Atterdag thought those new repeating rifles were intended for Benedikt Sveinsson."

Longarm stared slack-jawed at her, exclaiming, "We sure don't. Who in blue blazes is Benedikt Sveinsson?"

She answered simply, "The new leader of the *lythveldisk* or, you would say, Republican party, of course. How many times do I have to tell you Jon Sigurdsson is dead, probably murdered by the Danes?"

Longarm blew a thoughtful smoke ring and quietly asked her how long she'd been a U.S. citizen. When she told him she'd been away from Iceland as long as he'd been riding for the Justice Department, Longarm hummed a few bars of "My Heart Is in the Highlands," and told her point-blank, "I'm counting on you to put the interests of the U.S. of A. first, Citizen Jonsdottir. If I suspected for one minute that you'd cover for another Icelandic nationalist, I'd have to send you packing whether I could prove it or not!"

She shrugged her naked shoulders, a sight that might have been more tempting a few degrees cooler, and sighed, "Who would I be covering up for? One suspect is a Mexican. The other, even worse, is a Dane! I don't know anything about the political opinions of Pall Njalsson. I do know he took an oath to uphold the Danish Crown when he enlisted in those Royal Marines.''

Longarm poured more sangria for both of them as he muttered, ''I wish I knew more about him too. On the face of it, he had no call to run off like that. Nobody could have accused him of the assassination because he just won't work as the assassin. So what could he have been so afraid of?''

As he handed her some iced punch, Sigridur suggested in a far from interested tone, ''Perhaps he feared Count Atterdag might turn out to be an *afturganga*. People can be very superstitious on those wet rocks he grew up on. They tend to believe in trolls and elves or less attractive creatures of the night. An *afturganga* is a dead man who for reasons of his own keeps going on after death. They say one time a lover was drowned on his way to take his sweetheart to a dance. She was surprised when he finally showed up at her door, a little late and very wet. But she got up on his pony with him, and they rode quite a way before she noticed they seemed to be at the graveyard instead of the dance.''

''That could spoil a gal's evening for her,'' Longarm remarked.

Sigridur nodded and said, ''Fortunately, she jumped off, just as her lover and his pony vanished into an open grave. Pall Njalsson was raised on such bedtime stories. So how can we say what might have passed through his mind when he saw the nobleman he'd been ordered to guard flopping about on the blood-soaked pavement like a beached *hvalur*? I mean whale.''

Longarm said, ''I figured that might be what *hvalur* meant. A hostile witness spooked by a haunt makes as much sense as that letter somebody sent his sergeant from Laredo. In any case, we're looking for a fairly ordinary young man and a mighty unusual mare who may or may not have a bullet under her palomino hide. So I reckon I'd best start posting pictures of her around livery stables, horse markets, and such.''

He got up and moved to the corner washstand to make himself a tad less sweaty with a damp washrag and a dry towel as Sigridur protested, ''Surely you don't intend to go

116

out again! It's a sauna in here, I know. But it must be a furnace outside right now!''

He said, "When you're right. But the shops will be opening up again, and I want to have a photograph gallery run off a mess of prints for me. Then I have a ferry boat to catch. I ain't talked to that other suspect yet. But I have the address of his town house in Matamoros, and with luck he may be there. I know *I'd* want to stay close to my lawyer's office if somebody was trying to pin an assassination on *me*."

Sigridur gasped, "You are going to Mexico! Take me with you! I have never been to Mexico, and it can't be any hotter across the Rio Grande than it is on this side!"

He shook his head as he moved to gather up his duds, explaining, "It might not turn out a pleasure trip. I'll bring you back a lace mantilla to wear over your pretty hair, Lord willing that I don't get stabbed, shot, or both. There's folks down yonder who don't like me, for reasons having nothing to do with this mission. And there seems to be some folks on *this* side of the border who don't like me for reasons that *must* have something to do with this mission. They're likely to see my visit to a town where I can't call the law a golden opportunity. But meanwhile, the folks around here will see that you're as as safe as the Bank of England.''

As he sat beside her to haul on his pants, Sigridur sat up and threw her bare arms around his naked shoulders, sobbing, "I don't want to stay here alone. I don't feel safe. I feel bored, bored, and bored!"

He patted her bare back and said soothingly, "I know. I've often noticed that riding for the law can get boring as all get-out betwixt mighty exciting moments. When I say you'll be safer here, I ain't whistling no Vienna waltz. I told you about that Mr. John Brown from Kansas who made the mistake of following El Brazo Largo up a dark street in this *barrio*. Some Mexican folks call me El Brazo Largo instead of Longarm because their English ain't so sharp, but they remember past favors I'd as soon not discuss with a court recorder.''

He rose to stamp his boots on better and grab for a shirt as he told her he'd be back by midnight, Lord willing, and if it didn't hurricane.

She leaped to her bare feet in all her naked glory, an almost alarming sight, as she shouted, loud enough for them to hear downstairs, "You can't treat me like your old hat! To put on or fling aside whenever it suits you! How can you be so cruel to an *unnusta* who has given herself to you so *akafur*?"

Longarm removed the telltale handcuffs from the back of his gunbelt and strapped the belt on, quietly but firmly pointing out to her, "I brought you this far on a field mission for the Justice Department, not our honeymoon. I'd by lying if I said I wasn't enjoying the side benefits as much as yourself. But keep it in mind that the job comes first and that I expect you to soldier along with me, like a grown-up, when I'm on the job."

He put on his hat, but he'd already decided it was too blamed hot for his coat and vest. He moved back to the bed and bent over to kiss the part of her blond hair, adding, "You're allowed to act silly as a cuttlefish in heat when I'm off duty in your company. So hold the thought and, like the poem says, I'll come in you at midnight, though Hell should bar the way."

For some reason, that seemed to inspire her to throw a shoe at the door as he shut it between them. He sighed and headed down the back steps as he muttered, "If I live to be a hundred, I'll just never in this world understand the unfair sex. They piss and moan if you hump 'em too often. They piss and moan if you don't hump 'em enough. Had I been consulted by Creation at the beginning, men and women would have both wound up with something better than one another."

He went out back—she'd been right about it feeling like he'd just opened a furnace door—and saddled with his personal McClellan, the paint he'd hired up the coast.

The pony didn't want to take him anywhere in that late afternoon heat, even though it was a Gulf Coast mount. Longarm whipped its stubborn jug head with his hat a few times, and they seemed to get along better.

He rode to a photograph gallery he'd noticed by the waterfront, and asked the mousy middle-aged woman behind the counter if they'd be able to make him up two dozen prints without the negative plate.

She allowed that at two bits a print they'd be more than willing to take a picture of the picture and work from there. He paid her in advance, thanks to the late Mr. John Brown of Kansas, and allowed that he'd expect to pick them up the following day.

When she didn't argue, he went back outside, untethered the paint, and told it, "I'll be a sport and lead you to the ferry slip on foot. But don't you dare go shying as I lead you aboard. It ain't possible for the slip and ferry deck to meet dead level in a tidal estuary. But the step up or down won't harm us."

The paint didn't shy or hesitate as he led it into the cavernous lower deck of the side-paddle ferry boat. He noticed they had plenty of room. When a crew hand came to ask for their fare, Longarm casually commented on how few other passengers they seemed to have this trip.

The ferry boat man shrugged and said, "The greasers say it's fixing to hurricane. You know how superstitious they are."

As he turned away he added, "Ain't a wisp of breeze off land or sea, and the harbor's calm as a millpond."

Longarm saw that that seemed to be true as he stood just under the top deck's overhang, holding his mount's reins as he peered thoughtfully up at the sky. The sky was a tad overcast, accounting for the muggy late afternoon they were having.

It had been Mexicans, or Mexican Indians leastways, who'd given the world the word "hurricane." They'd meant a ferocious Taino god, Mr. Hurakan, who'd haunted this very coast in olden times and no doubt scared folks just as much and as often. He had this way of showing up unexpectedly.

Up on the Texas deck, they tooted the steam whistle to signify they were shoving off. Another gent as tall as Longarm and dressed for working cows must have wanted to visit Matamoros as much. For he came dashing across the cobbles at a dead run to leap aboard just as the ferry got a good full yard from the slip.

As he landed on his boot heels near the edge and kept

going at a brisk pace, Longarm nodded and said, "I admire a man who can jump so good in riding boots."

The stranger didn't answer. He barged past Longarm as if he hadn't noticed him, and tore up the stairs to the passenger deck.

Longarm shrugged and said to himself, "Up yours, Tex. I was only trying to be neighborly. I wasn't going to ask you why you had to get to Mexico so suddenly."

Chapter 17

The ferry boat ride last just a few minutes, and none of the gray-uniformed Mexican crossing guards pestered anybody getting off on their side. The Diaz dictatorship encouraged visitors, and anything they might want to bring into the country in their pockets. The guards had been posted near the ferry slip to watch for crates big enough to carry guns, Porfirio Diaz having commenced his career as a Mexican rebel against an earlier tyrant, and to make sure nobody *left* Mexico with anything more valuable than the knickknacks on sale along the waterfront. Mexico taxed silver and gold leaving the country, whether it had been dug from Mexican soil or not.

Not wanting to attract attention as a strange gringo in any *barrio* he wasn't familiar with, Longarm left his hired pony in a livery near the Matamoros waterfront, for the time being, and hailed a hansom cab he could get around in more privately. He gave the Mexican driver the address of that town house and sat back, screened by the high sides of the hansom, as they clopped along the dusty *calle*.

It was tougher to tell what sort of a neighborhood you were in down Mexico way because, rich or poor, Spanish-speaking folks liked their windows facing inwards. So you couldn't tell much about them from the street.

Mexicans spent more time outdoors than Queen Victoria

might approve of after dark. But they tended to congregate near the churches, cantinas, and little shops wrapped around the plaza each *barrio* or neighborhood came with. So the residential side street was deserted where Longarm got out as the sun was setting. He told his driver he'd find his way back on foot. It hadn't seemed far, and that last plaza they'd crossed had indicated they were in one of the better quarters of Matamoros.

The driver never argued. His regular customers hardly ever tipped him a whole Yanqui dime. As he drove off, Longarm approached the big iron-studded oakwood entrance, looking for a knocker. But then it swung open and a friendly female voice called out, *"Bienvenido, El Brazo Largo. Esté en su casa!"*

Since his unseen greeter knew his Mexican nickname and had invited him in to make himself at home, it seemed a safe bet they'd been expecting him.

He strode on into the cooler tree-shaded patio. Don Hernan Obregon had surely expected some damned body to question him about that killing north of the border by this time.

As the heavy gate swung shut behind him, he turned to see a kid in white cotton closing it, while the lady in black Spanish lace over red satin switched to English, sort of, to declare her husband was not in, but that she, Doña Felicidad with a whole tree of family names strung after that, would be honored for to entertain him and answer any and all questions the U.S. government might have to ask of anyone.

He allowed that sounded fair, and began by asking where her husband was, as she led him through some French doors her servant opened for them under the arcade around their private jungle.

Inside, the same kid lit some candles atop a grand piano near a furlong or so of tufted leather sofa. Another white-clad kid, this one a young gal, dashed in through another doorway with a salver of nachos and honest red wine. Longarm had noticed that the watery iced sangria didn't really do much when it got *this* hot.

Doña Felicidad sat him by the low table piled with food and drink, then sank down gracefully beside him. She was built for such graceful movement, and not bad-looking if you

122

ignored her pale greenish complexion or the way her heavy brows met in the middle. Longarm warned himself not to study another man's woman any harder than that.

When she told him where Don Hernan was, he knew he was just as glad she was only so-so. She said her man had gone up the river to Laredo, looking for the *pendejo* who'd dared to accuse him of shooting anybody in the back.

"Is a matter of honor," his hostess, who looked to be in her mid-thirties explained. "Hernan did not like Count Atterdag. In this he was not alone. Is true he called the arrogant Dane a species of dung beetle and challenged him for to fight. But that *cobarde arrogante* was not man enough for to back his insults with his blade or gun!"

She poured the wine as Longarm said he'd been told the late Count Atterdag had been unpleasant to everybody. He said, "I reckon growing up as a spoiled brat and then getting diplomatic immunity to back your play could turn the head of many a dullard. But did your man really feel it was wise to go gunning for another Dane entirely, on the Yanqui side of what you call the Rio Bravo, whilst accused in writing of the first shooting?"

She pressed the dish of nachos on him by gesture as she explained, "Hernan has diplomatic immunity for to deal in horses in the name of our own *federales* on both sides of the border. I asked him not to go after that *idiota* in Laredo, but he was very, how you say, *enfurecido*?"

Longarm allowed he'd be mighty vexed had anyone written a letter like that about *him*.

She paid no heed to his calming words and insisted, "Was *defamatorio premeditado*! Hernan can prove it! Was speaking to a *francesda* who works there when they both heard a shot and rushed outside together for to see the count already on the pavement! My Hernan could not be the murderer, even if he had wanted to shoot the fat *cabròn* in the back, *comprende*?"

Longarm took his notebook from his shirt pocket as he asked her if she could name any Frenchwoman who could alibi her man.

She couldn't. She said, "Hernan *told* me he was speaking with one of those *francesas* when that one shot rang out. I did not ask her name. There are questions one does not ask one's husband if he is an Obregon with a delicate sense of honor.''

Longarm put the notebook away as he allowed he followed her drift. It made sense that nobody from the French consulate had come forward to name any French gal a murder suspect might have been flirting with, before or after the distressing international incident.

As he tried to decide what to ask next, they both heard a distant rumble of thunder. So Doña Felicidad said, "You had better allow us for to prepare you a room, *señor*. We are overdue for that break in the weather and I fear it will get most *espantosa* outside, at any *momento*!"

He smiled thinly and replied, "I never argue with a lady about her own climate, ma'am. But I'm expected back in Brownsville by midnight, and I'd better study on getting there before the ferry boats go out of business because of inclement weather."

He drained his small wine glass to be polite, and rose to his feet in spite of her begging him to spend the night with her. He didn't think she meant it the way it could be taken, and even if it could be taken that way, no man with a lick of sense was about to mess with the woman of a man who'd travel two hundred miles to reply to a dumb letter that said nothing about his family matters.

It wouldn't have been polite to tell her that the little she'd been able to tell him hadn't solved a thing he was concerned about. So he thanked her for her help and got out of there as gracefully as he knew how.

By now the sun was all the way down, and the usual gloaming seemed to be missing as the clouds hung low in the gathering dusk. For the same reasons they didn't show off any house trimmings to a street a lot of strangers were likely using, nobody bothered much with street lamps away from the islands of lit-up plazas. So Longarm strode just seventy yards or so, and then ducked into a dark entryway to flatten out and make sure nobody was following him in the tricky light.

Nobody seemed to be. So he lit a cheroot and moved on, the night air much cooler on his shirtsleeves now as the overcast up above swirled as if some monstrous witch in the sky were stirring clouds in her Texas-sized cauldron.

"It's fixing to rain fire and salt!" he told himself as he picked up his pace. He was coming to that sort of fashionable plaza they'd passed through coming in. He idly considered buying a rain poncho on his way out. Such notions were cheaper south of the border, and he still had most of that money the late Mr. John Brown of Kansas had been packing.

He found a tiny shop where they offered him a saddle blanket at a bargain as well. He told them he already had a saddle blanket, and settled for a sort of piss-yellow rain-poncho of canvas, waterproofed with a mixture of beeswax and tallow. It smelled awful, and he didn't put it on until he'd strode out the far side of the modest plaza and got hit by what he hoped was rain instead of pigeon shit.

As he put the stinky but waterproof poncho on over his head, the gobs of rain were falling seriously. But the water-front wasn't all that far now. So he forged on ahead, more worried about wind than rain.

He knew the ferry boats would keep running in mere rain. But not if an east wind blew to pile whitecaps against the seaward current.

It was raining harder, but the wind wasn't all that bad as Longarm approached the waterfront livery where he'd left his paint pony.

As he did so, an old lamplighter was shedding more light on the wet pavement out front, dusk having fallen so early after sundown. The wan beams of the oil-fired street lamp barely made it into the doorway of the shut-down saddle shop next to the livery. But there was enough light for Long-arm to make out the figure standing there, dressed like an Anglo rider of above average height, with a casual hand resting on the grips of his side-draw six-gun. It looked like that rude cuss who'd jumped aboard the southbound ferry boat earlier.

It took the surly stranger longer to recognize the poncho-clad figure striding toward the livery, and him, in the rain. But when he did, he drew that side arm to throw down on Longarm without an eye blink's worth of hesitation!

Longarm had figured he might, and there was no law saying a man couldn't discreetly draw his own gun under the privacy of a mess of wet canvas. So he was glad he had as he fired first and barely made it. The stranger, who'd obviously been waiting for him to come back for his pony, shot 250 grains of lead off the pavement between them as Longarm pinned him against the door to slide down it with six hundred grains of lead in *him* all told.

Then, as the rain-lashed *calle* commenced to fill up with noisy Mexicans of all ages and both sexes, Longarm was crawfishing back from the street lighting, gunsmoke billowing from under his shot-up poncho, till he ducked into a narrow serviceway and shed the incriminating piss-yellow canvas, then ran the length of the dark slot, to skid to a stop and sort of stroll out the far side in his dark pants and lighter work shirt, already soaked to the skin.

As he turned to head toward the brighter lights of the waterfront, instead of scuttling for the shadows like a cockroach with a guilty conscience, a big wet Mexican with an official gray sombrero and a .45 U.S. Army Issue S&W Model #3m or Schofield, asked Longarm where those shots he'd just heard might have come from.

Longarm replied, "*Quien sabe?* Not back that way. It sounded as if they were at least one *manzana* over."

The *rurale* nodded and turned to head back to the closer corner. It was nice to know he didn't know this *barrio* all that well. *Rurales* tended to patrol on horseback between towns, bless their ornery hides. That one was likely just in town to get laid and couldn't keep his nose out of any gunplay.

Longarm drifted as innocently toward that ferry slip as he dared. Everyone else on the streets of Matamoros was dashing from cover to cover in the tropical downpour.

Had he had it out with that truculent rurale on his own side of the estuary, it would have only been a pain in the ass. But owning up to a shootout down Mexico way could result in a whole lot of trouble no matter how your story went. El Presidente Diaz didn't allow anyone one but his own uniformed thugs to shoot tourists.

As he paused beneath an awning near the ferry slip to consider his options, Longarm decided his hired pony would keep overnight in that livery near the scene of what Mexico might view as a crime.

So if he were to simply board the next ferry afoot, lay low for a spell on the Texican side, then come back in the morning, bold as a big-ass bird . . .

"Hey, gringo. For why are you hiding there, eh?" asked a mighty suspicious voice from behind him.

Longarm turned to see two Matamoros beat patrolmen eyeing him with those bland smiles Mexicans reserve for someone they just might want to stomp.

Longarm smiled back as coldly and explained, "I am waiting to run for the next ferry boat. As you see, there ain't one moored against the slip right now, and I'd sure look silly dashing for the river in this rain."

One of them seemed to feel that would be amusing to watch, and asked Longarm why he didn't take a running jump into the Rio Bravo.

The other one said, "I got a better place for you, gringo. Was a killing not far from here just a few minutes ago. For why you don't come with us to our *cuartel de policía* and tell our *sargento* where you were when somebody shot another gringo three times for to leave him dead in the rain."

Longarm tried for a boyish laugh as he replied, "You can't be serious. I heard the shots, if you're talking about mayhaps five or ten minutes ago. But nobody I know has been shot around *here* in recent memory."

This was the simple truth, as soon as one studied on it some. But for some reason they didn't seem to be buying his act. The one who'd asked him to take a running jump into the harbor stared down at the .44-40 riding cross-draw in the rain at Longarm's side. The Mexican was smiling in as he almost purred, "That other gringo was shot three times, with three bullets. No more. No less. Would you let me have a look at that gun you are wearing now, *por favor*?"

Chapter 18

It was two to one. They were spread and on the prod. And even if he won, Longarm knew he'd be in the wrong.

He didn't like them. He liked their government even less. Just the same, they were fellow peace officers doing their job.

On the other hand, it was a mite late in the game to plead self-defense. You weren't supposed to run away like a thief in the night with three spent cartridges in the wheel after you gunned anybody, in self-defense or even righteous indignation.

"We are waiting, gringo," purred the one who seemed to like him the least.

Then that same *rurale* who'd stopped Longarm came around the lamplit corner with a couple of scampering kids who seemed to enjoy the rain a lot more. The *rurale* called out, "For why are you two not searching for that killer? Was not a gringo. These *muchachos* saw him. I already questioned that *borrachón* on my way to the scene. He was on another *calle,* and as I just said, we know what the killer looks like."

One of the rain-soaked youths stared sort of slyly at Longarm as he volunteered, "Was an *indio,* in a *poncho amarillo.*"

The local lawmen didn't see to care. The one with the mouth turned on the *rurale* to demand, "Who invited you for to investigate the theft of a *centavo* in Matamoros? Are not you *rurales* supposed to patrol the country lanes lest somebody rape a chicken or murder a cactus?''

The *rurale* stood taller under his rain-soaked sombrero to shout back, ''You question my right to stride the shit-strewn *calles* of this village? You dare? Was in town for to see my *querida linda*, a woman of your town who would not spit in your mother's milk. Is it my fault you *pendejos* don't know for how to conduct a routine investigation?''

A crowd was gathering despite the way the rain and now some wind were picking up. Longarm figured he'd best get out of there before he drowned or somebody arrested him or picked his pocket. So it was easy enough to edge backwards slowly as the rain came down in sheets and both the wind and all three Mexican lawmen commenced to howl.

Longarm ducked around a corner, and paused under the awning of a sidewalk *cafetín* to reload his six-gun and figure his next move. They had candles burning on the far side of their storm shutters. So he knew they were still serving in there. But he was too close to those Mexican lawmen, and since the ferry was likely shut down for the storm as well, he had no sensible reason to tarry within a furlong or more of the waterfront and a recent shootout.

He started to move on, glad he'd left his coat and most of his papers with Sigridur at their *posada*. Everything he had on this side of the harbor was getting wetter by the minute. But it wouldn't have been smart to go all the way back to that shop for another waterproof poncho.

Longarm could only hope, as he hugged the storefronts to windward, that the plaza shop closer to the Obergon place was far enough from that livery stable. That *rurale*'s point about sloppy police work had been a low blow. If anybody in Mexico went in for brutal, sloppy methods, it had to be *los rurales*. The law in most border towns was designed to encourage visitors to come again, provided they had pocket jingle leastways. Nobody, Anglo or Mexican, wanted to be rounded up down this way with empty pockets. For why would anyone wish for to feed a prisoner who had nobody coming for to bail him out?

Light and laughter seemed to be spilling out across the

wet pavement up ahead. So Longarm headed for what looked like a roofed-over arcade of food stands, shops, and such. He'd explained to Sigridur how Mexicans stayed up later than most, weather permitting. It was no accident that you saw so many awnings and arcades down Mexico way. When folks couldn't congregate in the streets, they settled for doing it in as close to open air as they could get.

But before he could get to illumination and laughter, a mysterious but friendly-sounding voice called out from the pitch blackness between two blank walls facing outwards. "You do not wish for to go in there, El Brazo Largo. The people searching for you have fewer places for to search with this *chaparrón* sweeping everyone into less scattered piles, no?"

Longarm stepped into the narrow slot to see, as he'd suspected, that it ran way the hell back in the dark. Spanish-speaking folks laid things out that way, presenting rude back walls to the general public while providing them with convenient shortcuts. It likely made it harder to explain why you were cutting across somebody's property.

In the dim light he could barely make out what seemed to be a kid of the male persuasion. It wouldn't have been properly dressed in just those wet white pants, lopped off below the knee, had it been a kid of the *female* persuasion.

"Where do you reckon I want to go?" asked Longarm in a desperately casual tone as he tried to decide whether this one had been one of the young jaspers back by the ferry slip with that *rurale*.

The kid said, "*Vamonos.* I was told for to take you to some friends of your own. I shall tell you where if we get there. If we are caught, it may be just as well you do not know, *comprende*?"

Longarm decided to chance it. The kid knew who he was. Had the kid been inclined to turn him in to the Mexican law, he'd have only needed to point. The maze of narrow slots between wet stucco walls wasn't roofed over, save for a few buttressed archways they passed under, so Longarm wasn't any drier when the kid directed him through what looked like a closet door set in a thick outside wall. He found himself crossing a nice-smelling patio, where a fountain talked back to the rain and a mess of night-blooming jasmine really seemed to be enjoying it.

The next thing he knew, they were inside a nice-smelling house, and he was glad the floors were covered with red Spanish tiles instead of rugs for him to drip on. The smell came from mesquite wood burning briskly and popping, the way mesquite wood was inclined to, as it warmed and dried the air indoors.

His soggy young guide looked sort of like the urchins he'd seen near the waterfront. It made it easier to swipe things from market stalls when you all sort of looked alike. But whoever he was, he wasn't supposed to track around that house in his wet bare feet. A dry-shod moonfaced Indian lady, wearing a Basque blouse and gathered print skirting, came to fetch Longarm with a pro forma, *"Está en su casa. Acompañeme, por favor."*

He went along with her, casting a wistful glance into that firelit baronial parlor as they passed right by it and headed up a spiral staircase to the really private second floor. Longarm knew that, like Frenchmen, Spanish-speaking folks had Queen Victoria beat when it came to inviting guests who weren't family up to the sneakier rooms of their homes.

It got sneakier when what seemed to be their housekeeper ushered Longarm through an open doorway three closed doors from the top landing, then vanished back into her lamp, or wherever.

As he stepped into the dimly lit and pefumed private chambers of somebody who sure liked the smell of jasmine, night-or-day-blooming, the gal was lounging on a chaise upholstered with velvet a more refined shade of red than you'd find in a whorehouse. Her black lace wrap was expensive but tasteful as well, save for not covering her below the pearls she wore as high as some thought proper, in cool weather leastways.

She was a pure head-turner of around thirty. It wasn't true that all Anglo, Dutch, Irish, Mexican folks, or whatever looked alike. But he'd never yet met up with that peculiar combination of Ancient Greek features and skin the color of a ripe peach, fuzz and all, that hadn't come with a Spanish name.

As she sat up straighter to extend one hand and give him a better view of her statuesque figure, she told Longarm to call her La Abogada, which meant The Lawyer. Other members of *La Causa* he'd met in the past had been coy about their real names as well.

He smiled down at her, aware that this time there really was a rug to drip on as he allowed he sure could use a lawyer that evening.

La Abogada smiled back and firmly replied, "You could use a good soak in a warm tub as well. You must be a mass of gooseflesh under those clammy clothes."

She rose to her pom-pom-slippered feet—she stood about five feet and change—to wave him towards a lamplit archway you had to circle a big four-poster bed to get to. The bed and its mosquito netting smelled more like lavender than jasmine as he circled it. La Abogada led him into a piped-in bathroom, still a rarity in more modern parts of the world, where he found a big copper bathtub had been lying in wait for some time with its hot tap running—expensive as well as hospitable.

La Abogada moved ahead of Longarm to bend and test the water with one hand as she shook bath salts into it with the other. The view from where Longarm stood was inspiring. The shapely rump that black lace couldn't hide worth mentioning was like nobody's he'd gone dog-style with in recent memory.

She straightened up to turn and face him as he decided her proud breasts sort of reminded him of that opera singer he'd once sung duets with out California way.

She said, "*Bueno.* I shall come back for your wet things after I allow you for to get in, eh?"

Longarm replied, "That might be more modest, ma'am. But where did you have it in your mind to take my duds?"

She said, "For to dry downstairs in the *cocina,* of course. Would take forever and result in *moho* if we just hung them up in this damp weather."

Longarm began to unbutton his shirt, but thoughtfully observed, "I sure would like my duds dried and not mildew-rotted, ma'am. But since you know who I am, speaking as my lawyer, do you feel it's wise to hang my stuff in your kitchen right off the back door?''

She laughed—she had a happy-skylark laugh—and assured him she had an arrangement with the police captain in this *barrio*. He knew who she was, how many *friends* she had, and how many of them knew where *he* lived with his own wife and family.

Longarm allowed that was good enough for his shirt and pants. But after she'd left so he could strip down, he placed his wallet with his badge and identification next to his gun rig and pocket jingle on the marble washstand.

Then, having piled everything else handy for her on a towel hamper near the door, Longarm got in the tub. He'd forgotten how nice it felt to exchange wet socks for warm bathwater laced with perfume and those salts that made your skin all slick.

He found a cake of real castile soap, Spanish folks having invented modern soap, and lathered himself all over before he lay back in the big tub with a hand pinching his nostrils and just went under like a soaped-up beaver to rinse all the soap and dirt off his hide and out of his hair.

When he came back up, his duds, hat, and boots were missing. He hoped his dick hadn't been sticking up out of the water at her. He had no call for a full erection. But the critter seemed to have a mind of its own when he was suddenly slick and wet and warm without any cares that couldn't wait until morning.

La Abogada let him splash and wallow until the copper tub drained some of the warmth out of his bath. He turned the hot tap to make it cozier, feeling a tad guilty because he knew he was as clean as he was likely to get, while somebody down below had to keep the firebox stoked under the boiler he was abusing like a rich man.

But it felt so good, he didn't want to get out just yet. And then, as he lay back to soak as if he were a banker, or at least a mine owner, it came to him that nobody had told him what in thunder he was going to put *on* once he rose from all this luxurious water like Miss Venus from that seashell, although without hair long enough to cover his own privates the way she did in that painting.

Then, as if she read minds or had a keen sense of timing, La Abogada was back with what looked like a big black bearskin coat, until you looked closer and saw it was black Turkish toweling.

She said, "We have hung your things near the stove, except for the boots which we stuffed with corn husks after they'd been saddle-soaped. You still do not remember me, do you?"

To which Longarm could only reply, sitting up straighter, "If I ever laid eyes on you before, ma'am, I was passing through in a hurry and you had a different outfit on. I noticed you had more than one mirror hanging on your walls in yonder. So you don't need me to tell you how good-looking you might be."

She smiled down at him as she hung the toweling on a hook near Longarm and assured him, "No woman can be told too often what she looks like, provided she is not told too often she is ugly. You guessed right about the rags I was wearing and the frantic pace we were all moving in when I rode with you and the rest of La Mariposa's band on the far slopes of the Sierra Oriental. Was a close call we all had with *El Enemigo* that *Noviembre,* no?"

He grinned up at her and asked, "Lord have mercy, were you mixed up in that running gunfight just after the Day of the Dead in Mexico City? You sure must have been raggedy and dusty for me not to have noticed you!"

She smiled wider, moving closer, as she demurely replied, "You were most busy with La Mariposa, whenever nobody was shooting at you. La Mariposa still boasts of making love to El Brazo Largo and fighting for *La Causa* at the same time. Don't you wish for to get out of that tub and put on this robe now?"

He gulped and said, "You'd best go in the next room then. All this talk about love and war has made me feel sort of shy!"

She shrugged and shucked her own lace wrap in one graceful motion to show she wasn't shy about her own peach-colored and perfectly formed body as she answered simply, "*Bueno.* If you won't come out for to play with me, I shall have to get in for to play with you!"

Chapter 19

Longarm had promised old Sigridur he'd get back to her by midnight though Hell should bar the way. But he hadn't promised anything about Heaven, and it sure felt heavenly when La Abogada slithered her naked torso down his own to impale her old ring-dang-do on his old organ-grinder under the warm water, with one bare heel planted to either side of his naked hips as he slithered his slippery bare ass back and forth on the slick copper bottom of the tub filled with water and bath salts.

For this dusky-peach beauty was built as differently from the big blonde he'd been bedding as two human beings could get without one of them turning into a boy, and despite all the serious thought he and Sigridur had put into coming up with new positions on land and sea, they'd never tried it *this* way.

So thinking about a bigger, blonder gal's broader pelvis swishing sudsy water back and forth as she inhaled and exhaled tight and wet inspired his erection even more, and La Abogada, feeling the twitches with her sensitive sensual innards, sobbed, "*Sí, sí,* this makes me *loca en me cuna* as well! Why do we not go to bed together and let you *chinge me mucho y más rapido,* eh?"

That sounded swell to Longarm, once he'd ejaculated up

into her under the water while she sort of barked like a sea lioness.

He offered to towel her off some as he lifted her out of the tub with her wet legs still wrapped around him. But she just kept sliding up and down his semi-sated shaft as he toted her into the bedroom that way.

His shaft didn't stay semi-sated once he'd flopped inside those mosquito nets with her, both of them still wet, to soak her scented sheets or dry themselves off a mite while they tried all the usual positions, and a couple La Abogada had always been meaning to try.

As they took a break to catch their second wind and share a smoke in the form of a mighty powerful as well as expensive green cigar, La Abogada lay beside him with one peachy thigh across his belly and the other spread just as wide the other way as she aired her crotch and cleared her mind about his reasons for shooting other Anglos in her fair city.

Longarm passed the cigar back to her as he truthfully told her he had no idea why that rascal had been laying for him by the livery.

He said, "I'm sure he was following me around Brownsville. When I surprised him by boarding the ferry boat, he had to break cover just long enough to board at the last possible minute. I lost track of him for a spell. He must have made it ashore on this side whilst I was coaxing a pony off the lower deck. He watched me from a distance, and when he saw me leave my mount at that livery and hail a hansom, he must have decided that he who heads off is likely to head back. So he was laying for me in the rain with the edge of knowing more about who both of us were."

She snuggled closer to reply adoringly, "He must have wished for to commit suicide. The *muchacho* who reported the affair at the *estable* to me said you nailed him three times as he was still drawing. But he must have known who he was up against, and anyone here in Mexico could have told him you do not draw on El Brazo Largo face-to-face!"

To which Longarm could only reply, "Aw, mush. Gents who hire out as gunslicks tend to be long on confidence as well as short on brains. I sure wish I could find out who hired him, though. As it now stands, I dare not ask your Matamoros law who they reckon they have on ice, and I've no idea how I'll ever get back to Brownsville with that paint I paid a deposit on!''

She said soothingly, "Let me and your other friends help you. *La Causa* has eyes and ears everywhere. It has to, for because the *malvado vicioso* who stole our *revolución* from our sainted Benito Juarez has *his* spies everywhere!''

He took a drag on their big green cigar, blinked away his tears, and soberly replied, "I've noticed as much on earlier visits. But I'd be false to you and your friends if I let you think I was down this way on any business having to do with Mexico this time. The want I was sent to bring in may be *hiding out* on this side of the border. But he's neither Anglo nor Mexican. He's a . . . let me see if I can work this out. He's a military deserter from *Tierra de Hielo*?''

She said, "*Sí*, Iceland. I speak English more better than you speak Spanish, and we have heard of this Pall Njalsson the Texas Rangers are searching for, along with a small palomino mare called Lille Thruma.''

Longarm grimaced and declared, "That's one on me and the Justice Department then. I don't know why the infernal Rangers have to act so standoffish, just because the Reconstruction Acts put them out of business for ten years after the war. They told us they had no jurisdiction and didn't want any. How do you figure, you being a lawyer and all?''

She took a thoughtful drag on the cigar, as if she was more used to her brand, and decided, "They wish for the credit if they find a man wanted by both his own government and Tio Sam. But they do not wish for the *mierda* on their boot heels if they fail. The Rangers of Texas are supposed to be infallible. One way for to seem infallible is to never let anyone see you fail, no?''

Longarm sighed and said, "There have surely been times when I've wished I'd never set out after an owlhoot rider. We all fail. It's a fact of nature that nothing nor nobody can win every pot or kiss every pretty gal.''

She asked him to just kiss *her*. So he did. Then he said, "Hold the thought just a minute. We were talking about that killing north of the harbor. What can you tell me about Don Hernan Obregon, seeing you know so much about that other witness to the killing, and I'll be whipped with snakes if I can see why a horse trader ought to have diplomatic immunity!"

She curled her pretty upper lip and told him, "That one is another *malvado* in league with *El Diablo,* or El Presidente Diaz as the Devil is known in this country. But we are saving the smaller devils such as Obregon for the big fiesta we mean to have against a lot of walls when our turn comes at last."

Longarm patted her bare shoulder and said, "You folks sure have an exciting way of deciding elections down this way. What does Obregon do for the powers that be, aside from buying and selling horses on both sides of the border?"

She told him, "He moves gold and silver around as well. As you must know, there is no law forbidding anyone from bringing bullion or specie *into* Mexico. But the *puercos* we have yet to overthrow still demand the royal fifth on all wealth *leaving* Mexico. So a man moving back and forth on innocent business with diplomatic immunity is in a grand position for to conduct some not-so-innocent business for his friends in high places, *comprende*?"

Longarm answered honestly, "No. Why in blue blazes would the bad men running their own government like a gambling house need to sneak their own ill-gotten gains past their own tax collectors?"

She shrugged her smooth, now dry, shoulders and replied, "You just said the magic word. *Sneak* means the same as *salir,* no? The junta in the process of looting our country neither wishes for to make exact details a matter of record, nor do they wish for to share any wealth with tax and custom officials of lower rank. And so, whenever certain high-and-mighty thieves wish for to transfer funds to their secret bank accounts in other countries, they call upon a respected horse trader with diplomatic immunity and friends on both sides of the Rio Bravo. We are not alone in feeling not even a devil can live forever, and Don Hernan Obregon is that most intelligent species of criminal. He breaks no laws he does not *have* to, on either side of the border. He deals honestly in horseflesh, only takes a modest commission, and never pilfers when he smuggles contraband, and so far, he has never given us *revolucionarias* much reason for to assassinate him.''

Longarm asked how she felt about Obregon assassinating that Danish count. She asked, ''For why? We know he had some dealing with those *comerciantes danes* who wish for to sell children's pets as *caballos*. Does not matter if he bought any or not. He would have had no reason for to fight with anyone from their *consulado* that I can think of, and if he *did* have a reason, Don Hernan is not the sort of man who must assassinate his enemies in person. He must have over a hundred *vaqueros muy machos* riding for him.''

Longarm set the green cigar aside lest he wind up seasick in a bouncing bed, and began to absently roll one of her nipples between thumb and trigger finger as he mused, half to himself, ''Doña Felicidad, Obregon's wife, told me he'd headed all the way up the river to Laredo to clean the plow of a man who wrote a nasty letter about him.''

La Abogada took that hand by the wrist to lead it into further temptation as she replied in a tone of dismissal, ''Men tell their wives all sorts of things when they wish for to have a few days free for other pleasures. We heard somebody in Laredo had accused Don Hernan of murder. But for why would this upset a man of *la raza* so much? Nobody has offered to appear in court as a witness against him. Even if somebody did, no Texas court has any powers to put any Mexican with diplomatic immunity on trial, while no *Mexican* court is about to try a member of the ruling junta for killing an insulting drunk in another country.''

She parted her own love-lips with Longarm's fingers as she asked in as clinical a tone, ''Do you think I could take one of those odd little ponies down here? I have heard it said that some adventurous Roman women were able for to *chingar* with ponies. Do you think this possible?''

Longarm began to politely rock the boy in the boat for her as he replied, ''I read that book, in a plain brown-paper wrapper. It was called the Golden Ass, and those old-time Romans could sure write as dirty as that crazy Frenchman de Sade. But it was a jackass, not a small horse, those Roman ladies were fooling with in that book. There *is* a dirty book by some Arab lady, bragging about her and a full-grown stud. But I somehow have my doubts. A heap of those notions that a crazy man comes up with as he's writing with one hand and jerking off with the other seem more exciting than practical.''

The warm-natured and peach-complected La Abogada suddenly sat up to fork one shapely orange thigh across his lap, and settled her gaping but snug-fitting *bragadura* on his reinspired *palo* as she moaned, "*Ay, que magnifico*! I do not see how any other beast could feel any better. But tell me what those other women did in ancient times with that golden ass!''

He knew some gals liked to have a man talking dirty to them at times such as these. So he said, "They mostly fucked and sucked it. Roman dirty books stress size, frequency, and oddity of partners. They say that some old Roman gal poisoned her husband so she and her favorite slave could have more time in bed together. Some Roman emperor decreed that since they like to fuck so much, their punishment should fit their crime. They were tied across sawhorses in the arena so that trained bulls could fuck them both in the ass fatally. The book said the crowd loved it. De Sade had way more imagination, the poor sick bastard.''

La Abogada wanted more dirty bedtime stories as she slid her swell golden fuzzy torso up and down to the very limits of hanging on to him with her moist love-lips.

So he told her the tale de Sade had penned about this totally depraved child who'd strapped on a dildo to attack her own mother, and thus managed to commit rape, incest, and lesbianism at the same time. The disrespectful child had been named Justine by de Sade.

From the way La Abogada got to moving on top of him, she found the tale exciting. Longarm had never seen much point to it. He had to allow that any poor mother in such an odd predicament would be shocked and hysterical. For she, as the victim, would feel all the violation, and maybe forbidden pleasures. But what in blue blazes would any gal get out of scaring her poor old momma like that with an artificial pecker only the momma's raped pussy could feel going in and out?

He said, "Old de Sade finally got locked up in a madhouse

after he'd tied a housemaid up, cut her hind end crisscross with a razor, and then dripped hot candle wax all over her ass.''

La Abogada gasped that she was coming. That made two of them, and so he rolled her over on her back to finish right, with her sobbing and accusing him of trying to rupture her while, all the while, she was trying to run her bare toes through his hair.

After he'd exploded in her some and extended her some of the mercy she'd been begging for, Longarm decided, ''There must be something wrong with me. I just can't see why anybody would want to mistreat their own kin or torture the hired help. But whilst we're speaking of strange love notions, could you find out if either Don Hernan, the Danish officer holed up in the U.S. Customs House across the harbor, or our Mr. Andersen in charge of there enjoys a rep for sort of unusual views on slap-and-tickle?''

La Abogada lay limply in his arms with her legs loosely wrapped around his neck as she languidly replied, ''I shall have my friends on both sides of the harbor ask around. Are you suggesting that stink at the *consulado frances* was a lovers' quarrel between a bunch of *señoritas degeneradas*?''

He said, ''It's worth looking into. It might let Don Hernan off the hook, unless he's double-gaited and I missed something about his nice-looking wife this evening. On the other hand, that Andersen at the Customs House must have *some* reason for sticking his neck out for a former classmate at a fancy English school where the term 'fag' was invented.''

She sat bolt upright, demanding, ''You were with Felicidad Obregon earlier this very evening?''

He said, ''Of course I was. I told you I'd been there and . . . hold on, you don't think I got to know her *this* well, do you?''

So that was when the rebel gal told him that that sort of high-toned beauty he'd passed on would have certainly screwed him had not he escaped in time.

La Abogada explained, and he was inclined to believe, that society gals down this way didn't dare mess with the hired help, and thus seldom missed the chance to mess with a proper stranger their husbands might not know about.

But Longarm didn't care. Any husband who'd tearass two hundred miles after a cuss who'd insulted his rep was nobody you'd want after you for humping his wife.

Chapter 20

The following day dawned cool and clear. The ferry was back in operation, and that shooting by the livery had been chalked up to a holdup gone wrong, with the killer a Mexican in a piss-yellow poncho. But Longarm wasn't out of the woods yet.

He was enjoying a breakfast of *huevos rancheros con tostados* in bed, looking forward to enjoying La Abogada some more, when his mighty gracious hostess came back in, wearing her wrap, to tell him not to go back to that livery for his hired paint.

She said, "Is not *la policía municipal*. Is *los rurales*. They are most excited about that rifle you left in the tack room. Was not a good time for to bring rifles into Mexico. You, or someone else that may be able to reason with them, must satisfy them about that rifle."

Longarm asked, "How come? It's just an old Winchester '73. You can buy one like it in most any pawnshop cheap."

She shook her head as she sat down beside him, saying, "Not in Matamoros. Not right now! All this talk of repeating rifles, a *lot* of repeating rifles, has the ruling junta and the coyotes who ride for them *muy nerviosos*!"

Longarm had learned the hard way in other beds not to say too much just because a lady had been acting as if she liked him. For all her charms, La Abogada was a paid-up

143

rebel leader, and he'd already been the victim of a Prussian spy who'd wanted to know more about those infernal new Mauser repeaters. So he took another bite of his grub and chewed it some before he replied in a desperately casual voice, "Seems to me I did hear tell about some contraband arms being dumped on the local shady market. Can't say I know just how they got there, who's offering, or who's buying."

The pretty rebel sighed and replied, "Neither do we. As you must have been told by our other friends further west, *La Revolución* is not yet completely organized. So there are at least seven or eight more or less independent leaderships."

He smiled thinly and said, "Everybody wants to be a chief and not enough are willing to be Indians. Like I told El Gato out Sonora way, the main reason Diaz has held on so long is that he holds on tight and won't allow nobody else to promote his own self to commander in chief."

She replied defensively, "My people are a simple people. When a simple man has been told all his life he is a dog, it goes to his head when he suddenly finds himself in command of *anything*."

Longarm told her, not unkindly, "I don't aim to argue about that. It seems the same this whole world over. The Irish Fennians spend as much time fighting one another as they do the English. Queen Victoria rules the Indian subcontinent from her runty little island because, as much as they hate the British Raj, the Hindu leaders won't sit at the same table with any rebel from a different caste. I've just been talking with an Icelander who tells me Iceland is only ruled by a faraway Danish crown because the natural leaders of each Icelandic district couldn't refrain from fighting like cats and dogs. Folks who want to overthrow their rulers, good or bad, start by working together, the way our Continental Congress did. Just good enough to hang together lest they hang separately, as old Ben Franklin warned. Mexico will never rid itself of Diaz, or others just as bad, before she learns that when you don't get your way in politics, you're not supposed to shoot the cuss who won the argument, election, or whatever."

He could tell by her puzzled look that he wasn't getting

144

through to her on majority rule. There were some on his own side of the border who'd never grasped it either. So he said, "Never mind all that. Tell me what you do know about them Prussian rifles."

She said, "I have. Like *los rurales,* we have heard vague rumors of a great arms shipment, perhaps consigned to a border dealer in forbidden fruit we only know as El Turco."

"The Turk?" Longarm frowned, thinking back to some bulletins he'd scanned a spell back in Denver in connection with an earlier Texas case.

He said, "I've heard tell of El Turco, and you're right, he sells things. They say he'd sell you his grandmother's false teeth if the price was right. But he mostly deals in stolen goods, with notes to the teacher allowing they come from the estate of some dead plutocrat, a pawnshop going out of business, or whatever. So I reckon someone like El Turco would come in handy if you had at least a boxcar load of side-tracked Mauser rifles you wanted to unload in Texas or . . . Hold on, wouldn't it make more sense to unload them down the Gulf Coast a piece if they were meant for your rebel group or any other?"

La Abogada shook her head and said, "El Presidente's new steam cutters can patrol his own coast day and night, with four-inch deck guns and no fuss about constitutional rights if they spot a fishing boat riding low in the water with a load of fish, or anything else. For a gunrunner, is more better to land whatever you wish on the *Texas* shore. Your Yanqui cutters are fewer in numbers, they are less inclined for to shoot first and ask questions later, and most of all, your own government is not *loco en la cabeza* on the subject of modern weapons in the hands of the common people."

She heaved a vast sigh, reminding him of how much her tits remind him of the two halves of a split peach—when you could see them, that is—and continued. "As you say, anyone can buy a repeating rifle or a ten-gauge breechloader anywhere in Texas. Your cowboys and even your Indians go armed in a manner that would get them shot by your own *rurales* for no other reason. Men who rule by fear frighten easily. I think that is for why they got so excited when they discovered a pinto left at that *estable* with a gringo cavalry saddle and a repeating saddle gun, eh?"

He grimaced and said, "Damn, I put a lot of time into zeroing the sights on that Winchester, and I'll miss my old McClellan as well. But I don't see how I'm to recover them, or my deposit on that hired mount, without chancing some serious grilling, at the least, if I turned out lucky."

She told him how to work it. It was all in knowing the mind of her own brand of lawmen. He laughed, set the breakfast tray aside, and hauled her down atop him for dessert.

But while she kissed him vigorously, she sighed and told him it would work out better if they got him the hell across the harbor while the getting was good. She said the sky had dawned breathless but red in the east that morning. So there was just no saying how long the ferryboats would be paddling back and forth on a calm low tide.

He followed her drift, having taken part in an earlier salvage operation on these very shores a spell back, and got himself bathed, dressed, and back in Texas within the hour.

He paid a call on the town law to report his paint and possibles stolen and to make sure nobody was after him. Then he got to the *posada* to find Sigridur pacing up and down out front, as if she thought she was a fishing captain's woman with the weather glass dropping and his lugger long overdue.

When she saw him, she ran down the *calle* to hug him and kiss him, as Mexicans of all ages grinned from all around.

He said, "I'm sure glad you're up and about. I lost my paint pony in Matamoros last night. Let's get your own saddled up and I'll tell you all about it on our way back to that KHA pony paddock."

He did, leaving out the dirty parts, as they led her pony afoot as far as that remuda of Icelandic ponies nobody in Texas seemed to have any use for.

The same morose horse dealer came out to greet them. This time Longarm told Sigridur, "I want you to tell him who we really are, and then I want you to tell him I need another mount fast to do some canvassing and mayhaps to see what all the fuss is about when it comes to these cute little critters."

The KHA man cut in, speaking perfect English. "We knew who you were the first time, Deputy Long. You and Fru Jonsdottir were described to us, and neither of you answers the descriptions of elves. You say you want the loan of a *Smahestur,* Deputy Long?"

Longarm grinned sheepishly and replied, "I surely do, and that's a good one on us. Who told you we might come pestering you, or is that supposed to be a secret?"

The dryly smiling Dane shook his head and said, "Not at all. Baron Senderborg sent word from the consulate and told us we were to cooperate with you in every way. I confess I was a bit surprised when you seemed to prefer a charade, but orders are orders, and I just told you what the baron ordered."

So they shook on it, the Dane called a pair of hostlers out to lend a hand, and in no time at all they'd saddled and bridled a spunky mare called Kolsvartur because she was black as any black cat ever got, and about as soft and fuzzy-looking.

Longarm felt sort of silly forking himself aboard old Kolsvartur. She was a lot less horse than he was used to riding, although his heels didn't really drag the ground, once he had them in the steel stirrups of the flat-saddle provided. He doubted anyone would ever want to chance roping a Texas longhorn from aboard such a sweet little pet in any case.

One of the most appealing things about Icelandic ponies was the way they came up to you like friendly pups that wanted you to play with them.

They'd led Sigridur's bigger Texas scrub on over with a view to her riding it back. She wanted to ride with him when he said he meant to do some canvassing in and around Brownsville Township. He told her it was too big a boo, explaining, "I told you I was followed aboard that ferry boat and laid for on the streets of Matamoros, honey. I got enough to worry about without having to watch your pretty ass as well as my own. So you just wait for me where our Mexican pals can watch out for you, and I'll make it up to you come supper time."

She allowed she expected him to make it up to her a lot *after* suppertime and sundown. For she'd desired him just awful once that storm off the Gulf had cooled their bedding right for some loving.

He promised she'd live to regret such bragging as he helped her down and kissed her good in the *posada*'s stable. It sure seemed like a nice change, swapping spit with a big blue-eyed blonde instead of the smaller peach-complected spitfire of recent memory.

Once he'd made sure she'd stay safe, Longarm rode over to the waterfront and reined in at that photograph gallery.

When he went inside, the middle-aged gal behind the counter stared past him at the pony tethered out front to marvel, "What a dear little horse!"

Longarm sighed and said, "She ain't a horse, ma'am, she's a mare. Icelandic, like the palomino in that picture you said you could print up for me in quantity."

She nodded primly and replied, "We certainly could and we certainly did. Two dozen prints, just as you ordered, and I'll get them for you."

She ducked through a print cloth curtain, and came back with his prints neatly boxed for him, saying, "That will come to exactly six dollars, sir."

He paid her out of some of the money the late Mr. John Brown of Kansas had been packing in a dark *calle*, and when he had a look, he saw they'd done a swell job. With the smaller pony outside to compare with, he figured Little Thruma's Arab bloodlines had contributed the extra few inches at her withers, along with that creamy and somewhat less shaggy coat.

The older gal, who'd run off those twenty-four prints, followed him outside, saying they could print up some more from the same negative if he so desired.

He started to say something dumb. Then he considered how many more he might need before this wild-goose chase wound down one way or the other, and allowed that was good to hear.

The gal wanted to pet Kolsvartur. That stuff about negatives had just been an excuse. So he let her, wryly wondering why old maids seemed to fancy friendly critters so much when they were so afraid of being intimate with other human beings.

He wondered idly if he was being fair to the friendly old gal as she made silly noises at the black pony. For that lilac water she'd splashed on earlier smelled more schoolmarm than old maid, and if you ignored a few iron threads in her dark brown hair, she might not be all that old and frosty after all.

He let her pet his borrowed pony a polite spell. Then he told her he had to get it on down the road, and she blushed like a young gal and said she was sorry for acting so silly.

He said, "It ain't silly to be kind to animals, ma'am. I'd be proud to let you ride her if I had the time."

She clapped her hands and asked when. He said another time, of course, and remounted to get out of there before they *both* wound up looking silly.

It made more sense when canvassing to ride out as far as you meant to canvass and work your way back. That way you ended up at home as you finished for the day.

So he rode due north, away from the river and the last old chicken spreads on the outskirts of town, to find himself moving at a wondrous pace through the cactus-hedged corn or bean milpas of the Mexican produce growers within easy cartage of the river. Then on to higher and drier range, where clumps of palmetto and Spanish bayonet mixed with more scattered range cattle on a spring carpet of centipede grass.

He'd heard tell about the Icelandic pony's fifth gait, or *tolt*. So he figured that was what Kolsvartur was up to as they moved as if on tracks, slower than a cow pony's trot but way faster than a Tennessee's walk. It felt really nice to move that fast so comfortably. He said, "I'll be damned if we couldn't have used a mount like you on many a long market drive, Blackie. I ain't certain you'd have the weight for serious roping, but as a trail pony . . ."

Then he suddenly swung her off the trail, wishing like hell his saddle gun wasn't stuck in that Mexican tack room as he told the obedient little mare, "I aint tolting you through the sticker-brush to find out how tough you are, Blackie. We're being followed. I only have this .44-40 and a pocket derringer to deal with the son of a bitch. So I want us where the extra range of his own rifle might not weigh as much in his favor, see?"

Chapter 21

There was something to be said for riding a short-legged mount through palmetto and Spanish bayonet. For from time to time Longarm caught a glimpse of the high crown of the cowboy hat on their trail, and whenever he did so, he'd hunch down lower before that other rider could spy his Colorado-crushed Stetson and make another sharp turn.

Kolsvartur turned good. She seemed surefooted as a burro and if his weight bothered her, it didn't show. He'd noticed Icelandic folks ran to size, and Sigridur had told him they rode these small spunky critters over lava flats and such during their big fall roundups.

Icelandic stockmen raised a breed of Nordic sheep that thought they were wild American bighorns. Longarm didn't care. It was out Arizona way where sheep and cattlemen had started feuding recently over the limited grazing of marginal range. He hailed from West-by-God-Virginia, where country folks raised any fool thing they could get to grow, and *still* had trouble meeting taxes.

Glancing back, he saw that the small hooves of his shaggy black mount weren't leaving much of a trail. But they were leaving *some,* for a tracker worth his salt. The greened-up centipede, fescue, and little bluestem sod were as thick and springy as they ever got. But you could hardly ride over blue-stem without busting it up a mite, and hither and yon they just had to cross a bare patch, still soft from all that rain the night before.

He was searching in vain for some prickly pear. That cactus grew from deep in Old Mexico to the Great Lakes and Cape Cod. But it was seldom more than a few puny pads away from its natural home in the dry Southwest, where it could turn into a thorny jungle as high as the roof of a one-story house.

He saw no cactus half that high as he zigzagged through such cover as they could manage. But he and old Sigridur had screwed in a palmetto clump while riding in from the north. And even though the shaggy, more spaced-out trunks of such dwarf palm trees offered little in the way of bullet-stopping, a man forted up in the shade of a good-sized grove might get the drop on another riding through the bright sunlight all around.

So when he spied close to an acre of palmetto huddled around the remains of some long-dead parent, he rode past it at faster than that comfortable *tolt*, swung Kolsvartur sharply to the off-side, and tore back into those palmettos from the north.

He dismounted and tethered the fuzzy black pony to a shaggy green palmetto head that barely made her thirteen hands from its roots.

He told his mount, "Stay put here and hope I win. As dark as you are, you ought to pass for deep shade. But I sure wish those damned *rurales* had let me bring along that Winchester!"

Drawing his double-action Colt, which loaded the same .44-40 brass as his missing saddle gun but threw it less far and less accurately, Longarm dropped to one hand and his knees, crawling through the grove between the shaggy brown trunks in the deep shade of the spring-growth canopy. When he got to where he could cover his backtrail without sunbathing, he pulled his hat brim down a bit to shade his tanned face as he lay prone in damp sand with his six-gun gripped in both hands and steadied by his well-planted elbows.

A million years went by before, sure enough, a tall rider in a pale horse rode into view, staring down with interest from under a tall Texas hat, but riding with both his side arm and saddle gun well holstered.

So instead of bushwhacking him, Longarm called out, "*Buendias, hombre!* If you mean to live another fucking minute, I'd like you to rein in right where you are and grab for some sky!"

The other tall rider did as he was told, but shouted back as he sat his buckskin with both hands at shoulder height, "Good for you and the more fool me, Longarm. But before you gun me, be advised that I'd be Captain Travis Prescott of the Texas Rangers."

Longarm called back, "I see that bitty badge on all that sunlit white shirt, now that I've got you holding still. But leave those hands up whilst you tell me what call you have for tailing a fellow peace officer in the line of duty!"

The Ranger called back, "You ain't been acting all that natural, and a body gets to wondering why. How come you're riding that stuffed toy instead of the paint you rode in with? Before you tell me you told Brownsville it had been stolen, let me tell you *los rurales* have sent it back across the harbor, along with the body of that other Anglo they picked up off the walk just a hop, skip, and jump away."

Longarm replied, "I hadn't heard. What can you tell me about that mysterious jasper who seems to have ended his career down Mexico way?"

The Ranger answered, "I was hoping *you* could tell *us*. The county coroner says he was perforated three times with .44-40 slugs. What's this all about, Longarm? The way I heard it, Justice sent you down here to round up that one hostile witness and mayhaps that unusual mount that murdered diplomat was riding the night he died. So how come you've been acting as if you were working for Allan Pinkerton or Mr. Edgar Allan Poe?"

Longarm crawled out from under the palmettos and holstered his six-gun, for the time being, as he said, "You can put your hands down now. I feel more like those detectives Poe wrote about than any private dick. For this case seems to combine parts of the *Murders in the Rue Morgue* with *The Purloined Letter*."

Prescott dismounted to lead his own pony closer as he

asked with a crooked smile, "Are we after a superhuman trained ape that makes bodies vanish up smoke flues, or evidence hid in plain sight by a crook too clever by half?"

To which Longarm could only reply, "If I knew what the son of a bitch behind it all was up to, I'd have a better notion who assassinated Count Atterdag and how come."

As the Ranger joined him on the shady side of the grove, Longarm got out two cheroots and handed one over as he grumbled, "If you and your Rangers hadn't handed the whole shebang to me on a tin platter, I might not have to ride around in such mysterious circles. You got me asking questions *you* should have asked before I ever got here. I agree I ain't getting anywhere in my search for that hostile witness and that possibly wounded pony, but—"

"It's wounded," the Ranger cut in, adding, "I personally stood in the exact spot where that dead Dane caught a bullet in his back and had my boys do some measuring. We weren't able to backtrack the fatal bullet to its point of aim because the coroner's crew found the slug had curved some on its way through the old boy's innards. But it came out the front of him just under the breastbone as he was fixing to mount. Figuring that would place the exit wound eleven or twelve hands above the pavement, with the pony in the line of fire standing thirteen hands at the least . . ."

Longarm said, "I follow your drift. We're talking about a spent slug, mayhaps as light as a .30, hitting saddle leather and a felt pad high enough for both to be slanting some. By the way, I was told nobody thought to measure the entrance and exit wounds."

Prescott shrugged and replied, "The county was sincere about not wanting the tangle as a gift. And whether you hurry an autopsy or take your time, it ain't that easy to tell the puncture of a .30 from a .45. That old diplomat was wearing a corset under his full-dress uniform. He must have been as vain as some say. In any event, neither wound was as clean as you'd get when shooting at a cardboard box. The only way anyone but the killer can know for certain calls for recovering that fatal slug from the saddle leather or hide of old Lille Thruma. If the slug glanced off, or nobody ever finds her, that'll be the end of *that* line of investigating."

Longarm thumbnailed a match head to get both their smokes lit, and then he said, "I got some sepia-tone prints of the missing mare, if you'd like one or more."

Captain Prescott took a drag, let it out, and calmly answered, "We already had our own set made. Doubtless from the same photograph them Danes gave copies of. You ain't going to find her out this way. We discreetly canvassed every spread for a hard day's ride up and down this side of the Rio Grande."

"What about the other side of what *they* call the Rio Bravo?" Longarm asked with one brow cocked.

Prescott said, "We've questioned all the ferry operators as far upstream as Private Njalsson could have rid that peculiar-looking palomino. It ain't as if you can ford the Rio Grande this close to her mouth during the spring runoff, you know. We have *los rurales* watching for both pony and funny-looking rider, though. Just in case."

Longarm blew smoke out both nostrils, and tried not to sound too disgusted as he dryly remarked, "I heard you Rangers got along better with *los rurales* than the *peones* they ride roughshod over."

The tall Texan, who likely had ten years on Longarm, met his eyes without a lick of shame to reply, "I know they say President Diaz is a boy-buggering chicken thief under all that oily charm. But he's still done wonders and sliced cucumbers along the border. We used to have way more trouble with the greasers before Diaz and his junta took over to run Mexico with the firm hand she requires. The fool greasers get crazy-mean on that slimy *pulque* they brew, and I swear they would steal the cow shit off a Texican's heels if they thought they could get away with it. Used to be a whole lot of cattle raiding along the border before *los rurales* got to patrolling it better."

Longarm couldn't resist saying, in an innocent tone, "So I've been told. Was it your Colonel Doniphan or the irregular captain Cameron County is named after who brought back the bigger herds from Mexico in their travels?"

The Texas Ranger bristled and said, "That was in time of war, and them longhorns were reparations. Greasers raiding on their own in time of peace *deserve* to be shot down like dogs by *los rurales*!''

"I'm sure they often are." Longarm smiled, adding, "We were talking about Private Njalsson and Lille Thruma, neither of whom seem to be anywhere in sight. But I thank you for doubtless saving me some dumb questioning, Captain. I thought you Texas Rangers had refused to be party to the case.''

Prescott shrugged and looked away as he murmured, ''We were told not to touch it with a ten-foot pole. There's no glory to be gained when you ain't allowed to arrest nobody, and you look like a simpleton when you can't even *catch* 'em.''

"But you still did some canvassing on your own," Longarm insisted as a statement rather than a question.

Travis Prescott of Texas growled, "Aw, mush, don't ask me to explain the odd urges that come over me in hot weather. Mayhaps I'm in a family way. Lord knows Headquarters fucks me every chance I give 'em.''

Longarm smiled knowingly and said, ''I've had the same urges come over me. I reckon we're both like that third workman in the parable.''

"Say again?" the Ranger demanded with a puzzled frown.

Longarm explained. ''I ain't sure whether it's in the Good Book or whether I read it somewhere else. But they say that one day this angel of the Lord, or just a curious traveler, came upon three workmen going at it lickety-split with hammers and nails.''

He took another drag on his cheroot as he gathered his memories of a tale told long ago and went on. "The angel or whatever asked the first workman what he was doing. The first workman said he was earning a living for himself and his family. So the angel asked the second one, and *that* workman allowed he was nailing planks to a heavier framework. So the angel asked the third workman what *he* was doing, and the third workman allowed he was building a great ship to sail the seven seas.''

Longarm paused, then asked, ''Which workman do you reckon that angel of the Lord blessed, and which one would you rather be?''

The older lawman smiled sheepishly and tried not to blush as he muttered, "Well, shit, they only pay us a tad more than a rider could make as a top hand for a good outfit, and the least they can let us do is our gawddamned job! You're a lawman, Longarm. You know none of us would take such chances for so little if we weren't as curious as cats and sort of restless by nature."

Longarm chuckled fondly and held out his hand, saying, "Put her there, you poor curious cuss. I follow your drift, and I know about how far I can push my luck with my own boss. But can I write you up for an assist when and if I bring that hostile witness in?"

The Ranger looked horror-struck, and said, "Don't you dare. As far as anyone either of us ride for is supposed to know, we never had this conversation."

Longarm agreed. As he turned to head back to his tethered mount, Prescott called out, "That goes for any other conversations we might have if I find out any more, hear?"

So Longarm was laughing as he led Kolsvartur out of the palmettos and mounted up again. When he rounded the grove to ride back to town, the only sign of Captain Prescott was some faint dust drifting way out behind him.

Longarm rode back to the *posada*, and led the black pony into the stable, where she nickered up at Sigridur's bigger but not all that big cow pony. She sure was a friendly little thing.

Sigridur could have been better described as a friendly *big* old thing when he joined her upstairs, earlier than he'd said, to find here reading in bed, naked as a jay.

He agreed it seemed a tad early for supper as he shucked his own sunbaked duds to join her on the cool cotton sheets. He began to tell the big beautiful blonde why he'd gotten back to her earlier than he'd promised. But Sigridur said she didn't care because she'd missed him so—once it cooled off enough for more slap-and-tickle—that she'd wound up playing with herself during that big storm they'd had.

So he didn't feel quite as guilty when they commenced to play with one another. For what the hell, as long as they'd both been coming a lot at the same time the night before, he figured it was only fair to forgive her for cheating on him with her fingers.

Chapter 22

The most predictable thing about South Texas weather was its unpredictability. For after their cooler-than-usual siesta, it was starting to warm up again by supper time. The muggy evening breezes suggested that whatever might be going on way out over the Gulf, it wasn't finished with them yet.

So poor Sigridur, sporting her new spring outfit but looking a bit wilted, asked if they could sup in an ice cream parlor she'd noted in passing near the beauty parlor.

Longarm agreed it was getting a bit warm for hot tamales or even steak and potatoes. So they wound up seated in a shady alcove at a marble-topped table, dining on fresh-cranked vanilla ice cream under chocolate syrup and banana slices. Sigridur allowed she'd never had banana slices that tasted so banana. Longarm explained they likely came up out of Mexico. For bananas grew in gay profusion all through the Mexican lowlands, colored from canary-yellow through shades of orange, brown, and into purple. Large, small, sweeter than most Americans had ever tasted, some even starchy as potatoes and served with meat in their place.

The ones they were eating with their ice cream tasted just the way you always expected bananas to taste before you tasted them. So he ordered second helpings, and told Sigridur about his sneaky talk with Captain Prescott. He figured, since they'd been assigned to the mission by the same Attorney

General, he ought to be able to confide in her more than any Texas Ranger who wasn't supposed to be working with them. He told her, "I never mentioned that contraband runner they call the Turk because, had Prescott known anything about those Mauser rifles, and had he wanted me to know he knew, he'd have said something. But I have some Mexican pals trying to find out more about that angle for us."

She washed down some ice cream with the clear soda water they'd served with it, and said, "I've been meaning to ask you more about your night away from me in Matamoros. But up until now we've been . . . having too much fun. Where *did* you spend the night when you found yourself stranded there during that big *urkoma,* I mean deluge."

He said he'd been deluged a lot, and then sheltered by a sort of rebel leader down yonder. Then he told her that the less she knew about Mexican revolutionaries the less she'd have to answer for back up in Kansas once they'd finished down this way.

She sighed and said, "I would not care just when we finished, if only it would stay *cool.* When I was a girl in Iceland, a visitor from New England said Icelandic weather seemed like April in New England, only all year around. But April can't get this hot in New England if he was telling the truth."

Longarm said, "I reckon he might have meant to. The way I hear it, you can get sunny robin-bird mornings or a good snow in April up New England way. But I've never heard of heat waves and hurricanes around Boston Town that early in the year."

She smiled and said, "That sounds like Iceland at any time of the year. It has been known to snow in July. Yet our winters can be as mild as those in New York City. I spent some time there when I first came to America. The only difference I noticed in December was that the days were so much longer and brighter. We pay for our white nights of summer with black days around Christmastime. But it never gets too cold, or too warm, to . . . sleep comfortably with a friend."

He said with any luck the sun would be down before it could get any hotter. Before she could answer, Longarm spied a familiar figure pass by their alcove, trilling out a greeting to somebody else at yet another table just around the corner.

It had been that petite dark secretary from the Danish consulate. She'd exchanged her sedate black silk for a lavender skirt and snow-white blouse, with a tiny straw boater perched atop her upswept jet-black hair.

As she sat, unseen but just out of sight, he heard another gal say, *"Vi skal have fest i aften. Kommer du?"*

Longarm shot a questioning glance across the table at Sigridur. She nodded and silently mouthed, "Danish."

The Danish gal they knew of was answering, *"Tak, jeg vil gerne komme. Ma jeg tage en ven med?"*

Sigridur whispered, "The first one just invited that dark elf to a party. She's agreed to come, but wants to bring a friend. I recognize that other voice. She's the same one the first was talking to in the beauty parlor. From the conversations I've heard, I don't see how they can be working together at the Danish consulate. See if you can peek around that paper tree and tell me what she looks like!"

Longarm shook his head and told her, "That ain't the best way to work it. We don't want to scare them off, and you just said one's invited the other to some shindig. Did she say when?"

Sigridur murmured, *"I aften* means this evening. That would call for arriving around eight o'clock in diplomatic circles. But how are we to know where unless we find out who the other *Dansk tik* is?"

He said, "My way. If *Dansk* means Danish, what's a *tik*?"

She wrinkled her nose and said, "Your term would be 'bitch.' I'm sorry. I get annoyed when I hear those aristocratic airs they put on. When I was a child some Danes stopped at our farm for directions, and one of them said right out that it was a good thing I was running barefoot because it had saved the hides of two poor cows. They must have thought a *smabondi* didn't understand them. But I understand them, the *slunginn* snobs!"

Longarm caught the eye of a waitress in his line of sight, and as soon as she came over, he ordered iced tea to dawdle over. As they waited, he murmured to Sigridur, "They won't stay long if they both mean to go home and get gussied up for later this evening.''

He was right. They'd barely finished their first tall glasses of iced tea when the two Danish speakers around the bend tinkled a heap of *Farvels* at one another. Then the small dark one he'd already met hove into view without glancing his way, and swept on by. The gal leaving right behind her was a new face to Longarm, but not a bad-looking one. She was taller than her little chum, which only made her about normal height, and her hair was a warmer shade of blond than Sigridur's, which made her more persuasive as a Scandinavian. She never glanced his way as she swept by in her darker skirts, frillier summer blouse, and fancier veiled boater of brown straw with arificial ivy creeping around the brim.

Sigridur whispered, ''Aren't we going to follow them?''

He smiled across the table at her and said, ''Remind me to tell you a story about two bulls and a distant gap in the fence on a hot day sometime. I don't want the baron's secretary to know we were listening in on her as she accepted a party invitation for herself and some friend. Not before I find out more about the party leastways.''

He placed a silver dollar in plain sight on the marble tabletop before he caught that waitress by the eye again. When she came over, he waited until he was sure she'd spotted his astounding tip before he smiled up at her and said, ''We didn't want to interrupt that Danish lady at the table around the bend whilst she was chatting with that little dark gal we didn't know. But Miss Sigridur here is sure she works for that Danish consulate down the waterfront a piece, whilst I say she's with that trading outfit. So who's right?''

The waitress frowned thoughtfully and asked, ''You mean Madame du Prix? She comes in here all the time, and I think I did hear someone mention she was Swedish, Danish, or whatever before she got married. But she don't work no-wheres, Lord love her. She's the wife of one of those diplomats at the *French* consulate. You say you know her and you didn't know that?''

Longarm allowed he'd likely mixed the lady up with some other gal as interesting-looking. Then he helped Sigridur to her feet before the waitress could assume they were fixing to take the tip back from her for not saying what they wanted to hear.

She scooped up the dollar, better than a day's pay for her sort of job, as Longarm paid the cashier out front and took his change in mints for them to suck as they stepped back out in the late-afternoon glare.

He headed her back to their *posada*, explaining along the way why he wanted to go to that party alone later.

She didn't cotton to the notion at all. He left her gnashing her teeth and threatening to run off to the North Pole with the first Eskimo who'd have her.

Then he walked back to the town law's office near the town hall, and went in to ask about that other pony *los rurales* had "recovered" for him.

The desk sergeant said they had his saddle and possibles in their tack room. The paint was corraled out back with the rest of their stock.

As Longarm signed for his "stolen" property, the town lawman told him how the helpful Mexicans across the way had put the theft and recovery together.

The Texican explained, "Your pony, McClellan, and Winchester were abandoned in a Mex livery near the ferry slip, or so it seemed until nobody came forward all morning. Then the *rurales* watching for the owner of that repeating rifle got our report on the paint being stolen on this side whilst you were in that saloon like you said. They added it up easy, with a dead gringo of ill repute they'd scraped off the cobbles right next door to that same livery. A Mex who'd seen the dead man aboard the ferry boat the night before said he'd rid across without any riding stock. Mexico figures the late Ham Keller was in a hurry to do somebody dirty down their way and, needing transportation, just helped himself to a pony tethered near the ferry crossing. They say he was like that."

"Ham Keller, as in Hamilton?" asked Longarm, trying to recall the wanted flier he might have seen that name on.

The desk sergeant shook his head and said, "Ham as in Hamburg. He was a square-head seaman from Hamburg who jumped ship in Texas a spell back and took up life on the owlhoot trail. They say he never got the hang of roping. But he'd fit in that Franco-Prussian War, on the winning side, and there always seems to be outfits that can use a rider who's handy with a gun. When they ferried his body back to us this morning, they told us he'd been gunned by some Mex as he was standing in that rain, waiting for somebody more friendly most likely. They had it down as a robbery gone sour until somebody put his dead face and a seaman's tattoo together with a wanted poster printed in English. They might have thought there was a bounty on him. The Rangers only wanted to talk to him about a card game he was taking part in when all hell busted loose and a couple of cowhands and a tinhorn lay dead on the sawdust. Keller was more what you'd call a lookout man for more established gunslicks. As far as we know, nobody ever sent him after anybody on his own.''

Longarm got out some smokes to prolong that line of interesting conversation as he mused, ''Not as long as they had more established gun waddles, you mean. It's been a spell, and I hadn't connected those half-forgotten fliers until just now. But didn't Keller ride with a whole bunch of truculent immigrant youths?''

The Texas lawman, who'd been reading about the dead pest more recently, nodded and said, ''Yep, all disgruntled seamen who'd jumped all sorts of vessels trading out of the North Sea, Baltic, and such. Rangers figure one bad apple off one ship started the whole trend.''

Longarm scowled and said, ''I brushed with some Icelanders up Kansas way the other night, and a gent I met up with here in Brownsville looked sort of Nordic, albeit he was claiming to be a Mr. John Brown of Kansas.''

The Brownsville lawman smiled thinly and said, ''I give up. Was he claiming to be that old Bible-thumper they hung just before the war, or the Major Brown we named this town after?''

Longarm decided, ''Neither. Foreigners taking American names are inclined to just grab an American name they've heard out of thin air without concern for who might have had it first. I arrested a Polish killer one time who'd decided to be Jesse James right after he'd shot his boss and ridden off with the contents of the till. As I was cuffing him, he explained he'd seen the name on the front page of a newspaper and thought it sounded more American than his own. If you asked one of our own wayward youth to make up a Mexican alias on short notice, they might well come up with something like Benito Juarez or Antonio Santa Anna.''

He chose his next words with some care, deciding the old-timer on the evening desk was about what he seemed, and asked, ''By the way and speaking of immigrants gone wrong, have you heard tell of some dealer in stolen goods called El Turco by the Mexicans?''

The Brownsville lawman nodded without shilly-shally and replied as easily, ''Sure I have. Everyone in these parts has heard of Ben Hakim, also known as the Turk. After that, his history grows more murky. Some say he came over here from the Ottoman Empire with that herd of camels Jeff Davis sent west to fight desert tribes whilst he was still a Union Secretary of War. Others would have it Ben Hakim ain't no Turk at all, but a Jew, a Greek, or a Frenchman, depending on whether the one denouncing him hates Jews, Greeks, or Frenchmen the most. We've even heard him described as a Swede by a cattleman who once lost a gal and one eye to a big old Swede.''

Longarm started to ask how anybody could mistake a Swede for a Turk, or vice versa. Then he recalled that that Danish secretary was small and dark enough to pass for an escapee from a Turkish harem. So he just said, ''I thank you for a name to put with El Turco. Now if it's all the same to you, I'd like to gather up my possibles and riding stock. For I'm not expected at that party they're giving at that French consulate. But I'm going anyway.''

The Brownsville lawman rose from behind his desk, saying, ''I'll show you about out back. We heard they were having another shindig over where that Danish diplomat got assassinated. Let's hope nothing like that has been planned for this evening.''

Longarm trailed after him, muttering, ''Oh, I don't know. It would sure simplify matters if that killer returned to the scene of his crime, as some of them have really been known to do.''

The desk sergeant said, ''I've heard of that odd behavior.

What do you reckon inspires killers to behave like so at times?''

Longarm wearily replied, ''If I could figure out how the mind of a killer works most *any* time, I'd have this job half licked.''

Chapter 23

As he rode the saddled-up paint back to the *posada*, the air hung still at ground level, but the overcast sunset sky swirled above as the Great God Hurikan was stirring bloody orange vomit. So Longarm told his mount, "I'll bet they call off that shindig over at the French consulate. For they've been down this way longer than me, and even I can see we're building up to another stormy night!"

By the time they got to the stable behind the *posada*, it was warm and muggy as a steam bath. The Texas-bred pony Sigridur had been riding just stared listlessly over the rails of its stall. But little Kolsvatur looked as if she was fixing to die, all lathered, with her tongue hanging out like a foamed-up dishrag.

He found a Mexican *jaquima* hanging on a nail, and led her outside with the rope halter in hopes fresher air might help. But she just stared his way with a hurt expression, as if she blamed him for the suffering she was forced to put up with.

Leaving all three ponies secured, Longarm ran upstairs to tell Sigridur, "That little black mare's come down with some distemper on us. I still have time to get her over to that KHA paddock, and I hope they have a vet. Do you want to tag along and translate, if need be?"

She almost sobbed, "No! I am not going anywhere in this

vethur! You told me that heat wave had ended, *du stor lygari!*"

Life was too short to spend much of it arguing with a woman in English, let alone Icelandic. So he told her he'd get back to her when he got back to her, and lit out to rid himself of that Icelandic pony before he wound up having to pay for it.

But when he led the miserable lathered Kolsvartur back to her rightful owners, that horse trader told him she was only overheated.

Longarm demanded, "How come? I put her in her stall rubbed cool, and ain't ridden her since."

The Dane sighed, pointed with his big jaw at the cow pony tied out front, and explained, "That's a problem we've been working on. The Icelandic pony has a harder time becoming acclimatized to Texas than the Spanish warm-blood or even the European working breeds. Captain Steensen thinks breeding the Nordic with the Spanish barbs and Arabs should result in a stock pony with the endurance and comfortable gait of the Icelandic breed and the Texas cow pony's ability to take your dreadful Western climate."

Longarm checked the time with his pocket watch. He saw the sullen sky was lying about how late it was getting, and tarried to say he'd heard how seldom Iceland suffered a heat wave in April or, hell, August.

Then he asked, "Wouldn't it make as much sense to deal in things less complicated than untested breeding stock from Iceland?"

The KHA man sighed and asked, "What do you suggest? For all the bitching about free trade, Iceland's two main products are in direct competition with American producers. Iceland imports almost every product, but aside from mining some sulfur, which Sicily sells cheaper on the world market, Iceland's main exports, up until now, have been stockfish, dried cod or haddock, and a rather rough grade of wool."

Longarm winced and allowed, "Our own New England fishing fleet must be able to undersell dried cod from way off in the North Atlantic, and there ain't no shortage of fine merino wool raised from coast to coast on American graze. So I follow your drift. But cow ponies as can't stand the climate of the American West? It may not get this bad up Montana or Idaho way, I'll allow. But it does get hot, mighty hot, most everywhere across our short-grass open range by the Fourth of July."

The KHA man nodded, but insisted that they had a lot invested in the trade with Iceland and vice versa. He said, "Denmark broke up our monopoly in '56, and allowed the stubborn Icelanders limited home rule in '74. But they still blame us for the miserable conditions on a barely livable rock pile. KHA has to find *something* Iceland can produce that we can sell."

Longarm asked, "How come? Seems to me that if I had poor relations who kept complaining about the suppers I was serving, I'd just give them the freedom to rustle up their own."

The Dane insisted, "We *have* given in to almost all their demands! They still keep demanding total independence!"

Longarm shrugged and said, "Might save your folks a heap of pain if your government just let 'em go off on their own to sink or to swim."

"They would sink," the Dane insisted, adding, "I just told you Iceland has little to export. They have no coal, no industry, nothing to occupy their time but catching fish, herding sheep, and arguing politics. They would be lost without our guidance!"

Longarm smiled thinly and replied, "The English say the same things about the Irish and the Hindus. They used to say it about us. It must feel grand to be that sure of anything. But meanwhile, all those benighted ingrates are likely to just keep on fussing about freedom until you more civilized gents either kill them all or let them all go."

The Dane favored Longarm with a superior smile and said, "I hope you won't think I'm being sarcastic. But what you just said sounded a little strange, coming from an official of the U.S. government, in view of its attitude on good Indians."

Longarm sighed and said, "That was a fair punch. Mr. Lo, the Poor Indian ain't always your average literate churchgoer, but if it was up to me, we'd let him enjoy the freedom to win or lose in the game of life. Lord knows we've spent more on every Indian we've managed to kill than it might have cost to set 'em up in business as trappers, herders, farmers, or whatever.''

The Dane asked, "What would you do with Indians who refused to be that well behaved, Deputy Long?"

To which Longarm replied sincerely, "Kill 'em, I reckon. I just now said you could let folks be themselves or you could kill them if you just couldn't stand the way they were. There's just no way you can hold a whole mess of folks down against their will forever. I don't suppose you've heard tell about those Mauser repeaters from Prussia? The ones that fire fifteen times, bolt-action, from a prone position from cover? What sort of cover might a sniper use up Iceland way?''

The KHA man repressed a shudder and replied, "Heather, dwarf birch, and willow or volcanic rocks, a *lot* of volcanic rocks. We *have* heard something about a shipment of a new-model Mausers being auctioned off to the highest bidder somewhere in Texas near the border. Count Atterdag was looking into such rumors when he was assassinated at the French consulate. Our own Captain Steensen thinks such guns would be intended for the Mexican rebel movement. Mexico mines silver and gold. Iceland mines sulfur and a clear spar sometimes used to grind lenses for optical instruments. How many guns do you think the half cracked *Islenzk Fothurlandflokkur* could buy with barrels of sulfur or buckets of Iceland spar? I just told you there is no market for stockfish or raw wool here in your states.''

Longarm figured that was too dumb a question to bother answering. Nobody bought guns with natural resources. They *sold* their produce for cash and used the cash to go shopping for anything they wanted.

But that raised a more sensible question, to Longarm's thinking, so he asked, "How do those free-trading Icelanders get their fish or wool and such to market, seeing they're out in the middle of the North Atlantic and don't want to trade with your KHA?''

The Dane made a wry face and explained. "Trading vessels from our import-export rivals put in to Reykjavik, and the Danish Rigsdag says we can't do anything about it. Iceland has no merchant marine to speak of. But as I said, they have limited self-rule, and their shortsighted Althing will grant trading privileges to almost anyone. It will serve them right when they are cheated blind by Connecticut Yankees or two-faced Swedes!''

Longarm asked if the KHA man knew anything about a shipping outfit based in New York and trading between Hamburg and Brownsville.

The Dane didn't. So Longarm said he hoped their poor little ponies would make it through the coming heat, and rode off on the Texas-bred paint, uncomfortably, as she trotted.

He thought about dropping by the *posada* to pick up his frock coat. But even without the tweed vest it would sweat him witless, and he wasn't up to another fuss with the sweaty Sigridur. For the heat had gotten to her almost as bad as her fellow Icelander, Kolsvartur.

He had time to stop at a haberdashery, and sprang for a fresh shirt and shoestring tie, both dearer than he usually bought. Stuffing his honest work shirt in a saddlebag, he led his pony on foot to a barbershop near the French consulate to spring for the haircut he'd been putting off, a clean shave, and more bay rum than he usually stood for.

Then, smelling pretty, but already feeling the heat inside his new shirt, Longarm led his pony around to the back of the consulate, and tipped a colored stable boy to unsaddle and stall the paint with oats and water till he got back.

Walking around to the front of the good-sized complex, he saw he'd timed it about right. A berlin carriage was just letting out a fancy-dressed older couple. The gent had on a white Panama suit, and the old skinny lady with him was wearing a pongee ball gown and a surely fake diamond tiara.

Longarm followed them toward the long front veranda, designed to impress, with whitewashed wood columns and long wooden steps stuck like a steamboat promenade deck to the brick building.

As he followed the already wilting older couple up the steps, he took note of the French windows lined up all along the veranda. They had all but the center ones shut. Longarm figured they'd throw more of them open once they'd read everybody's invitation and things could start humming

169

smoothly for a spell. But even with every opening in a brick building like that flung wide, it was still going to be a bake oven on any night this hot, with that many warm bodies inside.

As he took his time on the wide steps, Longarm gauged the ranges from the doorways at either end. Assuming Captain Steensen and Don Hernan Obregon were fair pistol shots, either could have nailed any target standing about where that berlin had pulled in. But would a bullet fired from a better-than-forty-five-degree angle go almost *straight through* the softer parts of a man?

As sloppy as all the medical reports had been, they all agreed Count Atterdag had been shot in the back, close to the spine, with the exit wound just under his breastbone.

Allowing for the slight curve both the county coroner and the odd ways of spinning lead slugs agreed to, it would have made more sense had the fatal shot been fired from about where that snooty-looking butler was examining the engraved invitations of that older couple.

Longarm took a deep breath and pasted a smile across his face as he approached the priss in fancy red, white, and blue livery. There'd been no way to notice back at that ice cream parlor, but he saw now that the gal from the French consulate who'd been jawing in Danish had likely been passing out invitations as well.

Idly wondering how the skinny gray butler could stand there dressed sort of like George Washington, wig and all, without suffering a heatstroke, Longarm got his wallet out to flash his badge and identification instead of an invitation he just didn't have.

The butler called him *monsieur* mighty politely, but still said he couldn't come in because, even had he been properly dressed, he needed a paper invitation from the fancy folks in yonder.

Longarm knew the poor cuss was just doing his job. So he didn't pistol-whip him, but tried to sound just as polite when he said, "In that case you'd better rustle up somebody with some rank on you. I ain't here as no guest. I'm here as an officer of the law. Federal."

The snooty old Frenchman shrugged and said, "That well may be. You are still without proper attire or an invitation,

170

monsieur, and these premises are not subject to search or seizure on the part of your government or any other government. We have diplomatic immunity under international law.''

Longarm smiled wolfishly and said, ''Let's try her this way. You get me somebody higher on your totem pole to talk to right now, or we're about to have us an international incident out here!''

That worked. The snoot turned his white-wigged head the other way and signaled to somebody inside. So Longarm knew he was about to be treated either more politely or more rudely. But he didn't want to go for his gun unless he had to.

He was glad he was standing there so properly when that same honey-blond gal he'd seen at the ice cream parlor came to the door, asked the butler in French what was up, and turned to Longarm with a pleasant smile to say, with an accent more Danish than French, that she was Madame du Prix at his service, and that she wondered what he had in mind.

Longarm told her, ''I've been sent by the U.S. Justice Department to look into that assassination you had out front, ma'am. I know I ain't allowed to arrest you diplomatic folks whether I decide you're innocent or guilty. But wouldn't you rather have me write you off as innocent if you were really innocent, ma'am?''

She laughed, and allowed that while she could only speak for herself, she'd introduce him to the person in charge of the consulate and let *him* decide.

The butler sniffed like an old tabby who'd just missed the tail of a mouse by a whisker as the more easygoing Madame du Prix, dressed in almost sheer green silk and wearing an emerald tiara that almost matched the color of her big green eyes, took Longarm in tow and led him across a ballroom big enough for a railroad waiting room, where others were standing along buffet tables, none of them dancing.

He murmured, ''Wind's off the Gulf and it figures to get hotter before it gets any cooler.''

She softly answered, ''I know. But nobody ever comes to these ghastly affairs for pleasure, and some may find it amusing to just let their discomfort show for a change.''

Chapter 24

Most everyone sure looked uncomfortable when Madame du Prix led Longarm over to the bunch gathered at one end of the long buffet. It was easy to see why they were up at that end. That was where a big cut-crystal bowl of punch sat half empty, with slices of lime and chunks of ice floating in it.

The handsome gal introduced Longarm to a friendly old goat with a rusty iron beard and a wide blue ribbon across his starched shirt. He was Henri Bernier, and in charge of the whole shebang. A wilted flower of around forty, standing near Bernier, turned out to be Madame du Prix's husband, Andre. A short squat Frenchman who'd been issued the same make of beard, in a lighter shade of gray, was their doctor in residence. He answered to Monsieur Chirurgien du Marais. Longarm had met some French speakers up Canada way, and so he knew Chirurgien meant Surgeon. None of the other men and women swilling punch seemed all that important.

When Longarm told the ones who counted who he was and what he was after, Bernier made a wry face and declared that France joined Denmark in demanding justice for the murder of the late Count Atterdag. The sawbones said he'd tried to help the poor dying Dane, but there'd been no way to staunch the internal bleeding. Du Marais added that he'd naturally attended the autopsy at the county morgue, along with delegates from the Danish and Prussian consulates. He said that one round had severed the count's aorta, a big artery that sends blood from the heart and lungs through the body.

"It was, how you say, the shot of *bon chance*," he opined. "No other vitals but the liver were seriously damaged and the liver repairs itself *tres bien, hein*?"

Longarm replied, "If you say so, Doc. Were you or any of the other docs able to make an educated guess as to the caliber of the fatal bullet?"

Du Marais looked pained and said, "*Mais non*. You are not the first to ask about that. The human body is not composed of soap or cheese. Picture carving steak with a *tres* dull saw, and perhaps you may picture the track of a bullet through living flesh more clearly. The poor man had a weight problem he was attempting to compensate for with a laced canvas-and-whalebone corset. From the bullet hole in the back of the victim, one assumes the bullet, of whatever caliber, glanced off a whalebone stay and . . . how you say, entered in an *acrobatique* mode?"

"Keyholed," said Longarm without hesitation. "That would account for the curved course through the poor cuss. How about the exit wound?"

"Larger, but of course. One expects the soft lead to deform and tear a wider path as it continues through softer tissues and . . ."

"*Mon Dieu! Je suis malade!*" cried one of the old gals nearby as she tottered off with her mug of spiked fruit juice.

Longarm smiled sheepishly and said he was sorry for bringing up such a grim subject at a party, but he had to do the chores they ordered him to do.

Bernier agreed they had to be *practique* about the killing out front. Then he asked if Longarm felt comfortable in that *practique* white shirt.

Longarm allowed he'd feel much cooler without the tie, but doubtless a whole lot hotter under his tweed coat and vest.

The boss Frenchman said that sounded *practique* as all get-out to him, and proceeded to peel off his own clawhammer coat as he declared something *practique* in French.

Most everyone there laughed, and then most of the menfolk shucked their own fancy coats to stand about in their shirtsleeves and suspenders, grinning like schoolboys who'd just put one over on their principal. Andre du Prix and a tall, thin drink of water with a profile suited to some large species of rodent went on sweating as dignified as they knew how. It was hard to fathom how such a natural beauty as Madame du Prix could have married up with such a priss.

Feeling more comfortable, although not all that much, the older gents got back to the killing out front. But the more they jawed about it, the more convinced Longarm became that nobody there who knew anything new was about to say so.

He helped himself to some of that iced punch as the others continued talking. The cold crimson concoction turned out to be a French version of Mexican sangria, but stronger. No Frenchman who respected his mother would dilute *wine* with fruit juice, sugar, and such. So they'd used hundred-proof rum, likely from Martinique.

As he stood there sipping with a chunk of ice in his mouth, Madame du Prix and her French husband drifted out of ear-shot, quietly but hotly arguing about something in French. The resident doctor and old Bernier were arguing in French about something else. Longarm was wondering how he'd ever sneak upstairs without anyone fussing at him when a no-longer-young but not bad-looking French lady, with a ruby tiara over hair a shade less red, sidled up to him to observe that he seemed to be feeling neglected.

He almost told her he felt swell before it occurred to him he could use friends in high places around there. So he in-troduced himself and allowed that her low-cut ball gown of red brocade over coral silk looked mighty cool next to his own shirtsleeves.

She said, "Poof, I would be melting in this heat like the candle on the altar if I was allowed to stand here naked as the stork."

He assumed she meant stark naked, but didn't say so. She turned out to be their head bookkeeper, a Madame Laverne. She told him the first chance she got that she was a widow woman who had to be careful lest the younger gals who worked for her on the consular staff tried to take advantage of her own youth and carefree attitude.

174

He asked her if she'd like some punch. She confided that she had already had so much she was about to run for *le pissoir*. He asked her where the pisser was, seeing she'd brought it up, and she confided it was out back for guests, or upstairs, with locks on the doors marked *femmes* or *hommes* depending, for staff.

She asked him how bad he needed to go. French gals could talk like that to a man, and did, because French folks didn't confound their bodies' functions the way English or High Dutch speakers did. Up Canada way, he'd once seen some schoolgirls standing unconcerned while one of their fathers or big brothers took a leak against the wall behind them.

So Longarm said he was all right for the time being. Then he noticed that petite brunette from the Danish consulate coming in with a husky gent wearing a cutaway white jacket and a blond mustache. He knew who *she* was. He'd heard her accept an invitation and ask if she could bring a friend. So he asked the French gal next to him if she knew who that dapper cuss with her might be.

Madame Laverne said, "*Mais oui,* that would be Monsieur Steinmuller from New York. He is the, how you say, agent of Texas for a big shipping firm. The small black spider on his arm would be Madame Nansen, from the Danish consulate. They say she has buried two husbands, as young as she claims to be, *hein*?"

Longarm resisted the impulse to observe that the pretty little thing's husbands had likely died happy as he watched the pair join up near the door with that rodent-faced cuss who still had his stuffy coat on.

When he asked her, Madame Laverne said that was the Prussian consul in Brownsville. His name was von Braun. She didn't seem too pleased to share the same world with him.

Longarm said, "I heard about your Franco-Prussian war, ma'am. I heard old Bismarck and his Kaiser gave the Danes a tough time over a couple of border provinces earlier. Yet that Danish gal seems to feel comfortable with that prim and proper Prussian and an escort called *Steinmuller*?"

"Germanic-American, one assumes," said the French bookkeeper with one hand up to cover a yawn.

He got her to identify some other guests with the same lack of enthusiasm. He was surprised when a swarthy but sort of smooth and high-toned-looking gent in a stylish Panama suit turned out to be the one and original Don Hernan Obregon. For Longarm had pictured the Mexican in a *charro* outfit way upstream in Laredo. Obregon was by the French doors, peering down the front of a young gal's ball gown. Sure enough, they had opened the doors at either end for some air, now that most everyone on their guest list had arrived.

The high-placed horse trader was wearing concealed weapons, if he was armed at all. Longarm asked Madame Laverne if that other gal had been the one Obregon was messing with when those shots came from outside.

The well-preserved French widow shook her head and told him, "You are no doubt referring to Mademoiselle Pouchard, one of the stenographers under me. I was standing about here that night, and I spoke to her later about getting under a married man, and a species of Mexican at that!"

Longarm soberly replied, "I've met his wife. Your point was well-taken. Spanish-speaking wives are inclined to resort to acid, razors, and such. You say this Mademoiselle Pouchard is talking to somebody else right now, ma'am?"

The bookkeeper shook her henna-rinsed head and told him the gal Obergon had been flirting with the night of the killing had been sent to the county hospital, with France paying, after she'd come down with a mortified appendix a few days before. The gal the Mexican was flirting with tonight was married up with a gent from the British consulate. Some men just seemed to enjoy life along the edge of a cliff.

Longarm asked Madame Laverne to think back and tell him whether she was certain Obregon and that flirty stenographer had been inside the doorway at that end when the single shot rang out.

She said she was. But when he asked her how sure she was about a Danish captain standing alone at the other end of those windows, she wasn't as sure. He finally got her to admit she'd been looking all around at everybody and everything on a livelier night with the dance floor more crowded.

He said, "So in sum, you *ain't* sure, and I'd hardly expect

176

Obregon to say he was outside as either the killer or a witness now that he's told so many lawmen he wasn't.''

He sipped more iced punch as he stared at the center door, where that butler still stood, wig and all. He shook his own head and told her, ''A single shot fired from along the centerline of that long veranda out front works better than forty-five degrees from either end. But if the killer had been a third party, unobserved by either of our main suspects, that doorman yonder should have jumped when his gun went off.''

He sipped again, scowled, and put his mental notes away again, grumbling, ''The town law got statements from everyone anywhere near that dead Dane before you all remembered you had diplomatic immunity. A sneaky shot fired from the floor above won't work. The angle of that gory path through the old boy's innards would have been too wild. So what's left?''

She demurely asked if he'd like her to show him a basement air vent that just might work.

He allowed he surely would. So she told him to put down that cut-crystal glass and follow her.

He did. Nobody seemed to care as they swept out of the ballroom and along a less brightly lit hallway to what looked like a broom closet door until you opened it. Madame Laverne took an unlit candlestick from a ledge just inside, and asked him to light it for her.

He did, to see steep stairs leading down to the cellars under the sprawling complex. As he followed her through musty smells and cobwebs, she explained they were in a seldom-used service corridor leading to the *chambres de dossiers* or old records they only hung on to in the unlikely event somebody might ever want to dig them out.

He said the folks *he* rode for hated to throw musty old paper out. That was doubtless why they asked him to fill forms out in triplicate lest a single arrest report from years earlier go missing.

She knew her way around down yonder. She led him into a tiny room where a folding cot and a writing table with an unlit lamp on it shared space with big filing cabinets. The brick wall at the far end rose only two thirds of the way up to the wood ceiling, which she said was the bottom of that long veranda. More unpainted wood, top and bottom, framed a four-or-five-inch slit that ran the length of the little hidey-hole. A cooling draft was coming in from outside. It kept on coming when she shut the door, because of the open transom over the door and some jalousie slits in the bottom panel. She said she'd shut the door to prove a point.

As he stared out through the eye-level slit to see, sure enough, a carriage parked on the far side of that drive out front, Madame Laverne explained she'd set up the cot and work space once she'd found out how much cooler it could be down there during a Texican heat wave.

He was trying to decide whether you could really shoot a man in the back straighter from this low vantage point while he told her he could feel how much cooler it was half underground.

She confided, "*Oui,* I have often been *tres indescrete* about *mon habilier* down here alone. The door locks, and the air from under the veranda is so much cooler on the nude skin, *hein*?"

Longarm allowed it sounded mighty *practique* to keep books down here in the altogether with the door locked on a warm day.

Then he turned to see she'd lit the lamp on that writing table and shucked everything but her ruby tiara and white high-button shoes, and was lying naked as a jay on that folding cot, grinning up at him like a mean little kid who just didn't care if he noticed she wasn't a natural redhead after all.

He had to laugh, as most men would have.

Then he set his hat and gun rig on the writing table, and sat down beside her to shuck his boots, as most men would have.

She was begging him to hurry by the time he'd stripped down as bare. Her pale, lean, well-preserved body felt oddly cooler than the mighty muggy air as he took her in his arms. But there wasn't a thing cool about the way she kissed, or the way she insisted on getting on top because she didn't want their bellies to get all sweaty while she posted up and down his old organ-grinder like a mean little kid on a merry-go-round, telling him all the while they had to hurry and get back upstairs before they were missed.

So he didn't know why she wanted some more dog-style once he'd exploded in such swell new surroundings. But she did, and once they got going that way, he did too, as most men would have.

Chapter 25

Madame Laverne, who allowed he could call her Yvette after making her climax more than once, was as experienced at fixing her hair and smoothing her gown to look proper as she was at enticing strange men into cellars for what she called *la zig-zig*. But they split up out in the corridor before rejoining the party. For he agreed other women could always tell when a couple had been zig-zigging when they spotted them smiling or trying *not* to smile at one another.

Longarm felt sheepish enough about the surprise down below when that younger and blonder Madame du Prix caught up with him to ask, "Where have you been? I have someone here who wants to meet you."

Longarm tagged along after her, hoping nobody was expecting him to get it up again on short notice in this heat. It felt better as they neared those open French windows for, just as he'd hoped, they'd opened the entire row and a breeze no warmer or wetter than a cow's breath was coming in from outside, along with gnats that didn't bite and a meaner breed of salt marsh mosquitos that did.

The party that had been anxious to meet him turned out to be Don Hernan Obregon. So they only had to shake hands.

As Madame du Prix trilled off to round up somebody else, the Mexican showed himself more fluent in English than expected.

He got right to the point by saying, "I have just returned from a wild-goose chase. You must have heard about that Icelandic ingrate accusing me of a cowardly assassination by this time."

Longarm nodded, and suggested they step outside where they could smoke as he told the dapper Mexican, "Nobody seems to be buying that letter postmarked from Laredo as the work of Pall Njalsson. How come you called him an ingrate, and can I take it you never caught up with him in Laredo?"

Obregon followed Longarm out on the veranda as he replied, "I was unable to find a trace of him or anyone who'd spoken to any gringo with such a distinctive accent in either Laredo or Nuevo Laredo, south of the river crossing. I call him an ingrate because he *is* an ingrate! I helped him. I gave him money and offered him a job on a stud ranch I own a safe distance from here. Then he writes a letter accusing me of assassinating his superior, that pompous Count Atterdag! Can you believe it?"

Longarm started to reach in his shirt pocket for two cheroots, but Obregon beat him to the draw with a pair of Havana claros as Longarm was saying, "Not hardly. I just told you I have it on good authority that the letter accusing you seems to have been written by an educated Dane with some easygoing Copenhagen slang. I've noticed most Mexican folks who speak English just well enough to get by, no offense, speak it like a schoolmarm or make simple mistakes. You speak English like you were raised on it, but I'll bet it took you some practice. I'd learned enough Spanish to get laid or even buy a horse before I learned to say *buenoches* instead of *buenas noches* or leave the *yo* off *yo no sé,* the way you hear Spanish along the border."

Obregon struck a waterproof Mexican match of wax to light them both as he said, "Your accent is not bad, for a gringo. If I understand you correctly, that letter from Laredo was written more as a Dane or somebody who had spent much time in Denmark might have written those lies about me?"

Longarm took a luxurious drag on the expensive mild cigar, and told him that was about the size of it, adding, "You were going to tell me how come you'd been so good to that Icelander, right?''

Obregon blew some expensive smoke out over the driveway before he quietly observed, ''I assume you understand I have diplomatic immunity as a man who sometimes deals in remounts for the Mexican Army. So you could not arrest me if you wanted to.''

Longarm said, ''Oh, I could arrest you if I *wanted* to. They'd likely let you go and give me hell, but why not save us both the bother and answer my infernal question?''

Obregon laughed easily, and said, ''My wife told me you were most direct, although, fortunately for your health, most well behaved when you dropped by. Young Njalsson approached me. I was not the one who came up with the proposition. Perhaps I had better start at the beginning?''

Longarm said he wished somebody would.

So Obregon blew more smoke and began. ''It is not any secret that I deal in horseflesh, whether those I breed myself on more than one stud ranch I own, or perhaps those I obtain through other means.''

''Njalsson wanted to sell you a stolen horse?'' asked Longarm.

The dapper Mexican soberly nodded and replied, ''To be specific, that prize Icelandic-Hispanic cross, Lille Thruma. She was the only real *caballita* they had in that KHA remuda and she was not for sale. She was the prized experiment and personal mount of that Captain Steensen. He refused to sell her at any price. But he made the mistake of allowing me to ride her. He was trying to convince me I could breed others like her by allowing a good barb or Arab to service those furry dwarfs they are trying to unload.''

Longarm nodded and asked, ''Don't they have a swell fifth gait, though? I was riding a pure Icelander earlier. She wasn't worth shit once the day heated up again. But I can see how you might end up with fourteen hands, a smoother coat, and that mighty comfortable ride.''

Obregon shrugged and said, ''I wanted Lille Thruma. She *had* the best qualities of both breeds, and I do not like to wait for things I want when I see no need to. That pompous Count Atterdag arrived to inspect their trade mission and look into some smuggling charges. I was not interested in that. So don't ask me what they might have been. Atterdag commandeered Steensen's personal mount. One can hardly fault a big fat Dane for wishing to ride a more reasonable mount than any of the others. When I saw the count riding about with his marine bodyguard, I approached him, hoping he might be willing to make a deal on Lille Thruma after he was done with her. He cursed me as if I'd asked him to do something dishonest. Can you believe it?''

Longarm answered simply, "I can. He was an officer and a gentleman as well as a mean drunk. If you don't see nothing wrong with asking a visiting nobleman to steal horses, let's just say no more about that and get on with the story.''

Obregon shrugged and replied, "That is about all there was to it, as far as anyone but myself and that two-faced marine were concerned. *He* approached *me* later, in civilian clothing while off duty. It was Njalsson who offered to steal horses. He said he hated the Danish marines, Danes in general, and that Danish count in particular. Then he said he'd been planning for some time to desert and start over in America. But he needed money and a place to hide out until the Danes gave up looking for him. He said Denmark does not let even Danes get away with desertion and horse theft, if Denmark has a thing to say about it. But I swear on the beard of Christ I was never aware Njalsson planned to kill the count!''

Longarm said, "You're right. It's best to start from the first move and chew the apple a bite at a time. So to begin with, can this missing marine speak Spanish?''

The dapper Mexican shook his head and replied, "I don't think so. His English is very bad. But since I was speaking to his superior in English, Njalsson would have been able to follow the gist of our argument and devise his own alternate deal.''

Longarm said, "Makes sense. Let's get to the killing right out yonder in the drive. Private Njalsson was standing near the head of that palomino mare, facing this way, when somebody shot the count, facing the other way, in his broad back. So whether Njallson meant to murder a boss he hated or not, and if he was packing a rifle or side arm, which he was not

183

according to other witnesses, he'd have had to fire *this* way, shooting the count point-blank in the belly with the slug coming out his back and smacking into this very veranda, the bricks behind us, or one of the French windows, and on into a crowded dance floor. Is that the way things looked to you that evening?''

Obregon sighed and replied, ''How many times do I have to repeat myself? I was standing just inside, speaking with one of the French clerical workers, when we both heard the shot. I stepped out on the veranda, about where we are standing now. I saw Atterdag already down and Njalsson fighting to control the hurt or frightened pony. I saw Captain Steensen down there at the far end. He had his pocket pistol out. To be fair, I had drawn my own Colt for perhaps the same reasons.''

Longarm asked, ''How about gunsmoke? If you got out here right away, you should have seen at least some gunsmoke, down near Steensen or out in the open driveway by Njalsson. So which was it?''

Obregon gasped, ''Neither! I see what you mean. Stray bullets have a way of losing themselves in even whitewashed wood. But if Njalsson had just shot Count Atterdag in the guts, there should have been a small entrance wound in the front of his tunic, surrounded by powder stains, a bigger exit wound in the side facing Steensen and me, and most importantly, a cloud of gunsmoke hanging over him as he thrashed about on the cobbles, cursing and babbling in his own tongue!''

''I'd better ask Captain Steensen if *he* noticed any gunsmoke, next chance I have to talk to him. Unless he saw some close to you or that missing marine, all three of you could be off the hook.''

Obregon insisted, ''Damn it, *somebody* shot the count! I heard the shot! I saw him dying right out there in line with the main entrance!''

Longarm wasn't ready to tell anybody about that cellar vent under the veranda. But a lot of gunsmoke could drift about under all those beams and steps until it sort of got lost. The smell would be long gone by now too.

He said, ''Let's get back to that deal you thought you had

with my missing witness. Assuming you thought he only meant to steal that prize broodmare and bring her to you, then what?''

Obregon answered without hesitation, ''I was to pay him five hundred dollars, U.S., and allow him to hide out for as long as he thought he needed to as soon as he delivered Lille Thruma to one of my breeding operations, a hard day's ride up the Rio Bravo.''

''This side or the other?'' asked Longarm.

Obregon smiled boyishly and said, ''You're good. This side. I have properties on both sides of the border where a friend might relax as his trail grows cold. But as I told young Njalsson, *los rurales* would be more likely to pick up a strange gringo with no visible means than the Texas Rangers would.''

The smooth Mexican hesitated, then admitted, ''Aside from that, we know he rode at least as far as my O Bar O, just west of the Cameron County line. He rode in on Lille Thruma the next sundown after the assassination here. My *segundo* at the O Bar O had been told they should take him in, of course. So they fed him, sheltered him, and he rode on like a thief in the night sometime before dawn.''

Longarm consulted his mental map of those parts and decided, ''He hid out along the trail betwixt dashes if he only made a half day's ride in, say, eighteen hours. How do you know it was Njalsson unless you were there? Had you already introduced him to your foreman?''

Obregon shook his head and said, ''Of course not. There was no way he could have ridden that far *before* he deserted. But it had to be Njalsson. Who else would have ridden in on Lille Thruma?''

Longarm blew a thoughtful smoke ring and replied, ''Somebody who'd write in Danish like he knew the streets of Copenhagen better than an Icelandic fisherman. I've tracked down more than one deserter for our own army. Before such crybabies light out, they tend to bitch a heap to their fellow sufferers. So any number of pure-bred Danes with some axes of their own to grind could have helped themselves to that mighty swift and comfortable transportation and your generous offer for a hidey-hole.''

"Then where would Njalsson have been while this imposter was pretending to be him and ... *Jesus, Maria y Jose,* riding up to Laredo to post that letter accusing me of his own crime?"

Longarm shrugged and said, "Works just as well with Njalsson dead and buried, or paid off and on his way to parts unknown. I've yet to figure out why anybody would have call to frame you, unless it was to clear Captain Steensen, or lure him back so they could grab him and ship him back to Denmark. Works as dirty either way."

"Then we are dealing with a very treacherous Danish consulate as well as a murderous horse thief?" asked the dealer in stolen horses.

Longarm shook his head and said, "Not hardly. They sent *me* to bring Njalsson in, whether he did the deed or only witnessed it. So it's been nice talking to you, but I'd best go back inside and talk with somebody else now."

Enjoying a last luxurious drag on the swell cigar, Longarm tossed it out in the driveway, and turned to step back inside, where it wouldn't be decent to blow cigar smoke on a night like that.

Obregon shouted and shoved him sideways into the doorjamb as Longarm grabbed for his .44-40, heard the gunshot, and felt Obregon's big hand sort of twang against his own shoulder.

So as he bounced back from the shove and whirled to spy gunsmoke rising from behind the oleander hedge across the way, he decided he didn't want to slay the infernal Mexican after all. He pegged three shots into the hedge across the way as he dropped to one knee beside Obregon, who hunkered low and clutched his bloody forearm to his shirtfront, making a mess out of that as well, while he pissed and moaned about ungrateful *hijos de putas.*

Longarm grunted, "Let's get you inside. He may or may not have shot and run. Thanks for that shove. I needed it. But which one of us do you reckon he was aiming at, pard?"

Obregon moaned, "I don't know. I moved without thinking when I spotted his movements behind that hedge over there. Thank God it was backlit by the lamplight from the windows behind it. I don't know how I knew what he meant

186

to do when he stopped and then dropped into a slight crouch. But I managed to move both of us just as he poked the muzzle of his rifle through the stems and fired.''

Madame du Prix, their trilingual greeter, was first to reach them from inside, looking mighty horrified as she spied the blood dripping out of Don Hernan.

Longarm told her, ''Get Doc Marais and have everybody else stay well back from these French windows, ma'am.''

She gasped, ''What happened? Who shot poor Don Hernan?''.

Longarm was reloading as he grimly replied, ''That's what I'm about to see if I can find out, ma'am!''

Chapter 26

He didn't. Scouting around behind the hedge of the house across the way, he could still smell the lingering powder fumes. But the rascal hadn't even ejected a damned shell, and there were no footprints in the grass or gravel when he hunkered down and lit a match to make certain.

Somebody was yelling at him to get the hell out of the yard from an upstairs window. So Longarm rose to hold his open wallet and badge up to the light, shouting back, "I'm the law, sir. I know you didn't see anybody down here firing rifles through your hedge. You wouldn't be yelling down at me like this if you had."

The irate householder ducked back inside as another figure in a white cutaway jacket and blond mustache joined Longarm, Starr .38 in hand, to ask if he could be of any help.

Longarm grimaced and said, "The yellow bushwhacker's long gone, Mr. . . . Steinmuller, ain't it?"

The somewhat shorter and more thickset shipping agent nodded, but said, "Call me Sam. I asked who you were too, Longarm. What's going on around here? It seems every time the frogs give a party, somebody shows up with a gun and shoots somebody! Why were they after Obregon this time? Camilla says the Danes think Count Atterdag was assassinated by Danish rebels."

Longarm said, "They call themselves Icelanders. Who

might Camilla be? That Madame Nansen you came in with from the Danish consulate?''

Sam Steinmuller answered easily, "I came as her guest tonight. We were talking about the shooting of that Mexican, not my personal life."

Longarm said, "I know neither you nor that Danish lady took a shot at us from over this way. I saw you both in the ballroom as Madame du Prix was fetching the sawbones. What can you tell me about the medical outcome so far, seeing I left so sudden?"

Steinmuller shrugged and said, "I only stayed long enough to get the impression it was a small-bore flesh wound through the forearm. More blood and Ave Marias than real damage. Why don't we go back and just ask? Both our ladies will be getting anxious by this time."

As they moved along the inside of the hedge, Longarm said he hadn't come with any lady. Steinmuller allowed he and Madame Nansen had had the impression he and Madame Laverne were good friends.

To change the subject, Longarm said, "I was fixing to pay a call on you in any case, Sam. If you bothered to ask about my name, you know what they sent me down here to look into. We got conflicting reports on a screw clipper called the *Trinity*. One of your line's?"

Steinmuller sighed and said, "Welcome to the party. My New York firm owns the *Trinity*, the *Brazos*, and the *Sabine*. All three are named for Texas rivers because they trade regularly between Texas and more than one North Sea or Baltic port of call."

"Such as Hamburg, Copenhagen, mayhaps Reykjavik?" asked Longarm.

Steinmuller replied, "Yes to Hamburg, Copenhagen, and St. Petersberg on occasion. No to Reykjavik. Denmark has *officially* repealed its trade monopoly with Iceland, but try doing business there. The years under the thumb of the Danish KHA, paying prices inflated as much as five hundred percent, have left the Iceland market clannish and so suspicious that it's not worth going that far north of our usual route to Europe. Aside from that, they don't have anything to trade that we couldn't buy from American farmers or fishermen and . . . Why am I telling you all this? We both know what you're after. Both U.S. Customs and Prussian Military Intelligence have already talked to me about those mysterious Mauser rifles we're supposed to have laden aboard the *Trinity*."

"Is that sort of sharp-featured von Braun you were jawing with across the way with Prussian Intelligence?" asked Longarm.

Steinmuller said, "I think so. Not that Herr von Braun would admit the time of day if he didn't have to. His consulate has sent more than one snoop in Prussian blue and a spiked helmet to request a look at our bills of lading. I told them to go to hell at first. Then, since I know firsthand about how stubborn my own relatives can be, I wired New York and got permission to open the books to the sons of bitches."

"What did they find?" asked Longarm as the two of them stepped back out in the driveway again.

Steinmuller said, "Nothing Andersen at the U.S. Customs House a few streets away from our shipping office hadn't already told them about. We'd unloaded Texas tallow, hides, and bone meal in Hamburg, along with some Mexican trans-shipments of sisal fiber and pig iron. The vessel came back mostly in ballast, with a mixed cargo of modestly priced notions, from steel cutlery to Christmas tree ornaments. The cargo was inspected by U.S. Customs. You'd expect them to notice if we'd been carrying a boxcar load of military rifles."

As they crossed toward the crowded veranda of the French consulate, Longarm observed, "Smugglers have been known to hide things under a good load of ballast. I've read the old French Navy used to bury its dead in the bilge-soaked sand they used as ballast, and dig 'em up to plant more properly once they got back to France."

Steinmuller said, "You can ask Andersen and his American crew. The *Trinity* was ballasted with paving stones we then sold at a modest profit. You've surely noticed all the rough blocks or cobbles in this port, despite the deep delta soil all around. Andersen must have heard about that disgusting French burial practice as well. You don't land ballast or anything else in this port without them looking it over and

190

writing it down. So I don't know how that wild tale about Prussian guns coming in aboard the *Trinity* could have gotten started. I only know it makes no sense. You land contraband by moonlight on some deserted shore. You don't bring it into a port of entry and unload it in front of a customs inspector!''

Longarm didn't push that line of questioning any further. There was always a possible objection to any answer, and the cuss wasn't about to confess smuggling purloined Prussian rifles to a federal agent, whether he was some sort of stage magician or not.

Rejoining the now mighty informal gathering inside, they found Don Hernan had been carried upstairs to a bedroom and put to bed with his left forearm wrapped in clean bandages and riding in a sling. Longarm didn't crowd in to witness this. He took the word of Madame du Prix when she came down to tell him near the punch bowl.

He was standing near the punch bowl because somebody had refilled it and his mouth felt like the floor of a henhouse in dry weather.

Sipping strong punch with ice on his tongue helped him wash away the nasty taste of reined-in nerves. But it sure got tedious, telling one fool guest after another that he just didn't know who'd fired out front either time.

Madame Laverne came over to rejoin him in her ruby tiara and still-tidy ball gown, smiling as if butter wouldn't melt in her mouth. She likely figured anybody who'd seen them talking earlier, just before they'd dropped out of sight a spell, should have forgotten by now. A lot of folks dropped out of sight for a spell at such shindigs. Half the international plots the diplomatic community indulged in called for screwing one another's wives on the sly.

He saw Steinmuller had rejoined that little dark Danish widow in such a draft as they could manage near an open doorway. It sort of hurt to picture the heavyset shipping agent screwing such a pretty little thing, who was experienced enough to screw back tolerably if she'd really buried two husbands at her age, so he tried not to.

Madame Laverne said, ''*Une centime* for one's thoughts?

Your grin of a boyish nature *c'est tres intéressant, mon cher!*"

He smiled sheepishly down at her and explained, "I was just now thinking about the Brotherhood of the Ants, ma'am. A Russian lady up to the north range told me about this secret way Russian country folks have for getting rich off treasures you can get the ants to bring up from under the ground if only."

"If only what?" she demanded, explaining how she'd always wanted to be rich.

He said, "You can become a member of the Brotherhhod of the Ants, so that they bring you bitty gold nuggets, diamonds, emeralds, and rubies, if only you can manage one magic feat. You have to go out in the woods by yourself, sit on a stump, and not think about a big white bear for one whole hour. That's all there is to it."

She looked blank, started to ask the point, then laughed the way she had down in the cellar dog-style, and declared, "*Mon Dieu,* I have not thought of a big white bear since I do not remember when, *mais* now I can't stop picturing one—making lewd gestures to me as well!"

He tore his gaze away from that other pretty gal across the room, and told the fake redhead he feared neither one of them would ever be members of the Brotherhood of the Ants.

She said, "I have another suggestion. It seems to be cooling off just a little and that room down below was not too insufferable to begin with, *hein*?"

Her offer was tempting. She was right about the air outside sort of stirring in its sleep as if it meant to yawn and stretch a mite.

Somewhere in the night a ship's steam siren was sounding as she cast off to seek adventure on the high seas, or a change of scenery up the Inland Waterway leastways. And if you listened more closely, you could almost swear you heard thunder way off in the distance.

The thought of big blond Sigridur, waiting for him as the heat of the night seemed about to break, took his mind off Camilla Nansen and, come to study on it, this sort of angular French lady, as nice as she could move her bones. So he murmured, "Wouldn't be smart to try anything like that with a gunshot man upstairs and Lord knows how many local and state lawmen on their way by this time."

She looked so disappointed that he tried, "Why don't we get together later, after things calm down around here?"

She husked, "*Grrr*! I mean to eat you alive, or kiss all the spots I missed, *mon vieux! Mais* we must meet *tres discret*. You should have heard the things Madame du Prix said about poor Mademoiselle Pouchard and that married Mexican upstairs!"

That got Longarm to sweeep the crowd with his gunmuzzle gray eyes until they locked on the Danish blonde, standing with her French husband and that rodent-faced Prussian, von Braun. He'd have been more tempted to go over and ask von Braun where *he'd* been when Obregon got pinked in one arm if the older and likely wiser French gal hadn't just told him Margrethe du Prix was just another two-face.

He filled a cut-crystal glass for Madame Laverne, refilled his own, and told her he'd likely see her around town where nobody could gossip about them. Then sure enough, he heard a distant but real roll of thunder. So he added, "I'd best get me and my pony home before that rain we hear coming can get here. I got him around the back with no slicker on my saddle."

She asked where he was staying, and whether he thought he could sneak her in or not.

He laughed like a man who'd just drawn a straight flush in a game with strangers on a train, and lightly allowed he doubted it. He told her he had a big gal yonder that seemed interested in his comings and goings. Which was the simple truth as soon as you studied on it.

That got him out of her friendly clutches for the time being. He had to say good night to the consul, Monsieur Bernier, and then that ever-beaming Madame du Prix tore over to ask if he had to leave.

He wondered idly what made such a pretty gal insecure enough to spite a poor innocent stenographer with a mortified appendix, and that made him wonder how innocent Mademoiselle Pouchard might really *be* and what she *looked* like.

So he made his excuses and got out of there before he could work up a real hard-on.

It sure beat all how having a quick one early in the evening could leave a man feeling sort of unsatisfied in a ballroom full of other women.

He ducked outside, turned the corner carefully, and when he saw how dark the way around to the stable was, hunkered down by some handy garbage cans to see if anybody tore around that corner after him.

Nobody had by the time he'd counted to three hundred, with a Mississippi between each digit. It appeard that that skunk who'd winged old Obregon might have been after old Obregon.

He got back to the stable, took care of the stable boy, and rode his oated, watered, and rested paint back to the *posada* the long way round, giving anybody on his tail a chance to make their next move, if they had the balls, away from good old Sigridur.

By the time he reined in behind their *posada* and dismounted to lead the paint into its stall, he was feeling fond as all hell of old Sigridur. For Yvette Laverne had been hours ago, and built a whole lot differently. So Longarm was really looking forward to another sort of dog-styling entirely as he mounted the back steps two at a time, pleased as punch with his timing because it was just starting to rain again outside.

He opened their door, noticing the lamp wasn't lit as, up on the roof, little wet frogs commenced a war dance.

He called out, "Don't shoot, it's me, and it looks like we're not going to bake like potatoes tonight after all."

He flared a match to light the lamp by the head of their bed. That was when he saw the bed was neatly made and totally empty.

He picked up the note Sigridur had left for him on one pillow. It said she was sorry, but she just couldn't take feeling so useless in what she described as an eternal steam bath. So she was going on back to Kansas, and if they fired her, they fired her. From the way she'd borne down with her pencil, a man could get the impression she just didn't give a shit.

Longarm sighed and set the note aside, muttering, "Well,

I won't say nothing if *they* don't say nothing. But damn it, Sigridur, you let me pass up a really swell lay, just so I could come home and lay you swell. So *now* what am I supposed to do? That geezer who said virtue was its own reward never found himself in *this* ridiculous position!''

Chapter 27

The next morning's sunrise caught Longarm and the hired paint on the trail a good six miles west of town. For there was no saying how long the break in the early heat wave might last, and he knew there'd be no sign to scout for until he got as far as that O Bar O spread that Don Hernan had owned up to.

It was too bad in a way. For as the first slanting sunbeams hit the rain-smoothed trail ahead of them, Longarm saw that they were the very first to sally forth and leave fresh hoofprints in the drying mix of mud and sand.

He'd naturally asked around town before riding out in the wee small hours. So he knew Don Hernan was safely stowed in the Cameron County hospital whether he wanted a lawman questioning his hired help or not. As Longarm walked his mount up rises and trotted her down them, all long and gentle swells running in line with the coastline off to the east, but cut crossways by the river road and the nearby Rio Grande, he explained to the pony, "We call this the process of eliminating, paint. Marshal Vail taught it to me when I was young and foolish and inclined to chase my own tail around the stove."

He reined in to light a fresh cheroot and continued, "You always seem to have more pieces of the puzzle than you could ever make a sensible picture with. So you see how many suspects and how much you have down as material evidence you can simply *shuck*. Billy Vail and me have noticed more than once that once you've eliminated all the notions that don't add up to nothing, the notions left seem to just fall into place. So we're going out to that stud spread this morning to see whether that Mexican is a barefaced liar, or mayhaps telling the truth as he sees it. He told me a long, lean Icelander on a small blond mare rode this very trail right after he or somebody else shot his boss in the back. And look just yonder along this very trail and tell me if that ain't a Mexican drilling in a modest crop of Lord knows what.''

As they approached the Mexican with a seed sack on one hip and a dibble stick in his right hand, Longarm couldn't say whether the older gent was trying for beans, corn, peppers, or squash. For the freshly hoed milpa was just bare turned-over soil. But hardly any Mexican planted any other crops in these parts. So Longarm just reined in to call out, *''Buendias, viejo. Como está?''*

The older man allowed he was just fine, and asked where Longarm might be headed on such a fine morning.

In such Spanish as he could manage, Longarm confided he was a lawman looking for a horse thief.

He described his hostile witness and that missing experimental palomino as best he could, not daring to hope for much this early in the game.

But the Mexican hoe-farmer surprised him pleasantly by saying he'd been working the next milpa east the morning that Anglo had come by on that *caballito bonito*. He said, in his own version of English, ''Was a very nice pony. Nice for to look at and nice the way she trotted, very smooth trot, like a dancer gliding to that Vienna music. Her rider did not bounce in the saddle as they passed. Such a mount could take a man most far in a day, if it did not tire too soon.''

Longarm said, ''Her name was Lille Thruma and her breed doesn't tire worth mentioning as long as they don't get overheated. Her rider was a foreigner. Neither your *raza* nor mine. What can you tell me about him?''

The older man answered simply, *''Muy poco.* He did not have much for to say that morning. I remember I called out,

'*Buendias, caballero. A 'onde va?*' But he just kept riding, as if he had much on his mind.''

Longarm said, "He likely did. You're sure he was an Anglo, tall, lean, lighter coloring than me?"

The Mexican nodded and replied, "He lacked your manners as well. Since he refused for to talk to me, I don't know what he spoke like. You say he stole that *caballito bonito*?"

Longarm said that was about the size of it, excused himself, and rode on. He questioned others along that same trail all morning, and those who'd noticed a tall man on a modest mount described their encounters much the same way. Lille Thruma and her rider had been making damned good time, and more than one witness allowed that young Njalsson had pushed west along that same trail like a man with a lot on his mind, or his conscience.

But the pickings grew slimmer as he rode further west. For as the Mexican milpas and Anglo truck farms within easy cartage to the seaport gave way to cattle spreads large and small, there were fewer and fewer folks with roadside chores. Longarm stopped for water at more than one spread where they insisted on him having coffee, but didn't recall any peculiar cuss on an unusual mount.

Where the trail swung close enough to the river, Longarm could see at a glance through the gaps in the tanglewood along the bank that the Rio ran deep and wide as a no-shit river that far downstream at that time of the year. So he knew his quarry would have had to cross by ferry, where memories of him figured to linger, or chance swimming his Icelandic-Hispanic experiment across and hope Capatain Steensen had known what he was breeding. Longarm didn't have the least notion about the seaworthiness of Lille Thruma. So he doubted Njalsson would try that when he only had to swing north, away from the river, to put a whole lot of wide-open Texas between himself and any pursuit.

Longarm stopped around fifteen miles out to unsaddle and air his paint while he took a good shit and opened cans of Boston beans and tomato preserves for an early dinner. You didn't count on an outfit to feed you when you came barging in on them with a Winchester and a curious mind.

So there he was sitting, inhaling canned grub and tobacco

smoke, by the side of the trail while he grazed his pony, when who should he spy coming west his way but the one and original Captain Travis Prescott of the Texas Rangers.

Prescott reined in and dismounted nearby, quietly saying, "Howdy. Did you know another rider followed you out from the county seat this morning, Uncle Sam?"

Longarm replied in as laconic a tone, "Yep. I'm looking at him. Don't you have no kids your own age to play with, Captain?"

The Ranger tethered his handsome bay gelding to a handy cottonwood, and hunkered down beside Longarm, saying, "Nope. Heard somebody pegged another shot at you last night. So this morning I inquired as to your health. They told me you'd rid this way. As I tagged along after you, the rain-smoothed trail still virgin, I couldn't help noticing you seemed to be leaving two sets of hoofprints. I hadn't heard you were riding one brute and leading another. So I tried to catch up before morning traffic along the river road spoiled the game."

"What did you find out?" asked Longarm, holding out half a can of tomato preserves.

The Ranger shook his head and said, "Never touch the stuff. As to who might have been tailing you, morning traffic spoiled the game. I lost your tracks and his under other hooves and more than one set of cartwheels going both ways. I put the spurs to old Ned yonder, hoping I wouldn't come across you dead. I'm pleased as punch to see you alive and well. Albeit them sugared tomatoes are likely to play hell with your teeth in time. Where did you say you were headed, old son?"

Longarm said the O Bar O, and brought the Ranger up to date on his conversation with Don Hernan Obregon. For a man who didn't want the law to know he'd been out to steal a horse had no business telling a lawman he was a horse thief who didn't seem to see anything wrong with his ways. Having diplomatic immunity was likely to have that effect on a cuss who'd never been raised strictly enough.

The Ranger got out some makings and began to roll himself a smoke as he said, "I sure wish I was allowed to arrest that *ladrón*. We've scouted *his* trail ahead of you too. For all his faults, Obregon was likely telling the truth when he said he'd sent that deserter from the Danish marines along this primrose path. I've already had that out with the *segundo* at the O Bar O. Talked to the Chinee cook and the house *chica* whose favors I suspect they both share. Everyone at the O Bar O is going to tell you Njalsson rode in on that pretty little palomino just after supper time, stayed a part of the night, and lit out again before dawn. That's where the trail goes cold. Nobody up to the ferry crossing at San Juan owns up to having ever seen 'em. There ain't no ford this side of San Juan. Had he wanted to be *rafted* across, he'd have had to ask somebody who'd remember him if they know what's good for them. How do you cotton to him just heading inland, into more open range?''

Longarm said, ''Already considered it. Leaves us with one big question. How come Njalsson or some other foreigner sent that letter in Danish from Laredo if Njalsson and that palomino headed inland instead of upstream?''

The Ranger licked his cigarette paper to seal his crude smoke, and replied easily, ''You just now answered that. It was some other fool foreigner who sent that letter. Njalsson and the Mex were pals. That letter accused Obregon of murder most foul.''

As the Ranger lit up, Longarm suggested, ''Try her this way. The one who rode off on Lille Thruma could have been someone else entirely. The broodmare was valuable to all concerned. Anybody might have killed Count Atterdag, or Private Njalsson, to lay hands on her.''

''But the *segundo*, the Chink, and the play-pretty—'' the Ranger began to protest.

Then Longarm shushed him and pointed out, ''Nobody at that stud spread twenty-odd miles from where Njalsson was pulling guard duty to the day he deserted could have ever met the marine in person. They had orders from Obregon to aid and abet a horse thief. So let's say a killer who knew this took advantage of it long enough to behave as his own red herring?''

The Ranger took a thoughtful drag on his smoke, let it out, and decided, ''That works. Sending a letter signed as Njalsson might have simply been meant to make us all think

200

Njalsson and the stolen pony wound up in Laredo when all the time it was somebody else.''

Longarm finished his tomato preserves, and crushed the can under his boot heel to pound it into the ground to rust, before he declared, ''That's saying Njalsson ain't clever by half and sent the letter written Danish-style to make us *think* it was a forgery. A Texican doesn't talk like a Cockney from London Town often. But a Texican who'd spent some time in London Town and chose his words slow and careful might write a letter Cockney-style if he put his mind to it.''

The Ranger moaned, ''Lord have mercy if you ain't riding me around and around on a durned old roulette wheel. Make up your mind. Which is it going to be?''

Longarm kicked harder to make sure the crushed cans would stay buried until they'd rusted clean away, and heaved himself back to his feet as he replied, ''When my mind is made up I'll be in better shape to say. I don't even know all the questions I need to have answered! Whoever sent that letter postmarked Laredo, Don Hernan and all his friends in Laredo, Anglo or Mexican, never spotted Njalsson or that even easier-to-spot pony.''

He moved over to pick up his overturned and airing saddle as he continued. ''I reckon I'll ride on to that O Bar O and see if they tell me the same story. You want to ride yonder with me?''

The Ranger scowled and demanded, ''Have you sent your brains off hunting strays in high chaparral? I told you what they told me, and I wasn't supposed to care that much! Even if we could deliver that count's killer with a signed and sealed confession, there ain't a court this side of Copenhagen with the jurisdiction to *do* anything about it!''

Longarm asked, ''How do you know? More than one likely suspect may have diplomatic immunity. But we can't be sure the *killer* has before we *catch* him!''

''I tell you you're beating a dead horse,'' the Ranger insisted.

To which Longarm could only reply, ''Then why does somebody seem to want me dead? I don't seem to be getting anywhere, and by now I'd have been inclined to agree I was wasting my time if they'd just let me run around in circles.

201

But they must fear I'm on to something, or about to stumble over something. So like I said, I gotta just keep on chasing my own tail till I spy a better tail to chase.''

Prescott grimaced and said, ''Lord knows there's been many a rider on the owlhoot trail who'd have never been caught if he hadn't been so mean to lawmen. I've stuck my neck out as far as I dast. It looks like we're fixing to have another gully-washer, and I mean to get back to town before it hits. But feel free to ride on out to the O Bar O if you won't take my word for shit!''

So Longarm did. He met a fence rider along the way who recalled a stranger sitting tall in a funny-looking saddle aboard a sort of runty palomino. But nobody else Longarm met up with along the way could help him out. So he just kept going until, sure enough, he spied a sunflower windmill hovering above a sprawl of tiled rooftops off the trail to his right up ahead.

He swung off the main trail to catty-corner towards the O Bar O. A pack of cur dogs tried to cut him off, yapping and gnashing like they'd all gone mad at once. But his hired paint was Texas bred, and didn't shy as the mutts circled them like Comanches worrying a wagon ring. He saw six or eight figures had come out of the main house to stare silently in the noonday shade of the veranda out front. All but two looked to be male, dressed Border Mexican. The one gal was dressed Border Mexican as well. A lean and hungry-looking cuss dressed Texican with a six-gun on either hip stepped out in the sunlight as Longarm rode within easy shouting distance.

The Anglo, who seemed to be the *segundo* or foreman, called out to him, ''You're on private property, pilgrim. Whatever you're selling, we ain't buying. So why don't you just turn back and git back to the public thoroughfare, before we have to hold private services for you.''

It had been a statement, not a question, and the unsmiling cuss looked like he'd meant every word of it.

Chapter 28

Longarm rode closer and reined in near the hitching rail along the front of the veranda as the *segundo* scowled and asked, "Might you have a serious hearing problem, pilgrim? I just told you to *git*. I don't remember telling you to git off your fucking pony!"

As Longarm tethered the paint he calmly replied, "I hardly ever fuck ponies, and you don't want to fuck with me either. I am the law, federal. The Rangers know I rode out this way, and your boss, Don Hernan, told me where it was."

Stepping around his mount with a firm but friendly expression, Longarm continued. "He's in the county hospital in Brownsville, by the way. Him and me came under fire from the same source last night. So I doubt he'd want you to murder me and bury me under your outhouse. My name would be Custis Long and I'm a U.S. deputy marshal. Now it's your turn."

The *segundo* replied, "Why didn't you say so sooner? I'm Bowie Bickford, and El Patron sent a rider out from town in all that rain to tell us he'd been winged but not to worry about him. He never said we'd be visited by you, though, no offense."

Longarm said, "None taken. Just before he took a bullet in one arm, your boss and me were talking about that deserter from the Royal Danish Marines who rode out here earlier aboard that pale prize pony.''

Bickford suggested they go inside before it got hotter or rained fire and salt. South Texas was like that in April.

Once they were inside the spartan but well-kept main room, seated by a cold baronial fireplace while that one gal rustled up coffee, tortillas, and chili con carne whether Longarm wanted any or not, he brought Bickford more up to date on the events of the night before.

In turn, the *segundo* repeated Don Hernan's tale of the missing Pall Njalsson almost word for word.

Bickford added, ''Feel free to ask any of the help out of my own guidance, if you like. Every one of 'em, from Maria in the kitchen to the kid who shovels shit in the stables out back, will tell you the same tale. That Swede rid in around supper time, and we supped him and put him to bed in the guest chambers, just as we'd been ordered by El Patron. Next morning, before sunup, he was gone. He'd snuck that palomino out of the stall we'd put her in for him, as if he'd had experience as a horse thief. Go ahead, just ask all the greasers on the spread if you think I'm lying.''

Longarm said, ''He was an Icelander, not a Swede. But I reckon the rest of what you say ought to hold up in any court of law. For I'd be surprised if this was a theatrical company instead of a stud spread.''

Maria came in with their coffee, snacks, and an unfortunate smile. She'd have been sort of pretty if her front teeth hadn't rotted out, been knocked out, or whatever.

A man on the trail could always use strong coffee, and he was a bit surprised by how good a real warm meal went down after a cold-can noon dinner.

Being country-bred, both Anglos put away most of the tortillas and chili con carne and lit up to smoke with their coffee before they got back to the hostile witness Longarm was trailing.

Longarm said, ''I'll take your word most everybody out this way saw a gent answering to Njalsson's description ride in aboard that missing pony. That ain't saying he had to be the real Njalsson, but it would be harder to fake an Icelandic-Hispanic palomino mare. So let's talk about *her*. She might or might not have taken the same bullet as killed another foreigner fixing to mount her. That stable hand you mentioned should have noticed either way, right?''

Bickford banged his coffee mug on the low table in front of him until toothless Maria came back in looking worried.

Bickford said, *''Quiero Pablo. En seguida!''* Then she tore right out to fetch the kid. Bickford sounded bossy in any lingo. So she was back in no time with a scared-looking kid in *peon* whites.

As Pablo stood there, straw hat in hand, Bickford questioned him curtly in Border Mexican. Longarm pretended he needed another Anglo to translate. But the ruse failed to catch the unpleasant *segundo* in any fibs. The stable boy said he had indeed unsaddled Lille Thruma and rubbed her down before putting her in a stall out back with cracked corn and water. Longarm resisted the impulse to ask if the kid had been smart enough to soak the dry grain first. Had they bloated the pony after her long, hard *tolt*, she'd have never been gone the next morning.

Pablo agreed he'd have noticed any punctures in that golden blond hide of Lille Thruma, and again, Longarm resisted the temptation to tip his mitt. If the kid said the mare hadn't been hit, either he was lying, which seemed unlikely, or she hadn't been hit, which was unlikely as well.

When Bickford translated, Longarm said, ''Well, the coroner's report did say the fatal bullet ticked a corset stay and followed a curved path through his guts. When it keyholed out his belly, it only had to miss by a whisker or, hell, hang up in saddle leather if it was small-bore, slowed some by a lot of noble guts. I don't suppose Pablo here examined that military saddle for any such damage?''

Bickford asked. Longarm wasn't surprised when the stable boy admitted he hadn't looked for any cuts or bruises in cordovan leather under tricky gloaming light. When Bickford repeated this, Longarm nodded soberly and said, ''Don't really matter how the mare escaped serious injury. I'm glad she did, and now we know she's had time to travel far and wide at that mile-eating fifth gait of her kind.''

He took one of those sepia-tone prints of Lille Thruma from his shirt pocket as he added, ''Just let me make certain we're talking about the same mount before we get on to which way she might have gone from here.''

He showed them the picture of Lille Thruma. They both agreed that was the very pony Pall Njalsson, or somebody saying he was the runaway Royal Marine, had passed through aboard.

Longarm put the picture away again, having paid good money for it, and said, "I sure wish I had a picture of my missing as well as hostile witness to show around. Say the one who left here before the sun came up rode hard. How long might it take him to make her to the next ferry crossing upstream?''

Bickford thought and decided, "Too long, if all he wanted was to get across to Mexico. If he was at all anxious, he could have asked at a dozen spreads up or downstream from here to be rafted across for less than that ferry up by San Juan charges.''

"Wouldn't anyone who crosses the river informally now and again be likely to recall such a transaction?" asked Longarm.

Bickford shrugged and replied, "No more likely than the ferrymen up to San Juan. Mayhaps less. You ain't *supposed* to raft man or beast across the border so informal.''

Longarm rolled his eyes up at the beam ceiling to moan, "Oh, Lord, I wish you hadn't said that. You're right about looking like rain, and I just hate it when folks lie to the law, don't you?''

Bickford smiled for the first time since Longarm had met him, and dryly remarked, "Not hardly. I was riz by a moonshining daddy to lie to the law every time they asked about our family business.''

Longarm laughed, and finished his coffee so he could ride on. When he got back outside, the sky was overcast and the *segundo* who'd followed him out said he was fixing to get soaked. Bickford didn't sound as if this really worried him all that much.

Longarm allowed he had a slicker lashed between his cantle and tarp-covered bedroll. Bickford allowed he'd surely *need* it, as the tall deputy mounted up to ride on.

At least the afternoon was cool enough for comfortable

riding as the sky got really dark and the vagrant winds blew back and forth across the river road. He moved on upstream a mile or more, and no signs of human habitation were in sight, when he came upon a little gal in bib overalls, trying not to cry as she trudged up the trail ahead of him.

Longarm reined in to keep pace with her short legs as he smiled down to say, "Howdy, Miss Bo Peep. Might you be looking for a lost sheep, or have you left home to seek your fortune on the wicked stage?"

The six- or seven-year-old pouted. "My durned old pony throwed me and I mean to whup him good when I get home! We was out gathering in the herd ahead of the coming storm when a windblown tumbleweed spooked my durned old pony. He bucked me off and run for home, the big old baby!"

Longarm said he'd had a pony like that when he'd been about her age. Then he reined in and held down a hand, adding, "Let's ride you on home double and see if we can beat that rain to your door."

She hesitated and said, "I ain't supposed to go nowheres with any strangers, mister."

Longarm said, "I ain't no stranger, sis. I'm U.S. Deputy Marshal Custis Long. Do you want to see my badge?"

She did. So he showed it to her, and she allowed her name was Elsbeth Bean and she sure was tired of walking.

So he swung her up to sit his saddle roll behind him with her little hands hooked in his gunbelt. He walked the paint under the two of them, seeing she had no stirrups and had confessed to her own mount throwing her.

As they rode along, he asked if she didn't feel she was a tad young for a top hand.

Elsbeth calmly replied, "It can't be helped. My daddy got sick and died poor. So all Mamma has is our homestead claim and us three kids to help her. When it started to cloud up just after dinnertime, Momma said we'd best round up our stock and corral them till things quieted down again. My brothers, Ewen and Ian, are fanned out up the river to keep the fool critters from bolting down the banks into the tanglewood and falling in to be swept away by the current. Momma says any ponies that bolt inland are likely to come home on their own as soon as they recall how good she fodders them.''

Longarm nodded and observed, ''Open range don't offer much in the way of oats, cracked corn, and such. You say you and your small family are out here raising *horses*, short-handed as you must be?''

The little she-wrangler soberly replied, ''Momma says it's the only way we'll ever work our way out of debt. She says one grown woman and her three kids could never manage enough *cows* to matter. But horses sell for so much more, we just might make it if we pull together hard enough.''

Longarm had the picture now. It wasn't pretty, but it was all too familiar out this way.

The Homestead Act of '63 had been intended to help populate the West, not break hearts and starve children. The land management office let you claim a quarter section or 160 acres of unimproved federal land, good, bad, or indifferent, and ''prove'' it for five years as best you knew how before you could lease it, sell it, or do anything but try and get by on it. If you hadn't been run off by grasshoppers or devoured by Indians at the end of your first five years, the land was your own to cherish or never forgive, depending on how things had worked out.

The land office offered a little advice, a lot of it misinformed, and no material help at all to the homesteaders wise and foolish it allowed to sink or swim. Some made it. As many or more failed, slow or sudden, and had to give up and get a job, or go back busted where they'd come from.

So most of them worked harder, trying to make a go of their claim, than any slave driver with a bullwhip might have been able to get them to work.

The West was still dotted with the abandoned homesteads of a lot of folks Longarm would never meet up with.

When Elsbeth said the rambling collection of sod structures and pole corrals off the trail up ahead was her momma's place, Longarm swung toward it. A distant female figure waving a trio of scrub ponies through an open corral gate spotted her only daughter on a strange mount with a strange man, but had to finish her chore, as a bitty kid on a bay too big for him tried to haze another head of horseflesh toward the same gate. The frisky blue roan cut around the kid to crow-hop away as if it was laughing at him. It likely was. Cow ponies, like cowboys, were inclined to enjoy crude humor.

Elsbeth slipped down from behind Longarm to run over to her mother and help with the gate as the woman, a sort of gaunt natural redhead in a dark blue Mother Hubbard and sunbonnet, smacked one of the ponies with her sack and got them all in the corral. Off in the distance, her boy bawled about that frisky blue roan he'd almost had for the third time.

Riding closer, Longarm reined in to call down, "Howdy, ma'am. I am a U.S. deputy marshal hunting for another pony and its rider. But Miss Elsbeth explained your predicament as we were riding in just now. Might you have a roping saddle with, say, fifty feet of fairly new grass-rope handy, ma'am?"

She stared up at him warily. Her big eyes were hazel, and she was sort of pretty if you liked them long and lean. She finally nodded and said, "My late husband's saddle and a lariat he'd barely broken in are still in our tack room gathering dust. But why do you ask?"

Longarm said, "I can't gather stock with this cavalry saddle and no rope, ma'am. Loan me a fresh horse and the right gear and I'll see if I can't help your boy bring in that sassy blue roan to start with. You've likely noticed it's easier to fill a corral as soon as you get a good crowd waltzing around inside."

She looked as if he'd said something mean enough to make her cry. But she never did. She said, "I'd be Una Bean, and as you see, I'm a wee bit short of help. But I have no money to spare, and I don't see how I would ever reward you for that much trouble, sir."

Longarm said, "Call me Custis. That's what most of my friends call me. The government pays my wages, ma'am. We'd best get cracking before that storm hits, hear?"

She headed for the stable on foot ahead of him, calling back something about never being able to repay him. Poor but proud gals were inclined to talk like that. He told her they'd work something out later when they had more time.

Chapter 29

He'd have never done it without a good roping saddle and a fresh cutting horse, a fifteen-hands bay gelding called Crusader, with the instincts of an overgrown sheepdog.

The kids helped a lot. Even little Elsbeth rode mighty fine, and while her big brothers—Ewen, nine, and Ian, going on twelve—were a tad too small for roping, they hazed as good as many a full-grown hand, and as Longarm had told Miss Una, you only had to rope a few of the more sassy ones.

The Beans had a string of eight broke and saddle-trained mounts along with a remuda of eighty-two, from long in the tooth to foal.

With the kids cutting them off on the far side, Longarm roped and dragged in that troublemaking blue roan and seven more who seemed to feel that the Emancipation Proclamation included horses. Once the more frisky ones had been shown the error of their ways, things went smoother. But it was raining hard by the time Longarm and the three soggy kids joined the lady of the house in her kitchen for hot chocolate and shortbread.

She made all three kids change into dry outfits, stared thoughtfully at Longarm, and allowed that her late husband had been a smaller man whose dry duds might look sort of silly on Longarm.

He said he was used to sitting damp by a kitchen fire and

drying out. She insisted he at least shuck his wet shirt and try on her husband's wool cardigan. So he did, and she'd been right. The salmon-colored knitting was too small for him by half. So his arms, halfway to his elbows, and the front of him, from belt buckle up, were left exposed to dry as best they could manage on their own. For some reason it seemed to fluster his hostess. She looked away every time her gaze fell upon his naked hairy chest.

She'd hung his wet shirt over a chair by her kitchen stove. The stove was sheet iron and glowing red near the flue. One good thing about homesteading close to the Rio Grande was that you never had to burn cow chips for fuel as you did further north on the higher plains. Cottonwood burned bright and about as long as paper. But there was plenty of sour gum, swamp maple, and even oak to gather along the wooded banks of the lower reaches of the muddy brawling river.

It was just as well they'd gathered a mess of it. For by then it was really raining fire and salt outside. Una Bean kept getting to her feet to peer out her rain-spattered kitchen window and worry out loud about twisters. She said she'd grown up in Iowa. That was likely why she was so worried about twisters.

Longarm said soothingly, "April through to June is the worse time for twisters somewhat north of here, Miss Una. But to tell the truth, we're more likely to get hurricaned this far south."

She asked what improvement that added up to. He asked, and got her permission to smoke before he rose to fumble in his wet shirt, saying, "Hurricanes tend to drown you, whilst twisters tend to pick you up and tear you limb from limb."

He got out his last soggy cheroots, decided they'd best dry some before he risked trying to light them, and sat back down, wishing he chewed, to explain, "All told, a hurricane does way more damage. For it comes at you hundreds of miles wide, piling up tides, flooding streams and washes, peeling roofs off houses, and so on, whilst a twister comes at you hundreds of *feet* wide, but within that one strip of destruction, watch out! I don't know which is worse from a strictly business point of view. But I reckon I'd rather sit through a hurricane than a twister, this far inland leastways."

She repressed a shudder and said, "Speak for yourself, Custis! I wish we could afford to fence this claim in. But we can't, and this rain we've been having is making my stock too hard for us to manage!"

He didn't ask why. He'd ridden for bigger outfits than this in his misspent youth. He nodded and said, "I'd stick closer to home if I was forced to choose betwixt ranging free on summer brown grass or coming home to my corral for my supper of grain and timothy hay too. But I might be tempted to wander some in a wider world of fresh-sprouting salad greens."

Then he brightened and declared, "Lord love you, ma'am, that other pony I'm interested in might not notice how lonely open range around it might look, with the same greened up and with bluestem sprouting past my stirrups!"

She wanted to know more about Lille Thruma. So he was going over the complicated mission with her, leaving out the other gals, when her kids came back to the kitchen in dry clothes to listen in wide-eyed, making Longarm feel a tad guilty about the way he'd been comparing a natural redhead with the henna-rinsed Madame Laverne, both of them nude, in his mind's eye.

He'd about finished, finding it more tedious to himself than it was to the widow and her kids, hearing it all for the first time, when all five of them and the house around them were tingled and jolted by a swamping lightning bolt crackle-banging like a twelve-pounder field gun close as hell!

Little Elsbeth ran and dove into her mother's comforting arms as little Ewen rolled under the kitchen table. Big Ian, made of sterner stuff, just stood there ashen-faced and owl-eyed.

Una Bean managed to stammer, "Don't be frightened, dear hearts. They say lightning never strikes twice in the same place."

Longarm doubted she wanted to be told that "they" were full of shit. So instead of observing that lightning tended to strike the same high spots until it had flattened them out, he told them to look on the bright side. Lightning hardly ever came with hurricane winds.

212

Una asked, "What about twisters? I seem to remember thunder and lightning when we had this big twister carry our barn away up in Iowa when I was as little as Elsbeth here!"

Longarm repeated his earlier observation that hurricanes and twisters were not at all the same.

From under the table, little Ewen demanded, "What if you get a hurricane and a twister at the same time, Uncle Custis?"

Wondering who on earth could have told the kid he was his uncle, Longarm explained, "You just don't. I ain't sure why, Ewen. All I know is that I've seen fair weather and foul since I was your age and I've never yet . . . Great day in the morning, and if you ain't as clever a child as ever lived this side of Sir Isaac Newton, I'll eat my hat!"

"What did I say?" asked the bewildered boy.

His mother and siblings wanted to know too. So Longarm told them all, "I've been guilty of mayhaps adding one and one to get one!"

Little Elsbeth declared from her mother's lap, "That's silly. One and one is two. So there."

Longarm said, "I know. They sent me down this way to find that hostile witness and see if he could say who killed the count he'd been guarding. Along the way I stumbled over some razzle-dazzle rebel plot involving those repeating rifles I just told you about. I might not have if somebody else didn't jump to the conclusion I'd been sent to look into *that* instead of that assassination. I just as naturally figured it was all one big tangle of unmatched yarn. As if there was a hurricane and a twister blowing at the same time!"

Una Bean frowned and asked, "Well, haven't they been? From what you just told us, there has to be some connection between that Danish count, the Icelandic rebels he'd been sent to investigate, and those Prussian rifles you assume the same rebels are interested in."

Longarm nodded, but asked, "What if I've assumed wrong and there's no such connection? What if I've just been seeing tigers in the roses or cracks in the plaster I've taken for spiderwebs?"

She told him he wasn't making much sense to her as she set little Elsbeth back on her feet and added, "Mother has

213

to think about making supper now. You'll be staying for supper, Custis. Mayhaps some solid food will clear your mind of spiderwebs and tigers in roses, of all things!''

As she rose from her seat across from him, but only moved as far as the dry sink and work counter, Longarm explained. "We all see tigers in the roses, Miss Una. It's a natural condition of the human way of looking at the world around us. I only use tigers in the roses by way of illustration. One time, when I was little, I was staring up at this floral wallpaper. I forget where. I was that little. But I still remember this pattern of red roses, red leaves, red baskets, and such. It was cheap wallpaper. I can still see the big growly tiger that was suddenly staring off the wall at me. Even though I knew full well that the artist who designed that floral pattern never had any fool tigers in mind. He only meant to draw roses. He only *drew* roses. I saw a tiger instead, because I wasn't paying attention to his old roses and my kid brain and sleepy eyes inspired losts of dots and blotches to just fall into place as a big old growly tiger, see?''

"I'm scared!" Elsbeth complained.

But Ian suddenly blurted out, "I saw a flying horse in the clouds one day. It had a horse's head with big white wings, a mane, a tail, and everything but hooves!"

His mother stared at Longarm thoughtfully and declared, "There was this cracked plaster wall back home in Iowa when I was still in school. It was the exact shape as the continent of Africa. I thought I was just imagining, until I compared the cracks in the plaster with my eighth-grade atlas. A few little coastal features seemed a tad off, but the pattern was still an almost exact fit. Is that what we've been talking about, Custis?''

He nodded and said, "Our human minds can't stand a total mess. We tidy things up by deciding we must be looking at *something*. Had not you seen Africa in those plaster cracks, you'd have seen something else, such as Australia, an Irish harp, the sign of the cross, or a funny face. It's tougher to just stare at a pattern and admit you can't make a lick of sense out of it.''

She asked how he felt about fried hash with peas and

214

carrots. He had to allow it sounded like a change from what he'd been eating along the border of late.

So she grubbed them and made more hot chocolate while the wind and rain lashed at the windows all around and made the stovepipe moan like a love-struck spook. Longarm refrained from mentioning spooks or the tangled web back in Brownsville because he was trying to untangle it into tidier separate piles in different corners of his mind. The problem was deciding where to snip a thread free or leave it connected to another. The notion that Pall Njalsson had joined the Royal Danish Marines instead of a home-rule party cut a lot of threads connecting him to those purloined Prussian rifles. That Mexican horse dealer had admitted he'd wanted to buy Lille Thurma if the unhappy marine wanted to steal her. Njalsson could have been just as tempted if Count Atterdag had been investigating the sex life of the Texas armadillo or the nesting habits of the horned lark. A horse thief steals horses from the one who has the horses he's out to steal. But if that was all there was to the missing prize pony, who'd shot Count Atterdag in the back as he was fixing to mount the pony? And above all, why?

"Try her this way," Longarm muttered to his peach-cobbler dessert. "That malcontent marine was waiting his chance, then somebody shot his boss for other reasons entirely, and the kid just took advantage of all that confusion."

"I beg your pardon?" Una Bean asked.

Longarm said, "Sorry. Talking to myself again. I know you ain't supposed to. Everybody does it just the same when they have a lot on their mind."

She softly answered, "Don't I know it! You should hear the conversations I have in here after the children are all in bed at night!"

But she only seemed to want to talk to Longarm after the three kids had been tucked in for the stormy night down at the other end of the rambling soddy. Longarm tried to talk about the weather outside, and then, failing that, the mission he was on. But she kept asking questions about him, his life up in Denver, and whether he had any serious sweetheart yonder.

They somehow wound up seated together on a sofa in her

parlor by the time he'd finished telling her about coming west after the war, knocking around sort of restlessly, and winding up a senior deputy for the Denver District Court. He felt no call to talk about another widow woman on Capitol Hill or that younger but more possessive matron of the Arvada Orphan Asylum. Una wasn't wearing perfume like that French gal had the night before. But her red hair was natural, and she smelled of naptha soap and clean female sweat. So the next thing he knew his free arm was up behind her on the backrest of the sofa and the story of *her* life was turning out to be less cheerful.

When she got to a handsome no-good who'd comforted her a lot after her husband's death, Longarm stopped her to say, "I wish you ladies wouldn't rub our noses in other scoundrels, Miss Una. Telling a man you know *he'd* never treat you half so mean could be defined as cruelty to dumb animals. Men always want to use and abuse women. It's the nature of us beasts. Just like making us feel guilty about it is the nature of *you* beasts, bless your pretty hides."

She laughed, and suddenly popped up to kiss him, bold as brass, and ask if that made him feel guilty.

It did. He said, "Miss Una, I'm a worthless catch with a shifty job. If I said I didn't want to use and abuse you, I'd be lying. But we'd both be sorry in the cold gray dawn, and I got to look at myself in the mirror every time I shave."

So nothing much was happening while, miles away under a dripping trailside live oak, two men hunkered out of the wind, if not out of the rain, with primed and cocked repeaters under their dark ponchos.

After another flash of lightning revealed a furlong of empty trail to the west, one of them said, not in English, "He's not coming. For he would have been here long before now if he'd turned back from that Mexican's place. What if he has gone on towards Laredo?"

His partner in intended crime grinned wolfishly and replied, "Who cares? If he has ridden off into Limbo, it does not matter to us. Our orders are to stop him from returning to Brownsville. If he comes our way tonight, we kill him. If he does not, we can't. Must I explain such simple tactics to a man who claims to be a professional killer?"

Chapter 30

Longarm rode into Brownsville at high noon the next day with a clear conscience and a raging hard-on after a night alone on a sofa and half a day posting in a McClellan saddle.

Such saddles had been designed by the good quartermaster and awful field commander who'd modified and improved a Hungarian cavalry saddle he'd noticed while a military attaché on duty at the U.S. embassy to the Hapsburg Empire. Longarm used his McClellan for the same reasons the U.S. Cav did. It was easier on the horse than a stock saddle, although hell on a rider's crotch if he didn't stand in the stirrups while trotting.

He unsaddled and rubbed the paint down out behind the *posada,* then went upstairs to get his frock coat, missing old Sigridur a lot after all that infernal virtue. The April day after that storm off the Gulf had turned out nice and springlike, with cool breezes wafting off the harbor estuary.

But he mostly put on his formal frock coat, without the tweed vest, to look more official now that it was practical to do so.

Not wanting to worry about tethering and untethering in a town as compact as Brownsville, Longarm walked over to the Danish consulate, not bothering to hug the shady sides on such a swell day. A snooty Dane in snooty livery let him in, but made him wait while he went to fetch that little brunette in black silk, Camilla Nansen.

She smiled up at him friendly enough, but told him her boss, Baron Senderborg, was over at the U.S. Customs House, trying to talk that Captain Steensen into coming home. Longarm told her he'd come to chew the fat about that letter from their missing marine. So she led him into a side office, sat him down at one end of a desk, and offered him a skinny black cigar and some more of that *akvavit*— both Danish exports, she said, as she sat down at the desk as importantly as any man.

He asked if that KHA monopoly saw to it that they got nothing but the best from home. She nodded, and reminded him he'd said something about that letter.

Longarm put the fancy cigar away for later, but took a sip of their firewater to be polite before he told her he'd established Njalsson's line of flight, as far as the far side of the county line, well enough for most grand juries.

Then he said, "If somebody's trying to flimflam us into thinking Njalsson lit out for Laredo, they went to a heap of trouble, considering how they worded that letter that set out to clear Captain Steensen. I reckon you know why Steensen suspects it was a ploy to get him back here so the baron can arrest him?"

The dark little Dane nodded gravely, but pointed out, "Baron Senderborg does not arrest people. He does not write his own letters or shine his own boots. He has us to attend his every need, and I assure you, he has not ordered anyone to arrest Eric Steensen. Eric and that other . . . *varmbror,* Andersen, are just being silly."

Longarm wasn't ready to ask her to translate that term yet. He suspected he already knew what she seemed to suspect. He told her, "I had an American translator who could talk and read both your Danish and that missing marine's native Icelandic. I lost her to the weather we've been having down here."

Camilla sounded just a tad catty as she smiled like Miss Mona Lisa and said, "I know. There certainly was a lot of her, wasn't there? Is there any point to this conversation? I know you had her follow me around and listen in on my conversations. What did she accuse me of saying?"

Longarm answered easily, "Nothing. Her being in that beauty parlor and ice cream parlor when you spotted her was an accident both times. I might have know that since she could spot a gal your size, you'd have no trouble spotting a gal *her* size. But she never low-rated you, and she's gone back to Kansas. So the *point* I was out to make was that she told me Captain Steensen had a point in suspecting that letter had been written by a Dane instead of an Icelander. How might you feel about that, Miss Camilla?"

The dark brunette shrugged her shapely silk-covered shoulders and replied, "Private Njalsson was a Royal Danish Marine, writing a letter to his Danish sergeant. He'd naturally write it in Danish."

"How easy would that be for an Icelander from a humble fishing village?" asked Longarm.

She smiled like Miss Mona Lisa again and said, "Don't underrate our rustic Icelanders, Deputy Long. They're notorious chess masters, and inclined to greet visitors who don't speak Icelandic in Latin, if not the visitor's own language. The first Basque dictionary ever was compiled by an Icelandic farmer with a shipwrecked Basque sailor and those long winter nights on their hands. They read more than most common folk of their class. As I said, long winter nights. *Northanfari,* their radical nationalist newspaper, is quite well-written and edited, as well as very subversive. I don't think an Icelander stationed any time as a Royal Danish Marine in Copenhagen would have any trouble composing a letter in conversational Danish."

Longarm must have looked unconvinced as he sat there sipping his white lightning. For she suddenly declared, *"God dag. Hvordan har De det?"* followed by, *"Godan dag. Hvad segirdu gott?"*

Longarm decided, "I give up. Was that Danish or Icelandic, ma'am?"

She said, "Both. I just said, 'Good morning, how are you?' in both Danish and Icelandic. It's as much a choice of words as vocabulary. Think of a Bostonian saying, 'how do you do?' and a Texan just saying, 'Howdy.' "

"That all the difference there is?" he asked.

She hesitated. Then she said, "Perhaps a little more. Danes have a little trouble following the distinctive lilts of Icelandic or Norwegian. It's easier for them to follow Danish because it's spoken somewhat flatter and, like English, forgives a reasonable ammount of uncertain grammar."

Longarm allowed he'd noticed French Canadians laughed at Americans trying to speak French, and decided, "In sum, that letter postmarked Laredo could have been managed by any halfway bright Icelander or a Dane trying to sound sort of country?"

She shook her head and said, "There were no grammatical or spelling mistakes in that letter. I typed up the manifold copy to be cabled to Copenhagen myself. It was a simple handwritten note, addressed to a Danish sergeant in everyday Danish. The same Danish we heard those Royal Marines speaking while they were here with poor Count Atterdag."

He nodded, and asked what sort of military guard they had at the moment.

She answered simply, "None. Some of the staff and most of the liveried male servants have had some military service and keep guns in their quarters, should they be needed. But we mostly depend on your Brownsville police to guard our lives and property. This is only a modest consulate with a small staff. We issue visas and offer advice to Danish travelers and merchants down here at the tip of Texas. We don't really have a lot to do between assassinations."

He grinned back at her. She had a better sense of humor than most beautiful young things. Getting married up a couple of times had no doubt taught her not to take herself too seriously.

He said, "I've been showing pictures of that prize pony the count was fixing to mount when somebody shot him in the back. It's paid off a time or two. A photograph of that Private Pall Njalsson might be of even more help, ma'am."

She nodded and said, "Anyone can see that. But I'm afraid we can't help you. As I said, those marines were with Count Atterdag as his bodyguard, for all the good it did him. We had no occasion to have photographs taken of them. If any were, they've been taken back to Denmark with all their equipment and Count Atterdag."

He grimaced and insisted, ''You still saw more of them than I ever did, Miss Camilla. What does a Royal Danish Marine on duty look like, and more important, can you tell me how they were armed, or should I ask one of the menfolk on your staff?''

Her nostrils flared a bit, but she managed not to look sore as she calmly replied, ''They rather resemble the toy soldiers American children still get for Christmas. Tall shako hats with chin straps, much like those your West Point cadets still wear, with similar short jackets, crossed white webbing, and full-length white pants. Do you really expect to find Pall Njalsson in full-dress uniform at this late date?''

Longarm said, ''Not hardly. What can you tell me about those *arms* I just asked about, ma'am?''

She answered without batting an eye, ''Your own Remington rolling-block rifle, and don't think the Danish firm of Jorgensen hasn't made a fuss about *that* choice! I believe the cheaper Remington ammunition, together with the strong, simple design, were the deciding factors. A Danish gunsmith named Krag has been trying to sell our military on a repeating-rifle design. But there you have it, as far as our Royal Marines are concerned right *now*.''

He asked about side arms. She said marine officers packed swords and pistols. Marine privates were issued neither. They might sport their sword bayonets without the rifles on ceremonial occasions.

He asked if such sword bayonets might be curved, like, say, a cavalry saber.

She said they were straight, about eighteen inches long, and broad as butcher knives. So there went a grand notion, and you wouldn't hear a gunshot from such a weapon in any case.

The petite brunette seemed as open as any pretty gal with a clear conscience might act. So Longarm asked if she could tell him what that assassinated count had been sent all that way to look into.

He wasn't astounded to hear her answer, ''Gunrunning. A rather silly rumor about rather silly Icelanders coming to America to buy arms for that revolution they'd been talking about for generations.''

221

He said he'd heard they'd tried and failed in 1808.

She made a wry face and replied, "That was no revolution. That was a comic opera farce. A British trading vessel put in to Reykjavik while our navy was tied up in those Napoleonic Wars. The royal governor in Iceland told the British to go away, and threatened to punish any Icelanders who traded with them. An Icelandic crew member on that British trading tramp, a vagabond who called himself John Johnson, led a shore party of a dozen English ruffians, or translated for them, and announced he'd liberated Iceland and that he'd be pleased to run the place from then on. Nothing much came of the burlesque. For a time the British merchant seamen held the royal governor in a cabin aboard their vessel. Then, since it *was* during the Napoleonic Wars after all, a real British naval vessel put in. Its Anglo-Irish commander told them not to be silly and put everything back the way it had been. But the Danish Rigstag did take note of the apparent discontent, once things got back to normal in Europe, and slowly but surely began to put things right. The KHA that everyone makes such a fuss about was actually set up by the Danish government to rein in the more greedy Danish traders, and by the mid-1850's the Rigsdag ended restrictions on free trade entirely."

Longarm said, "Captain Steensen told me the same. He seems to feel the Icelanders should have been more grateful."

She wrinkled her pert nose and declared, "Even a *varmbror* has to be right some of the time. Denmark admitted trying to abolish the Icelandic Althing in 1800 was a mistake. They allowed it to assemble again under Danish supervision, and finally granted almost complete home rule in '74. So why can't they simply shut up about paying too much for Copehagen snuff generations ago? Europe, from Ireland to the shores of the Black Sea, has been able to forgive their Viking ancestors. Why can't they forgive long-dead traveling salesmen for only *cheating* the unwashed louts?"

Longarm sipped more *akvavit* and suggested, "Mayhaps *almost* home rule doesn't feel the same as *total* home rule. Ain't it true Norway was given, or took, total independence from the Danish crown back in . . . Was it 1815?"

She grinned like a kid with a hand in the cookie jar and

told him, "You know full well when it was. That big fat blonde was a very good *kennslukona*, I see."

That sounded dirty. He said, "I asked Miss Sigridur to fill me in on Icelandic matters and she tried, Miss Camilla."

The petite brunette replied, "That was what I just said. There is some lingering discontent in Iceland, and some rabble-rousers have tried to take advantage of it from time to time. Count Atterdag had been told a subversive group of Icelandic malcontents, funded by gold strikes Icelandic immigrants had made in your American West, had contracted with *Prussian* malcontents to arm themselves here in Brownsville with Prussian repeating rifles. Captain Steensen, with our trade mission before he began to act silly, said the whole story was madness. Baron Senderborg and I had to agree. Why would anybody plot to buy contraband Prussian rifles in a remote American seaport when they could buy all the rifles they needed, legally, in any much closer New England town? Where do they think the Danish troops get *their* rifles, from Tibet?"

Longarm reached absently for that *akvavit*, decided he'd had all he needed, and said, "The Remington rolling block is a fine single-shot rifle. The logistical points most armies still make in favor of single shots spaced six to a minute are well taken. But maybe those chess-playing Icelandic rebels read about the Lakota Confederation having Spencer repeaters at Little Big Horn. A way harder-hitting Mauser with a fifteen-round tube magazine, handled bolt-action from cover in a prone position, sounds sort of ominous."

Then he pointed out, "If there was nothing to the rumor, we're left with Count Atterdag getting shot in the back before he could prove it right or wrong. And somebody's tried to shoot *me* more than once. So they must be worried about me tripping over something bigger than desertion or horse theft."

She demurely said, "If there is anything *I* can do for you, seeing you have lost your rather large translator, don't hesitate to call on me."

He said he would as he got to his feet, feeling that *akvavit* she'd been dosing him with. It would have been impolite to tell a lady you'd trust her about as far as you'd trust a bitty black widow spider in an outhouse in the dark.

Chapter 31

Longarm's next stop was the waterfront Western Union, to wire a progress report to his home office and see if they'd sent anything new to him in care of the telegraph office.

They had. Marshal Vail was getting discouraged by the way the can of worms had turned into a bucket, and wanted the government to put more field agents on the case or let Longarm come on home.

Longarm sent a longer day letter, and wired some questions to the other government offices he'd considered of late. Then he stepped back out in the bright but tolerable April sunlight, unaware of a lazy-looking cuss in dockworker's garb they'd posted across the way lest Longarm do what he'd just done.

At the hospital they told him Don Hernan had left on his own and hopped the ferry boat back to Matamoros the morning after the shooting. They told him at the desk that the only way a flesh wound killed you was if you got gangrene. Longarm already knew that. So he asked to see Mademoiselle Pouchard from France.

A plain-faced but nicely built nurse in a starched white cap and apron led him down a corridor reeking of naptha soap and phenol to where the stenographer from the French consulate had her private room and a whole lot of flowers.

Her pals had every right to worry about her. The Prophet

Brigham Young of the Latter-day Saints had been able to afford the best of modern medicine, and his mortified appendix had still killed him.

Nobody knew what in thunder the human appendix was good for. A body could live without one, although taking it out was a dangerous procedure indeed. That Professor Darwin had suggested it could have evolved from something like the blind gut of a sheep they made those expensive condoms out of.

It was easy to think of condoms when you were smiling down at a small French gal with ribbons in her taffy-colored curls and firm perky tits barely hidden under her thin white hospital gown.

Longarm handed her the bag of gumdrops he'd brought her as he introduced himself and made sure, praise the Lord, she spoke some English. She asked him to sit a spell. So he did, and got right to the point.

He said, "They tell me you were standing near the front windows, talking to Don Hernan Obregon, the night of that ball when Count Atterdag got shot out front."

She nodded thoughtfully and decided, "*Mais oui, monsieur le agent*. I remember the incident well. I heard the shot when someone shot *le pauvre bet*."

Longarm had known French Canadian gals in his time. So he was able to ask, "*Bet?* You're sure that pony was hit too?"

She shook her pretty head and replied, "I meant to say beast. The words are so much the same in both tongues. I referred to the species of Danish beast someone shot that evening, *Monsieur le agent*. The fat species of *danois* had insult half *les femmes* of Brownsville during his short time in Texas, *hein*? That same night at the ball he is ask me if I have ever tasted Danish sausage, and if I had desire to see his."

Longarm whistled softly and said, "I heard he was a mean drunk. A mean drunk with a mouth like that could surely make a bunch of serious enemies in a short time. But you were witness to the simple fact that Don Hernan Obregon was inside, talking to you about something a mite more refined, when you both heard that one shot, right?"

She said, "*Mais non,* not exactly. I have been over by the corner of the ballroom you inquire of me, breathing air of freshness after a *tres fatigué* polka. Don Hernan have come over to request of me the next dance. *Mais man programme,* he is filled for the next six dances. So perhaps he goes to ask someone else. Perhaps he is only steps away. I do not remember even thinking about that married Mexican when I hear the shot, glance outside, and see that poor dying beast out on the pavement."

Longarm whistled again and decided, "You just knocked down a whole house of cards I'd been building, Lord love you, *mademoiselle.* I'd been told you and Don Hernan were gossiped about around your consulate."

Mademoiselle Pouchard looked as if her appendix had acted up again, and sort of sobbed, "*Mais* he must be almost forty, and *married*! Why would I wish to be with a married man of middle age? I know who told you that, the species of cow! *Eh bien,* two can play at gossip most vile! Madame du Prix has only been spreading those stories of me and her Mexican lover to keep her own husband in the dark!"

Longarm blinked and asked, "Do you know for a fact that Madame du Prix and Obregon are lovers, or did you get that from somebody I might have talked to earlier?"

Mademoiselle Pouchard insisted, "I caught them myself. Only kissing, it is true. But what would two married people be doing in a private office, kissing with the door locked, if they were not more than friends, *hein*?"

Longarm smiled thinly and decided, "I doubt either her husband or his wife would see it any way but your own, *mademoiselle.* But no offense, didn't you just tell me they'd locked the door first?"

She answered simply, "*Mais oui.* It was the private office of Madame du Prix. I opened the door with a key she had given me. I did not of course know anyone was in there when I went to see if she have left me any typing on her desk. I naturally knock on the door before I unlock it. They must not have hear me, *hein*?"

Longarm kept a straight face—it wasn't easy—as he dryly remarked the couple had likely been too busy making plans to go farther, right there or somewhere else. He decided,

"Somewhere else sounds more *practique*, as you folks say. I know Madame du Prix is inclined to stray all over town without an escort, and a rogue such as Obregon must know more than one handy place for some slap-and-tickle in a town this size. But I reckon that's their business and none of my own. Do you have anyone aside from that Danish-born wayward wife at your consulate who could manage the Danish language like a native?"

She looked sincerely confused and said, "*Mais non!* Monsieur Henri only gave the position of translator to a diplomat's wife when they told him she spoke such an *autre* language. Why do you ask?"

He said, "Hell hath no fury, and Obregon is rich as well as a good-looking snake charmer. Somebody wrote a letter about him in Danish and posted it, or had it posted, so everybody might think it came from a hostile witness I've been hunting. I wouldn't have been sent after him if it hadn't looked as if he'd witnessed the killing of Count Atterdag from an angle of vantage. The letter allows he did, and that Obregon was the killer. You just punched a hole in Obregon's big fib about you being ready and willing to alibi him."

"Then why do you not arrest the villain as the assassin?" she asked in a perfectly logical way.

Longarm said, "Obregon has diplomatic immunity. And I have it from more than one Danish speaker that the letter was penned by somebody totally at ease in a Copenhagen beer garden. I'd like Madame du Prix as the letter writer better if Obregon had insulted her with remarks about his hot tamale, or had taken his hot tamale back and left her feeling sore. How do I find out if the two of them are still swapping spit in her office, *mademoiselle*?"

The young stenographer suggested he ask her superior, Madame Laverne, who was paid to keep an eye on every female worker in the place.

He didn't tell her he'd already talked to Madame Laverne. But he had to grin as he considered talking to her some more. Sigridur lighting out on him and a night on a sofa with a real redhead bedded down so near and yet so far away had

227

given him renewed respect for the way that henna-rinsed old gal could move her bony rump.

He excused himself from Mademoiselle Pouchard, and asked if there was anything he could fetch for her from the outside world. She smiled up at him, said *"Non, merci,"* but invited him to come back and see her some more before they shipped her home to France.

Outside in the hallway, he asked that no-nonsense nurse how things looked for the little French gal. The nurse asked if he was kin or "involved" with the patient, and once Longarm had told her more about who he was and what he'd been doing in there, the nurse said simply, "She's dying. Seventy-two hours at the most."

Longarm stopped, swung to face her, and demanded, "How can you say that? She looked fine to me just now!"

The nurse replied, gently but firmly, "You're not a doctor, or even a nurse. She has no temperature. There is not the slightest sign of pus in her sutured incision. She has a good appetite and claims to be feeling fine."

Longarm replied uncertainly, "I just said that."

The nurse said, "There is *always* post-operative infection. When we have to go in after a mortified appendix, and a good many doctors don't think the new procedure is worth the risk, you expect and hope for what we call laudible pus. As a sign that the body is fighting those microbes Pasteur has been investigating, speaking of France."

Longarm said, "I've had me some pus-cuts and boils in my time. I wasn't sure they were *good* for me, but now that you mention it, they told me at a place called Shiloh to pray for pus in a bullet wound."

The nurse nodded and said, "Straw-colored laudible pus. Green pus is a danger sign. No pus at all means septicemia, or blood poisoning."

"Can't anything be done for her?" Longarm demanded, adding, "She's so young and pretty!"

The nurse looked away to murmur, "A lot of them are pretty, and the ugly ones want to live just as much. Maybe someday we'll be able to cope with Pasteur's little pets a bit better, but as I just told you, seventy-two hours at the most."

Longarm thanked the nurse anyway, and blundered outside for some fresh air and sunshine, telling himself he was too big to cry.

It was best to keep busy, and he had more chores than you could shake a stick at. So he figured he'd go over to the U.S. Customs House and talk to those two old school chums some more. Camilla Nansen's suggestion they might be more than that to one another was spiteful, even if it was true. But it sure might explain a few things, if only he could decide one way or the other about that.

It was starting to warm up a tad. Not enough to make him shuck his frock coat, but enough to inspire him to cut catty-corner across the cobbles to the shady side of the street.

Before he reached the shade, a voice rang out behind him loud and clear, *"Achtung, Long! Duck!"*

So Longarm did as all hell busted loose, too close for comfort. He dove headfirst to the cobbles and horse apples, drawing his own side arm as he landed on his left shoulder and rolled to land prone with his gun muzzle following every shift of his eyes as they took in a swirl of movement obscured by gunsmoke filling half the damned street.

A bearded raggedy cuss sporting a Texas hat, a Schofield .45, and red splashes on his dirty work shirt emerged from the gunsmoke like a shot-up battle cruiser from a fog bank, staring goggle-eyed at Longarm as he called him something in some outlandish lingo and swung his six-gun up to back his hostile words.

So Longarm shot him, and he staggered back into the smoke to whatever fate awaited him there.

After a time, police whistles commenced to chirp like robin birds on a misty morn as the gunsmoke slowly cleared.

After he could see well enough to matter, Longarm saw one tall figure standing alone with three other gents laid low between him and Longarm. The man's smoking six-gun hung down at his side politely as Longarm held his fire. The man called out, "Where have you been hit?" in a slight accent.

Longarm called back, "Nowhere. Was that you just now who told me to duck?"

The mysterious stranger pointed casually at one of the

229

three men he'd just gunned, and answered simply, "I thought it wise. They were about to shoot you from behind just now."

Longarm got to his feet and holstered his own .44-40 as he moved closer to the now-more-familiar outline. He said, "That's three I owe you and I'm much obliged. Ain't you that Herr von Braun from the Prussian consulate?"

The lean and hungry-looking rodent-faced Prussian, in a frock coat that Longarm would have had to save for all summer, clicked his heels, bowed his straw planter's hat slightly, and said he was at Longarm's service.

Longarm said, "I reckon you've already served me about as much as one man can serve another, without acting queer. But can you tell me why? I don't mean why you *saved* me. I never said you weren't an honest officer and gentleman. I meant can you tell me why these fools were out to backshoot me just now."

Before von Braun could answer, they were joined by a pair of blue-uniformed copper badges, who naturally demanded some explanations.

The Prussian began to calmly reload his big horse pistol, a European make Longarm was unfamiliar with, as he told the Brownsville law, "I am Herr Kurt von Braun of the Prussian consulate here in your city. I have diplomatic immunity."

The older and more weary-looking of the copper badges sighed and said, "We never asked you if you had a hunting license, Dutch. We want you to tell us who shot them, how come, and who they might have *been*, dad blast it!"

Von Braun finished reloading as he told them, "I shot all three of them. I had to. They were about to shoot this other gentleman here."

Longarm had already reached for his wallet, but before he could flash his badge the disgusted-looking older patrolman said, "We know who you are and we we told to steer clear of you, Longarm. Has this something to do with that assassination you're working on? The three of them look more like saddle tramps than international whatevers."

Longarm honestly replied, "I've never seen any of 'em

before, but I seriously doubt they could be riders of the Texican persuasion.''

The junior copper badge hunkered down to start patting down the handiest cadaver. Von Braun put his gun away in his newfangled shoulder holster and said, ''Don't look at *me*. If they had been Prussian secret agents, I would not have had to shoot them. Perhaps they were simply vagabonds, as you suggest, with some grudge against this other American law officer.''

The copper badge on his haunches held open a wallet to declare, ''This one was passing himself off as Mr. Tom Jones of the Indian Nation. He sure don't look Indian or even breed to me.''

Others were crowding closer by then. Von Braun nudged Longarm and murmured, ''Come. They can't stop either of us, and there is nothing here for us now.''

Longarm said, ''Hold on. I'd like to see if I can figure out who they were and how come they were out to gun me more than just this one time!''

The rodent-faced Prussian insisted, ''I can tell you who they were. I can tell why they had orders to kill you. So why don't we go over to my office and have the private conversation we probably should have had earlier?''

Chapter 32

Von Braun's private office was on the cooler top floor of the nearby Prussian consulate. He had a spiked helmet mounted on the wall, as if he'd shot another Prussian, or more likely his fool self, and mounted it yonder as a trophy. All the other trophies on that same wall were elk antlers. They didn't have elk in South Texas. A man who had his hunting trophies shipped in from other parts took his hunting seriously.

The desk was bigger than it needed to be, and the diplomatic drink of the day seemed to be iced lager, laced with a stronger hard liquor. Von Braun sat Longarm in a guest chair that Billy Vail was going to hear about, a batman in Prussian blue brought him some sausage and rye sandwiches, and then von Braun himself dug out a swamping rifle and placed it on the desktop on Longarm's side as he said, "The experimental Mauser eleven-millimeter repeating rifle. A blend of their reliable bolt-action Gewehr, '71 single-shot and your own Winchester's expired patent."

When Longarm set aside his beer stein to pick up the handsome new rifle and work the bolt, he saw it was empty.

Von Braun said, "It loads eight rounds in the tubular magazine and carries one in the chamber, very carefully."

Longarm frowned and said, "I was led to expect fifteen rounds in the tube and one in the chamber, like my Winchester."

The Prussian shook his close-cropped head, and explained, "Your Winchester loads glorified pistol rounds. This military model loads with a worthy rival to your own army's .45-70, meant for serious work at longer ranges. So naturally you can fit fewer longer cartridges in a magazine about the same length. That tubular magazine is one of the sticking points our General Staff has asked the Mauser brothers to rethink. The percussion cap of a .44-40 resting on the blunt tip of the bullet behind it seems to work safely enough. A string of eight high-powered rounds going off like noisy dominoes could make quite a mess in the center of a military column, *nicht wahr?*"

Longarm grimaced at the picture, shut the bolt, and set the repeater aside to pick up his stein again as he asked, "What *are* you boys in Prussian blue shooting folks with these days, if you ain't ready to buy modern repeaters?"

Von Braun circled the desk to sit down himself as he replied in a sort of smug tone, "The reliable Gewehr '71, of course. The Mausers based their improved brass-cartridge single-shot bolt-action on the more delicate Von Dreyse Needle Gun of 1840. We walked all over the Danes, Austrians, and French with the Needle Gun, but its weak spot was those paper cartridges. Once reliable brass was developed by your own Remington firm, the Mausers found it possible to do away with that long delicate firing pin of the Needle Gun, and the General Staff has been most content with their Gewehr '71."

"Then how did this repeater come into being?" asked Longarm.

Von Braun said, "All the major arms makers have been trying to push repeating rifles for years. To begin with, they can charge more for them. Our General Staff should not be thought of as a bunch of crusty old crabs. Ask the people Herr Bismarck has been so forced to reason with how old-fashioned we Prussians are. Your own experienced marcher, General Sherman, has come down on the side of single-shot breechloaders in the ongoing heated debate. It is true the Indians at Little Big Horn had some repeating rifles, along with their bows and arrows. It is true the Turks cut up more than one Russian column with repeating Winchesters in '77.

But it becomes a matter of logistics. A matter that has yet to be solved.''

He sipped some suds himself, and continued. ''A trained soldier can get off six rounds a minute with a single-shot breechloader such as our Gewehr '71 or your Springfield .45-70. That means over three thousand rounds a minute for a regiment, or thirty thousand rounds in the average ten-minute skirmish.''

Longarm nodded soberly and said, ''I read the *Army Times* now and again at the Denver Public Library. I was in a war one time. I know that when you talk about bringing up more ammo, you're talking *tonnage*.''

The Prussian said, ''Exactly. I was in action against the French at Sedan. Their Chassepots were about as good as our Needle Guns, if the winners had not written the history books. We won because, as one of your own Confederate generals advised, we usually got there *fustess with the mostess*. We were helped a great deal by Napoleon the Third assuming he was Napoleon the First and assuming personal command. But I can tell you it was often a near thing keeping our troops in light paper cartridges day after day. Can you imagine the ordnance problem any army would have if all its troops were happily blasting away with repeating rifles?''

Longarm said, ''Yep. Like you just said, repeaters worked swell at Little Big Horn and the Russo-Turkish War. I've sent some wires out on that shady arms dealer they call El Turco, by the way. Do you reckon Mr. Ben Hakim was there when his countrymen cut the Russian Army up with repeating rifles?''

Von Braun sniffed and said, ''Flukes don't count in military science. Our military observers study such events first-hand, or interview any survivors they can get to talk about such matters. It is true your Seventh Cavalry rode into battle armed with six-shooters and single-shot carbines. It is true your Colonel Custer refused to drag a pair of Gatling guns along. They would have fired twelve hundred rounds a minute between them, and Custer's column pack mules were already heavily laden with all the ammunition they could carry.''

''It wasn't enough,'' said Longarm quietly.

The Prussian nodded and said, "My point exactly. As you have to know, the Indians only wiped out a third of the regiment that noisy day in '76. The third of the Seventh that died on Last Stand Ridge with Custer left us no detailed records of that action, and one doubts the conflicting Indian accounts could all be right. From what I have read, and from my own experience in the field, I would say Custer had the right idea with the wrong subordinates. He would seem to have begun the action according to standard cavalry tactics. But his last dispatch to Benteen's separate column was misunderstood, and I would have found Major Reno guilty when they court-martialed him for not even trying to ride to Custer's aid."

Longarm shrugged and said, "Mayhaps he was too busy over on Reno Hill. Those Indians with those impractical Spencers and Winchesters kept him and Benteen pinned down for close to forty-eight hours."

The Prussian said, "Exactly. Two thirds of the Seventh dug in with their Springfield single-shot .45-70s and held the Indians off until they *ran low on ammunition* and had to withdraw. Those Turks had the same problem the next year against the Czar's slow but steady fire."

Longarm nodded, but pointed out, "Those Icelandic rebels may not have been to military school. I understand the Danish military agrees with you on single-shot hardware and, logistics be damned, I'd hate to be caught on some old glacier with a Remington rolling-block while I was getting peppered with a high-powered repeater!"

Von Braun made a wry face and said, "Mauser is working on a safer design for us, based on the more recent patent of your own James Lee."

"You mean that newfangled box magazine?" asked Longarm. "I read about that notion in *Scientific American*. A bolt-action rifle with that bottom-loading spring-fed box magazine sounds like a real pisser. But if that's what your General Staff is holding out for, how come those Mauser boys made up whole boxcar loads of these deadly rejects?"

Von Braun replied, "They *say* they *didn't*. They tell us they only ran off a dozen or so samples, subject to approval by our ordnance experts, and I told you what they thought of that dangerous tubular magazine.''

Von Braun stared at the rifle between them with distaste and said, ''Perhaps that is what they believe, the supervisors anyway. But a handful of Mauser machinists, working overtime when the lights were low, may well have run off a good many more on their own. As you can see, the experimental model is simply the Gewehr '71 with some simple adaptations. The spring-loaded tube inserted in an easily routed groove in the original forestock, the basic bolt action remachined with a few complex but very small parts, and—''

''You mean somebody went into business for himself,'' Longarm said, cutting in. ''How do you boys know all this, seeing that the Mauser boys say it never happened?''

Von Braun said, ''Prussian Intelligence pays people to *tell* what has been happening.''

Longarm smiled knowingly and asked, ''What did that Heidi Durler you boys set me up with have to tell you about yours truly?''

Von Braun chuckled despite himself, and made no bones about it as he answered simply, ''She reported that you were completely in the dark about the things I've just been telling you. She said you'd been sent to locate that possible witness to that assassination at the French consulate, and that you seemed to know next to nothing about Iceland, or Herr Ben Hakim, alias El Turco. I am telling you more than we really wanted anyone to know because we don't want you to keep thinking we have had anything to do with the several attempts on your life.''

''So who's been after me if it ain't you gents?'' asked Longarm in as delicate a tone as he thought the situation called for.

Von Braun said, ''We know who *some* of them were. Those two you smeared all over the railroad tracks that night in Colorado *were* in fact Icelanders, albeit listed as common criminals by the Danish law authorities.''

''You Prussians have sources amidst the peace officers of other countries?'' Longarm asked mildly.

The rodent-faced Prussian stared right back at him to answer they had spies amidst the *war* officers of other countries, and went on to say, "Be that as it may, Ben Hakim seems to have recruited a ragtag band of sinister types, trying to avoid those with American criminal records. One of those I just shot today was a Hollander who jumped ship after stealing everything that wasn't nailed down in the crew's quarters. The other was a Swede, wanted for manslaughter in Stockholm. The one you shot down in Matamoros had established a Hamburg identity, but he was actually born in Norway."

Longarm asked how anyone knew he'd shot anybody down Mexico way.

The Prussian just smiled across the desk at him.

Longarm said, "Ask a stupid question and you don't deserve much of an answer. Tell me more about this Ben Hakim cuss. I've heard tell of him, but not much. Ask any two informants along the border and you get three descriptions. He's here, he's there, he's doing this, or nope, he's doing that. He reminds me of the tales you hear about old Juaquin Murieta out California way. He was a simple peace-loving Mexican the forty-niners wouldn't leave alone, he was a proud grandee who'd lost his *rancho* to a gringo sharper, or mayhaps he never existed at all. That head in a jar in that Frisco flea museum could have come off most anyone, and there's this Mexican lady who swears it was her true love, an honest young *vaquero* the posse just shot for the reward."

Von Braun said, "Ben Hakim is all too real. We have transcriptions of his dossier, compiled by the Constantinople police. They want him on every charge but incest, and they say that is only because nobody can find where he hid his mother's body. Nobody knows just when or how he arrived in America. He first surfaced in Mexico right after your Civil War, selling guns to both sides in the Mexican revolution against that ridiculous Austrian Archduke Maximilian. Since then we know he has run guns to the Canadian Metís separatists, the Irish Fennians, and of course the Mexican rebels who keep rebelling against the ones who rebelled against Maximilian. We live in exciting times, *nicht wahr*?"

Longarm said, "Somebody who ain't supposed to have one is always in the market for a gun. You figure some crooks at that Mauser plant in Prussia produced Lord knows how many of these wicked weapons on their own and sent 'em to El Turco to sell to the Icelanders?''

''Or Mexicans,'' von Braun replied, explaining, ''He's said to sell to the highest bidder. Count Atterdag suspected they'd been unloaded here in South Texas, with access to either rebel movement, with some sort of auction in mind.''

Longarm blinked and said, ''You'd gotten to that Danish count too? I'd heard he was looking into complaints from your government, but I had no idea you were so close. Didn't you have a war with the Danes one time?''

Von Braun said, ''More than one time. I first met Svein Atterdag when he was a prisoner of war in Berlin. Before you ask, anything you may have heard about him being a nasty drunk, a womanizer with neither the looks nor common sense required, or an arrogant bastard to his fellow Danes are all true. But he was a bulldog at investigating the irregularities of others, with a keen grasp of the military sciences.''

''Then you figure El Turco masterminded his assassination?'' asked Longarm.

The Prussian replied without hesitation, ''Why not? Hasn't his gang been trying very hard to assassinate *you*?''

Longarm studied on that before he decided, ''That's what it looks like. I'd just started working on it as horse theft. I don't suppose you know whether El Turco deals in horses as well as guns?''

The Prussian said he'd heard nothing like that, or even where on earth the sinister but mighty secretive Ben Hakim could be hiding out. He said, ''The last firm location we had on him was over in the Sierra Madre Occidental. He'd been selling guns to the Yaqui and Apache, to fight one another, when the Yaqui attacked his trading post and wiped it out.''

Longarm said, ''I'm glad. Those Indians might not raid so much if there was nothing expensive to buy with their loot. But what in hell is El Turco doing on this coast if the Yaqui wiped him out to the west?''

Von Braun answered simply, ''I told you. Selling guns to the highest bidder. He naturally got away from those Indians. Since then, he seems to have set up shop somewhere here in

Cameron County. We are still trying to find out just where that might be.''

"So you could turn him over to the Rangers?'' Longarm asked. Then he caught the look in the Prussian's cold gray eyes and quickly added, "Never mind. Ask a stupid question and guess what the answer from a cuss with diplomatic immunity is going to be.''

Chapter 33

La Siesta had set in by the time Longarm left the Prussian consulate, knowing more but not nearly enough. Despite the hour, the April day had never gotten past balmy. So Longarm walked over to the French consulate. Fooling with a pony could be a bother when it was a French lady you had in mind for fooling with. He told himself he had good cause, as a tracker, to make certain nobody had fired that fatal shot at Atterdag from Madame Laverne's love nest under those front steps.

When he got to the corner of the block the French grounds took up, he paused in the noonday shade of a street tree to finish the cheroot he'd lit along the way. So that honey-blond Madame du Prix didn't seem to notice him as she suddenly popped out the front of the consulate to tear across to those oleanders and hug them as she headed the other way.

Longarm got rid of his smoke and crossed over to hug the same shade as he tailed her, muttering, "That's about when *I'd* light out unescorted if I was up to something I might not want my husband to know about."

The Danish gal married to the French diplomat ducked around the next corner. So Longarm was free to lope after her along the deserted street. He reined himself in at the same corner, risked a peek around it, and caught Madame du Prix and Don Hernan Obregon swapping spit and hugging fit to bust by a buckboard pulled over in the shade of another street tree.

Then the married Mexican helped the married Dane up to the sprung seat, and went around to climb up beside her, gather the ribbons, and drive off at a goddamned trot as Longarm cursed himself for having left both ponies at the damned *posada*!

He waited until they swung around another corner before he broke cover and ran after tham flat out. He had long legs and low heels to work with, but it was still a near thing as he made it the next corner and just had them in sight. He was wondering how long he could keep such shit up when he saw they were pulling over, Lord love the two of them!

Risking a closer approach along the shady side, Longarm saw Obregon had handed the reins of his team to a Mexican kid so he could take the blonde by one elbow and steer her toward the entrance of a sort of seedy hotel.

As Longarm drew closer, he decided, ''After you've been dining high-toned on white linen all your life, hot tamales wrapped in newsprint might tickle your fancy just fine.''

He approached the hotel taproom with a separate entrance on the street, and ducked inside. But instead of ordering a drink, he eased over to the archway leading to the hotel lobby, and sure enough, neither one of them were to be seen. The sly dog had paid and registered in advance. It reminded Longarm of a couple of times *he'd* been as sly.

Striding over to the hotel desk, Longarm flashed his badge and identification at the small, bald day clerk and said, ''Before you tell me you don't have to tell me without a warrant, I can *get* a warrant, and I'll bet you a silver dollar you can't tell me nothing about that couple as just came through this lobby.''

The clerk replied without hesitation, ''That would be Señor and Señora Herrero of Matamoros. They've stayed with us earlier. Before you say it, I know Herrero means Smith in Mex. Business is business, and I only work here.''

Longarm snapped the promised cartwheel on the fake marble desktop and said, ''I'm glad to see we're getting along so well. I got another dollar says you can't tell me which room they're in and let me set a spell in the room next to it."

The clerk said, "Give me *two*, and the dollar-a-day room is yours until noon tomorrow."

So Longarm did, and pocketed the key, allowing he'd see if they served any sandwiches in the taproom next door before he went on up.

They did. Longarm had them make him up a ham and cheese and a sardine and mustard, both on rye, and bag them for him to sneak up the stairs with.

As he turned around, he spied Camilla Nansen from the Danish consulate seated in a booth with that Sam Steinmuller from the shipping line. They were both staring curiously at him. So he went on over.

He said, "Howdy. Small world, ain't it?"

Steinmuller smiled awkwardly and said, "All right, we followed you. Never run past people that fast if you don't want them to wonder a tad about you."

The petite Danish widow in black silk and matching sun-bonnet said, "We know who you were running after. That brazen Margrethe du Prix and that married Mexican passed by just ahead of you! Are they somewhere upstairs in this den of wickedness?"

Longarm set his bag on the table and sat down by Steinmuller, across from her, to reply, "Room 207. I was just fixing to carry these sandwiches up to Room 208. I ain't interested in the noises next door before they die down to pillow conversation."

Steinmuller said, "See here, Deputy Long, that's hardly the sort of thing a lady wants to hear about!"

Camilla said, "Speak for yourself, Sam." She turned back to Longarm. "What do *you* suspect them of, aside from funny noises? *I'd* like to know why a Danish woman is doing anything with a Mexican suspected of killing a Danish count!"

Longarm said, "That's about the size of it, ma'am. Madame du Prix would make a swell suspect if she'd had any reason to write that letter posted from Laredo. But would you write letters calling a man you were kissing behind your husband's back a murderer?"

She demurely replied, "I only cheated on my second husband, but now that you mention it, I never accused the sweet young officer I'd taken up with of murder."

Sam Steinmuller looked flustered and declared, "I wish you folks wouldn't talk that way in front of us children. I do business with Don Hernan, and what he does with other men's wives is no business of mine as long as it's not *my* wife up there with him!"

He asked Longarm to let him out of the booth, and told Camilla he had to get back to his office.

She told him sweetly to go ahead. So he did. As soon as they were alone in the booth, Longarm smiled uncertainly and said, "Correct me if I'm wrong, but ain't you and old Sam . . . you know?"

She said, "You're wrong. There are occasions when we'd rather use Sam's American shipping line, and you just heard him say he had a wife. As he told you, we were across the way, having met on the street by chance, when first that buckboard and then you tore past us at a pace to arouse anyone's interest. Don't you think we should go up to your room and see if we can hear what they are up to?"

He didn't say anything about those wooden steps he'd been meaning to investigate with Madame Laverne. He helped her out of the booth, and paid the tab Steinmuller had left him—along with Camilla, Lord love him.

The room upstairs was dark and dingy. Longarm allowed it would be safer to sit on the top surface of the chenille comforter spread across the brass-framed bed. Camilla whispered that like every woman who'd ever read a "realistic" novel, she'd often wondered what it would be like to stay in a sordid hotel with a strange man.

He whispered back, "Aw, I ain't so strange. Keep your voice down, and we'll use these two hotel tumblers by the water pitcher to see if we can hear through the wall."

They could. They had to take their hats off to press the open ends of the tumblers to the plaster and lean their ears against the glass bottoms. Voices from the other side sounded faint, but clearer, and the first thing they heard was that gal demanding, "Deeper, damn you! Shove it all the way up my ass and come in my bowels!"

Longarm tried not to blush. The petite brunette whispered, "Why would she want him to do that? Wouldn't it hurt?"

To which he could only reply, "I've never let nobody do that to *me*, Miss Camilla."

"Nor I," said the widow woman who'd surely had some experience with at least two men. Three, if you counted that officer she'd owned up to without being asked.

He straightened up and suggested, "Let's share those sandwiches. I doubt they'll be talking about assassinations or gunrunners for a spell."

She whispered that she wanted to hear more. So Longarm got out the two sandwiches, cut each in half with his pocket knife, and silently offered her a sample of both.

She whispered, big-eyed, "He's committing a crime against nature! She let him sodomize her and now, in return, he's trying to make her climax with his tongue, and he has a mustache!"

Longarm managed not to laugh out loud—it wasn't easy—and handed her some grub as he whispered, "Most Mexicans do. Mexican gals say kissing a man without a mustache is like eating an egg without salt."

You didn't need a tumbler against the wall to guess what they were up to now. Madame du Prix was one of those gals who couldn't come without letting the whole neighborhood know about it. It was small wonder Obregon liked to eat her a couple of streets over from her husband's office! It was giving Longarm an erection in spite of the distaste he now felt for the two-faced honey-blonde. He had a vivid imagination, and she had a mighty graphic way of describing the way she felt it in her toes when he sucked her nipples so hard.

Camilla had put aside her half-sandwich and put her head and a tumbler against the wall again as Longarm sat on the bed to eat the other sandwich and a half. He'd finished when Camilla came over to hand him the last bit of sardines and mustard on rye as she whispered, "I don't think they were plotting to assassinate anyone or run any guns to anybody after all. I think they've fallen asleep, unless they've managed to kill one another. What on earth could have made her that wild? I am not a blushing virgin, and all couples experiment, within the bounds of common-sense regard for life and limb. But those two . . ."

Forbidden fruit," Longarm said, softly explaining, "If those two had all the time they could need for making love to one another, they'd likely sneak off to go *loco en la cabeza* with somebody married up with somebody else. They ain't getting as much out of one another as each lets on. They're both showing off. He's playing the Latin lover making love to a Viking princess. She's the respectable wife of a diplomat giving herself barnyard-style to a greaser in a third-rate hotel. They say those Ancient Romans with all the slave girls and boys they wanted took to fooling around with critters, one another, and anything else for a new thrill. What's that the French might say at her husband's consulate about *vive la* whatever?"

Being a diplomat, Camilla said, "*Vive la différence!* But I've always thought an occasional change of *partners,* behaving in less disgusting ways, might be nicer."

She glanced around at the dingy plaster and tattered window shades to add with a sigh, "I don't know why. Perhaps it's because this horrid little hotel is not at all suitable to refined romance, but it's a good thing you're here because, if I were alone right now, I might end up playing with myself!"

Longarm rose from the bed to take her in his arms as he smiled down at her upturned smile and said, "That makes two of us. Are you by any chance a Prussian spy, ma'am?"

She stared up thuderstruck and replied, "Good heavens, what gave you that idea? Of course I'm not a Prussian spy, you big silly!"

He said, "In that case I reckon it's all right," and then he kissed her.

She kissed back a lot, and commenced to rub her black silk against his brown tweed. But then she pulled back and said, "Wait, Custis, I wasn't serious about wanting to masturbate in a dingy little hotel!"

He said he'd never ask a pal to do anything like that when they had one another to fall back on. Then they both fell across that comforter so he could run his free hand over her compact, silk-covered curves as he kissed her some more.

She twisted her lips just free enough to murmur, "Please, Custis! I was only teasing you. Maybe I was teasing both of us. I don't know what I mean. This whole sordid scene has me so confused!"

He said, "Me too, ma'am. But if you want to get up from the table as the cards are being dealt, so be it. I only meant to play a friendly game with a lady I took for another sport."

As he let go of her and sat up, Camilla just lay there, pouting up at him. "Is that all this is to you, a *game*?"

He said, "Never mind what a mere man says at times like this, Miss Camilla. I've learned the hard way that you ladies tend to twist anything we say into what you want to say we said. I reckon you're right about those game-players next door. They've shown one another how dirty they can talk and now they're sleeping it off. So I'd be proud to see you back to your office or anywhere else you'd like to go right now."

She murmured, "I don't want to go back to my office, and it's siesta time. Almost everything will be closed until later this afternoon."

He shrugged and said, "I got nothing more exciting to suggest, seeing you don't want to spend your siesta the way I thought you did. The more fool me. You're right about one thing. A body does need privacy to satisfy his or her fool self by hand."

She began to caress herself through that sheer black silk as she sobbed, "I know. I can't stand it. I want you. I need you. But please take me slowly and gently at first. It's been so long since I've been with a man and, oh, Custis, I'm so frightened and confused!"

So they started over, slowly and gently as she'd asked, until he had her out of that black silk and just as beautiful in the altogether as an ivory statuette.

Then he had his own duds off, and she began to cry when she saw what he'd been saving up for her to pleasure. But of course, once he got it in, with a little effort, she proceeded to move under him with all the enthusiasm she'd likely shown two husbands and at least one lover. So if they didn't hear her in the next room over, they were likely sound sleepers indeed.

246

Afterwards, as Longarm and Camilla lay there sharing a smoke, she wanted him to take her back to his *posada* to spend the night. But he told her he had to go down to Matamoros again, now that he was starting to figure lots of things out at last.

Chapter 34

Once he'd parted with Camilla in front of the Danish consulate with a discreet handshake, Longarm legged it over to the Western Union to send more wires and pick up the few answers commencing to trickle in. Then he went back to that photograph gallery, and asked that nice old well-built and sweet-smelling lady if it was safe to assume members high and low of Brownsville's considerable foreign community had pictures of themselves taken in Texas to send home.

He hit the jackpot. Or leastways, they had a studio portrait of Private Pall Njalsson on file. She said he could have it for two bits because they had the glass negative in the back.

He paid her willingly, and allowed he owed her more. The sepia-tone print was that of a young cuss in what really did look like the outfit of that toy soldier described by Mr. Hans Christian Andersen, complete with crossed white webbing that held a cartridge box on one of his hips and a sword bayonet on the other. The face under the high-peaked shako looked younger and dumber than Longarm had been picturing. But you couldn't tell from his picture how well he spoke Danish.

The nice-smelling gallery gal asked what the law needed the picture for. She said, "I hope Private Njalsson hasn't done anything wrong. He seemed like such a nice boy."

Longarm said, "Well, at the very least he seems to be

guilty of desertion and horse theft, ma'am. But neither are federal offenses. I'm just looking for purloined letters. Things that could be right out in front of you if only you knew what you were looking at."

She didn't seem to follow his drift. He didn't blame her. That process of eliminating could be a bitch for a paid-up lawman. He asked if they took many pictures of Icelanders, Danes, Norwegians, and such, seeing there seemed to be a Scandinavian community there in South Texas. She said that if there was, it was news to her. For most of South Texas had been settled by Mexicans or Scotch-Irish, with High Dutch and Black Irish, who'd come over in the late '40's, a lot more evident than Scandinavians.

He said he'd noticed folks from northern climes seemed less able to take the heat that far south, and they parted friendly.

He went next to the U.S. Customs House to ask Harold Andersen if he was any relation to the late Hans Christian and to say he had just a few more questions.

The Treasury man sighed and said, "No, Eric is not here and neither one of us parts our hair that way. He was mighty upset to hear Baron Senderborg had sent a letter to Washington accusing me of sheltering an old school chum because I was a sodomite and he'd been my fag at Cambridge. To begin with, we were both in the same class, and one of the reasons we became such good friends was that we two and a half-dozen like-minded lads stood up to the upper-class sodomites."

Before Longarm could ask, Andersen said, "There weren't as many as some think. Most of them were decent enough to stay out of the fight. But it did leave Eric and me old comrades in arms, and anyone could see they were trying to frame him for that puffed-up nobleman's murder."

"I wanted to ask him about that," said Longarm. "You say he's gone off, risking his immunity from arrest?"

Andersen answered simply, "He's gone off to St. Paul, Minnesota, where he has some Norwegian friends who have a pretty daughter. Eric was already disgusted with his almost feudal monarchy before that pompous ass Atterdag helped himself to Eric's favorite mount without bothering to ask the favor. He says it will serve Denmark right if the Icelanders, the Eskimos, and the cane cutters over in the Virgin Islands all revolt and pepper the Royal Danish Marines with repeating rifles!''

Longarm said, ''Private Njalsson didn't think much of his future as a Royal Marine either. So let's talk about how you'd move a whole lot of Mauser eleven-millimeter repeating rifles from hereabouts to Iceland. Sam Steinmuller says none of the vessels with his shipping line put in to Reykjavik as a regular port of call. It would be noticeable if one was sent there *irregularly*, right?''

Andersen looked pained, and insisted, ''Damn it, I've had this dumb conversation with that ass von Braun more than once! I don't care *how* many Prussian police informants say they saw those rifles go aboard that screw clipper, the *Trinity*. They were never aboard her when she put in here, and this was her only port of call this side of Hamburg!''

''How can you be so certain?'' Longarm demanded. ''Seems to me I could stop just long enough to unload a few cases of most anything up the Inland Passage a piece if I was the skipper of any oceangoing vessel.''

The customs inspector shook his head and said, ''You could if you were able to captain and crew a three-masted sail-and-steam clipper all by yourself! Common seamen talk, unless they're paid so much you'd hardly call them common seamen. I told you I had this out with von Braun. He admits the Iron Chancellor's police spies would have told on any skipper carrying a Prussian cargo stopping anywhere but the port it had been assigned to. It was a long tedious sea voyage, with more than one of the American crewmen refusing to ever go back aboard. But the *Trinity* put in here with her cargo intact and agreeing with her bill of lading. Are you going to accuse me of taking part in some crazy Icelandic plot because of my part-Danish ancestry?''

Longarm shook his head and said, ''Not hardly. Like you said, crew members talk, and nobody suspects you inspect cargo holds all by yourself. Does the name Ben Hakim or El Turco mean anything to you?''

Andersen said, ''Of course. I have some wanted fliers on him filed away somewhere. He was a notorious smuggler who sold duty-free guns to Mexican bandits and wild Indians. We've been given to understand he's dead, according to the Mexican *rurales*."

Longarm said, "So have we. But you never know. Might you have a county business directory you could spare me, pard?"

Andersen said, "Business, residential, and shipping, if you'd care to tell me why. Are you expecting to find Ben Hakim listed under gun sales?"

Longarm smiled thinly and said, "Anything's possible. But I was told outlandish names are sort of rare in these parts, and I ought to be able to figure out Turkish or Icelandic names. Icelanders would spell Andersen with an extra S, wouldn't they?"

The Danish-American said, "I think so. Their logic is that it means Ander's Son and so that's how it ought to be spelled. Eric says they can be stubborn as well as backwards."

So Longarm was soon on his way with the thin directories in a side pocket. He had supper at a stand-up tamale stand, and saw he'd timed it about right when he boarded the ferry boat to Matamoros with a crowd of seamen and cowboys off to purchase a straw *vaquero* and mayhaps get laid.

His own hopes were dashed a mite when he got to La Abogada's *casa* and they made him wait downstairs like a bill collector for a good half hour. When a servant finally took him upstairs, he found his peach-complected old pal fully dressed and looking sort of vexed as she asked if he wasn't taking a lot for granted.

He handed over the candy he'd bought in Texas while waiting to board the ferry boat. He said, "They were selling fireworks for the May Day parade in a few weeks. I'd have brought you some sparklers if I'd known you were in such a dark mood, honey. What have I done wrong?"

She grumbled, "You should send advance word when you are coming. Just because you have been inside a woman does not give you the right to feel she is at your disposal at any time of the day or night. We are trying for to mount a *revolución* here. This is not a *casa de putas* for any *gringo chingado* for to drop by anytime. I have business with other people, you know.''

He said, ''I figured things had to be coming to a head. I've been eliminating like hell. You want to tell me where your pals with the *dinero* are supposed to meet El Turco with the *fusiles repetirantes*?''

She said she didn't know what he was talking about, and commenced to take off her clothes. So he knew she knew what he was talking about.

She beat him into bed. He sat down beside her and took his own duds off, as most men would have, because she sure looked swell and two could play at that same game.

As he spread her peach thighs wide, hooked an elbow under either knee, and let her take the matter in hand to guide it in, he was struck by the wild contrast between her softer and more ample tawny curves and the compact ivory charms of the brunette he'd spent La Siesta with earlier.

He'd spent so much of it with Camilla that he had a time coming as soon as usual in La Abogada. But fortunately, she seemed to take that as a compliment. She moaned, ''Oh, I can feel your passion! Do not hold back, *toro mio*! Let your *palo grueso* rage inside me until I overflow with your lust! *Chingeme! Chingeme mucho!*''

He did his best, as most men would have. She was really as juicy as her peach complexion promised, and lovely to look at while a man was at her. So he found it easy enough to stay stiff as he straightened his arms, raising her thighs and peach-fuzzed rump higher while he watched his wet old organ-grinder sliding in and out of that sliced-peach part in her soft, darker fuzz down yonder.

When he'd shut his eyes to picture whiter skin and more pubic hair of an even darker shade, it drove him wild but, damn it, he wasn't able to come just yet.

He was running out of steam. He didn't want to admit it any more than any other man would have. So he paused at the top of a stroke to demand, ''Tell me where El Turco is holding that auction. It has to be on our side of the border, right?''

She gasped, ''*Dios mio*! Is this the time and place for to speak of *La Causa*? I am almost there! I wish for to die of rapture supreme in your arms and on your *pitón*!''

He shoved it all the way in. She moaned, *''Sí, sí, mucho mas!''*

Then he took it halfway out again and said, ''Let me see if I have it figured straight. Your band has been approached by El Turco with an offer to sell a boxcar load of Mauser eleven-millimeter bolt-action repeaters to the highest bidder. Did he say they'd been rechambered for the U.S. Army .45-70 rounds your own army fires one shot at a time?''

She said, ''*Sí!* Put it back in and tell me how you found that out later, after *yo brinco*! If you are tired, let me get on top!''

He moved in her faster, not wanting to let her take control, as he said, ''I've got most of it figured out. I told you I'd been eliminating like hell. So I figure all these secret visitors you've been having have to mean your big deal is coming to a boil. I know you can't tell me how much you've scraped up to bid against those Icelanders El Turco may sell those guns to if you can't match their top bid. I don't care how many such rival rebels he may have lined up. I don't give a rat's ass whether Iceland or Mexico overthrows any government I don't ride for. I only need to know when and where everyone will get together to bid on those goddamned guns!''

She pouted, ''Stop teasing me! Stop teasing us both! I know you wish for to come in me! I can feel the way it is twitching with desire as you pretend to feel so cold.''

He really wanted to come. So it was easy enough for him to run it in and out a half-dozen times, making her moan with mingled pleasure and frustration, before he paused again in mid-stroke and demanded, ''Just give me a hint. Just tell me which side of the river, doll!''

She sobbed, ''I won't! I can't! You want for to arrest El Turco just because he sells a few guns to Los Apaches for the livestock he can exchange for cash. We do not *wish* for you to arrest so clever a gunrunner. We may need him for to get us more such guns before we win. So I shall never betray El Turco. You may tease me all you want. You may take it out and abuse yourself while I have to do the same. But I shall never tell you which side of the border. Never, never, never!''

She already had, so he proceeded to pleasure her as best he could with such remaining wind as he had. She'd have never been so stubborn had the meeting been planned for the Mexican side of the border. She knew he had no jurisdiction there, and wasn't about to work with *los rurales* because he could only trust a handful and wasn't too sure about *them*, thanks to that bounty certain Mexican sore losers had posted on El Brazo Largo.

As he concentrated on pleasuring the excited beauty with his sated shaft, he discovered that, as many a good-natured whore had on similar occasions, the feeling of unselfish giving could feel sort of nice in itself, the way petting a hound that really enjoyed it could give pleasure to both the petter and the pet. He liked La Abogada, and what the hell, it wouldn't hurt to just screw her till she came, fake coming in her, and then question her some more.

But the funny thing was, when he felt her wet warmth contracting with passion as she gyrated her shapely peach-fuzzed rump in time with his fake passion, his old organ-grinder began to really feel swell, and the next thing he knew he was fixing to come his ownself.

"No más! No más!" she begged him as he commenced to really pound his way to glory.

She moaned, "You are killing me! I can't take any more! You have made me climax and I feel so sensitive and—*ay, carramba*, I am going for to come again!"

That made two of them. But even as he felt himself ejaculating in her down to his insteps, he said, "If you can't tell me where they'll be meeting to hold that auction, at least tell me what time *mañana* they intend to meet!"

She moaned, "Please let me catch my breath *por un momento*! I never said anybody was meeting anywhere *mañana*. You cannot trick me just because I have feelings. I told you I would not tell you when or where that auction is to be held and I meant it, *comprende*?"

He kissed her and just let it soak in her for now. She'd told him the auction would be on his side of the border, and that he had more than twenty-four hours to work with. So what else could he ask for, an egg in his beer?

254

Chapter 35

Late the next night, after the moon went down, the master-mind and eight henchmen were gathered in an empty warehouse at the upstream end of the Brownsville waterfront. The only lights in the cavernous space came from glowing cigar tips and a single coal-oil lamp on a good-sized stack of packing crates with High Dutch markings.

The slicker who'd come up with the complicated negotiations for the transfer of wealth adjusted the bandanna covering a lot of his face and warned the man beside him, near the lamp, "Don't you try any of your Border Mex on our expected guests, Turk. We can't get around letting them see your face and having you do most of the talking. But the light in here is tricky on purpose, and witnesses forced to parley in an unfamiliar language are less likely to feel sure when asked to recall a suspect's voice."

The shorter, darker henchman complained, "You've told me all this before. If we played this game by *my* rules, we wouldn't have any witnesses to worry about."

The mastermind laughed, and sounded more silky as he replied in a sardonic tone, "I've always admired your smooth ways, El Turco. Hasn't anyone ever told you it's not nice to shoot a customer when you might be able to get more money out of him?"

A skinny kid with a feed sack over his head came over to

tell them, "They're coming along the quay. Gordo just called out the password, and they called back the countersign we'd agreed on. Do we open up to them, Boss?"

The mastermind replied in a disgusted voice, "Why, no, we leave them out there with the mosquitoes until they get discouraged and go back to Mexico. Open the freight entrance to them, like I said, and make sure it's slid shut and covered by Mike and Al, like I *said!*"

A few minutes later there came the grating groan of a massive sliding door, and a quartet of shadowy figures materialized in the tricky light. One was tall, in a dark, Anglo suit and Stetson, while the other three were dressed like prosperous *vaqueros.*

The mastermind nudged the one called Turk, who called out, "Where might your, ah . . . lady lawyer be this evening, gents?"

The tall visitor replied with no trace of a Mexican accent, "La Abogada couldn't make it. I'm holding this here carpetbag in her place. So can we commence the bidding? I take it the guns are in those crates?"

The one called Turk said, "They are. I take it you brought enough in that carpetbag for a serious auction? I warned La Abogada the bidding starts at a hundred dollars a rifle."

The Anglo spokesman for the Mexicans marveled, "That sounds a mite steep, no offense. We could buy us a spanking-new first-class American-made infantry rifle for less than half of that!"

The mastermind couldn't restrain himself any longer. He called out, "Step closer to the light and let us see you better."

When their visitor complied, the mastermind swore and demanded, "What in hell are you doing here, Longarm?"

Longarm calmly replied, "Same as you, Sam. Attending this here auction. I thought you'd invited some rebels from Iceland to look at all your wondrous Prussian weapons and bid on them against my Mexican pals here. But I reckon you felt no call to carry this confidence game that far, eh?"

"Who might this Sam you mentioned be?" asked the mastermind in a mighty sick tone.

Longarm chuckled and said, "Ain't you Sam Steinmuller,

the sly dog I've been following around for the better part of a day? You got old Sam's business suit on. You set this meeting up in this warehouse he hired in the name of his shipping company a month or so back. Who are you if you ain't Sam Steinmuller?''

The two-faced Steinmuller drew a four-shot whore pistol from under his frock coat and almost purred, "I'm the man who's never liked you since you horned in between me and that spicy Danish pastry, and you are just too clever for me by half. So why don't you tell us what makes you so smart? Who told you what was going on here?"

Longarm said, "Elimination. Once you set aside all the suspects that couldn't be guilty, you wind up with the few who *could*. I knew *I* wasn't guilty, and commenced from there. The Prussian government was tipped off about a big shipment of advanced Mauser rifles being stolen from the factory and shipped to the port of Brownsville aboard one of your outfit's vessels, the *Trinity*. But you'd think the Mauser boys would notice if anybody lifted four figures of regular locks, stocks, and barrels. They said they'd neither made up nor lost that many eleven-millimeter experimental rifles, and they had no call to lie. So that takes us to the captain and crew of the screw clipper *Trinity*. Ain't you going to take that rag off your face on such a warm night, Sam? Your foolish face is sweating considerably."

Steinmuller pulled down the stuffy bandanna without aiming away from Longarm as he hissed, "Nobody aboard the *Trinity* told you shit. None of them *knew* anything!"

Longarm said, "That's good to hear. I'd suspected as much, but I like to write up my official reports neat and tidy. Nobody aboard the *Trinity* knew anything about those Mauser repeaters because none ever came on board in Hamburg. If they had, U.S. Customs here at the other end of the line could never have missed a pile of crates *this* size!"

He patted the nearest crate thoughtfully and asked, "Is there anything in any of these used shipping crates you'd saved up from lawful cargo, or were they easier to cart over this way empty?"

"Never mind what's in those crates, damn you!" Steinmuller almost wailed, going on to demand, "Who told you? Who gave me away?"

Longarm answered easily, "I just told you. *You* did, once I shaved away the Mauser boys, the screw-clipper crew, and U.S. Customs. All of them eliminated easy because it's complicated as all get-out to keep such secrets betwixt so many plotters. You were the first rock in the stream, or the first one who could sell a convincing story and set some wheels in motion with your own smaller crew."

Longarm glanced about, not able to see just how many might be covering him and his brave volunteers. He shrugged and said, "From the ones who came after me and lost, I've long known you recruited most of your little helpers off the decks and docks of Scandinavia, the Dutch ports, and such. You only needed one sneak in Hamburg to start that false rumor about purloined Prussian rifles and Icelandic rebels headed off to the Mexican border to bid on weapons they couldn't get from the usual sources, the same as the Irish Fennians or pissed-off Russians. The waterfront rumors about Icelanders was only meant to get this carpetbag across the border with enough in it for some serious bidding. But as you should have expected, you created your own ruin in the resulting diplomatic uproar. The Prussians told their old Danish enemies that Icelandic rebels were out to swipe their repeating Mausers and, shit, you know how things went to pot from there!"

"Who told you all this?" Steinmuller repeated in a stubborn whine.

Longarm smiled thinly and said, "Salesmen tend to buy goldbricks. Devious plotters always suspect somebody is plotting against them. I told you it was your own fool cleverness that eliminated everyone else I could think of. Had you kept it simple, hardly anybody on this side of the border would have *heard* about your confidence game, you simp! Had you only had this fake El Turco approach La Abogada as a known arms dealer with the usual hardware for sale, she'd have sent these boys with less, it's true, but I'd have never been able to boil it down to the only cuss in these parts with connections in Hamburg."

Longarm started to reach for a cheroot as he added, "Shit,

we'd have never *heard* about your double cross up Denver way."

Steinmuller snapped, "Keep those hands where I can see them. All four of you. I never expected anyone to send that Danish count to snoop about and get himself killed! But they did, and he did, and the next thing we knew the damned State Department had sent for *you*, and you sure were a hard man to stop!"

He shifted his gaze to the carpetbag as he said, "But we've got you now, and whether we forgive you or not depends on what's in that bag for us!"

Longarm said, "Hold on. Let's see if I got this right. There ain't any Mauser repeaters here. There never was any Mauser repeaters. But you're demanding the price of all those Mauser repeaters at gunpoint?"

"That's about the size of it," purred Steinmuller in the silken tones of a slicker feeling mighty slick.

Longarm raised his voice to announce, "I hope all you crooks in here see Mr. Steinmuller has just upped the ante from confidence game to armed robbery!"

Nobody there seemed to give a shit.

Steinmuller sneered, "Did you really think any of my boys would throw in with you? Half of them don't speak English, and you *shot* more than one I sent after you, you dumb bastard!"

Longarm said, "Leave my family out of it. I mean that. As to how dumb I am, there ain't no money in that bag. Once I'd scouted you and these others long enough to figure out where you'd be meeting them, I laid for my more trusting Mexican friends in the dark. La Abogada was mighty chagrined to learn you and this gunrunner you brought back from the dead were aiming to flimflam her and *La Causa*."

Steinmuller stared at him owl-eyed and marveled, "Your balls must be machined from case-hardened steel! You fuck up a job we've been planning for months, then you walk in here like a big-ass bird to *brag* about robbing us?"

Longarm modestly replied, "I thought *you* were out to rob *them*. So I sent La Abogada home with the money, and none of you want to show your faces south of the border for a spell. As to how brave me and these volunteer decoys might be, I repeat what I just said about you upping the ante."

He called out in a calm voice of reason, "Up to now, the most I could hang on most of you in court would be participating in a scheme to bilk foreigners. There's no way any of you will ever *share* in such a bilking. So should you let your not-so-bright leaders kill us, all you'll have to show for it is a heap of our pals, Anglo and Mexican, out to avenge the shit out of us."

He let that sink in, and added, "On the other hand, I can always see my way to postdating my deputizing of any of you who'd rather be on the winning side."

The only reply was a distant, heavily accented suggestion he do something mighty vile to himself.

Longarm shrugged and said, "Reckon I'll have to run the whole bunch of you in then."

Steinmuller laughed incredulously and sneered. "I was right about you! You earned that rep for being brave by really being lucky and stupid!"

Waving his whore pistol, the crooked shipping agent added, "We've got the drop on you. Two to one. Front and back. So now we're going to all take a stroll over to the river and watch the tide roll out."

Longarm shook his head and said, "Not hardly. I can see why you'd like to avoid messing up this warehouse you hired a month ago. But you're under arrest, Samuel Steinmuller. Would you be willing to come along like a good sport if I didn't snap my cuffs on you?"

Steinmuller hissed, "All right, since you insist on right here and now, I reckon we'll just have to mop the floor afterwards."

But Longarm's announcement of arrest had been the agreed-upon code. So a top crate popped open, and Captain Travis Prescott of the Texas Rangers sat up like a corpse in a ghost story with a ten-gauge Greener leveled at Steinmuller as he snapped, "That's enough for Texas and me! Drop that gun and grab for some rafters!"

Steinmuller gasped, "Oh, shit!" as he swung his four-shooter to cover the Ranger way too late.

Prescott fired both barrels of number-nine buck at short range.

As the fake El Turco went for his own side arm, Longarm beat him to the draw and shot him in the head as well.

Then both cadavers lay sprawled at his feet as Longarm shouted, "That's enough! Every damn one of you freeze!"

So everybody did. The other Rangers popping out of the places a clever captain had selected for them before the moon had set had as chilling an effect as Longarm's words, not to mention the hide, hair, and brains spattered across bloody cement as far as Steinmuller's hat against the far brick wall.

Captain Prescott rolled out of the crate he'd hidden in to eavesdrop on the meeting as he said, "You *heard* me tell him to drop that gun. But did you have to shoot his partner in crime? When I have to answer for disregarding informal instructions, I'd sure like to tell them more about that murdered diplomat."

He brightened and added, "At least neither of *these* sons of bitches had diplomatic immunity! Now all we need to do is sweat the details of that assassination out of these here survivors, right?"

Longarm said, "Wrong. I doubt even Steinmuller and this other con man knew much about that killing at the French consulate."

The Ranger gasped. "Jesus H. Christ! Are you trying to tell me you've been working two separate cases all this time?"

Longarm said, "That was what had me mighty confounded up until recently. Have you ever worked on one of those newspaper puzzles where you have to connect numbered dots with your pencil to see the whole picture?"

When the older lawman nodded, Longarm explained. "I read a couple of numbers wrong. When you connect the dots the wrong way, you just wind up with a tangle that makes no sense and seems more complicated than it really needs to be. But now that I have this many dots lined up in order, I can see there's more than one picture."

Captain Prescott looked sort of worried.

So Longarm said soothingly, "I doubt I'll need as much help with these last dots. I already have some of them numbered in correct order. So they shouldn't be as much trouble to connect correct."

261

Chapter 36

The next morning dawned cool and overcast. April was like that along the Gulf Coast. So Longarm got an early start, wearing his frock coat and vest with plenty of pockets after a good five hours of lonesome sleep.

He went back to that photograph gallery and asked the sweet-smelling old gal behind the counter if she'd let him paw through a lot of their older studio portraits. She said he'd have to come on back where they had them filed away. So he did. He was mildly surprised to discover there was nobody else working back there. She'd been using that royal "we" to make it sound like she was a bigger firm than she really as. As he went through one old picture after another, back to tintypes older than her glass gelatin plates, he learned through casual questioning that she'd married the gent who'd started the business before the war, and had inherited it from him a few years back. But he hadn't come there to console widows, and he finally found a good enough picture of a young Texican in a Confederate Cavalry uniform.

She said the kid had been killed at Chickamauga, riding with Hood. In a town that size, all the old-timers knew such things. He got out the more recent picture of Private Njalsson in his Danish uniform, and placed the two pictures side by side as the sweet-smelling owner and operator stood beside him.

He drew a line across both grinning portraits, and asked if she could adjust the scale so they were both the same size, then print the top of one negative and the bottom of the other so that the missing Dane's top could be joined at the waist with the lower half of the dead Texican.

She said she'd have to do some retouching to make the results at all realistic. He told her to go ahead and charge it to his office, as much as she felt fair.

She said it would take a spell if she got right to it. So he left and legged it over to a Mexican arcade where they'd sell you anything, from wax matches to a silver-mounted saddle, and bought some cactus candy. Then, while he was at it, he bought a package of those red and green firecrackers the kids kept setting off between Easter and May Day for reasons known best to kids.

When he got to the hospital, that same nurse told him Lola Pouchard hadn't made it. He wanted to slap the gal's smug face as she bragged about being right about blood poisoning. But he handed her the cactus candy, and asked her to see it went to any kids they had on hand that morning.

Then he went and found a sit-down beanery to see if he could get rid of the sour taste in his mouth with Texas chili over a surprisingly tasty cut of goat meat. A lot of Texican cooks marinated goat meat in milk for a spell to cut the gamy aftertaste. The Good Book said the Children of Israel weren't allowed to do that. They must have liked their goat meat and mutton pungent.

After some tuna pie with two cups of black coffee, Longarm went back to the photograph gallery to find it stunk up with chemicals and its owner wearing extra perfume. She seemed proud of the way she'd made one military figure out of two. She pointed out how she'd blended the two shades of darkness behind them with her camel's hair brush.

She'd made up a dozen prints, as he'd asked. While she was putting them in a gray card folder for him, she asked why she'd just done all that.

He said, "Purloined letter, ma'am. I don't know if you've read that detection story by Mr. Poe, but it has to do with a sneaky crook hiding things in plain sight."

She said, "Heavens to Betsy, you surely don't think that

263

Danish boy once rode with Hood's Texas Brigade, do you?''

He chuckled and replied, ''I want to find out how many others notice the impossible full-dress uniform of a Royal Danish Marine.''

He didn't have time for further explanations, as sweet as she might smell, bless her dear old heart.

He found a pawnshop near the waterfront that didn't have exactly what he was looking for. A second one did. He didn't buy anything. He only needed to know you could along the waterfront near the Danish consulate.

He didn't go on to the Danish consulate, much as he might want to kiss Camilla and see if he'd recalled her right while in bed with La Abogada. He wanted to get on over to the *French* consulate while he could snoop around better. They'd told him at the hospital that the services for poor pretty Mademoiselle Pouchet would start early enough to plant her before La Siesta. Being a stenographer, Mademoiselle Pouchet didn't rate the long voyage home to France canned in lead. But since she'd been on the staff, they were likely to be giving her a respectful send-off at the Catholic cathedral by that plaza across town.

When he got to the consulate, he found he'd guessed right. That old butler, who knew who he was by this time, let him in, but allowed the the entire staff was attending a funeral.

Longarm explained he'd left something in the cellar, and the butler never blinked. He said that was between Longarm and Madame Laverne, and crawfished off, even though Longarm had never said who he'd been down in their cellar with.

He made his way to her downstairs love nest, and found the door had been left locked. That was no problem for a man who'd had one blade of his pocket knife ground scientifically by a Denver locksmith.

He let himself in, and moved over to that long narrow slit that served as air vent and skylight. The blinds were open. He peered through to see mostly dirt and debris under the front steps and the veranda above. Most of the bits and pieces scattered across the bare dirt beneath them were different shades of rat shit and belly-button lint. But off about a yard and half, he did spy what looked like a bit of green confetti.

He got out a cheroot and that package of firecrackers. He lit up, tore open the package, and unfastened one green-papered cracker from the string. He knew kids were told the green ones were louder. They were all made with the same powdered zinc and sulfur, wrapped tight in the same cheap binder, and finished off with red or green tissue.

Longarm lit the fuse of the greenie, and tossed it out under the veranda. It went off with a pretty good pop. But far less smoke than would go with a black-powder bang drifted thin and blue under the veranda's beams. The bitty new specks of green paper matched.

Longarm nodded soberly and said, "Late at night, who'd have been able to see such thin smoke if they'd been looking?"

He heard footsteps on the veranda above as somebody tore out to investigate that bang out front. Longarm smiled thinly, enjoying his cheroot, and turned to see Madame du Prix standing there in the open doorway, wearing a housedress that matched her honey-blond hair and a quizzical smile.

He said, "Morning, ma'am. I'm glad you didn't feel up to going going to church with the others. I got something to show you."

She shut the door and threw the bolt, allowing she could hardly wait to see it.

She seemed confounded when Longarm showed her one of his doctored sepia-tones and asked if she noticed anything odd about it.

She never reached for it as she wrinkled her nose and told him, "It seems to be one of those Danish soldiers Count Atterdag brought with him. I understand they've all gone back to Copenhagen. Why were you firing your gun down here just now?"

Longarm said, "It was a firecracker, ma'am. I was eliminating. You were upstairs the night that old cuss was killed out front, ma'am. Are you sure you don't recognize this particular marine, not a soldier?"

She shrugged and asked, "Why should I? They all look alike in those uniforms. Isn't that supposed to be the point of uniforms?"

Longarm put the picture away as he replied, "It sure is,

ma'am. The one I just showed you a picture of was the missing witness holding the count's mount for him when somebody shot him in the back, or so we were led to believe. Neither you nor likely half the others who dashed out on the veranda that night could have picked Njalsson's face out of a crowd because they were *used* to seeing Royal Danish Marines out front in those toy-soldier uniforms.''

She said that was all mighty interesting, she was sure, but didn't he mean to take advantage of this unusual opportunity they had to get better acquainted, seeing everyone else with any call to come down to that cellar room would be headed out to the burial grounds after the church services.

He blew smoke in her face and said, ''Not just yet. Let's first eliminate that letter you wrote, in your native lingo, accusing Don Hernan Obregon of shooting Count Atterdag that night.''

She asked, ''What are you talking about?'' as she loosened the sash of her housedress to open it wide and make him say ''Ah!'' She was a natural blonde all over, and built breathtakingly from there up.

He sighed and said, ''Some lonesome night I promise I'll jerk it a couple of times with you in mind, ma'am. But right now I'll tell you what I'm talking about. I'm talking about somebody who can write in Danish like a native and who doesn't know or care that a native of an Icelandic fishing village would write it more formally. Folks who wrote Danish and *knew* that could be eliminated. A swamping number of Danish-talking folks could be eliminated as soon as I asked myself if they were likely to know Don Hernan and have any sensible *motive* for wanting to frame him.''

She placed her hands on her shapely hips, the full front of her still exposed, to demand, ''What possible reason might I have to see poor Hernan in trouble? We're very good friends, you *koldtfish*!''

Longarm said, ''If that meant cold fish, you are right on the money when it comes to my feelings about *you*, Miss Margrethe. I have met a heap of gals with your taste for variety, but seldom one as spiteful at the game of musical beds.''

She moved closer, and would have wrapped her arms

around him if he hadn't pushed her back and said, "Don't go rubbing that cunt all over my tweeds. Lord knows where it's been since last I heard you going sixty-nine with that married Mexican. I had another witness with me who heard the way the two of you were carrying on the other side of that hotel wall. You shouldn't shout dirty instructions to a lover if you don't want others to know what you're doing, ma'am."

She drew herself up proudly and wrapped her beige shantung around her charms as she coldly demanded, "All right, what do you want of me, if it's not my body?"

He said, "Elimination. You really numbered some dots wrong on us when you wrote that letter, signed Njalsson's name to it, and had it posted from Laredo. Who ran that errand for you, some other local talent who likes to get sucked off?"

She snapped, "*Hvornar?* Why would I do such a thing? I don't mean why would I suck my beloved Hernan, since I see it's no use to lie to you about that. I meant, why would I try to get him in trouble? You just confessed to listening to us making love!"

Longarm nodded and said, "It sounded like fun. I doubt you spit in your husband's face whilst *he's* fucking you either."

She gasped, and stamped one foot to demand if that was any way to speak to a lady.

He said, "No, ma'am. But you ain't a lady. You could best be described as a vicious slut. Not because you like to screw around. Some of my best friends like to screw around. But you screw around really dirty and low!"

He blew smoke out both nostrils like a disgruntled bull, and told her, "Variety is the spice of life, and I know how much fun musical beds can be. But you weren't content to marry up with a Frenchman and cheat on him with a Mexican when the variety wore off. You got tired of *that* variety of lover and wanted to move on. But tell me if I ain't getting warm when I tell you old Hernan wasn't as easy to shed as younger diplomats who didn't want trouble with your higher-ranking Andre?"

She started to brazen it through, then gave a sigh of self-

267

pity and sobbed, "I was trying to save my marriage. I kept trying to tell Hernan my husband was asking questions about my unescorted errands in town. But he refused to hear of ending our affair, and alas, I don't have much willpower once a man's hands are all over me and I might as well enjoy it."

Longarm nodded soberly and said, "I was wondering about all those visits to beauty or ice cream parlors where you found it so easy to trip over other gals from the diplomatic community. Don Hernan kept acting like Don Juan, and wouldn't give up his blue-eyed-blond brand of variety. So when you thought you saw the chance to at least have him thrown out of the country, you took it. You wrote your letter in what you thought would be taken as working-class Danish, and had it sent from Laredo just to hide the fact it had been penned here at this consulate. I see now you never set out to get anybody *else* in trouble. But I do have the dots connected right, don't I, Miss Margrethe?"

She sank down on the bed to cover her face with her hands and sob that she felt so ashamed.

He said, not unkindly, "You have call to feel ashamed, ma'am. For you are one nasty cunt. But seeing you've been truthful with me, for a change, I won't tell Don Hernan what you wrote about him in that letter. We got enough killings around here to clear up, and he'd kill you for certain if I told him."

Chapter 37

He left the French consulate before Madame Laverne could get back from church. So he was still feeling the effects of all that naked blond flesh as he made it to the *Danish* consulate before La Siesta set in.

Camilla had likely been worried about him doing that. She headed him off out front and said, "Custis, I told you back at that horrid hotel that we have to be discreet! I'm personal secretary to Baron Senderborg, and he'd have a fit if he found out about you and me! I had enough trouble convincing him Captain Steensen was a sodomite!"

Longarm made a wry face and said, "I was wondering about that. You Danish gals sure cover up for unwanted lovers with a lot of imagination. I just got your pal, Margrethe du Prix, to admit she was the one who wrote that letter to Njalsson's sergeant."

Camilla sniffed and said, "I might have known. But Eric Steensen and I were never more than good friends. We'd run in the same crowd back in Copenhagen. I told the baron that Eric liked boys when the baron asked me what was going on between us. But never mind all that. I can't tell the baron *every* man he catches me alone with is a *varmbror,* and I want you out of here before anyone notices you."

Longarm said, "I didn't come here to see you today, no

offense. I came to tell Baron Senderborg he's been barking up the wrong tree.''

He had a sudden thought, grimaced, and said, ''That's what's so bad about malicious letters. Their poison spreads like the ripples in a cesspool. Steensen thought the baron had forged that letter to trap him, and I have to own up to considering that. Let me show you something before you carry me in to the baron.''

He got out one of his doctored photos. When he showed it to her, Camilla studied it, or seemed to, then handed it back, saying, ''This looks like a picture of that Private Njalsson in his dress uniform. Are you going to have reward posters printed?''

He shook his head and said, ''Not hardly. Nobody's posted any bounty on a military deserter and possible witness to a crime. If they had, that new Ben Day process that lets you print photographs is costly. Ain't any such posters out on Billy the Kid or the James brothers to date. I had this print made up to illustrate what Mr. Poe wrote about purloined letters. Let's go show it to your boss and see if he spots the clear and obvious as soon as you really look at what you're looking at.''

She led him to a side room, checked to see that her boss wasn't playing with himself or reading a good book, and ushered Longarm in.

Baron Senderborg went on puffing his pipe while Camilla poured *akvavit* for the two of them. Longarm brought the boss diplomat up on all he'd just found out about his junior diplomats, leaving out their personal lives, and handed over the photo as Camilla hovered by, looking puzzled.

The stern old veteran of the Dano-Prussian wars held the sepia-tone up to the light for a long unwinking stare, then snapped, ''*Til Hel og hvorfor?* Those pants are not Danish issue, and what is a mere private doing with an officer's sword at his side? He should be armed with his regulation sword bayonet!''

Camilla said something in Danish, and the old diplomat handed her the picture. She took one look and said, ''My heavens! That *is* a sword, not a sword bayonet, hanging from

270

his left hip! But why didn't I *see* that when you showed me this same picture a few minutes ago?''

Longarm explained, ''You weren't expecting to see it, ma'am. In that story by Mr. Poe, the detectives are searching the suspect's home for an important letter they think he stole. They poke about for all sorts of secret panels. They roll up the rug and lift the pillows off the chairs whilst, all the time, the rascal has left the letter on his desk blotter with other papers, in plain sight, if only they'd been expecting to see it *there*.''

Baron Senderborg protested, ''I saw it at a glance. When one has inspected as many guard mounts as I have, one sees a brass button that was not polished properly. Are you suggesting any Royal Danish Marine could report for guard mount and be posted in front of another consulate out of uniform, without the sergeant of the guard noticing that *cavalry saber*?''

Longarm said, ''I'm sure he reported for Guard Mount in proper uniform, Baron. You can buy old cavalry sabers in many a pawnshop in town. Knowing in advance where he'd be guarding Count Atterdag's life and tending his mount, Njalsson only had to get there ahead of Tim and cache the more serious weapon in the stable around to the back.''

He let that sink in and continued. ''Most any time during the night of that ball, when the sergeant of the guard was paying mind to more important chores, Njalsson found it easy to replace his issued eighteen inches with a secondhand forty-one-inch blade. Nobody saw the purloined letter when he went to fetch the old drunk's mount for him in tricky light. I mean to ask when I catch up with Njalsson. I ain't too clear whether he was just a mighty mean horse thief or had some personal grudge against such a popular boss.''

Camilla protested, ''Count Atterdag was shot in the back. Nobody stabbed him with a sword, Custis!''

Longarm shook his head and explained. ''When his nibs came out of the ballroom alone, Njalsson was waiting with that full-length blade, and that was barely enough. You can see how awkward it had to be for him, holding the reins of Lille Thruma, whipping out a saber to thrust home before an old soldier could come unstuck, then lobbing a lit firecracker under the front steps to make it sound like somebody else had fired a shot. That's how come so many folks bought the fatal wound as the path of a bullet fired from *behind* Atterdag. The tip of that saber barely punctured the back of the vain count's corset. The hole a saber lunge left in the *front* of it looked more like an *exit* wound.''

The baron gasped. ''That accounts for the *curve* we took for the path of a bullet tumbling end over end, as well as that keyholed exit wound, which was really the entrance wound! It was Njalsson, a rebel Icelander, who assassinated that Danish nobleman!''

Longarm said, ''Let's not go jumping to any more hasty conclusions, Baron. You've already cost your service a good diplomat by accusing poor Captain Steensen.''

The crusty old cuss smiled sheepishly and said, ''I'm not certain Steensen had any future as a *diplomat*, after reading the letter of resignation he sent us, suggesting what His Majesty could do with Steensen's commission. But I hope he does better as an American, now that I know him to be innocent.''

He grinned up at Camilla to add, ''Of *murder*, at any rate.''

She blushed and looked away.

Baron Senderborg got to his feet, saying he had to get over to the Prussian consulate and fill von Braun in on these last few details. He told them, ''This should more or less ice the cake for the Prussians, now that we all know no Mauser repeating rifles were ever diverted here to Texas. If Atterdag's death had nothing to do with that investigation, we can consider the case closed.''

He told Camilla to have Longarm dictate a more detailed report and type it up in triplicate. Then he went upstairs to get dressed, and Longarm said, ''You heard what the man said. Your place or mine?''

She stepped over to him to kick up one high-button shoe like a sassy French dancer and hook a shapely ankle over his right shoulder as she boldly answered, ''Let's go somewhere we won't be disturbed as I take all the dictation you want to give me.''

He made her pay for her sassy over at his *posada*. Once

he had her upstairs, he dared her to do that again. So she did, and just as he'd suspected, and hoped, a tall man *could* get it in a short gal posed so French, if he spread his own legs wide.

Then she said his tweed pants and her frilly unmentionables were scratching her clit more than she needed. So they both undressed like old pals, and got back together bare-ass romantically.

She allowed she could write things down pretty good from memory, and he felt no call to repeat himself, verbally, as they wriggled and jiggled together in a way that should have gotten boring, but never seemed to before you'd come at least thrice.

After she'd come the last time on top, they just lay there that way, with her little cupcakes no burden at all to his hairy chest as she crooned to him in Danish a spell, then asked him in English how long he'd be staying in Texas, now that he'd solved the whole thing.

He said, "I never said I'd solved the whole thing. I solved the mystery of how so many guns the Prussian Army never ordered could be purloined and smuggled through U.S. Customs. I solved that mystery about the letter accusing Obregon, and I'm pretty sure I know who really killed Count Atterdag. I was sent to find Njalsson, whether he witnessed the killing or committed it. I'd like to recover that prize mare, Lille Thruma, too."

She said, "They could be in California by this time, and Lille Thruma was Eric Steensen's personal mount. Neither this consulate nor that KHA trade mission has any legal claim on her."

He patted her bare derriere, which was sort of spread apart for the ceiling beams to admire, as he growled, "I don't cotton to the notion of a murderous horse thief having her either. Even if I did, I was told to find that fool Icelander who stole her, and I've been getting better at connecting dots."

The door swung open. That was the trouble with giving keys to willful gals. So there stood big old Sigridur Jonsdottir, who started to say, "I know what you must think of me, Custis," before she saw him flat on his back, naked as a jay, with the petite bare-ass Camilla Nansen perched on top of him with his semi-erection up her old ring-dang-do.

Longarm felt sort of silly, as most men would have, but he had a clear conscience as he said, "I believe you ladies know one another on sight. If you don't, Miss Camilla Nansen, may I present Miss Sigridur Jonsdottir, who came down here to work with me, but ran off when the weather failed to agree with her."

Camilla grinned up at the big blonde with Longarm still inside her as she demurely answered, "I'm so glad for us all." Then she asked Sigridur something in Danish. The big blonde gasped, blushed, and then they were both laughing like hell, and Longarm felt left out as they gushed back and forth like schoolgirls, with Camilla showing off by moving her hips like that.

Longarm gathered the gist of the conversation when Sigridur put down her bags, shut the door behind her, and commenced to shed her hat and summer frock as she explained in English, "I suppose we three *are* going to have to be good sports about this, since I came back to you with another naughty night in mind and *she* won't leave until she satisfies her *own* naughty needs."

Camilla said, "Eric—I mean, an old friend in Copenhagen—told me one time that every man dreams of a night in bed with two women, and I must confess I've always wondered what a real orgy might be like."

So they had one. Longarm never admitted he'd behaved this wild before, with Indians and both Anglo and Mexican cowgirls. *They* pretended it was all new, strange, and wondrous to *them* as well. Although a man had to wonder how so few words in Danish could inspire two strange gals to act so strange. But as he stood with his bare feet on the floor, throwing it dog-style to the big blonde while she "experimented with the forbidden arts of Sappho" as the petite brunette lay under her in reverse order, head to crotch, he consoled himself with the thought that only they knew how silly *he* must look, and enjoying gals was only natural, whether they were blond and broad or brunette and little-girlish. Then Camilla said something in Danish, and the next thing Longarm knew, he was tossing it to *her* little dark derriere while she pleasured that big blond twat he'd just come in with some more of that Saphhic stuff.

As best he could recall, Miss Sappho had been a lady poet on this Greek island called Lesbos. Miss Sappho had written lots of love poems, the genders of the lovers sort of left up for grabs. Longarm suspected they'd gotten around to regular sex now and again, since those Greek lesbians, in real life, seemed to be men, women, and children, mostly catching olives and cultivating fish. You could read things like that in the Denver Public Library the last few evenings before payday.

Longarm couldn't tell whether they were starting to show off for him, or experiencing a whole new wonder, when they just commenced to make love to one another while he insisted on pausing for a breather and a smoke.

He sat there watching for a while, and it did seem sort of inspiring when they got to breathing heavy and moaning things in Danish, or Icelandic, that had to be dirty as hell. So he offered to finish off the loser of their contest in coming, and that inspired each to do her best to make the other come. So a fine time was had by all as Longarm had to console Sigridur some more when the peppery brunette came way ahead of her. But by the time he'd made Sigridur climax, taking longer now for some reason, old Camilla was hot again from watching, and demanding he treat *her* like a natural woman some more.

He did. It wasn't easy. Then, as the three of them lay all a-tangle in that one modest bed, they both wanted to know what he planned to do about all this once the three of them got some rest.

He got a cheroot going—that wasn't easy either—and thought a lot about the question before he answered it. Then he said, "I got to go track down that prize palomino mare and the murderous rascal who stole her. We'll talk about who does what to whom after I get back, ladies."

Sigridur hadn't been keeping up with the case as well as Camilla. So it was the petite brunette who demanded, "But Custis, where will you start? You told us you'd traced him half a day's ride up the Rio Grande and lost his trail completely!"

Longarm gripped the smoke with his teeth and patted both their bare behinds, large and small, as he muttered, "I know. Lately my poor brain's been awhirl with decisions, decisions!"

Chapter 38

That evening Longarm drifted off the ferry boat afoot, amid other drifters. He made it through the balmy scents of night-blooming jasmine, chili peppers, and shit of all species to his grateful rebel pals without incident. La Abogada said she'd be proud to fix him up with a mule, a *charro* saddle, and a Winchester '66 Yellow Boy. She offered him more than that. But he didn't have the time, nor had Camilla and Sigridur left him the lifting powers required.

Nobody there could do more than remount and arm him. Nobody knew where each and every damned Obregon holding might be. So he rode to the address he had in town to ask damned old Obregon.

When she received him upstairs in her quarters, Don Hernan's sort of green-faced woman, Miss Felicidad, seemed upset about something, but mighty glad to see Longarm. She ran over to him in her fluttery black lace to throw both arms around him and kiss him full on the mouth.

French.

Longarm kissed back in the same lingo, as most men would have, but when they came up for air he felt obliged to gasp, "Hold on and let's study on this, Miss Felicidad. I wouldn't want you to take me for a sissy, but I draw the line at ladies with a husband in residence."

She went on clinging to him as she purred, "He is not

here. He is never here. He thinks he is so smart with his Danish pastry and his diplomatic immunity. He despises both of us. Why don't we teach him a lesson by going out on the patio, where the servants can catch us in the act?''

He had to smile at the picture. But he said, ''No offense, but I'm out to catch somebody else. Before you answer any questions, ma'am, I feel I ought to caution you that I don't have any jurisdiction here on your side of the estuary. I can't make any promises about your Don Hernan ever being allowed back in the U.S. of A. if what I suspect him of can be proven. Having said all that, I might be able to prove him innocent if I could say I'd paid an informal visit to that one Mexican *rancho de caballos* you only hear rumors about from others.''

She said, ''You mean the place he has not filed a land deed on in his own name. For because it came to him from my people, as part of my . . . *dote?*''

Longarm nodded down at her and said, ''We call it a dowery, ma'am. How come your groom never took formal possession, and more important, can you tell me where it might be?''

She sounded pissed as she answered, ''He needed a place for to let stolen horses cool down, and he no doubt felt was better for any such disgrace to fall upon my people. I spent much time there as a *muchacha*, and so of course I know the way. Let me get dressed for to ride and I shall show you the way, no?''

He said, ''No. I'm hoping your man and his diplomatic immunity won't be there. But I'm looking for a horse thief inclined to commit cold-blooded murder, and I don't want you tagging along, no offense.''

She nodded grimly and said, ''*Sí,* I heard Hernan and his *segundo* from his Texas *rancho,* the O Bar O, talking about that. When a woman is used as an ashtray and sangria pitcher, nobody worries about her listening as they smoke and sip sangria. I heard Hernan say that *ladrone* from the frozen north had stolen the palomino Hernan wanted, with added problems nobody had foreseen.''

Longarm nodded soberly and said, ''Njalsson wasn't expecting the sensitive bright-eyed mare to spook at the sudden

278

flurry of movements, the smell of blood, and a sort of ferocious firecracker. Had she not fought him so, he meant to just lead her off amid all the fussing over a backshot diplomat, and allow he had no notion who might have stolen her. Are both Njalsson and the stolen pony hidden out at your maiden family holdings, Miss Felicidad?''

She said, ''I know the palomino is. I heard Hernan boasting that she is so beautiful he wished he had a bigger *palo*. He said this in front of me, his own *mujer*, and I do not care if you have to kill them all!''

Longarm could see her point. Being a rich widow had to have being an ashtray beat. One of the reasons you had to be cautious about Spanish-speaking gals was that they hated just the way they loved, with all their hearts and souls, and they'd forgive a man for busting their nose before they'd forgive him another *mujer*!

She seemed to take his considering for doubt. So she not only gave him detailed directions to the spread in question, but drew him a map on a scrap of paper.

She insisted on kissing him again, and told him to ride with God as he rode out. He didn't ride straight for the Camino Real down the coastline. He circled some through the streets of Matamoros to make sure he hadn't fallen for one of the older tricks of the same Castilian blue bloods the Borgia bunch had hailed from. The fact that lots of folks felt Miss Lucrezia Borgia had only been doing what her wicked brother and prince of the Church told her to do wasn't going to bring back any of her poor Italian husbands and lovers.

But after he'd wasted about as much time as he cared to aboard a bewildered cordovan saddle mule, Longarm headed out by moonlight, where a man could see what might be laying for him up the road a piece.

Matamoros lay on the same vast coastal plain that stretched from Mexico to New Jersey, wide or narrow as the higher inlands warranted. It wasn't as dead flat as a lot of Nebraska or the Great Basin west of Salt Lake City. Aside from being cut by many a river wending seaward, the coast plains had a sort of grain to them, called *cuestas* by the survey teams that studied such matters, running more or less in line with the seashore off eastward. This meant some stretches of the ever-so-gently rolling plains lay low and marshy, while others stood high and dry, covered with jack pine or scrub oak north of, say, the Carolinas, and palmetto, sea grape, and such as you trended south into honest tropical mangroves and saw grass.

This close to a big border town, the range all around had been hard hit by charcoal makers, and overgrazed until it looked more arid than the climate really called for. He knew that April grass along a poorly kept highway would grow saddlehorn-high if left to its own druthers. It looked like the short-grass prairie around Denver in the moonlight. When he came to a wooden shrine to the west of the road, immune to the charcoal makers if they valued their immortal souls and mortal asses, Longarm reined in, walked the mule around to the far side, and hunkered by the old oaken *santo* with his borrowed Yellow Boy armed and alert.

You had to spot targets sooner with the '66 Yellow Boy. Its brass action worked the same as more recent Winchester models, and it packed seventeen rounds to the '73's fifteen in the same-length magazine. But the rounds were .45-28, the same as the army preferred for a recruit's cavalry pistol, lest he hurt his little wrist. Hence Longarm knew the longer barrel would only give him a little aiming edge against a gang of mean-drinking *vaqueros*. If he ran up against serious shooters, he'd have to get close as hell before the fun could begin!

Nobody seemed to be tailing him in the moonlight, unless they were so far back that they were taking a chance on losing him. He considered a moonlight scamper out across open range to throw anybody tailing off completely. But it wasn't that cool, they had a good ride ahead of them if they stuck to the Camino Real most of the way, and bless her helpful map, old Felicidad would have told them where he was headed if she'd set out to betray him instead of her husband.

Knowing he and his mount would seem just a blur in the moonlight with their outlines broken by the higher shrine, Longarm waited and then waited some more. After it felt like way too long, he heard the pounding of hooves and spied the running lights and massive black blob of the night-mail coach heading south to Vera Cruz under a cloud of moonlit dust.

Longarm mounted up, tore out to the Camino Real, and headed south ahead of the coach at a lope. He knew the six mules pulling the big mail coach would leave many a hoof print and the fresh ruts of four steel-rimmed wheels across any distinctive tracks his borrowed mule could possibly leave.

They called a stagecoach a *stage*coach because it moved at a steady nine-mile-an-hour average few others could match without changing mounts or teams staged every fifteen miles or so along your route. A thoroughbred racehorse could run more than three times as fast as a coach team trotted. But for no more than a mile or so. A good saddle mule such as the one he was riding could outpace a coach team for the better part of five, or match their gait for fifteen to twenty miles before it was just plain through for the day. So once Longarm had a quarter-mile lead on the mail coach, he reined in to a steady trot, kept that up for another half hour, and turned off into a palmetto grove to let the big rig thunder by.

Patting the sweaty neck of his spunky cordovan, Longarm assured it he wasn't fool enough to run the full eighteen miles to the spread Felicidad Obregon had mapped out for them.

He took a trail break in the palmettos instead, removing the comfortable but heavy *charro* saddle to rub the critter down and water it before he allowed it to graze. The grass and forbs all around looked greened-up enough. But you couldn't tell, by moonlight, how much dry roughage the critter was putting away. It didn't hurt a grazer as smart as a mule to eat dry fodder on top of all the water you'd seen fit to offer. But when you let a critter stuff its gut with dry bulk first, *then* poured water into it, grazing critters could bloat up and die on you.

That hardly sounded like the best way to finish an eighteen-mile night ride. So Longarm didn't graze the resting mule more than ten minutes.

He reversed the saddle blanket and cinched the center-fire *charro* rig securely so he could stand in the stirrups as they

281

lit out some more, repeating the process once every hour.

Longarm knew he was pushing his mount. He'd warned La Abogada she might never see the critter again. So he had her permission in advance to swap her mule for a fresh mount or, hell, a broom.

They'd both understood the reasons a working *vaquero* rode a string of at least seven *jacos* during *rodeo* time. Nobody expected a single mount to carry him far or fast for more than eight or ten hours without feeling broken down for the rest of the week.

Longarm pushed on harder than he might have because he aimed to scout Obregon's spread before the moon set that particular night. His almanac allowed he had until nigh an hour after midnight. During the war a stupid patrol leader had taught him you had to keep moonlight or the lack of it in mind while riding at night.

The moon waxed and waned from new to full thirteen times a year, with a full moon on a different night each month, and that thirteenth "blue" moon showing up near the end of any month that started with the moon shining full. You got an all-night moon when it rose after sunset. It set before dawn if it was already on high at dusk.

Braced *vaquero*-style in the stirrups with the Yellow Boy across the exposed cottonwood swells of the Mexican saddle, Longarm came at last to a wash across the Camino Real that old Felicidad had drawn on her crude map. He reined his mule to a walk and rode up it to the northwest as she'd suggested, aiming to circle in from behind. You were more likely to be greeted by barking dogs when you rode onto private property from a more traveled route.

He rode with his mule's lop ears below the level of the weeds along either rim of the wash, with his own head just high enough for him to see where they were going. So he spotted weathered corral poles and the rambling mass of a Mexican ranch house in the moonlight before he heard a pony whinny to his mule.

He reined in and tethered to some Spanish bayonet as he whispered he and old Yellow Boy had best go on foot the rest of the way.

The mule didn't argue. So that was what he did, gliding

along the corral poles to see that there surely was a petite pale pony in there with the others. He paused and softly called, "Lille Thruma?" and damned if the critter didn't come over to the rails like a friendly pup that knew its name.

He petted the Icelandic-Hispanic cross on her velvety muzzle and told her, "I'll be right back. Just have to make sure I guessed right about that simp who stole you."

He eased on to where lamplight gleamed through a small but clean glass window set deep in a stucco wall. He lowered the muzzle of the carbine lest it clink on the waterproof stucco they had to use in these parts, and rested an elbow on the window ledge for a gander at the ranch hands gathered about a table in the kitchen, nursing black coffee as if they'd gotten orders to stay up late.

He spied Bowie Bickford, the foreman of the O Bar O up Texas way. But he didn't see Don Hernan Obregon or that horse thief and killer they'd had down as no more than a hostile witness.

He wasn't surprised. Nobody had much use for any man who'd stand there smiling as he held your horse for you, then stab you in the guts with an old and likely rusty blade.

He told himself it was time to get out of there while the getting was good. Nobody was fixing to produce the murderous Pall Njalsson in these parts, dead or alive.

But as he eased back from the window, he heard the snick of a rifle being cocked, and something hard as a broom handle and cold as death was poking him hard under his back ribs. So he'd frozen like a statue before a familiar voice purred, "So good of you to drop by, El Brazo Largo. We were told you were on the way, and this saves me the trip to Brownsville I was planning. I was not sure my diplomatic immunity gave me that much, how you say, leeway?"

As Longarm turned to face Don Hernan Obregon, one of the two ranch hands flanking their *patrón* to either side took charge of the Yellow Boy. The other stepped in to unbuckle Longarm's gun rig as Longarm tried, "Like I told your wife before she triple-crossed me with that mail coach, I was as interested in proving you innocent as guilty. We know it wasn't you who killed that count and stole that pony."

The smooth-talking Mexican said pleasantly, ''Of course you do. Start walking, *pendejo*. We do not wish to encourage flies around the kitchen door, and our garbage pit is over *that* way.''

Chapter 39

Longarm demanded, "*Por qúe?* Didn't you just mention diplomatic immunity, and didn't I just say that missing Danish deserter doesn't seem to be down here with you gents? That pony you value so highly has been deserted as well, in a way. Her owner, Captain Steensen, ran off to seek his fortune in America without her."

Obregon snorted in disgust and asked, "Did you really think you could spy on me and my Danish pastry in a hotel I almost own without anyone even mentioning it to me later?"

Longarm said, "I wasn't spying on you. I was spying on *her*, and I just got the impression you have a mighty understanding wife."

The philandering Mexican shrugged and said, "She has no choice. I give her none. I knew you would not rest until you had found this *rancho*. I told her to betray its location to you when, not if, you came snooping around. You were right about her sending a servant ahead of you aboard that night coach. He is holding your carbine as we speak. Is there anything else you wish to know before you die?"

Longarm said, "Yep. Just for the record, what happened to that Icelander you made that deal with?"

Don Hernan sneered, "What would I want with a *ladrón* who would betray his former *patrón* and did not speak a word of Spanish? I let him steal Lille Thruma for me as we had agreed. He rode out to the O Bar O as we had agreed. He enjoyed a last good meal, and then just a few of my most trustworthy followers tucked him into bed for the last time. You may tell the recording angel his body should be nicely composted by now in that *other* garbage pit.''

Longarm was about to observe that Pall Njalsson had hardly made that exact deal when the kitchen door flew open to spill lamplight across the backyard while Bowie Bickford yelled, ''What's going on out here?''

Everyone turned their heads that way without thinking long and hard about it. Longarm didn't have time for much thinking either, but his fighting skills were inspired by desperation as he grabbed for that Yellow Boy and kneed the Mexican holding it when he didn't let go.

The Mexican let go, sobbing in pain, even before Don Hernan whirled with a curse to send 250 grains of lead where Longarm had just been. It parted the skull of the bent-over Mexican instead. Then Don Hernan caught a .45 short with his mustache and the roots of his front teeth as Longarm fired the Yellow Boy up at him and kept rolling in a swirl of yard dust as he levered another round in the chamber.

The *segundo*, Bickford, got his own six-gun out, and might have shot anybody in all the confusion if Longarm hadn't jackknifed him with a slug that played hob with his belt buckle as well.

Then the ranch hand who'd been holding Longarm's gun rig dropped it to run somewhere in the night, yelling at the top of his lungs, ''*Socorro! Asesinato! Llamen a los rurales!*''

Longarm knew he'd nailed two of the bastards, and didn't aim to wait around for any *rurales*. So he scooped up his gun rig and lit out at a run for that corral between him and his borrowed mule.

All that gunplay had the remuda milling wild-eyed around inside the poles. Longarm cradled the Winchester on one elbow, and swung open the gate as he called out Lille Thruma's name in a soothing tone, not sure it would work.

It worked. The unsettled palomino came his way like a big scared pup uncertain about the way its master felt about that puddle on the rug. Longarm grabbed her by her almost-white forelock as he asked her nicely, "What's a nice little gal like you doing in a place like this? I want you to meet a pal of mine, Miss Lille Thruma."

The pony came along almost willingly, with Longarm just hanging on and telling her how lovely she was whenever she dug her hooves in. He could see the late Pall Njalsson had known more about stockfish than horseflesh. For he got her over to that wash without a serious fight, and as she and the mule nickered and rubbed muzzles, he switched the saddle and bridle to the fresh mount, telling the more-spent mule it was on its own and advising it to head for home, as both horses and mules were inclined to if they *had* homes.

Then he mounted up, gathered the reins, and told the pony, "It's time to see if you can move half as good as your little black pal, that fuzzy Kolsvartur!"

She could. Bigger than the petite, pure Icelandic pony Longarm had tried before, Lille Thruma loped up the wash a ways and then, as she saw he didn't mind, slowed to that odd Icelandic *tolt* gait.

That fool cordovan mule tagged after them, just plain trotting with no load to carry through the cool night air. So Longarm muttered to it, "Have it your own way. But we ain't aiming for Matamoros by way of that Camino Real. There's telegraph poles as well as stage stops along that route, and I've already been suckered that way this evening!"

He thought back to his meeting with the two-faced Felicidad in black lace as he wondered how far she'd have gone to convince him she was out to play her husband false. She'd surely been a convincing actress, or a gal who hankered for her own stuff on the side. He told the night winds and two critters, having nobody else to tell, "That'll learn me to behave myself. I might have wound up with a good piece of ass, and wound up walking into that trap an hour or so later."

They tolted on, and on, with his unusual mount showing no signs of tiring as he navigated by the stars. That got easier after the moon set, as more stars than he'd seen earlier came out to stare down at them. He could see why some Indian nations prayed to the stars while others were afraid of them.

As a white man who could read, he knew what they were. The clear moonless sky still looked mysterious, lit up from one horizon to the other and not casting enough light on the trail to matter, if they were *on* any trail. Lille Thruma tolted so smooth you couldn't be sure. Sigridur had told him that back home in Iceland the old-timers could ride as much as eight days to the Althing gatherings, over ice packs and lava fields and through a sort of dwarf willow and heather chaparral, without foundering their mounts. But he still reined in to get his bearings and rest both mounts two hours northwest of the Obregon spread.

A night bird cussed them, and the mule panted like a logging Shay locomotive hauling a heavy load as Longarm lit a cheroot and watered the two of them with the last of the ten-gallon canvas bag he'd been packing. If Captain Steensen's breeding experiment was in trouble, she didn't show it yet.

He compared the starry sky with the mental map of the Mexican state of Tamaulipas, and told his pals, "This range around us is cow country for now. The way ahead will get more settled as we approach the river, and there's a telegraph line following the river as far west as Del Rio, which is too fucking far to consider. So we want to duck under the wire betwixt guarded crossings before first light, and if you can't swim, Lille Thruma, I'm in a whole lot of trouble!"

He remounted and pushed on. The mule failed to follow them further. Longarm was neither surprised nor too worried about that. Mules were smart as dogs when it came to finding their way home to fodder, water, and familiar surroundings.

Lille Thruma tolted on and on under him, letting him and his own common sense decide when they should break for a few minutes.

They had to swing wide of lamplight and dog barks now and again, but he was still making time that would have done the old Pony Express proud, without having to change mounts every ten miles or so.

Cutting catty-corner for the border, they had twenty-five miles or more to cover in the little over six hours of darkness you got in April down this way. Those detours made them tolt even further. He figured that odd tolt moved a rider's ass six or eight steady miles an hour, when he wasn't resting his mount at least once every hour and a half. He had to wonder if the astonishing mare could tolt like that on a hot border day. But since it was a cool night, he didn't really have to worry about it. He felt sure he'd outdistanced anybody trailing them on mortal horseflesh.

He was almost right. A company of *rurales* had cut his trail by the light of the subtropical moon, followed it until moonset, and built a night fire to brew coffee and their grudge against a *gringo chingado* who'd just blown away a personal friend of El Presidente, a man who'd enjoyed diplomatic immunity as well!

They didn't sleep. They were too intent on bringing down that famous El Brazo Largo the *pobrecitos* thought so highly of. So their night was a drawn-out ordeal until, at last, there was enough first light to track by, while far out ahead of them, but not as far as he wanted to be, that same false dawn caught Longarm still tolting along on good old Lille Thruma, an unusual mount one could recognize as such from telescopic range. So he told her, ''We can't hope to scout up a raft tied up to the bank, because ain't nobody fixing to tie one up more than a mile from their infernal house! I sure wish I'd paid more mind to old Sigridur when she was holding forth on those long cross-country tolts up Iceland way. She did say they had lots of rivers, wide, swift, and cold as the high-country ice caps they flowed down from. So did any ancient Vikings ford such streams the wet way, or did they cross rivers the same way they crossed oceans, in boats?''

Lille Thruma couldn't say. Her rider might have felt better when they approached a solid line of treetops in bright morning sunlight had he been able to listen in on a conversation a good ways back.

The *rurale* sergeant had reined in to point down at the spent smoke and trampled dust, declaring, ''They've split up. El Brazo Largo is the one we want, and he is a big man who was seen riding down from Matamoros on a big mule. Those larger hoofprints are making more for Matamoros than those smaller ones. He has too great a lead on us if he intends to hide in town. But we can try, and if he tries for to board the ferry boat back to Brownsville, we shall have him!''

"What about those other tracks?" asked his corporal.

The sergeant shrugged and said, "What about them? What charge do we have on the unknown rider, perhaps a woman, mounted on such a child's pet? Our river patrol has a description of that peculiar animal. When or if they spot it, they can ask its mystery rider for why he or she was riding with El Brazo Largo."

The corporal said, "Forgive me, I mean no disrespect, but don't you think some of us ought to follow both trails, *Sargento mio*?"

To which his superior coldly replied, "If I thought we should split up as well, I would order us to split up, *cabron*! The reason *they* split up was to tempt *us* to split up so that they might pick off fewer, at a distance, with those high-powered Prussian rifles we heard about! We shall all ride together after El Brazo Largo. Let the river patrols worry about the one on that dwarfed palomino!"

So that was what they did, and Longarm would have made it down through the riverside tanglewood, or been shot out of the saddle, if the three cocky *rurales* coursing along their own Rio Bravo hadn't spotted him first and ridden out at an angle to head him off in the fallow corn milpa he and Lille Thruma were tolting across.

Not at all clear about that message they'd received at dawn about a tall gringo on a mule, one of them hailed the tall gringo on a very unusual horse with: "*Buendias, caballero! Are you taking your dog out for a walk or trying for to ride it?*"

Longarm knew there were riders along the border you could talk nice to, riders you could bluff your way past, and *los rurales*.

So, as many an Anglo survivor had done before, Longarm simply reined in, dismounted to kneel with his saddle gun, and commenced to fire and then fire some more until his Yellow Boy's magazine was empty and three *rurales* and one police mount lay still in the morning sunlight.

He was sorry about the pony. He didn't have time to salvage any guns. He knew the local citizenry would help themselves to the dead bastards' money, guns, and boots before they reported the skirmish, trying not to smile.

Longarm spotted figures in *peon* cotton and straw, moving out of his way through the cottonwoods and crack willows as he dismounted at the tree line to lead the pony through the tanglewood on foot. For you didn't really want to be in the saddle when you spooked a cottonmouth or timber rattler. He probed the shin-deep weeds with the barrel of the now-useless carbine, and tossed it aside at the water's edge.

He led Lille Thruma into the reedy shallows so they could peer across the Rio Bravo or Rio Grande.

By either name, it was a serious river this close to its mouth. A furlong and a half or more across, and nine to twelve feet deep in mid-channel. Longarm led the breeding experiment into the coffee-and-cream current, saying, "I know your Moro-Hispanic ancestors could swim. If your *Nordic* ancestors couldn't, and you drown us both, I'll never speak to you again!"

Then he took off his coat and gun rig, lashed them to the wooden dally horn of the *charro* saddle, and tied the big stirrups up across the tree, figuring the horse would have enough to worry about in midstream.

Then he looped her reins loosely around the cantle, moved back to grab her long silky tail, and slapped her on the rump, yelling at her that she was in charge for now.

He had to slap her once more and shove her pale rump the right way before Lille Thruma figured out what he wanted. Then, being a friendly pony as well as smarter than most he'd met chasing outlaws, Indians, or cows, Lille Thruma was off for the U.S. of A. so suddenly he almost lost his grip on her tail as she pulled Longarm off his feet and proceeded to swim at the same pace she tolted, easy-going but steady as clockwork, while the current carried them downstream at a forty-five-degree angle or more.

This went on way longer than Longarm had been hoping for. Then, at last, she was dragging him through the muck on the far side as she struggled to higher ground with him cursing her to slow down and let a man get his infernal feet under him.

She stopped, knee-deep in the swirling brown river, to look back at him with a hurt expression.

Longarm waded forward, regathering the reins, to give her

291

pretty blond head a friendly hug as he said, "I'm sorry I cussed you, honey lamb. For you are one hell of a pony, and as annoyed as I was with old Obregon, I see what he meant about wishing he had a bigger dick!"

Chapter 40

The Widow Bean was beating a rug out back when Longarm rode the tuckered but still spunky Lille Thruma in from up the north bank of the Rio Grande, feeling as if he'd been dragged through a keyhole backwards. For he'd done a lot of riding since last he'd slept, if you counted Sigridur and Camilla.

Una Bean sent her kids off on chores, and rustled up some fodder for the both of them as Longarm told her some of what he'd been up to since last they'd met.

He told her he didn't know who in blue blazes that prize palomino belonged to now, and said, "I'll swap her to you for a few hours rest and a fresh mount, Miss Una. A broken-down scrub pony will do me back to town, and you'll wind up ahead."

He demolished more ham and eggs before he explained Lille Thruma's odd bloodlines and suggested, "If I was breeding her, I'd cross her with an Andalusian, or better yet, a Barbary. I just can't say how she'll stand up to Texas weather in August. But she's sharp as a tack, and never seems to tire in cool night air."

So the horse-breeding young widow said they had a deal, and might have joined Longarm for forty winks had her kids been in bed as well, or had he asked her.

But they weren't, and he never did. So by noon he was

on his way down the river road to Brownsville aboard an older but no wiser version of his hired Texas paint, who was waiting for them in town.

He considered avoiding the home spread of the O Bar O as he rode in from the west. But with its owner and ramrod both dead in Mexico, he felt no call to ride that far out of his way.

Not until it was a bit late. Then he figured he'd look even more suspicious if he acted bashful in front of those other riders jawing with that toothless Mexican gal on the front veranda.

So he rode on in to howdy Captain Prescott, a couple more Rangers, and a son-of-a-bitching *rurale* officer in a big sombrero and matching slate-gray uniform. Two less-dapper *rurales* were sharing one smoke.

As he dismounted to tether his borrowed mount next to all the others assembled along the hitching rail, his laconic Ranger pal called out from the veranda, "You've not the least notion how glad I am to see an honest young lawman aboard that livery paint on this side of the border, Longarm. This here is Captain Morales out of Old Mexico, and we've been trying to convince him he's packing a warrant on the wrong man."

Longarm joined them on the shady veranda with as innocent a smile as he could manage with his mouth that dry.

The Mexican lawman wasn't smiling as he flatly stated, "Last night the owner of this *rancho* and his *segundo* were murdered in Mexico by an *hombre* answering to your notorious description, El Brazo Largo."

Captain Prescott removed his hat and soberly said, "They was both fine gents and they'll purely be missed. I understood you to say the tall, tanned Anglo as gunned them did so with a .45 and rid off on either a mule or a palomino pony, depending on who you ask? I don't see nothing but a paint pony yonder, and that sure looks like a Colt .44-40 this suspect seems to be packing. I fail to see a saddle gun of any caliber aboard that paint, Longarm. But ain't your Winchester '73 chambered for .44-40 rounds?"

Longarm said, "It is. I left it at that *posada* if you'd like to ride on into town with me, gents."

The laconic Ranger said, "You go on alone if you've a mind to. Our Mexican . . . associates say they've heard tell about some other murder that *segundo,* Bowie Bickford, might have known about. So I reckon we ought to nose around out here some."

Longarm was sorely tempted to suggest they probe the garbage pit. But he knew that once the Rangers started scouting a place, they'd scout it till they found something. So he quit while he was ahead and rode on, making it into Brownsville before supper time.

He was over at a waterfront cafe, seated outside under their awning as he washed down his paella of chicken, sausage, mussels, clams, lobster, rice, tomatoes, and red peppers with seriously black coffee, when Captain Prescott caught up with him.

The Ranger sat down across the bright blue table uninvited, and got right to the point. He said, "We found a dead body out yonder, right after you'd left. I had a time convincing that *rurale* you couldn't have done the poor cuss in because you ain't been in Texas as long as he's been rotting in that garbage pit. What's left of him answers to the descriptions of that hostile witness you were sent to find. Your turn. Unofficially."

Longarm told Prescott how Obregon had admitted right out that he'd made a deal for Njalsson to steal that prize pony and then ordered his *segundo* to double-cross him.

Prescott agreed that would surely have to *stay* unofficial, and they decided it would satisfy the diplomatic corps, and rough justice, if they just chalked all the dead horse thieves up to a falling-out among thieves.

That left a few loose strings official, but left all the lawmen involved looking good enough.

Longarm allowed he had a few last chores to wind up there in town, and asked if the Ranger cottoned to some *cascos de guayaba* dessert.

The Ranger allowed he had to get along. So they shook on it and parted friendly.

After Longarm had washed his guava preserves down with an extra cup of coffee, the waitress came out, her blouse having suddenly sort of slipped off one tawny shoulder, to ask how he'd liked her service so far.

He said, *"Mil gracias por una cena exquisita!"*

So she said, *"Por nada.* I get off duty in two hours."

He tried not to laugh. She was a pretty little thing, if you liked them sort of plump, and he knew some lonesome night in another time and place he was going to kick himself. But that particular evening the notion of taking yet another gal back to his *posada* didn't make much sense. So he left a handsome tip to prove he hadn't found her ugly, and ambled on to find most of the shops and saloons open for business in the cooler shades of evening.

Somebody was frying frijoles, and somebody else was strumming a guitar in the distance as he entered that photograph gallery to ask that sweet-smelling older gal how she felt about photographing a sort of stale cadaver.

She allowed she'd already done so for the county coroner on more than one occasion. They fished lots of corpses out of the harbor.

He still felt obliged to warn her, "This one's been swelling up under kitchen scraps, coffee grounds, and worse, ma'am. But if you're up to it, I'd like to carry a full-length portait of the late Pall Njalsson back to Denver with me. They sent me to bring him back dead or alive. I doubt they meant that literally."

So ten days later Longarm was seated across the cluttered desk from Billy Vail as the bullet-headed older lawman stared with disgust at the sepia prints Longarm had handed in with his report. Vail set the pictures of the bloated corpse aside and muttered, "I wish we could just dry up like jellyfish at the end. But we can't. So let's get to this usual terse report you handed in. I went over it this morning as I was waiting for you to drop by this infernal office. Have you any notion what *time* you got in, you casual cuss?"

Longarm refused to glance at the banjo clock on the oak-paneled office wall. He flicked tobacco ash on the rug Billy Vail refused to protect with one damned ashtray on this side of his damned desk, and calmly said, "It's all in there, Billy. The hostile witness you sent me to round up wasn't a witness to the assassination of that Danish count. He was the killer.

He wasn't the Icelandic rebel those Danish diplomats were concerned about. He was a pure and simple horse thief cum deserter, and you could almost say he got what was coming to him when his partners in crime double-crossed him."

Vail said, "I wasn't concerned about Njalsson. You done us proud, and the State Department is pleased as punch that you solved that murder for the Danish government. Njalsson's rank didn't entitle him to diplomatic immunity, and even if it had, you weren't the one who killed him on U.S. soil, so what the hell."

Longarm looked away and said, "I didn't think you wanted me to spell out in so many words the way that immune Mexican, Obregon, seems to have met his end on Mexican soil at the hand or hands of *La Causa*. I mean, once I eliminated most everyone else as the killer of Pall Njalsson, there seemed no call to put down every bitty detail."

Vail grimaced and said, "That's the way Obregon's estate seems to see it. My Ranger pals tell me his widow seems to be bearing up better than you'd expect, and she doesn't seem to care to have such details printed in the papers either."

He shot Longarm a knowing look and asked, "By the way, how was she?"

"How was she what?" asked Longarm sincerely.

Vail snorted blue smoke like a wise old cuttlefish and insisted, "Come on. You never would have found out so much about her man, ah . . . unofficially, had not somebody close to him told you, and who's left? Before you fib, I know you were by their place in Matamoros at times the man of the house wasn't home."

Longarm smiled easily and said, "Your Ranger pals do have big ears. Or Mexican servants have big mouths. But you have my word I never messed with old Felicidad, and I'm glad. For she was sort of treacherous, or scared skinny of her brutal husband. In either event, she's earned his holdings, for as long as *La Causa* lets her and her kind enjoy such holdings."

He sat back to just blow smoke rings as he waited to be dismissed so he could go out and play with another rich widow up on Capitol Hill.

He saw Vail didn't seem satisfied, so he said, "It's all in

there as far as that confidence game the late Sam Steinmuller was trying to get away with, Billy. That famous arms dealer he was backing was a fraud. The Mauser brothers only ran off a few samples of that cross betwixt their Gewahr '71 and a Winchester. Steinmuller planted tales of crooked machinists running off hundreds more and smuggling them into Texas by way of a vessel Steinmuller knew for sure to be pure as the driven snow. The captain and crew of the *Trinity* were innocent. Nobody working for U.S. Customs in Brownsville knew shit about any Prussian eleven-millimeter repeaters because they were never smuggled anywhere at all.''

Vail still seemed to be waiting.

Longarm frowned and asked, ''What are you asking for, an egg in your beer? I put down all that mythology about Icelandic rebels gathered in Texas, of all places, to buy arms diverted clean across the main ocean and the Gulf of Mexico. Njalsson was really an Icelander. At least some of Steinmuller's American, High Dutch, and Scandinavian gang spoke Icelandic. After that, we were just connecting the wrong dots, and the story about Icelandic and Mexican rebels bidding against one another for those mythical Mausers was only meant to assure that the Mexicans brought plenty of money across the border to be robbed.''

Vail wearily blew smoke out both nostrils and rumbled, ''I've been waiting to hear more about your romantic approach to duty in the field.''

So there it was, out in the open like ashes on the rug, and old Billy could be such a fuss when you told him to mind his own damn business.

Longarm leaned back and said with a sigh, ''I sure wish you hadn't been a Ranger in your own misspent youth. I don't know what those Texas gossips told you about this child, Boss. But you know I sent that court recorder back to Kansas ahead of me, so I could wrap up such chores as those photographs of the man you sent me after.''

Vail shrugged and said, ''Sigridur Jonsdottir is free, white, way over twenty-one, and works for our same Justice Department. So let's not get into her, whether you got into her or not.''

298

Longarm said that sounded fair, and said, "I put down how that Danish gal married up with a French diplomat sent that silly letter I wired you about earlier. If any of your old Ranger pals told you I messed with Margrethe du Prix, they're full of shit. I'm particular who I mess with. Dumb beasts and women who think they're that smart just don't appeal to me."

He waited, wondering what he'd say if Vail brought up old Camilla from the Danish consulate. He didn't see how anybody down yonder but old Sigridur could have spilled the beans about him and that petite Danish gal, and last time he'd looked, Sigridur and Camilla had been acting mighty fond of one another.

Vail said, "All right. I did ride against Comanche with Captain Coffee Hays, and my old pals keep me posted. So ain't you ashamed of yourself about that poor old widow woman who took these pictures of this rotting corpse?"

Longarm shrugged and said, "She was wearing plenty of perfume and all the windows were open. I warned her it might be bad. But she was game."

"So they tell me," Vail slyly observed as Longarm decided to stare at that banjo clock on the wall after all.

Vail waited, then said, "I understand the two of you went back to her place to develop those plates on a Friday, and then nobody saw either one of you until she opened up again on a Monday. Now what have you to say about *that*, you sly dog?"

Longarm shrugged and said, "Nothing. It was getting crowded at that fool *posada*, and I really had a heap of chores I had to wind up before I could leave town."

Vail demanded, "Do you call screwing for three days a way to wind up chores, old son?"

To which Longarm could only reply, "I do. I just told you how crowded things had gotten at that *posada*, and a man has to get a few winks of sleep *once* in a damned while!"

Watch for

**LONGARM AND THE
COLORADO COUNTERFEITER**

241st adventure in the LONGARM series
from Jove

Available now!

LONGARM AND THE RED-LIGHT LADIES

242nd novel in the exciting LONGARM series
from Jove

Coming in February!